Bounded Rationality

A Novel

Praise for *The Edge of Chaos*
the first volume of The Santa Fe Stories trilogy:

"I was a trustee of the Santa Fe Institute for 14 years, so I'm familiar with the science and scientists in this wonderful yarn, and with Santa Fe. I can vouch for the author's verisimilitude...AND it's a page-turner."

—Stewart Brand, editor of *The Whole Earth Catalog* and author,
The Clock of the Long Now: Time and Responsibility

"I honestly can't recall another reading experience which touched so many different parts of my mind and emotions. It's absolutely saturated with ideas and brilliant observations...and makes me think that the author has had her eyes very wide open for a very long time. I'll be buying many copies of this book. I can't think of anyone I know who wouldn't like it."

—Brian Eno, composer, musician, producer

"*The Edge of Chaos* is one of those rare books in which a keen sense of place, fully rounded characters, and the realms of scientific theory and intellect are fused in a seemingly seamless alloy. Pamela McCorduck's passions and sure-handed writing radiate in every direction in this irresistible novel."
—Jane Hirshfield, author of *Come Thief*, and *Nine Gates: Entering the Mind of Poetry*

"Pamela McCorduck has created not one, but two memorable characters, whose thoughts and doings absorb and fascinate—a rare thing in fiction at any time. I was astounded by the depth and range of her knowledge across many learned disciplines, but the greatest pleasure reading the book was seeing how things turned out..."

—George Newlin, author of *Everyone in Dickens*,
and *Everything and Everyone in Trollope*

"*The Edge of Chaos* takes on many meanings in this beautifully written story of complexity in human affairs: love, marriage, discovery, death, and more. The science of complexity is told in human terms as it unfolds in Complexity's Jerusalem, the Santa Fe Institute.

—Edward Feigenbaum, Stanford University

Bounded Rationality

A Novel

Pamela McCorduck

SUNSTONE
PRESS

SANTA FE

Also by Pamela McCorduck

Fiction:
Familiar Relations
Working to the End
The Santa Fe Stories:
   The Edge of Chaos
   Bounded Rationality

Nonfiction:
Machines Who Think
The Fifth Generation (with E. A. Feigenbaum)
The Universal Machine
The Rise of the Expert Company
   (with E. A. Feigenbaum and H. Penny Nii)
Aaron's Code
The Futures of Women (with Nancy Ramsey)

Sunstone books may be purchased for educational, business, or sales promotional use. For information please write: Special Markets Department, Sunstone Press, P.O. Box 2321, Santa Fe, New Mexico 87504-2321.

Book and Cover design › Vicki Ahl
Body typeface › WTC Bodoni
Printed on acid-free paper

Library of Congress Cataloging-in-Publication Data

Library of Congress Cataloging-in-Publication Data

McCorduck, Pamela, 1940-
  Bounded rationality : a novel / by Pamela McCorduck.
    p. cm.
  ISBN 978-0-86534-883-7 (softcovers : alk. paper)
  1. Children--Death--Fiction. 2. Grief--Fiction. 3. Santa Fe (N.M.)--Fiction. I. Title.
  PS3613.C3823B68 2012
  813'.6--dc23

      2012011393

WWW.SUNSTONEPRESS.COM
SUNSTONE PRESS / POST OFFICE BOX 2321 / SANTA FE, NM 87504-2321 /USA
(505) 988-4418 / ORDERS ONLY (800) 243-5644 / FAX (505) 988-1025

"Bounded rationality is the notion that in decision making, rationality of individuals is limited by the information they have, the cognitive limitations of their minds, and the finite amount of time they have to make decisions."

—Wikipedia

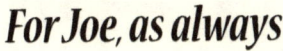

For Joe, as always

I

The Initial Conditions

1

A hundred and twenty-five million years ago, this plain might have been the bed of a mighty sea, bullied into flat submission by the slow, irresistible forces of water. On the littoral, volcanoes would have belched violently. Or maybe this basin is all that's left from a colossal meteor strike, reshaped by wind and water over unthinkable time. Geologists shrug. Immense amounts of silt, borne over the eons by water, by wind, occlude the real story.

Mighty sea or trembling meteor depression, geologists do know that far beneath this mysterious basin, the great North American tectonic plate has been fissuring for thirty million years, forcing the legs of the Rockies apart into two ranges, the Jemez, and the Sangre de Cristo. The Rio Grande Rift is a portal to the deep underworld of the earth's mantle. Whatever it was, this plain is now a place of slow, covert violence.

But the surface is calm, monotonous desert. The river is narrow, shallow, and seems well mannered; the persistent wind only hints at history. That wind also bears dreams—like prayers, like longing—for the green fecundity far to the south.

This place of ancient secrets, portal to what lies beneath tectonic plates, is now the municipal airport of Santa Fe, New Mexico, too modest for commercial traffic, and casual about security. Two travelers have been driven on to the apron to board one of the small private jets that can land and take off here. Aboard, they have the cabin to themselves. Eight seats in all, upholstered in soft pale gray leather, but the man sits down beside the woman, takes her hand. She turns to this stranger—well, stranger in some ways, not in others—this man she has agreed to go to Europe with, and returns his slight smile. They keep silent.

Outside, under the brilliant mineral clarity of the noon sun, the Jemez mountains to the west, and the Sangre de Cristo mountains to the east—both ranges snow-topped after a storm last night—are without depth to the human eye, a child's cutouts pasted against an improbably blue sky. But the mountains are real, and have claimed more than their share of human bones.

Somehow the luggage disappears. The captain steps out of the cockpit to welcome them, the man by name: "Always good to have you aboard, Mr. Molloy. Is all well?" Mr. Molloy nods courteously: all is well. "We're scheduled for just over three hours to Teterboro. A great day for flying. Maybe a little turbulence in the Mississippi Valley, a nasty blizzard there, but we'll do our best to climb over it."

Molloy's companion, a woman of his own middle age, puts her head back and stretches out, feeling a little bit stupid. When the captain closes the cabin door behind him, she murmurs: "You must've thought I was an idiot, offering you my frequent flier miles. I didn't realize..." She lets it go.

"I thought it was very practical of you. Very dear." He squeezes her hand gently.

She senses he isn't entirely at ease. He's begun on the *Wall Street Journal*. She opens the *New York Times*. Each of them knows this is a qualitatively different step. More significant. She lowers the op-ed page and watches him furtively as he reads, that taut face that's always seemed to her like a helmet, so self-protective. In the past eighteen months, she's sometimes thought of him as thug. A desperado. An outlaw. Sumi-brush eyebrows (the only expressive part of his face, when he allows himself expression) top those brilliant, unreadable black eyes of his. In the last few weeks, however, the helmet has softened; the pouty bust-of-Apollo mouth has opened to smile with warmth. With heat. With joy. And then some.

But today the helmet is securely back in place. If it used to offend her, she's lately learned that it's only a sign: it falls swiftly over his face when he fears, even suspects, he'd better guard himself. No, she thinks. I will not hurt you. Not now. Reconsiders. Well, not intentionally.

Exhaustion hits her yet again, and somehow, as the plane strains to climb, and she's staring down far below them at the snowy Pajarito Plateau, home of atomic Los Alamos, the Valle Grande caldera behind it, she's asleep.

Later she wakes. Molloy has moved, where he can work on his laptop. His face is invisible, bent over a screen; she can see only the top of his head, his coiled black hair like a thousand tiny fists. She dozes some more.

At Teterboro it's already dusk, quickly turning dark. They move effortlessly into a black SUV with heavily tinted windows that's awaited them on the apron— again, someone else sees to the luggage, the details. Someone else is driving, who also seems to know Molloy.

On their way into Manhattan he says: "Hope you don't mind New York for a couple of days before we go. I have some things to wind up. We're set for Munich. Where do you want to go after that?"

The question seems imponderable to her. Overwhelming. She can't even muster an answer.

He watches her carefully; those eyes that seem to absorb everything around them. "We can decide as we go along. Leave it to me." He examines her face, reaches up to touch her cheek gently. "You're exhausted, Judith. You really need this. You should've done it yourself months ago." It could be a scolding, which he gentles with a slight smile. "Though I'm glad you waited for me to take you." She gazes back at those eyes, oversize for his face, the imploring eyes of, oh, a baby seal, a colt. As a human being, she knows she's hardwired to respond automatically to such eyes. Neoteny. The scientific term swims up from somewhere. Oversize eyes, excessive fuzziness—in Molloy's case, not fuzziness precisely, but very generous amounts of body hair. Be careful, she tells herself. The very adult brain behind those infant-like eyes has wrecked national economies, helped to bring down whole governments.

She shrinks back on the car seat, wondering what she's let herself in for, what obligations this journey will entail. Sex, yes; but the only time she's felt alive the past few weeks is in this man's arms. Talk? The very idea exhausts her.

The SUV is moving swiftly south on Riverside Drive, and she gazes through the window. They pass a fine old 1910 brick-and-limestone apartment house, almost Gallic with its wrought iron balconies, its mansard roof. Jonathan and I lived there when we were married, she thinks to say, but doesn't. Why would Molloy care? Ancient history. She knows he too lives on Riverside Drive, but not in the Morningside Heights academic ghetto—farther south, the ritzy part. She wonders how long he's had this place of his, whether, by chance, they once lived simultaneously on the same long drive, when she was a young assistant professor of mathematics at Columbia, married to—an old professor of mathematics. When Jack Molloy was already a wealthy man, shuttling back and forth between New York City and Frankfurt, married to a woman who's now dead.

They stop somewhere in the low eighties—it's too dark to tell exactly where—and once more, polite and competent persons open doors, murmur welcomes, see to things. He walks her into the apartment's lobby—respectable, but hardly deluxe. In her deep fatigue, she can hardly stand up and he supports her tenderly. The elevator opens into the apartment itself—so she knows he has the entire floor. What she doesn't know, but learns, is that it's a triplex, three stories. Incredible luxury in Manhattan, where every square foot costs a ransom. His Santa Fe compound—house, outbuildings, guest houses—is spacious, but compared to this, modest.

"You really need to sleep," he says with concern. "I'll show you where the bedrooms are." She follows him across a wide living room, up the first flight of stairs. On the landing he says, "This floor has the kids' rooms." The kids are out of college. She knows his daughter lives in a loft downtown; his son, she's heard, lives in Santa Fe, where they've just come from, but she hasn't met him. Father and son have issues.

They continue to the top floor. He stops now, and looks at her worriedly. "Judith. If you—you don't have to sleep with me. You can sleep in Lindy's room. We each had our own. Hers even has an adjoining room for the maid—we used it for her nurses the last few years." She can see from his face that he's deeply conflicted, wanting to do the right thing, whatever that is.

She sighs, speaks from the heart. "Jack Molloy. Where else would I sleep but with you?" The relief on his face is so sweet she could cry.

When she wakes the next morning—ten, very late for her, but only eight, body time—he's gone. She vaguely remembers he got up and got into sweats, later came back for a shower; but he must have gone to his office, someplace in midtown. He'd sold his Manhattan firm before he even arrived in Santa Fe, but keeps a small office in midtown, a personal assistant on his private payroll who knows him well enough to make sure his life runs smoothly. He's principal in a modest firm he took over in Santa Fe, called New Business, a kind of consulting and training enterprise, which brings managers of established firms into the new economy. He also runs a hedge fund in Santa Fe, his micro-firm, he calls it, with few enough traders that they could gather around a kitchen table. Not that they actually do. These, she knows, are peripheral interests to him; his real interest now is his new foundation.

There's a note on the toilet lid. "Call me." A Manhattan number, not his mobile. She laughs out loud. In a few minutes she calls him.

"Did you sleep well?" The basso voice has always stirred her, sometimes to her consternation. Rested now, she enjoys some pleasant sensations.

"Very well, thanks." They're still shy with each other. If the last few weeks have been flooded with erotic extravagance, it's only after a year of denial, evasion. By her, not him.

"Breakfast's in the fridge. Celeste always puts stuff in there before I come in, but she knows what I like. I didn't know what to tell her for you. You and I haven't eaten that many breakfasts together." He snorts softly, and she detects discomfort. "You're a couple of blocks from Zabar's, from H and H. You can—"

"Jack, I lived on the Upper West Side for more than a decade. I'll manage just fine. When will I see you?" Even the use of his given name is strange on her tongue. Like everyone else in Santa Fe, she's known him up to now only by his surname. "The years I spent in Germany," he'd explained laconically. True. European men address each other by their last names, mostly, and so he's all but lost his given name.

He teases: "When would you like to see me?"

"Right this minute. We need to make up for lost time."

"And whose fault is that?" The laugh comes. She hasn't heard it often. It delights her. Makes her feel powerful, in some odd way, that she can evoke a laugh from this somber man. "Hold that thought," he says softly. "I'll be home before five. Think about where you'd like to have dinner. I gave you a key, right?" Of course he's given her a key. His attention to detail is faultless. She smiles at that, I'll be home before five. Jack Molloy has always set his own timetable. The insistent, the focused, the forceful Molloy, who always gets his own way in the end. She relaxes, decides everything is going to be just fine.

2

After she dresses, she explores the apartment.

The views are compelling: each room on the three floors seems to have a terrace she could walk out onto if it weren't so bitterly cold and windy on this gray winter day. The terraces look west to Riverside Park, the Hudson River beyond it, New Jersey across the river, full of new high-rise apartments perched on the Palisades.

Since the building is on a corner, other terraces look south to midtown. If she's willing to stretch a little, she can even look north, see the George Washington Bridge. Always the river, the glorious river. It flickers and flashes beyond the bare treetops in the park. He'd bought the place, he told her, because he loves rivers, grew up on one, had worked beside rivers here and in Europe. Rivers soothe him. She guesses he's a man who often needs soothing.

But the apartment's interior shows the neglect of the last years. At some point it had been "decorated"—soullessly, she thinks, a museum of the most correct style circa 1980—and the chintz upholstery is fading, shabby. The tables, fake Queen Anne, repel her with their curves and ball-and-claw feet. Nothing against curves and ball-and-claw: it's the impersonal decorator-ishness of it all.

The only personal touches are family photographs in the living room, and these she studies with interest. A wedding picture. An impossibly young Jack Molloy in striped trousers and cutaway escorting a pretty young woman in an elaborate bridal gown down the steps of St. Ignatius. Judith can't really tell it's St. Ignatius; he must have told her—his wife's family had lived on the East Side; were in art somehow. Later pictures: mother and young children, posed stiffly, formally, the woman in a tediously proper sweater set, pearls, her face looking as if she'd been lobotomized. Or is that just a little posthumous cattiness? She reproaches herself silently. This is history. Nothing can change it. A later picture, all the family on skis. As penance for thinking that Lindy looks lobotomized, Judith restrains from reading the faces in this picture. Photographs can be subversively misleading. But someone had thought framing this picture was significant, that it somehow caught the family just then. It's the Alps. Maybe St. Moritz. But of course, she thinks mockingly. St. Moritz. But of course.

A rush of shame stops her. She's spent more than enough time mocking this man and his money. Little by little, she's been forced to reassess, to admit that Molloy is a man with much more to him than his net worth. Not JAWS— Just Another Wealthy Shithead. The fierce defenses she raised against him have wasted stupid amounts of time. And whose fault is that?

One night, perhaps a week earlier, he'd asked playfully why she'd finally yielded to him. That was his old-fashioned word, yielded. Was it significant, a coincidence, he asked, that it was the night celebrating the formation of his foundation? The foundation a sign that he wouldn't have so much money after all? She'd been stunned. Was she really so simple-minded? He'd continued evenly: "If so, too bad. It isn't all gone, so don't think it is. I was born poor and spent my first twenty-five years poor. I've lived poor up close, and the romance of it never captured me. I won't be poor again. You're entitled to your own views, of course."

Forgive me, Jack. Now and evermore, no matter how this little trip turns out. It wasn't really the money, which was only an impediment of convenience. It was—she doesn't want to pursue it, even in the privacy of her own mind.

On the walls she can see that paintings have been removed. Their ghosts linger in shadows of wall paint protected from fading. She knows Molloy has brought his collection of contemporary art to Santa Fe, though most of it is in storage. From what little she's seen of the collection, she can't imagine how any of those superb paintings once lived here with the cabbage roses and fake Queen Anne. Maybe his late wife had olde English hunting scenes up instead.

To the bookshelves. Books in English, German, a few in Italian and French. Many about art and artists. Serious numbers of history books, mostly European and Classical, but Asian history too. A shelf full of mythology: Grimm's *Deutsche Mythologie*, the Edda sagas (but in English, thank God), half a dozen collections of Greek myths, also in English. Various dictionaries—a contemporary German Duden, an old-fashioned Cassell's German-English with Gothic script, a French-English dictionary, English etymological dictionaries. Even a Latin dictionary. Doesn't the man stoop to the occasional thriller? Apparently not. In the study, books about finance, ugh. Then she sees Merton's *Continuous Time Finance* and must smile. Molloy had picked up a copy of that book from a table at her house the first evening he'd ever come over, confessed he'd tried to master it one summer in Switzerland, tutored by a graduate student at ETH, the Swiss technical university in Zürich, but had pretty much crashed and burned. He was quick to grasp most financial mathematics, but this eluded him. She'd told him it was difficult even for professional mathematicians, and feels a rush of tenderness for his failed effort. "Do not worry about your difficulties in mathematics," Einstein is supposed to have said. "I assure you mine are far greater."

That was the first inkling she had that Molloy was not what she'd thought, but—what he is. She collapses on a couch in the study, opens Merton, and begins to nod.

Like all responsible couples, they'd dutifully gone to get tested for HIV (both negative, thank you) but Judith's doctor had told her she was noticeably anemic. He prescribed some iron, tutted that the extreme exhaustion she complained about was not just physical. No wonder. The recent death of her best friend. The breakup of a ten-year relationship. Maybe other problems. She must say yes to sleep for the next few weeks—sleep, the great healer. Doctor's orders. A vacation with a friend? Do it. She awakens only when she hears the elevator doors, and Molloy appears. He smiles, knowing he's woken her up on the couch. "Prove any good theorems today?"

"I didn't even prove I could stay awake for more than an hour."

As they're on their way out to dinner, they meet one of the neighbors in the lobby, an elderly woman introduced to her as Mrs. Siegel. "Meet my friend, Dr. Greenwood, Judith Greenwood," Molloy says formally. That use of the term doctor. He won't stop it. She's told him more than once that though it's almost required by law in Germany, in the U.S., it's pretentious, and anyway, one of these days somebody is going to need CPR in a restaurant, and she's going to sit there unhelpfully reciting the Fibonacci series instead: zero, one, one, two, three, five, eight, thirteen…

Mrs. Siegel peers at her closely, not entirely with kindness.

A car is waiting for them. She still isn't used to this. She expected to stroll over to West End and hail a taxi. "Does Mrs. Siegel have her eye on you, Jack? I felt a certain—not hostility, exactly, but—"

"Be serious." He settles into the back seat with her; the driver already knows where they're going.

"No, you're right. It was something else. I've seen that look before. Judith Greenwood. Originally Gruenwald?" Her German accent is impeccable, though southern.

"Was it? Originally?" he asks casually.

"Would it make any difference?"

He grabs her and kisses her hard. Then: "No difference whatever. Just interesting, if so."

"It's a long story. But not a very interesting one." Untrue, on both counts.

Of course he's known about Judith's intellectual achievements—a little dossier commissioned even before he got to Santa Fe, outlining her contributions not only to mathematical finance but to many other mathematical fields too, especially what's now called the sciences of complexity; her research position at the think-tank called the Santa Fe Institute, which has become known worldwide as the mother church of these new sciences of complexity. They've worked together for a year at a small start-up called New Business, where he's still a principal, and formally, she's still a consultant. Even now he's wryly embarrassed, amused by himself: how energized he used to be to wake up every Wednesday morning, knowing that this was the day Judith Greenwood came to the offices of New Business to consult. Like being a teenager all over again, except after nearly thirty years in finance, he's accomplished at masking his feelings, so he believes no one ever knew.

At the beginning too, he'd awkwardly asked her to tutor him in complexity, what it meant, his excuse that he'd been invited to be on the board of her home institution, and wondered whether this was a good use of his time. It was true about the invitation to the board. It was true that he needed to know more about complexity and the Institute. She'd been an excellent tutor.

But it wouldn't have mattered to him if any of this were so or not. He just yearned for the connection with her. He'd come to Santa Fe in the hope of finding her—or a woman like her. A picture in a trade magazine had caught his eye, come to obsess him: a lovely woman in a wide skirt, boots, a cowboy hat, a dazzling smile, accompanying an interview about her work, which he admired. He wanted to be where such women could be found. With such a woman, he wanted to put an end to his lifelong loneliness. He wasn't committed to Judith Greenwood necessarily, so much as he longed for a companion he imagined—on the ludicrous evidence of one magazine interview, one picture—this woman to be. When he met her, he was dashed down that she wanted to do most of the tutoring by email. That she had a longtime lover. That she was so elusive.

And then, in a beautiful garden one evening, that finally changed.

What he hadn't at all expected was that they share a history of stretches of living in Germany, and both speak German fluently. He's gradually come to discover that they love the same kind of art and music. (He thinks his own tastes are wider, but she's teachable, surely.) He's been frankly surprised to find her generous-hearted, at least once they got past all the resistance, which he still doesn't quite understand. The money, she'd claimed, as if it were some kind of repellent deformity. He wonders. Still, as a companion, she's so easygoing that he's allowed to plan everything, which suits them both perfectly. Once plans are made, she takes immense delight in them, no second-guessing. Immense delight in life itself, he amends.

From time to time he scrutinizes her, not quite believing that the unreachable Judith Greenwood, the golden girl, Queen Judith, is here beside him, getting ready to spend some indefinite period together. Very much together.

For a new and unexpected discovery has frankly dazed him: Judith's ardor. It's persistent, high-spirited, playful—he's never laughed like he laughs these nights—and wildly imaginative. She has no shyness. He sometimes feels as if he's watching her explore and colonize the dark continent of his body, taking possessive delight in every inch she claims. For years he's suspected that his physical self is subtly objectionable—maybe the generous body hair, a turnoff for many women; maybe something else. But Judith devours his body with gusto, teases him about it with deep affection, praises, pets and flatters him into believing he might be desirable after all. He inhales the scent of her body greedily, a musky wild thing, primal and direct, that penetrates to someplace seldom before touched. What rises to consciousness has been buried for years under layers of responsibility, gravity, above all, profound melancholy. Its disinterment is a heady gift. Its name is joy.

Or maybe, he reflects, it's just his lack of experience. God knows he'd been a randy young guy, but had married early, to a woman who was willing, if not quite passionate. Then after the birth of their second and last child, Lindy all but said that sex was something he ought to get over, outgrow, put behind him. Hurt, frustrated, he did just that. He poured himself into work instead, and made a legendary fortune. It took desperation—and the help of a wise and sympathetic New York City psychiatrist—to open his eyes to the dark side of that iron self-discipline, the severe depression that had slowly crept upon him, then gripped him without mercy for years. It took desperation to make him see the price he'd paid in indifference to most of the world's sweet pleasures. To open his eyes to the devastating cost of a vanished libido.

When he arrived in Santa Fe to begin his life over, an impulse that puzzled everyone who knew him (what would possess the urbane Molloy, welcomed all over Europe in the palaces of princelings, the villas of barons and counts, the hunting lodges of tycoons, to go off to live with the cowboys, the Indians, and the cactus?) he was still deeply unsure of himself. It seemed a miracle to meet Judith at the first Santa Fe dinner party he was invited to, the very woman whose picture he'd seen in a trade paper, the very woman who'd come to symbolize what Santa Fe, and life, might offer him after all. He could hardly breathe at that dinner table, not only because in the flesh she was lovelier than he'd imagined, smarter, more nuanced, but because for the first time in years, desire stirred unequivocally.

But to his great disappointment, Judith proved resistant. She was openly contemptuous of his wealth, politely indifferent to him personally. Inanities would blurt from his tongue, schoolboy nonsense that mortified him, and he couldn't help himself. Which only reinforced her indifference. He met her longtime lover, an archaeologist, and despaired. Yet sometimes he imagined he saw something in her eyes that said she was not so indifferent, that she could possibly be persuaded, that she hesitated for unspoken reasons. Since he didn't know those reasons, he could think of no way to get past that except the way he had always done things, with dogged persistence.

So he roamed Santa Fe and bedded hungrily, knowing he was lonelier now than he'd been during that desert of the soul when women—and the world—had failed to interest him at all. He began to think he might have made a terrible mistake, leaving New York for this profound and paradoxical little town of Santa Fe, New Mexico, in the high desert of the American southwest.

When Inéz, a beautiful but troubled young woman, agreed eagerly to move in with him, he gave himself over to a sexual fever with her that he hadn't felt for a very long time, partly out of relief, partly because what else was there to do? But it left him deeply sad, because Inéz was not who he wanted to be feverish with. Within weeks, he was bored with her, and had no idea how to disentangle himself. Just write a fucking check, any of his colleagues would have said, but he didn't. When he discovered that she and his son, newly arrived from the East, were having an affair under the same roof they all shared, he waited, asked himself what he really wanted.

At the time that he was pondering this dilemma, a gallery owner, Nola Holliman, whom he'd also met at that very first dinner party in Santa Fe, invited him to see, perhaps evaluate, a strange rose-colored cave, sculpted out of the sandstone formations about an hour north of the city. He'd been fond of Nola since he'd first met her. She was one of the few people easy for him to talk to, perhaps because she bore burdens of her own—a desperately sick child, a despicable husband and father of that child—and she understood that all matters weren't always sharp with moral clarity.

It became an afternoon of great intimacy. Though they began by talking art, he felt moved to confide in her about the situation at home. As he talked, he came to understand what this covert *ménage à trois* really meant to him (not much at all) but that he must act, for his son's sake if no other. Then, in that rosy womb of the earth, he and Nola Holliman had made love, an outcome he understood she'd expected, perhaps hoped for, though for him it was less passionate than comforting. Good enough. A few days later, he threw his son and Inéz out. But he said as clearly as he could that he welcomed the young man's return someday. Without Inéz.

He turned himself back to work, always his drug of choice, and laid down the strategies that would form his foundation. He disciplined himself to think of Judith only as a charming colleague.

Then, the night of a party at an old Santa Fe estate, celebrating the formal launch of the John B. Molloy Foundation, he found Judith alone in the elegant garden. It was mid-autumn, and the aspens had lost their leaves; the dead stalks of long-gone flowers were colorless. Even so, an unusual warmth happened to linger that evening, and the full moon transformed the dead garden into something enchanted, as if by this, the fates were offering one last chance for something yet to be born before the onset of cruel winter, and irrecoverable death.

There, slowly and reluctantly, beneath the full moon, she confessed: she was tired out, on the verge of giving up research, would go back to Germany to work as a science administrator for the German government's network of Max Planck research institutes. He could sense her bone-deep fatigue, her raw defenselessness. A place he'd been himself not so long ago. They made love at last, and then he persuaded her to take time off, let him take her to Europe to recover. Not to give up on herself yet.

So here she is, the mind and body he's longed for, first as a kind of dream, and now a delectably fleshy reality. Even more amazing, she longs for him. As physically and emotionally spent as she is, she's never too tired to make love. She tells him it energizes her, and maybe it does. Early in the journey, as one night he's caressing her, he stops and whispers: "I'm here to make you well, not to molest you. If anytime you—" She puts her fingertips over his lips, laughs, and surprises him.

The second morning in the Riverside Drive apartment, he's startled, and then profoundly embarrassed, that she follows him into the bathroom. It almost stops him in midstream. No woman has watched him pee since he was three. But clearly, she's there deliberately. She stands behind him, her arms around his waist as he finishes, her face buried in his bare back, murmuring to him affectionately. At this moment he understands it isn't just sex, but intimacy she brings him. Later, he admits to himself that this is unprecedented in his life. When the affair ends, it's what he'll miss most of all.

3

They fly first to Munich, where Judith spent her girlhood, and left only when she went back to the United States to college. In the Cold War days, she's told him, her father had worked for Radio Free Europe, headquartered here in the grand public park known as the Englischer Garten—for, instead of the formal layouts of Italian parks, it imitates the quasi-wild landscapes of English parks. The manager at the Hotel Vier Jahreszeiten comes out to welcome them personally, having known Herr Molloy many years; bows gallantly over Judith's hand, and is too smooth to show surprise when she speaks to him not only in his native tongue, but with a decided Bavarian accent.

"We'll want opera tickets later in the week," Molloy says, "and restaurant reservations tonight." He appraises Judith. "No. Room service tonight. The lady is very tired."

But the lady is not too tired to want to walk in a city she loves. As they dress for the chilly winter evening, he puts on a Persian lamb astrakhan, and she claps her hands in glee: "You can't tell where the lamb leaves off and Molloy begins! I love it! You look so handsome!" He supposes she's right about where the lamb stops and his kinky black hair begins. The handsome part? Maybe not. She herself is in a beautifully cut black wool coat, a close-fitting hat and a bright pink scarf. He's sometimes felt bold enough to tease her about her devotion to chic: can she really be a serious mathematician when she dresses the way she does? In fact, it gratifies him. He's always loved soignée women. She'd come to business dinner parties at his Santa Fe house dressed not in the regional costume of Navajo skirt and grand silver jewelry—which he rather liked, regional costumes disappearing everywhere—but in dramatically simple silks, even more dramatic jewelry, though from European ateliers, not the branded Cartier-Tiffany-Winston stuff. Yet he'd also see her at the Institute in jeans, a tee shirt and athletic shoes, if all she was doing was workaday science. Whatever that was. Chameleon woman.

From the hotel they stroll arm-in-arm along Maximilianstrasse, chatting naturally in German, because German is in their ears. Their walk takes them past the handsome opera house, behind it, the Bavarian king's Residenz, or palace, and then they turn toward Marienplatz, the main square in Munich. Because it's the season, the Christkindlmarkt fills that noble square, with fairy lights, jolly booths selling traditional Christmas ornaments, carved crèche scenes, the smells of gingerbread and glüwein in the air. Crowds of holidaymakers push around them. They get cups of the warm spiced wine, a gingerbread man to share, stop to listen to a brass band playing Christmas carols. Above them in the Rathaus Tower, the Glockenspiel starts up, a two-tier diorama, the finely carved figures in the upper section celebrating a royal marriage; the figures in the lower section celebrating the city's deliverance from the plague, symbolized by the brave coopers who went into the streets and danced, to show the townspeople it was safe.

"Amazing, isn't it? " Judith says, "In this day of TV, video games, virtual reality and super-graphics, thousands of people still stand here enthralled by these little clockwork figures?" He hasn't thought of that. She's right. As he considers it, he realizes that this has been his experience all over Europe, that the sweetness, the simplicity, the stately human pace of animated clockworks still charm human beings.

"Does this bring back memories?"

"Oh, yes." But she doesn't elaborate. He can see she's beginning to shiver, and insists they return to the hotel. "We can come back tomorrow night," he promises, as if he were bribing a child. "Please, yes," she says. "I'd like to pick up a few Christmas decorations for Ron and Gabe." En route home, they see that the great provender, Dallmayr, is still open, and they stop in, buy chocolates for later. Again, he's struck by what a pleasure she takes in these small things, laughing out loud when they choose together. Who was the last woman he knew who laughed with pleasure about bon-bons?

But the next night the concierge has got them tickets for the opera. "*Lohengrin?*" she says. "A tad on the dreary side for the Christmas season, wouldn't you say?"

"We don't have to go."

"Of course we'll go."

The Bavarian State Opera House is a neo-classical gem, though rebuilt several times—almost from the ground up after World War II. As they wait for the overture, they silently compare its intimacy to the cavernous spaces of the Metropolitan, even their own Santa Fe Opera. "This is how it should be," she murmurs to him. He knows exactly what she means. Even at the worst of times, they've had a history of being able to read one another's minds.

Onstage, a single figure in tee shirt and warm-up pants sits working on a drawing. Judith and Molloy glance at each other skeptically. Munich is infamous for restaging the classic operas, but what's this? They soon understand that this young man in the athletic wear is the evening's Lohengrin, playing not a medieval knight but a contemporary architect, and his lady, Elsa, joins him onstage wearing bib overalls. "Oh fuck," Molloy says under his breath. But Judith has her hand over her mouth, and the swelling Wagner covers her light laughter. At the intermission, where they sit down to the first course of supper in the opera house cellar, she can't control herself. Now he has to laugh too, shakes his head. "We're not going back?"

"Of course we are. Let's see if it can get worse."

It can. Lohengrin-the-architect's house, symbolic of his grand vision as a holy knight, is built bit by bit onstage, the supers pretending, with various degrees of success, that the Styrofoam bricks are heavy. When it's finished at the end of the second act, it turns out to be the most banal of suburban villas. Lohengrin carries a stuffed animal swan under his arm. The chorus appears variously dressed as "courtiers" (in blazers), as football fans, as construction workers. Judith and Molloy break for the second intermission, dessert, and German sparkling wine, Sekt.

"Oh, God. The architect as hero. Almost as original as the financier as villain. Can we go now?" But he says it with a smile.

"You go. I'm staying to the bitter end. I want to see that swan do something useful. My mother gives stuffed animals like that to her golden retrievers."

"Maybe the stuffed swan will inspire Lohey to redesign that pitiful dump into something decent."

"It's all so modern and re-imagined—hideously re-imagined—yet the acting: so wooden and nineteenth century. The voices are okay. His is good. Very good. With a competent director, he'll be a fine performer. Poor Elsa. Don't know if there's any hope for her."

"She ought to ask him not who he really is, but where the hell he went to architecture school." He shakes his head, joins her for the last painful act. It's something to laugh over for days.

In Munich they fall into a daily routine that they'll follow all during their European trip. He goes out for a run in the morning, returns just as she's waking up. After museums or galleries and an elegant lunch, he lulls her into sleep with sweet love-making. When she wakes, there's tea in the early darkness of

European winter afternoons, a time to talk. It's here they begin to tell each other their stories, the parts no one else knows. Into her care he pours a flood of tenderness that he's contained all his life, tenderness he's always known belonged somewhere, but has never found a place for expression.

On Christmas Day it snows lightly. He's asked casually whether she opens her presents on Christmas Eve or Christmas Day. "The morning," she'd said. "Very Episcopalian." And so that morning he presents her with a silver box, inside it a luxurious pale blue silk nightgown and robe. She thanks him, seems disconcerted. "I apologize that there's nothing under the tree for you. I haven't been—myself."

"Your company is the best Christmas present I've had in years, Judith," he says with such simple dignity that she won't even tease him.

Nothing is open except the churches, and they stroll along Sendlingerstrasse to the small Asamkirche, to attend mass within its ornate interior. The silver and crimson opulence is almost dizzying: twisted columns enclose the high altar, and before it, the life-size wax figure of St. Johann Nepomuk in his glass casket is just bizarre. Yet Judith has told him she loves this jewel of the baroque, used to come here as a young girl to sit and take it all in, so much the opposite from the austerity of Protestant churches. The sanctuary is so small—the Asam brothers had intended it for their private chapel—that the incense is suffocating. "The whole thing's like eating too many chocolates," he says when they come out.

"Over the top, agreed. That's exactly what I like best about it. Such fine instruction that worship of the divine is mostly worship of the ego."

"How do you normally spend Christmas?"

"Normally? No such thing as normally. With friends, I guess. Ron and Gabe always have a party on Christmas Eve because they live so near to the *farolito* walk. We all do the walk, come back for eggnog and things. Then I have them over on Christmas Day. If I'm in town. Sometimes I'm traveling. Sophie would come." Her dead friend. "She and Ron would declare a Christmas truce. I've never understood why the people I love don't love each other. Well, no Sophie now, to irritate Ron, or get irritated by him. Have you—did I pull you away from one of Santa Fe's best Christmas attractions?"

"I did the walk last year. I'll do it again in the future," he says agreeably. It's true, the walk among the adobe walls, each topped by rows of brown paper bags that hold lighted candles, *farolitos*, is ethereal, evanescent.

"And you? How do you usually spend Christmas, Jack? Are you religious? You certainly seemed to know what to do during mass."

He laughs a little self-consciously, made aware that he'd followed along and responded automatically as each stage of the mass was enacted. "Not at all. I was raised in the faith, went to parochial schools, and then we raised the kids in the faith—so they'd have some ethical foundation. And frankly, so they'd have something explicit to rebel against. I fell away a long, long time ago. As for Christmas. Well, since the kids grew up, I've been alone, mostly. Sometimes I ski." Sometimes, he thinks, it's just something to get through. He shrugs. She doesn't reply.

They walk through the very cold and now empty streets, toward the warmth of the hotel. "And you, Judith. Are you religious?"

"That's a very, very complicated question."

"The question is simple. Perhaps the answer is complicated."

She turns, reaches up to kiss his cheek. "As a mathematician, I appreciate your precision. Maybe over tea this afternoon."

4

Late that afternoon, she wakens as she normally does; tea arrives as it normally does; and they settle in the sitting room. He repeats the question.

She breathes slowly, as if in meditation. "Remember how your New York neighbor, Mrs.—what was her name?"

"Mrs. Siegel?"

"Mrs. Siegel looked me over without entirely approving of me? I'm sure she thought I was trying to—what's it called, pass?" She picks at a few *Lebkuchen* that have arrived with tea. She wears the Christmas present he gave her, exactly the same blue color as her eyes, fine against her pale skin, her silvering hair.

Molloy, who is much practiced in tactical silences, keeps quiet, allows himself to consider her. From the moment he'd laid eyes on her, he'd thought she was a beauty. It isn't a conventional prettiness that captivates him: to that he's indifferent. It's the sense of accomplishment that radiates from her, a woman who's challenged the world and triumphed. He loves that radiance, and sometimes even envies it. He loves her erotic energy, the new discovery. A woman to admire as well as love.

She smiles, leans forward, as if to share a joke of a secret. "It's like this. Before my father became Henry Greenwood, he was Heinrich Gruenwald." She stops, but he's silent, impassive. "Born a German Jew." He nods, perhaps only with his eyes, to say he's heard her. "Got to the United States as a kid in the late thirties. The family was totally secular. Couldn't begin to fathom why—or how—the Nuremberg Laws would apply to them. They kept putting off leaving—they considered themselves completely German. A grandfather had died in World War I for Germany; uncles, cousins survived, were decorated with the Iron Cross. What else did you need to prove your patriotism, your loyalty? But as you know, those laws did apply, and the family was infinitely lucky to escape when they did. My dad was thirteen, maybe fourteen. They settled in New York—Washington Heights, of course. So many Jews there, he told me, they all thought that Hitler had a special bomb just for Washington Heights. By the time the war broke out, my father was frantic to do something, do his part, help his new country. Help destroy the maniac who was murdering so many of his not-quite co-religionists.

Anyway, he enlisted, and somebody smart figured out a young guy like that, native speaker and all, could be a serious asset in counter-espionage."

Molloy listens without reaction, sips his tea from time to time.

"He'd been an ordinary GI, but now he was plucked from his outfit, put into a special program, and began very elaborate training." She stops for a moment, resumes. "Including bringing him up-to-date on his colloquial German. Counter-espionage tricks, of course. Parachuting. Electronics—such that it was in those days. How to kill, hand to hand. Knowing my father, he was all primed. Then—"

She puts down her cup and saucer, looks into the distance. "Then it all turned to farce. The guys he'd trained with, also young German Jewish refugees, their orders got bollixed up. They got sent to North Africa instead of Europe. But at least, as he heard later, they could talk their way onto a troop transport from Algiers to Italy. They were then flown secretly to Austria, dropped on to a glacier, and incredibly, made their way to a nearby town in the Oetzthal. Extremely rugged country. I've hiked it in the summertime. Maybe you have too. But this was the dead of winter. They actually passed themselves off as German officers, got a lot of good intelligence back to the Allies. Their story is heroic, a fabulous yarn. The kind of derring-do that ought to be a movie, except it was classified for so long. Meanwhile, and this is hard to believe, my father alone got orders to go to the Pacific."

"The Pacific?" His incredulity breaks his silence.

She nods. "He protested. No good. He appealed. No good. He apparently yelled and screamed. No good. He was heartbroken. It was such a stupid wartime fuckup. I mean, both fronts were the war, yes, but what good was all this intense, expensive training going to do him or his country in the Pacific, for God's sake? And then, to add insult to injury, to a desk job. A guy who could garrote a sentry in utter silence?"

"He was in the OSS, then?"

"You know about them?"

"Military history is a little interest of mine." She remembers all the history books in the Riverside Drive apartment. He adds: "Strictly a spectator sport: I never served. And then?"

"Long story short, he came back to New York after he was discharged, got a scholarship—it was more than the GI Bill—and after he graduated, pestered Radio Free Europe to take him on. Meanwhile, in school he'd fallen madly in love with a young woman who, I'm told, was very beautiful. But—Park Avenue Episcopalian!" She laughs now at the absurdity of it. "His family, being totally secular, didn't much care. But hers was appalled, raised all kinds of fuss. Even with a lovely old English name like Greenwood, Henry had been born a Jew. A Jew! The scandal, my dear! What would the neighbors think?" She turns back to look at him, her face softened in a distant compassion for this young couple who would eventually be her parents. "But love will have its way; he converted, and he married her. My brother and I were born. Eventually we came to Munich, RFE headquarters, and he finally got to do his thing against the Germans—well, the East Germans by then. The Communists, not the Nazis."

"My God, what a story."

"Even more complicated than that. He'd never lost his love for his boyhood home, his boyhood language. The Nazis weren't Germany, in his mind. Of course in some very real sense they were. But my father—overlooked that. He was so happy to be back here. Well, as happy as he ever got. I think all these things— these near misses—had undermined him somehow. He suspected he'd actually been washed out of the unit, without anyone telling him. Anyway, he was never the hero he hoped to be, not during the war because he never had the chance. Not afterwards, because he fell into writing propaganda, a kind of hack advertising. You could say making propaganda was important, or you could say it made no difference whatsoever in the world. But whatever you say, it wasn't heroic. It wears on a man. At least if he entertains ideas about his potential heroism. He drank a lot in middle age, was always, at some deep level, disappointed with his life. With life in general. He died of Alzheimer's. Very sad."

He lets her ponder silently until she looks up, smiles at him. "So you see, I fall between the two chairs. According to the Nuremberg Laws, I'm Jewish enough to be packed into a boxcar. By Jewish law, my mother not being a Jew, I just don't qualify. So I'm really not anything. I was brought up Episcopalian, but like your children, it was something explicit to revolt against."

"Hybrid vigor." He adds softly: "Those are the formalities. What is it you believe—or wish you could believe?"

"That's the complicated part. Another time." They sit in silence, and even in the dark can see that snow is falling heavily now. "And your family?"

He finally feels at ease enough with her to tell her the truth. That he's never known his father, who disappeared before he was born. That his mother, so broken by this desertion, vanished into her bedroom for essentially the rest of her life, and that he'd been raised by a loving aunt and uncle in a small town outside Pittsburgh, in the Monongahela Valley.

When he's finished, she laughs. "We're quite the well-bred couple, aren't we?" He smiles at least. But they're saying to each other: You are not who I thought you were. You are not what I feared you were. With you, I might be able to be who I really am.

At first a small dark doubt hovers at the back of his mind: what if she's a permanent invalid, like his first wife? His only wife. He's been drawn to Judith by her strength, her independence, her considerable scientific accomplishments; that she's so fully formed as a human being. She never bores him; she endlessly fascinates him—her work, her opinions about art and music, her broad collection of miscellany (the etymologies, the folklore, the new things just learned about brain chemicals) that she presents to him daily as little gifts. Having done more than his share of childcare, he's finished with that, wants and needs an adult companion in his life.

To his vast relief, in the New Year, she begins to recover herself. After a few weeks, her wry outlook on the world emerges once more, her happy curiosity (which leads to further diverting miscellany—the lifespans of newts; just exactly when celibacy had been introduced into the priesthood; the best arguments for rule of law). Her boldness returns; gradually, even her energy. He loves to hear her laugh. It comes up from somewhere deep within, a woman's, not a girl's laugh, unrestrained but in no way uncontrolled; joyous, rich; the laugh of a happy woman. He's delighted that this old-fashioned rest cure, like something out of *The Magic Mountain*, is actually working (minus sitting outside in the snow, she notes tartly, when he mentions it to her—and he loves her for that too).

Yet at the same time, he also begins to fear that once she's entirely herself, she'll no longer need him. Two phrases rise persistently in his mind, unbidden, like stubborn melodies he wishes he could forget.

First is an old Latin phrase, *Et in Arcadia ego*, with its equivocal meanings. Perhaps the voice of the dead: I once lived in Arcadia. Or is it the voice of personified death? I exist, even in Arcadia.

The other phrase is Faust's fatal words: *Verweile doch! Du bist so Schön!* Stay moment! You are so beautiful! Say that, and everything ends. He tries not to.

Since art is one of the things they both love, the journey becomes a pilgrimage to the great museums—they go from Munich to Vienna, from Vienna to Rome, to Madrid, and as the weather begins to warm up a little, they go north to Cologne, to Paris, to Brussels and Amsterdam. He teaches her some of what he knows about art, which is a great deal. "Some women," she says with a smile, "demand a diamond as big as the Ritz. Well, I can buy my own diamonds. I'm much harder on a man—I want him to teach me something."

"Do I make the grade?"

"Elegantly, Jack. Altogether elegantly."

Tentatively, they introduce each other to their European friends, usually over small dinners. One of these dinners results in an invitation to a grand ball at a palace outside Stuttgart. "You didn't say yes?" he asks incredulously. "Of course," she says. "I've always wanted to do this." He snorts, remembers without pleasure how frozen his wife was at such events during the brief time she joined him, when he was first working in Germany. But Judith, fluent in German, will not be frozen; already her smile is wicked. "Do you think *der Graf* has had a Jew under his roof since the family last summoned a money-lender in 1136?"

"They've probably had a Jew—not that you quite qualify, my love—more recently than a mathematician."

Beneath chandeliers that have illuminated gala dances since the late eighteenth century, they learn for the first time how well they dance together, that as they waltz, they close out the world save its music, speak silently to each other in a graceful, bewitching language of movement over time, over space. Time and space encompass not just the duration of the dance itself, not just this splendid ballroom, with its cream, scarlet and gold décor, but whole centuries of the past, an entry into the interior life of history.

Though he'd balked slightly when she accepted the invitation without asking him, now he's resentful when the music changes, becomes what he danced to as a young man—or what the young are dancing to now. He only wants to waltz this evening, hold a woman he loves in his arms, remain bewitched by music and the moment. Or the past.

She seems to have enchanted their host, *der Graf*, the Count, who regrets that Molloy no longer handles the finances of his friends—how pleasant it would be to do business once more, to see the lovely Judith, the gracious Judith, from time to time. Molloy smiles slightly, notes that it's not even Frau Greenwood, but *die gnädige Judit*. He's always liked, though never trusted, *der Graf*, and is relieved that such days are over.

So these brief meetings with friends are successful events. Yet afterwards, they gladly resume their seclusion with each other, tacitly understanding that this is a time for them alone, that its essence will be the heart—or death—of whatever comes next.

5

On the promise of spring, they fly down to Sicily, where, as a mathematician, she can teach him something, walking in the steps of Archimedes. Along one of the narrow cobbled streets of old Ortigia, the ancient part of Syracuse, where they've been exchanging grins about the Pizzeria Archimedes and the local cookies called eurekas, she suddenly says: "Do you remember quoting Schiller to me once at your house?"

For a moment, he's puzzled, then remembers. *"Wer um die Göttin freit, suche in ihr nicht das Weib."*

She nods. "Who'd woo the goddess doesn't seek just the woman in her. I was floored. So immensely flattered. Maybe that's the first time I ever heard you speak German. Anyway, did you remember it's from Schiller's 'Archimedes'?" He shakes his head—just a poem he'd been forced to memorize in a high school German class. The quote had bubbled up from nowhere, he tells her, maybe because he felt himself sitting next to a goddess at last. In Syracuse, he begins to call her what will be one of his favorite nicknames for her, English or German: beloved goddess, *geliebte Göttin.*

Above the old city is a public park, with the ruins of both a Greek amphitheater and a Roman stadium. They climb across stone seats, and he explains the differences between Greek amphitheaters and Roman stadiums. Further along are cliffs that enclose a high-ceilinged narrow cave, the so-called Ear of Dionysius, named not for the god of wine, but after a brutal tyrant who once ruled Syracuse. Molloy turns somber, tells her tales from the Peloponnesian Wars, the thousands of Athenian soldiers, prisoners of war, who perished at the foot of these cliffs once, of hunger and thirst in the shadeless, unforgiving sun. For him it's a solemn place, and so, for her too. "I can't really explain why the deaths of these Athenian soldiers thousands of years ago move me so much," he says thoughtfully. "This was going to happen again and again in other places. Maybe it's because they died as a result of a very stupid decision by their government—Athens was already failing on one front in the war against Sparta, so it stupidly opened a second front here in Syracuse, and lost bigtime. Maybe it's because wasteful death is infinitely sad to me."

In the hotel that night, they're looking out on the legendary bay, where Archimedes is said to have set the Roman enemy's fleet on fire by training on its sails a mirror, reflecting the sun. "Not entirely nonsense," Judith remarks. "Some geeks at MIT tried to replicate the experiment, and if it had been early in the morning, a very hot sunny day, and if the fleet stayed motionless for ten minutes…"

They lean against the balcony railing, gazing out at the bay as the dusk gathers, the distant seawall with its green and red warning lights that mark the channel between the bay and the Mediterranean. He has his arm around her waist, imagines he can feel the gauzy dress the breeze pushes against his trouser leg. "*Geliebte Göttin*," he says softly. "Come sit. I need to tell you one more thing."

They move to an extravagant velvet couch, so Italian, she'd murmured when she first saw it. With what's become familiar affection, she fingers his springy hair, watching, in amusement, as it obediently coils back on itself.

He looks away. "I need to tell you about one more strange episode in my life."

She falls back on a cushion with a merry smile. "Oh, another true confession? You left someone else on an Alpine glacier, and this one actually didn't survive?" She's teasing. He's told her such a story as an unedifying sign of how single-minded and heedless he knows he'd once been.

No. He turns so they're face to face. He needs to see the reaction to this. "I told you that Lindy and I drifted apart—she was in the U.S., I was working in Germany. I was almost a weekly commuter, especially when she got seriously sick and the kids needed a real parent. Still, I was alone a lot. It wasn't a good thing for a young man—unnatural, really, to spend so much time away from his family."

"You broke your marriage vows? Is that what you're trying to tell me?" She says it lightly.

He exhales. "I think you'd understand that better…than what I'm actually about to say. No. All that solitude—that loneliness—made me very sad. In the middle of it, I had no idea what was happening to me. It seems that very slowly, over some years, I slipped into a tremendous, almost debilitating depression." He watches to gauge how she's receiving this. "I'm alone. My wife and kids are across the ocean. No. No, I didn't break my marriage vows. Not because I'm a paragon of virtue, but because my libido had just plain disappeared, poof. A typical symptom, they tell me." He gets through that quickly, low-key. "Then my

35

best friend is murdered in the carnage that was the war on capitalism in Germany in the late seventies. The Baader-Meinhoff Gang—you remember, though this particular assassin was only a wannabe, a friend of the family, which is why Jürgen let her in the door. That was…devastating."

He pauses in recollection. "Yet I still didn't get it, because work was okay—in fact, work was what got me up in the morning and kept me going all day, and I'm functioning fine there, I must be, because the money is rolling in by the bushel basket." He takes a deep breath. "Yet outside of work, life was hardly worth living." He doesn't want to get into details; he's already got misgivings about bringing this up at all. "What kept me going was I had two little children, and who would look after them if I disappeared?"

What he sees in her face is horror. As he guessed she would, she understands the unspoken part. But he can't read what else is there. Is he suddenly loathsome to her? Pathetic? He can't stop now.

"Lindy was very sick by this time, so I brought the kids over to Germany and put them in the best boarding school in the country. They had to know they had one functioning parent. I went down to the Bodensee every weekend to be with them. Sometimes Lindy pulled herself together enough so that we could have a family holiday, but that didn't happen too often. After a while, not at all. By the time the kids were ready to start college, I'd wound down most of my work in Germany, had started my New York firm, and was still wondering what the fuck my life was all about. And whether it mattered. When Lindy died, that was it; I finally went to see a shrink. Who gave me my life back."

She says nothing. Her face is unreadable, and it disconcerts him. He's the one used to concealing himself, taking the measure of the face across from him, placing bets thanks to his very fine antennae. She's indecipherable. He can only speculate, which edges him toward despair. He can think of no good outcome.

"That's all. I've tried more than once to tell you about this, and now—now I have." In the darkening room, he searches her face hopefully. Maybe she'll dismiss the whole thing with her usual charming skepticism, laugh it away. In some weird way it is laughable. But she's a strong woman, the lapse that brought them here to Europe all but over. She doesn't seem the kind of woman who'll stop to bind up a man's wounds. So maybe he's despicable to her after all.

At last he asks her to say something, anything. She nods gravely, no smile, no teasing, takes his hand, pulls it to her lips. Now he can see her eyes are filled with tears. She's close enough to put her forehead on his chest. She speaks so softly that he can barely hear her. "I can't imagine. I simply can't imagine." She raises her face to his. "Dear, dear Jack. I'm so deeply sorry that you were ever that unhappy."

They've traveled for nearly five months, and for all his ambition to get his foundation up and running, he would gladly do five more years of this. He's needed a cleansing break from the last thirty years, devoted as they were almost solely to making money. It's a devotion he looks back on ambivalently. He's proud he reached the top of the global financial system through his own will alone, without the advantages of the superb education and early contacts his colleagues all seemed to enjoy. At the same time, he's felt demeaned by a devotion to something as base as mere money. When he'd first known Judith, and she'd expressed such disdain for his fortune, he felt justly stung. Now he can tease her about it, a little. Now he can tell himself that the past is what it is, and at least he won't be poor ever again, while he turns that same intelligence that got him his money to doing some good in the world. He's begun to sense Judith's nascent restlessness, has found her scrawling formulas on hotel stationery. "Just a thought, just a thought," she'll say lightly.

It's time to go home. Neither of them has mentioned the future.

They make a final trip to Berlin. As they come out of the Berlin opera one mild spring evening, walking arm in arm along Unter den Linden, he's singing softly to her, bits of *Rosenkavalier*, which they've just heard. He starts to take her in his arms, waltz with her there on the pavement as they did months ago under *der Graf's* chandeliers.

She stops him. "Jack, I understand something important, and let me say it here and now." She gazes up gravely, this woman he's admired and then adored— and sometimes fears, for her power over him, a power she's unaware of, a power she uses carelessly because she doesn't know about it, he dare not tell her. Then she smiles, a slight, embarrassed smile, not at all her usual self-confident dazzler. His heart lurches, dreads what's coming. He composes himself: automatically his face is unreadable. He'll endure the end of Arcadia, if he must. He also knows that he'll be destroyed. He isn't a man who can live on memories. Best not to have begun, but too late now.

"Let me say it in English, because I want to say it exactly right."

He doesn't even trust himself to nod.

"I behaved very badly at the beginning," she begins. Yes, he thinks, and his mind races to what might come next: that the first impulse was right, even if all this has been very nice. Appropriate that he's been singing an aria of that self-deluding idiot, Baron Ochs, *Ohne mich, ohne mich...* Without me, without me, each day drags on so long.

She takes a deep breath, stands immobile on the pavement, which demands silently that he stop with her. "You asked about my—resistance to you. It wasn't the money. The money's okay, the money's fine. You're not an asshole about it."

He swallows. "Thank you. I guess."

"Do you remember the first time we went skiing in Santa Fe? It's so vivid to me. You're down fixing a binding, and you're looking up at me—goggles, black ear-band, I can't see anything but your smile—which just stuns me, takes my breath away. And at one level, I think, this man's broken hearts. Not mine. Oh, please, not mine. But at another, a much deeper level—I understood I'd broken through a membrane of the known world. The cosmic egg had cracked open for me. Chaos."

Chaos. Child of time and necessity. Well, so say the Orphic myths, he thinks, drawing on a lifetime's love of Greek mythology. But he doesn't break the silence between them.

"I knew, Jack, I knew. At that very moment I knew I was so vulnerable to you. Would be, from here on out. I was so very afraid of that. I can remember frantically digging my poles into the snow and holding myself up so I wouldn't collapse, faint, whatever was happening to me. And yet. And yet, I'd been looking for something...something like this." She cannot finish.

He exhales slowly, still says nothing.

She's forced to go on. "Sometimes a dream come true is overwhelming. It frightened me; you knew that. But it was—it is—a dream come true. I've looked for you all my life. No, that's not right. I never had the imagination to dream you. You're so much more than... To say I love you is—inane, absurd, stupid. Meaningless. You're my other self." She stops. "Call it love. We don't have a better word. I love you so very, very much."

Infinitely relieved, himself wordless, he holds her to him, tears of joyful gratitude he still feels obliged to camouflage.

Legalizing it all is a small bump in the road.

"If you really want this, Jack."

"I do. I absolutely do."

"I'm here to stay. A formal ceremony won't make any difference."

"If it won't make any difference, humor me."

"Well, a pre-nup, at least?"

"Everything's tied up in the foundation. You're getting a pauper. Ah, you want to protect your assets. Well then, of course. I know a superb law firm." A small and silly joke: Molloy's money is famously deep and wide. He's already told her he never intends to be poor again. While her assets hardly match his, she's comfortable, and has recently inherited more from her dead best friend, which she's dedicated to a scholarship fund for women in science, named for that friend.

But Molloy isn't being entirely honest that everything is tied up in the foundation. The papers are indeed drawn up, the organization set to start. He means for the major part of his fortune to go to the foundation. But in his heart of hearts, Jack Molloy is having difficulty letting go—not of his money, but of the control he's always exercised over it. While he knows he could assemble a pliant board of trustees that would do his bidding, he's also honest enough with himself to admit that this is contrary to the point of a board. But to yield such power to anyone else is deeply trying for him. He hasn't yet completely formalized things.

Judith Greenwood, who does not know this, and wouldn't care if she did know, rolls her eyes, and agrees to a civil marriage.

But before this happens, Molloy is obliged to speak about something Judith has never considered. "Some security issues you should know about, being attached to a high-net-worth individual."

"You can say rich guy to me."

He nods gravely, ignores her jest, which had been no jest for so long between them. Thus Judith learns about the security surrounding a rich man— code words to be used in emergencies, telephone numbers if and when. He hopes but doesn't insist she'll learn how to handle firearms. He decides not to mention Krav Maga.

Molloy has always cherished his privacy, has never wanted to be encumbered with bodyguards (though there were years in Germany when he had no choice, and for a while in New York City he'd kept a dog that was both a family pet and a trained attack dog). He wants only to move through the world like a normal person—go to the movies, the opera, and the theater, eat out when the mood strikes him. He's managed to accomplish this for many years by living with a deliberate lack of ostentation; by employing chicanery to dodge various lists of billionaires; and he's furthermore imbued his children with the same ethos— neither of them dresses particularly well, he tells her, or drives a flashy car. He hasn't been able to cure them of private planes, but he hasn't been able to cure himself either, and his prospective wife, whose frugality is otherwise admirable, has already exhibited delightful talents for travel. He hasn't told Judith that it had originally pleased him that she herself lived well within her own means—in her case because she was too preoccupied with her mathematics to think much about getting and spending. But the formation of the foundation has given a distinct signal to those who can read it, and security arrangements must be made.

"Very cheering," Judith says when he's finished. "Can I rethink this whole damn thing?" He looks stricken, and she laughs, hugs him. "Just kidding, just kidding."

The church wedding is a little more difficult. "Jack, I am so *not* religious. I'll laugh in the priest's face. I thought we got that all clear." But for him, she does it, and does not laugh in the priest's face. In fact, Molloy is the one who laughs, but only to himself, to see that she's far more nervous for that than she'd been for the civil ceremony. When they finally return to Santa Fe, they repeat the wedding service at Cristo Rey, their landmarked adobe parish church, for all their friends to celebrate. She trembles there too.

Judith's mother has balked at her daughter's marrying an Irishman in a Catholic church (though God knows an improvement over Judith's first wedding in New York's City Hall to that eccentric old Jewish mathematician the family never saw more than twice). Dear Henry might have been born Jewish, but at least he converted. And he was never a bogtrotting Irish Catholic.

Two things coax her away from her Episcopal loyalties. First, her new son-in-law sends a private plane for her and Judith's brother, a musician in San Francisco, to be at the Santa Fe wedding ceremony. Then, he is himself so courtly to her that she has to wonder how her bookworm of a daughter ever landed such a catch. But the way this dashingly handsome man dotes on Judith persuades her that the marriage might last more than a week.

"That's a lovely necklace he gave you as a wedding present," she says to her daughter the night before the ceremony.

"Oh, mom, this one's just a copy. The original is too valuable to wear—it's in the vault. Eventually it'll go to a museum."

Her mother looks doubtfully at the simple gold circle around Judith's neck.

"It's called a torque. Something the ancient Celts always wore, a sign of the tribe. Never took off. Were buried with. The original of this one got dug up in Germany somewhere. My husband has taken me into his tribe."

"And what did you give him, dear?"

"A book."

"Only a book?"

"It's out of print. Hard to get. The original, the first edition of Pokorny's *Indogermanisches Etymologisches Wörterbuch*. A fundamental etymological dictionary. He was thrilled. Very. I also got him the updated version to go with it."

After the ceremony, bride and groom lead a procession, European country-wedding style, of all their family and friends, over a bridge of the Santa Fe River and down East Alameda under the green cottonwoods, returning the waves of people in Msgr. Patrick Smith Park who've stopped their soccer, their volleyball, or their dog walking, to wish them well.

They wind up at their own compound near the river for the reception. Before they cut the cake—their second wedding cake—Molloy holds up his hand for silence. "I'd like to recite a poem. It's by the Latin poet Ausonius." He turns and addresses Judith.

"Wife, let us live as we have lived, and let us keep
 Those names we took when first in bed alone.
Nor let the days see changes wrought in us by age,
 When I cease to be your lad, and you my lass.
Though I am more advanced in years than old Nestor
 And you outdo the Sibyl of Cumae,
Let's stay oblivious to what old age might hold:
 Let's prize the passing years, not count them up."

She can't hide her tears. Nor does she wish to.

The actual logistics of this marriage are a little odd—Judith doesn't want to give up her small house with its view to the Sangre de Cristos, but Molloy's bigger house, his compound, less than a mile away, nestled down near the Santa Fe River, makes more sense as their dwelling. She's brought some beloved pieces of art to his house (their house, he keeps correcting her) and they use hers as a kind of guesthouse for visitors, or a retreat when she really craves solitude.

The bigger place takes more household help than she'd prefer. There's a fulltime gardener/handyman whose wife does the housekeeping, except for cooking. They have a cook. Only part-time, but still. A bookkeeper comes in weekly just to manage the household accounts. Molloy's curator comes each month with a helper or two to take pictures down, put up new ones, rotated out of storage. She shrugs. It isn't bad; truthfully it's pleasant luxury. But it makes life more complicated.

Molloy realizes he can again have a dog. Of course it isn't just any dog. It's a German shepherd, a *Schutzhund*, specially trained first in Germany, and then in South Carolina. Its ferocity has been deliberately channeled away from establishing its own dominance into protecting its owner. It's already named Wotan ("not that pompous character in the *Ring*, I hope," he tells his wife, "but the original Wotan, leader of the wild hunt, the god of ecstasy, a Germanic Mercury, a Germanic Dionysius") and Molloy continues its training himself. In German, of course. For a few weeks, commands and praise ring through the house and garden: *Sitz! Bleib! Platz! Fuss!* And seldom, but vitally necessary: *Packen!* Seize! For this, he needs an assistant from the Santa Fe police's K9 group, with protective gear. *Brav*, Wotan, *brav*.

As Molloy's foundation work and staff grow, he'll soon move his enterprise out of their compound to another compound near the Plaza; and as it grows even more, to a former art gallery with a splendid garden, a brisk fifteen-minute walk from home. Wotan goes with him faithfully, at first frolicking, and then as he matures, seeming to understand that he should emulate the dignity of his companion, be a good dog and *fuss*, heel. He becomes a somewhat aloof dog, also like his companion, and understands that his job is to protect the family. "Wotan loves me," Judith will say with amusement, "but he worships Alpha Dog." It all works smoothly.

So, against expectations, does the marriage. They've begun as two people who could hardly say civil words to one another; so urgent was their attraction to each other, so profound their need, so cautionary their histories. "It won't be easy," she'd warned him when at last they reconciled—or rather, she seemed resigned to them as a couple. He'd agreed that it was never easy. But he's better at taking risks than she is, has had more experience at it. She's long understood—and indulged—her own sexual ardor; with her, he's discovering the depths of his. That such a passion should come upon them in midlife is almost unbearable, sometimes comical.

Unspoken is the impetus of time: time lost, and never to be recovered; time's limits in the future. *Et in Arcadia ego.* Instead they joke with each other: "How would the Pope feel about all this fucking around with no chance of issue?" she asks him. He pretends to ponder the question. "I believe there's a Latin statement *ex cathedra* that translates roughly to keep it up."

6

The same summer that Molloy brought his bride back to Santa Fe, and married her yet again to make sure it really took, a young city planner there—as it happened, a colleague of Judith's at the Santa Fe Institute—looked up from his computer and cried out. "Good God, papi's coming here."

His wife, Adriana, was sorting laundry. "For a vacation? That'll be nice. The kids will be very happy to see him."

"No, for good."

A sock dropped. "With—with us?"

"He's rented Benito's house until he builds one of his own. ¡Ay dios!"

Adriana resumed sorting socks, kids' overalls, underwear. "It may not happen. Your mother played with living here until she found out what the winters were like."

"I don't get it. Santa Fe is so totally inconvenient for him. He's on planes nine-tenths of the time. Papi, what are you thinking?"

"Let me guess. He wants to be close to family. Wants to settle down. Wants to find—"

"The reason my papi loves you is because you can read his mind and spare him the trouble of talking."

Adriana pushed her thick black hair out of her face, scooped up the sorted laundry, started toward the babies' bedroom, stopped. "The Torres men aren't entirely opaque. Choose one or more of the following: His latest girlfriend just dumped him. His fabulous new commission will not be built after all. His worst rival won the Pritzker Prize, and Lee not. So far. The deeper version: He's always felt rootless. Once he thought that growing buildings up from the ground was a good substitute for sinking roots; he now sees it isn't. So Santa Fe and his beloved son and family get to help anchor him. Ground him. Oh my. Oh—fucking—my."

Mikey had slumped. "I love him, you know I do, but goddam, the man just sucks the oxygen out of the room."

"Maybe the universe is saying—well, who knows what the universe is saying? He can certainly be overwhelming," she added judiciously.

"He won't like it," Mikey said hopefully. "It'll be too quiet, too backward, too unappreciative. The locals will lionize him, he'll think they're hicks, and then he'll get bored. Go back where he belongs. Wherever that is."

"Miguelito…" She was smiling in sympathy.

"It could happen."

"Did he ask you if it was okay, or did he just—declare it?"

Mikey looked at her in exasperation. Of course his father had simply declared it. *Basta de* New York City, *basta de* Madrid, *basta de* all the world's capitals where his buildings were among the most celebrated on the planet. Especially *basta de* the nonentity towns that were on the map thanks to his glorious buildings—and they were glorious, no one could deny it. *Basta, bastante, assez* and *genug.* Papi was coming to settle in Santa Fe to be close to his children and grandchildren.

Adriana smiled. "It'll be fine. It really will. I have to say, I enjoy Lee. I don't have to be married to him, or be his kid, so I can savor that ego. Be amused by it. Tease him about it. And Mikey, he is one accomplished dude."

"He'd be the first to agree."

Mikey's father, Leandro Torres, slipped in to his distant cousin's vacant little house on Canyon Road in Santa Fe, New Mexico, and declared himself ready at last to be the paterfamilias of his son's family. Not in so many words, of course—Leandro Torres was capable of great subtlety, as any architectural critic would gladly say. The same critics would also point out his capacity for drama. Melodrama, said the more spiteful. He didn't do the chorus line, he told one interviewer. He only did the stars. True enough—a city full of Torres buildings would have been vertiginous.

Mikey's prophecy about the lionizing did not come to pass, at least not immediately. As predicted, his father was on airplanes nine-tenths of the time, and when he came back to town, was too exhausted to do much more than drop in for a family dinner, play with his son's babies, and get into reasonably good-natured arguments with his son. Who often posed questions he didn't want to answer.

"Why did Communism build such crap?"

"For the past fifty years, Mikey, everybody built crap. Debased modernism, international style on the cheap—it celebrates crap. But capitalists get to pull their crap down after ten years and build new crap. Thank the tax laws. So while you're looking at fifty-year-old Communist crap, you're looking at only five-year-old capitalist crap."

"Papi…"

Mikey's irritation was justified; it was a retort for a design charrette, not for a son who was posing a serious question. They agreed that the architectural legacy of international Communism was disgraceful. Some places the Party hadn't built anything; had barely been able to maintain the fine old structures handed to them by history.

"Okay, okay. They built by the numbers; that's part of it. The ministry needs an office building, so we use People's Approved Plan #72 for this wing and People's Approved Plan #403 for the middle. Nobody cared; nobody was accountable; that's another part of it. No funds to maintain the old places, or the new, no matter how crappy they were. The old ones didn't get torn down because nobody had the resources to replace them. The new ones were out of sight, out of mind, on a city's perimeters. The commissars themselves were hardly aesthetes, so who cared? No art of distinction thrived under international Communism; it wasn't just the architecture that sucked. Now, Mikey. Are cities elephants or mice?"

"Shostakovich," Mikey said equably, ignoring the dig about elephants and mice. "Yet you're going ahead in China."

"It's different."

"You think? Everybody knows the construction there is crap. Your great and memorable building's gonna mortify you in ten years. If it's still standing."

Leandro Torres was uneasy that Mikey might be right, and parried. "I've got a good team on the ground. A first-rate project architect. At least they'll put rebar in the concrete."

"Rebar? I thought you were using Ductal."

"I am." That fatherly expression of impatience: don't split hairs.

"Where's it being manufactured?"

"There, of course."

Mikey shrugged elaborately. "Jesus, papi. Q.E.D. And do you have just a little hesitation about helping these people to proclaim themselves *Número Uno*? Given a few small details like human rights and what have you?"

Torres was uneasy enough about the materials being manufactured in China; chose to suppress whatever concerns he had about his clients' human rights record. But what really dismayed him as an architect was the Chinese indifference to a sense of place—they wanted a building that would say Now, but not Here. Didn't they understand that Now changed continuously, whereas Here had a history? Not that this made the Chinese unique. To be successful as an architect, to climb into the architectural stratosphere, the biggest point he'd yielded was a sense of *terroir* about his structures—Abu Dhabi, Beijing, New York. However elegant those structures were, they could be anywhere. It violated something deep inside him. Well, a man must eat.

Forced to think about it, he'd say to himself that the work was certainly good—what else were the prizes, the commissions about? But he knew the good work had once been great.

In those late, great days, Leandro Torres been the perpetual runner up in the competitions, a cult hero nourished only by ego and the words of those who assured him that he was the best—too good for the grubby real world of zoning laws, budgets, and cranky clients, which was why the commission had finally gone to less gifted architects. He was a cult hero supported by a working wife. And sometimes by money whose origin he didn't like to think about. In those days of greatness, not mere goodness, he could pretend that whether the building he'd designed actually got built was beneath his notice, or anyway, inconsequential; and no one automatically assumed he was crazy. An exhilarating time, that disengagement from consensus reality, a time to try anything. He was architect and client simultaneously, an excellent state of affairs, because while everyone knew a building was only as good as its architect, it was also only as good as its client.

As a student he'd long ago got seriously into computers. Unlike his fellow design students, he loved his engineering courses. He learned to program early so he could write software he really wanted to use, software that expressed what he wanted to do, not the off-the-shelf stuff that restrained him as much as it set him free. Other people's software could be treacherous. Software, he'd say, is not a pencil.

But he also loved the materials courses, learned all he could about any material, getting down, if necessary, to the molecular level to understand, to absorb its properties, get a gut feel for what the material might be made to do. Then, having learned all he could, the structure would grow organically under his hand, delighting him. His fellow engineering students, tone-deaf to the poetry, oblivious to the vitality, insensible to the potential in those materials, left him speechless with contempt.

When he became a fully licensed professional, his fellow architects, who sketched a design, then turned to an engineer and said off-handedly, make it work, filled him with rage. How could you call yourself a professional—how could you practice—without knowing and controlling everything? Leandro Torres, an abusive gutter brawler to his colleagues, loved every aspect of his work, was meticulous to the point of lunacy about controlling each detail. In a Torres structure, roofs did not leak; heating, ventilation and air-conditioning worked without complaint; windows fit. Above all, people within were unusually content. That is, in the handful of structures that actually got built.

Yet he was an architect, not a comic book fantasist. He did want his buildings to be born into the real world. He longed for the feel of something built under his hands, filling his eyes, spaces he had designed to walk around in, to shelter, to inspire. He wanted recognition. He wanted some money.

A compromise here, a concession there; a long and useful affair with a journalist who promoted his work in major publications (their parting, just about when he won his first major commission, was mere coincidence, he told her, told himself). This was a breakthrough, and he was suddenly acknowledged as a man for signature projects. More commissions began to come his way; people he wasn't necessarily shagging wrote important articles about him. He found and trained junior partners so attuned to his way of thinking that he could speak a kind of gibberish to them, wave his hands, and be confident they'd deal with issues of mechanicals, zoning laws, budgets, and contractors as he would. His halo was significant enough—and he paid them well enough—that they endured his occasional tantrums. Soon his small firm had more projects than it could handle, and it began to grow. Branches were established; project partnerships formed with other architectural firms, glad to sign up. He had polyglot assistants for everything, including at least two people to wrangle his phone calls, emails and text messages. Leandro Torres had become a celebrated brand. All it cost him, he thought, was his soul.

To inhabit his new success, he was forced to give up gutter brawling and invent a new persona. Not the fussy gnomic professor in the circular eyeglasses (somebody else—a multitude of somebody elses—had already claimed that role, those props); not the foul-mouthed imitator of a hard-hat site boss, Timberland boots, flannel shirt under a shabby down vest (again, already staked and claimed, and anyway, too close to the gutter brawler he'd once been). He didn't want to be the mouthpiece for impossible theories, propagating buzzwords that let the cognoscenti know he was one of them, "coherent and differentiated paradigms," "replacing long-lasting epistemologies of conservative systems with non-isolated complex models," "deconstructing the vocabulary of architecture" (a deconstruction that led, in the case of one of his rivals, to a roof being put on upside down—this supposed to be a profound statement of some sort, incomprehensible to the hoi polloi, who only understood that within a decade, this profound statement had allowed the interior structure beneath to rot completely). And on and on.

No. His new persona was Old World: the courtly Spanish *caballero* who worked to a soundtrack of the *cantes* and staccato *palmas* of flamenco, his designs driven by the souls of Gypsy ancestors, the tragic view of life. It was distant enough from the real thing to give him some diverting moments. But in his new role of courtly Spanish *caballero*, he must now forego losing his temper and threatening to shit himself on somebody's god, somebody's mother, or insulting their marriage, their forebears, or their sexual heritage.

Paradoxically, he could see how the courteous Spanish *caballero* might have offended the wife who'd supported him through the lean years. She'd married—who?—El Cid? Began to think she'd got Francisco Franco instead. He woke up one day to find her gone. It wasn't enough that he shared her contempt for those people who commissioned his easy, second-rate work. She passionately believed he shouldn't have yielded to them. The sexual adventures she could tolerate; men would be men. But to compromise your work! Ah, Angustias, with such impossible standards, you should've married a priest, not an architect.

But the fact remained that for all his success, he lived in a state of low-level irritation these days. He was irritated that the field was full of younger people who weren't yet doing better, but should. Maybe would. He was irritated by having to get up at 4:00 a.m. to get to Albuquerque for an early plane to L.A. or the East if a client hadn't sent a private plane to fetch him from the Santa Fe airport. He was above all irritated with his son, who not only kept asking questions he didn't want to answer, but who himself was far too theoretical in his city planning models.

Yes, he'd come here to be with Mikey and Mikey's family, because a chilly loneliness had crept up on him, and he had no idea how to remedy it. He'd come to Santa Fe on impulse, but already sensed that he mustn't impose himself tiresomely on the young ones. He tried imagining his own father in such a situation, and averted his eyes. But the loneliness was palpable, and depressed him. He was grateful for the worldwide building boom that kept him so busy.

So in Santa Fe he'd been paying his taxes, if not quite in residence, for almost a year when he met Lucie Marchmont.

7

They sat across from each other in a booth by the checkout counters at Whole Foods, beside each of them the modest grocery bags of the single person. Hers was a neat canvas bag she'd brought from home, being mindful, he assumed, of the environment, green-and-groan, et cetera, et cetera. He hoped she was single. The small orange juice bottle was a good sign.

He'd seen her at the Farmers Market a few days earlier, shopping, he was sure, for one person. He'd tried a conversation over the heirloom tomatoes, suggested lunch—always a safe feeling around lunch—but she didn't do lunches, she said, or dinners either: a polite but clear turndown. Last night he'd seen her again at the chamber music festival, though with another woman. At least she'd returned his smile: no hard feelings about the Farmers Market. Now he'd run into her once more in the Whole Foods produce section, introduced himself yet again, persuaded her to stop a moment for coffee, share the fetching view out the window into the anarchy of the parking lot.

He accused her playfully: "You wouldn't even have coffee with me until you saw me at chamber music. Is it the theory that axe murderers and other lowlifes don't like chamber music? Or is it that everyone who goes to chamber music is too old for mischief?"

Lucie laughed. "Both."

"But at Whole Foods and the Farmers Market, look out for axe murderers?"

"Probably at chamber music too." But she was still smiling.

He'd liked her looks each time he'd seen her. The eyes were splendid—big, well shaped, brown and inquiring, a strong center to her face. The mouth was fine too, a subordinate center. The nose was an axis to order all the rounded elements, eyes, mouth, cheekbones, elements that echoed and played off each other, framed when he first saw her at the market by a big-brimmed hat. At chamber music he'd noticed the braid down the back—a little earth-motherish for his tastes, but the glossy chestnut hair must anyway be long, something to fondle. He liked it that she liked chamber music too; that she had at least one friend (he hoped it was only a friend); that she was somehow a part of what he'd come to value about this small city.

"Be at ease," he said with what he hoped was affability. "No leading questions, like what you do for fun or profit, what part of town you live in, what your phone number is. Not even your last name, okay? We'll stick to Brahms. Did you like that quartet the other night? Of course you liked the music; I should ask if you liked that particular version. Jesus, the string players are getting younger and younger."

He stared at her full breasts, voluptuous inside the chaste white shirt. Not the breasts of a young woman, but he longed to touch them, and felt generous, almost high-minded about that. He wondered why more women didn't understand the sexiness of chaste clothing.

She disregarded Brahms. "Lucie Marchmont. I'm a translator. Legal documents, contracts, stuff like that, German to English, English to German, French likewise."

"You wouldn't think anyone could make a living at that in Santa Fe, New Mexico."

"I do my work on the Internet."

"How did you train for that?"

"The Internet? It isn't so hard." His mobile face said no, silly, the legal documents. "I was a legal interpreter in Germany. I'm certified in New York and New Mexico. But I don't want to work as hard as I used to, so I just translate documents."

"Are you German?"

"No." No further explanation. "My turn. What do you do for fun or profit?"

"I'm an architect."

"That sounds harder than trying to make a living here as a German translator."

He shrugged. "I work less these days too. Slowing down. Real chamber music material." He was lying. He'd never worked so much—so hard—in his life. As he spoke, he occasionally moistened his lips. "I still travel, but not as much. My son is here—works at the Santa Fe Institute, the think-tank here in town." Lucie nodded; of course she knew what it was. "He's an urbanist."

"An urbanist? Is that an order started by one of the Popes Urban?"

He laughed aloud. He liked that, happy his impulse hadn't misled him: not just a pretty face. "What we used to call city planning. But it's not quite. He thinks he can study the metabolism of cities: cities are big—so are their metabolisms like big animals, elephants? But cities are fast—so are they like mice? It's not about zoning laws, like it used to be. Yes, my son and his family are here. Maybe I can give my grandchildren what I never had time to give my kids. Then a distant cousin was here too—I don't know, is the son of your mother's cousin also your cousin? But he left unexpectedly to take a job in Arizona. Driven out of town by a broken heart, I hear. The lady went off with a gazillionaire. Which my cousin most definitely is not."

"Really? What does this quasi-cousin of yours do?"

"Archaeologist. Actually, the Arizona job was fortuitous; I've been living in his house for a year. On Canyon Road."

"Benito? Benito is your cousin?"

"Truly, you know Benito?" His hands were wrapped around the coffee cup as if he'd throttle it, for sure wring more than caffeine from it. He spilled a bit and hissed at himself.

"I know Benito." He heard calm down in different words. She handed over some napkins, and he understood he was to wipe up his own mess. "I always liked him," Lucie went on. "I know the lady; I like her fine too. I know the gazillionaire. They're good friends of mine. It wasn't about the money."

"No?" Big brown-eyed Lucie might not think so, but it was always about the money, eventually. From the corner of his eye, he watched the shoppers push their full carts away from the checkout stands, start to the exit. This was a town center in a way Santa Fe's main plaza had ceased to be. He liked the groceries sold here, but the structure and its layout drove him nuts. Sometimes he played with offering his services to redesign it just for his own mental health.

"To be blunt," she continued, "your cousin and the lady—her name is Judith—were together for a decade or so. I don't know why, but it never moved beyond a certain, uhm, deep affection. But Judith and Molloy, they're soul mates. Not a phrase I use lightly. They eventually got married. Idiosyncratic in this day and age, wouldn't you say? Benito knows this? About the marriage, I mean? I'm sure Judith did the decent thing and let him know." She shook her head disbelievingly. "Making it legal. It was the gazillionaire, Molloy, who insisted—not just city hall, but a priest to bless them, the whole thing." As if she were describing the behavior of an unusual tribe, as if marriage were a quaint but fundamentally inexplicable ceremony. As if he didn't need to worry she'd ever entertain something as odd as marriage. "Judith is a kind of scientist, an applied mathematician, actually. An ardent nonbeliever, and she really balked; but Molloy is used to having his way. Anyway, they came back married after a long trip abroad, and then did it all over again at Cristo Rey in your neighborhood for all their friends. Do you speak German?"

"In a half-assed way. I've done work in Germany, but every time I open my mouth, some local rolls his eyes and says, ve shpeak English, okay? Why?"

"Judith and Molloy have these terrific gatherings every month or so, German-speaking usually. Molloy has the best of connections, flies people in to give talks or demos or whatever. Artists, scientists, politicians, musicians here for the opera—even for the chamber music festival if they're not too feeble," she added with a smile. "You might like to come sometime."

"It's the audience at chamber music that's geriatric, not the musicians. Yeah, I might. How do I get an invite?"

She didn't answer that. "Look, Lee—it's Lee, right?—I like Benito a lot, and I'm sorry it broke his heart and all that, but he had ten years to make his move. What was he waiting for? Whereas when you see Molloy and Judith together, you know it was meant to be. Give me your phone number and I'll see what I can do."

"I'll be out of town for the next few weeks, but maybe after that?"

"Going someplace nice, I hope?"

Concealed in the pleasantry he was gratified to sense a flash of disappointment. "Beijing. Then Dubai. A couple of projects."

"You're not in the oil business, are you?"

"Architect. You weren't listening. Anyway, no oil in Dubai." With irritation, he pulled a business card out of his wallet. He regretted this; he'd hoped for a slower glidepath into this and wherever it might lead. The last thing he needed was another panting architecture groupie. He was getting too old for that. It bored him. But the lady apparently needed to know he was not an axe murderer. He slid out of the booth, the irritation, the disappointment, out of proportion, yes, but more than he wanted to put up with. "You can Google me."

She looked at the card, then up at him, standing next to the table. "Lee for Leandro."

"San Leandro. Canonized for his bureaucratic talents. My parents missed the boat on that one."

8

She'd been taking him in too. While it didn't quite qualify as charming, his persistence had disarmed her. If he was forty-five, he'd weathered some hard times. Sixty, he'd done all right. She couldn't tell. His face was rough, well-lined, eyes almost hidden by lids that looked as if they could use surgical intervention, and probably permanent dark shadows underneath; hair a steel gray that only people who've begun with deep black hair are blessed with. He was slightly simian around the mouth, which made him look as if he was ready, any moment now, to kiss. She had an ear for accents, but couldn't place this one. Compared to his weathered face, his long fingers were incongruously soft, sensitive, yet they suited him. The work shirt, the work boots: an affectation? Not another Viagra Valentino, oh please.

In the course of their conversation, she'd watched him moisten his generous lips again and again, and conceded to herself: she might want to know that knowledgeable tongue, those generous lips, a little better. Her own tongue came out in imitation, licked her lips. Talking about Judith and Molloy, she was slightly shamed to realize, was a proxy for the real agenda. But tongue or not, she sensed this was an old-fashioned man, and needed to be the hunter. Intuition warned her that this was a man greatly self-absorbed. Well, even that might have its possibilities. Of course he'd said architect; she knew perfectly well. But in the role of prey, she must let him think she didn't care enough to remember. All too easy to sink back into these games. Dismally easy. On the other hand, his present irritation puzzled her. He was the one who'd begun the chase. When he stood up she was displeased to see bits of belly peeping out from between the buttons of a straining shirt.

"Are you a modernist?"

He made a face, looked distantly out at the parking lot. "If I were a modernist, I'd be practicing historicism, wouldn't I? Given that, by now, modernism is more than a century old. Historicist is about the dirtiest word you can fling at an architect. Right up there with child molester. Axe murderer."

She didn't know why she felt slightly humiliated by that. She tried another question with multiple purposes. "What do you think of the new plans for the

Farmers Market?" Soon to be built, in what had once been a rail yard.

He stood beside the table, looking down at her, calmly considering his answer, or maybe calmly considering her. "My professional opinion? Not bad. Not great. I appreciate the railroad references. But if you dropped me from a helicopter, I couldn't tell if I was in Santa Fe or Omaha. Eh, the weather's better here, but an architect can't take credit for that. I'm old-fashioned; I like some sense of place in my buildings. You don't have to hoke it up with *vigas* sticking out of the wall and a chile *ristra* hanging from every nail to capture a taste of the *terroir*." He shrugged. "I've done a few contemporary railroad stations in my day. Mine wouldn't look like that. I have a drawer full of awards for those places."

Modest of you not to display them on your chest, she thought. "Could you have worked with the budget here?"

"Probably not." He didn't smile. "But they'd have got a complex that was a knockout. A destination in its own right. Change the way people think about the place."

His egotism was breathtaking. She tried again. "It's better than what might have been there—high-rises, say."

"No doubt. The park will probably work. Or at least it might when the vegetation grows in. Those pergolas—I don't know. Meant to reference the telegraph lines over the railroad? All very nineteenth century. It's good they plan to keep the *acequia*; I approve of the rain harvesting. Good use of native plants. But the Farmers Market? Okay. Not great. True to the original buildings. Come on, the original buildings were factory pre-fabs, thrown up all over the country. All over the world, for that matter. I'm not a guy who's real sentimental about the railroads. If the Santa Fe city planners had had their way back in the sixties— this is according to my son, who's a city planner, sorry, an urbanist—these rails would've been torn up." He leaned down on the table, closer to her. "Does this stuff interest you?"

"Yes, it does."

He reconsidered, sat down again across from her, cracked a half-smile, opened the eyes somewhat wider. "Well, then. Let me give you a walkabout. The New Urbanism in Santa Fe. What works. What doesn't. Never fear, I'm chamber music material, okay? What are you doing this afternoon?"

"Working."

"Tomorrow, then."

"You're in a rush."

"I told you I was leaving town in a few days."

"Okay, tomorrow." Lucie paused. "Let me ask you two questions. You can answer tomorrow. How come when this country was at its poorest, in the Depression, public architecture was so fine? Post offices, like the one near St. Francis Cathedral—it was handsome enough to be turned into a museum when it had to be replaced with something bigger. By then the country was flush, and yet look at the post office we got to replace it."

He hesitated. "That's maybe an economic question." Yet he knew exactly what she meant. The city had also recently built a new convention center downtown, an unexceptional building clad in the usual brown stucco, the usual *vigas*. Okay, if not brilliant. He understood that conventioneers wanted a shorthand version of the Santa Fe experience; he understood that city fathers didn't routinely commission unusual civic structures. He appreciated the courtyards, which allowed natural light into meeting rooms, allowed people to step outside for a moment into Santa Fe's brilliant sunshine. Having spent many years in Spain, he appreciated the touches of Spanish colonial revival—the building edging toward the sidewalk, the *portales*, the covered walkways.

But at the back of the building, which wasn't discreetly hidden, but was on a major street, and faced that same ugly sixties-era main post office that Lucie had meant—on that backside, somebody had unthinkingly slapped on a factory-built parking control apparatus: a little free-standing metal guard's booth, the barrier arms, ticket dispensers. It was as if, once the building was completed, it came as a complete surprise to designers that something must control the traffic coming into and out of the underground parking—itself an aperture, an orifice, that reminded Torres of nothing so much as an asshole. He'd said to his son: "It's like the convention center has pulled down its pants and, boil on its ass and all, is mooning the post office. Well-deserved, but does that kind of discourse have any place in civic architecture?"

Lucie cleared her throat. "My second question is: how come you professionals all love the buildings the rest of us hate?" She smiled winningly.

9

"Against the charitable gesture there is no defense." The man most people know as Molloy, the gazillionaire, has memorized certain passages from a book, also called *Molloy*, by Samuel Beckett, and likes to mull those passages over in his new, mid-life role as philanthropist. "Let me tell you this," the memorized passage goes on. "When social workers offer you free, gratis, and for nothing something to hinder you from swooning, which with them is an obsession, it is useless to recoil." Nobody has yet recoiled from anything he's offered. But he wonders how well he can spend all that money, which, as he was warned, was much easier to make than to spend effectively. The man known as Molloy sighs.

His wife, stretched out next to him in their bed, takes the sigh as an invitation to put her own book down and talk. "Lucie Marchmont mentioned a new guy for the salon." He's deep in his thoughts, prompted by his reading on the theory of philanthropy. He doesn't answer immediately. "An architect. Lee somebody. Spanish name."

He puts down the book. "Not Leandro Torres?"

"That's it. You know him?"

"I know of him. A starchitect, as they say. No idea he was in Santa Fe. Icy Lucie knows Torres? The world never ceases to amaze."

"She's not so icy, Jack. Well, not really. I think they may have something going."

"My God, that woman sails into a room like the figurehead on a dreadnaught."

"You need to raise your eyes above her chest, Jacko. She's quite beautiful." He grunts. His taste is for a face animated by energetic curiosity, accomplishment, a face that has seen something of the world, and conquered it too: the dear face beside him. The frozen symmetry of Lucie Marchmont's face doesn't do a thing for him. "Besides, I don't think dreadnaughts had figureheads," his wife adds decisively.

"I'm an inland boy; my grasp of the nautical is hazy. Maybe he'd be willing to give a talk." He means at their salon. "You didn't recognize the name?"

"Not something I follow." She reaches over and rubs his forearm. "Jack

Molloy, you are *such* an attractive man. No wonder I can't keep my hands off you."

He leans to kiss the hand affectionately, studies his wife's face fondly. "You know, when I kiss you—" and gently he demonstrates, "I feel like I'm kissing a Gainsborough lady. No particular Gainsborough lady, but any of them. That serene hauteur; that perfectly straight, by no means shy, nose; those knowing eyes—"

"And instead of a powdered wig, it's the real deal. Honest gray hair."

"With a sense of humor. Still, I keep thinking a museum guard is going to yell at me for defacing the painting." He strokes her face. "You should be Georgiana. Caroline. Philippa. Elizabeth. But Judith works. Lady Judith. The quintessential cake."

"Cake?"

He laughs softly. "Western Pennsylvania slang in my youth for WASPs. Cake-eaters. Cakes. Maybe only the Italians called you people that. All my friends were Italian guys. Where were we, *bella signora*, *chère madame*? Leandro Torres. The structures—buildings, bridges, train stations, stadiums, all sorts of things— are so very beautiful to me. They're biodynamic without quite being biomorphic, if you know what I mean."

"No. Afraid that one goes right by me."

"Sometimes they look to me like some fabulous flying animal has alighted just for a moment, and is about to take off again. Sometimes like some elegant musical instrument waiting to be played by a sweet-fingered giant. They're almost airborne, defying gravity, but in a breathtakingly beautiful way, not a disturbing way. He's said to take his inspiration from nature—sometimes they look like they've just grown there out of a field, or something. Even the train stations, the heart of the machine age if anything is, look so supple and organic. But they're—I mean, I'm no engineer, but they look to me so beautifully engineered."

"Jack, you're waxing positively poetic."

"Oh, I really love his stuff. It isn't that they look like any of those things— birds, eyes, musical instruments. It's that..." he hesitates, searching for words. "They capture some living essence of such things. He's an artist. Not just an architect or an engineer. An artist. Sometimes I think I'd like to add one to my collection. But what in hell would I do with a train station? Or a bank? He did a really magnificent thing for Deutsche Bank in Hamburg, I think it was. A weird but interesting building in Berlin. I think he's got a big one going up in Beijing. He's all over Spain, of course. Madame Genius, you know everything: you really didn't recognize the name?"

"Even better, I had no idea he was related to Benito."

While Molloy hasn't been entertaining carnal thoughts, he could, he certainly could. But Benito's name stops him. He falls away from her, clicks his tongue. "This village, as you like to say. Since you don't know anything about Torres, you wouldn't know the usual rumor is, his father was once the biggest scumbag dictator in the Caribbean. In that league, that's saying something."

Before he'd married Judith, she and the archaeologist Benito Jiménez had been longtime lovers. He can barely tolerate hearing Benito's name on his wife's tongue. Thus the gossip is really a bite at Benito, who has nothing whatsoever to do with the rumored dictator father of Leandro Torres, and he's a bit ashamed of himself.

"He was?"

"Hardly anybody knows that. I think Torres is his mother's last name. His origins—if this is true—aren't exactly widely known." He pauses. "At least he'd know who his father was." For all his success, his calm and love-drenched mid-life, this issue still nibbles when least expected. And maybe it's a kind of apology to the absent Benito and his blameless cousin, Leandro Torres. "The old guy ended up in Ibiza or someplace, sitting pretty on all the pesos he mugged his own country for. The architect, the son, did it all on his own. He's related to Benito? I'll be damned." He feels a sudden need for reassurance, a need that has been slowly disappearing; reaches across the bed, takes her book away.

Before they go on to other things, he murmurs, "I'll invite him to lunch." The salon is something he runs out of his back pocket, a little diversion for himself and Judith. If he isn't personally acquainted with the candidate he's considering as a speaker for the salon, he always begins with a lunch, a pleasantly informal way of making an assessment.

The monthly get-togethers, the salon, the *Freundesverein*, had started as a way of collecting people who wanted to keep their German and their minds fresh. It's true that Molloy has great connections, especially in Germany, where he'd worked in finance for some two decades. Into the intoxicating high desert air of Santa Fe, he flies in unusual speakers, gives them a few days to get used to the time change, the aridity, and the altitude, then presents them to a small audience willing to deal with significant issues.

A number of such circles can be found in Santa Fe—small, invitation-only groups. Beneath the veneer of Kokopelli *tchochkes* and fake adobe, invisible to the casual tourist, an important part of Santa Fe is intellectually driven. Not only do the opera and the chamber music seasons sell out, but public lectures put on by the think-tank called the Santa Fe Institute are always jammed, and the museums are well-endowed by private donors. The invitation-only groups exist even further under the surface, some devoted to reading classics (as he and Judith have the previous summer, bending their minds with a few friends to try to understand what an exiled pre-Renaissance poet named Dante Alighieri imagined Paradise might be like). Some groups discuss current affairs, since many old State Department hands end up in Santa Fe (plus an undisclosed number from the intelligence services too, but those keep very privately to themselves). The significant contingent of movie industry people means that other groups discuss movies, and there are "friends" of every kind of art imaginable, who meet, discuss, and visit art installations and private collections. A privileged few have been permitted to come to the compound and see Molloy's extraordinary collection of contemporary paintings, these very infrequent tours led by Molloy's fulltime curator. Amateur musical groups make music of nearly every kind. Talk has started of beginning a sing-around-the-piano group, Broadway tunes, American standards, but it isn't yet off the ground. A small number of science discussion groups, with scientists from Los Alamos, from the Institute, from Sandia Labs, offer Judith invitations: some she accepts and goes to, some fewer she takes Molloy to. In this, Santa Feans of a certain kind are old fashioned—they like to entertain themselves and each other with home-grown amusements.

The German-speaking aspect of their salon has been more often honored in the breach—the participants, whether German or not, all speak English, and it's too easy to lapse into the lingua franca. Thus whether Leandro Torres speaks German isn't interesting, but Molloy is very interested in an internationally celebrated architect whose work he knows and admires. He wonders how Lucie has met him in the first place, Lucie Marchmont, to his knowledge, having no interest whatsoever in architecture.

He reaches to embrace his wife, still a little bit surprised that she lies beside him, there for the reaching; that she reaches in return. As she moves across the bed to his arms, she murmurs, "Every woman in Santa Fe knows I go to bed nightly with the best in the Southwest. Maybe on the whole continent, but I don't think a complete search has been done. A case of bounded rationality— we can only decide something based on the limited information we have, our cognitive limitations, maybe even our psychological limitations. Don't you see the stark envy on their faces when we say goodnight at the end of a party?"

"Every woman in Santa Fe?"

"You've got only yourself to blame for that one. When you first got here you were one busy boy. You know how women will talk."

He pulls back a little. "They do? Well, I had a lot of lost time to make up for."

"Jack, forgive me if I find that legend of your earlier detumescence a tad implausible. Given subsequent events."

"Every word of it's true. Finally, when I saw you—when I was imprinted with you—libido came back with a rush. That's why no other woman would do in the long run. That's why we're stuck with each other."

"Maya even wanted me to call an old friend of mine in San Francisco, a retired plaster-caster, so she could come down and make a cast of this remarkable—uhm, phenomenon. The ladies were thrilled to think that the petroglyphs aren't all fantasy." He has to laugh. The southwest is full of beautiful etchings on the desert stones, often of males with phalluses that are longer than their legs. "An all-purpose general symbol of fertility," a colleague had once told Judith pompously, who laughed: "Not my all-purpose general symbol of fertility is bigger than yours?"

He pulls a pillow over his face. Takes it away again. "Jesus. I may fucking die of the mortification."

"I think that's a tautology," she says with mock gravity. "Add in the Elizabethan meaning of 'to die' and it's really quite clever." Silence while she lets him stew in his own embarrassment. Or pride. "Well, really, Jack. Maya. How could you?"

He groans. "It was sort of a hostess gift."

His wife laughs merrily. They'd first met at a dinner party at Maya Sinclair's. "And all I got when you came to dinner at my house was that lousy bottle of wine?"

"It was a very good bottle, as I remember."

"I'd rather have got what Maya got."

"You were otherwise occupied." Benito.

"All's well that ends well."

For, initial frictions past, they've settled into a joyous and harmonious partnership, finding with each other a love that leverages everything they do, alone or together. Judith, depleted when he took her to Europe, has come back to Santa Fe with fresh ideas for her research, fresh energy; Molloy has turned his ever-formidable will to spending his great fortune well.

10

Leandro Torres arrived for the promised New Urbanism walkabout in a BMW sedan with what Lucie thought was a hired driver, but was his son, Mikey, whom he introduced as a researcher at the Santa Fe Institute. Lee held the door to the front passenger seat for her, climbed into the back. "He knows his way around town better than I do. Anyway he's the city planner. I'm only an architect."

Mikey smiled that was not a smile. "Papi's modesty is so endearing." He looked over at her in the passenger's seat. "So, Lucie. Have you heard of the New Urbanism?" He was a younger, more polished version of his father, the hair still black, eyes alert, with an air of quiet self-possession—so different from his father's ego-forward bluster—that she warmed to him at once. Say this about the Torres men, she thought: leading-man looks ran in the family.

Yes, Lucie had heard of the New Urbanism, even if she couldn't name its precepts. Santa Fe, it seemed, had gone through a significant amount of development just as New Urbanism was catching the imagination of real estate developers. Some efforts worked, or almost worked; most didn't. "The question before us today," Mikey said with mock solemnity, "is which ones and why."

They drove north of Santa Fe for their first stop, a development designed by a well-known Mexican architect. Unlike most of Santa Fe's traditional pueblo-style buildings that mimicked the hand-molded corners of the old adobes, these townhouses and studios were sharply angled cubes that climbed up the desert hillsides. They were also painted shades of sand, umber, orange and gold, with bright accents of deep blue, red, hot pink, and yellow.

"What do you think?" Lee asked her from the back seat.

"I like the colors," Lucie said, "I like them very much." She stopped, wondering if this was a trap, that the architect was some dear friend, even Lee himself—she remembered the architect's name was Hispanic. Why dodge it? "I'm sorry. There's something so—sterile, so deadly about the whole place. Maybe it'll look better when the plants finally take hold." Hadn't he said the same thing about the new rail yard park?

From the back seat, the architect growled. "Walking. New Urbanism is all about walking to a center. But look at those garage doors! A Great Chinese Wall of garage doors. That's all you see. Anything duller? Anything less appealing to the pedestrian? Abandon all hope. I get a migraine just looking at them. So let's say you press on past the Great Wall of Monotony to where? *Zócalo* means main plaza in Mexican Spanish. Here's your main plaza—" he waved derisively at a small patch of struggling plants at the entrance to the development, intended decoratively, not functionally: no place to sit, to stand, to walk; no shade. "Or maybe they mean it's here, where the dumpster is."

Lucie had unconsciously screened from her gaze a large metal dumpster at the entrance, commonplace urban furniture. Now she saw its ugly carelessness, a garbage can on the front porch.

"This guy can be so good. Look at the detailing in the windows—proportions just so, placement just right, beautifully done. I like the colors too. I love the colors. But otherwise, the whole thing is just a barren mess. Nobody in their right mind would take a walk here. Would live here." Though contrarily, many people did.

Mikey added, "No porosity. You're not going to take a bike up that hill to get out here and connect with the rest of Santa Fe unless you're a Tour de France contender, and even so—you'd be roadkill in five minutes. Nobody in Santa Fe has any reason to come here."

"D minus," said his father with exasperation. "Next, please, Mikey."

As they drove south, they passed great tracts of desert that had been turned into gated housing projects. "We won't even bother talking about these. Just American big-lot suburbia in brownface. But give them their due: the developers didn't aspire to anything more ambitious. We're going to skip some other places, where you have to drive past the laundromats and the U-store places just to get there. You can guess the problems with all that."

"But hey, papi, things have really improved here. I was looking in the city planning archives, and you know? In this little paradise, back between 1935 and 1945, the average annual death rate from typhoid, dysentery, and infant diarrhea was twelve times greater in Santa Fe than in the U.S. generally."

"That's shocking. But why?" Lucie asked. "This is the desert."

"Badly built cesspools, septic tanks and privies right next to wells and other water sources. As late as 1947—this is three years after the atomic bomb is built up on The Hill—there are still areas inside the city limits without sewers or running water. The city dump was perpetually smoldering at the southern end of Galisteo Road, thus nasty air pollution. The arroyos were full of cars and other garbage. There was even a junkyard at the corner of Guadalupe and Montezuma, which the new city planners said ought to be moved, or at least screened." That corner was now at the center of a fashionable shopping area. "Santa Fe was no paradise then, believe me."

"Totally third world," Leandro Torres laughed. "And didn't you tell me, Mikey, that even as late as 1967, the city planners were saying that privies inside the city limits really must go? And the junkers in the arroyos? You'd hardly think you were in the United States. Would you call this city an elephant or a mouse?"

Lucie listened attentively not only to the observations, but to the man's accent. She turned back to him. "Where do you come from, Lee?"

"Born in New York City. Grew up abroad. Latin America, Europe. In my voice is my history. Sort of." He became less robotic. "I did that to my kids too. Mikey was born in Hawaii when his papi was working on a project. His sister was born in London. Went back to live there eventually."

Lucie nodded, not entirely satisfied. Turned again to observe him in the back seat. "I left you with two questions yesterday, Lee."

He grinned. "So you did, Lucita, so you did. I'll get to them today, I promise."

She faced front, the new nickname a bit presumptuous in her ears. Stop it, she told herself. This was being too, too Brit. Worse, colonial Brit. She had to watch that.

From the highway they reached a frontage road. At a place called Aldea ("the village, the hamlet," Lee translated) they turned from the frontage road and drove about two miles across the desert hills to what was indeed a central plaza. But except for the real estate agents who hoped to sell plots and houses, the storefronts around the plaza were forlornly vacant. As inviting as the plaza might be—some struggling trees, a fountain, benches—not a soul could be seen.

"No porosity goes without saying, but no density, either." Mikey said glumly. "Everybody's away all day because there's no place to work here. Damn, they did some things right. No Chinese wall; you get to your garage from a back alley. Streets meander. But the whole thing is way too tied to Santa Fe Style, so no architectural variety—you'd think the historical review board actually had a say this far out of town. The developers say that's what the people want. Maybe. But try giving them something wonderful with both memory and invention: you'd sell. Above all, the fatal flaw of the automobile culture. You can't get here without a car. You can't get away without a car. That really sucks."

"A technical term?" Lucie asked. Mikey laughed. "I hear you're studying the—metabolism?—of cities? Whether cities are like mice or like elephants?"

Mikey grinned. His father's summary of his work. "Yeah. Cities are big agglomerations, so they're like elephants. But organisms like elephants have slow-moving metabolisms just because of their size. Mice are small, and have fast-moving metabolisms. The number of heartbeats each animal is allotted over a lifetime turns out to be—on average—the same. About a billion and a half. The hearts just beat at different time scales, depending on the size of the animal. A whale's heart beats once every three minutes, a mouse's heart, like 800 times a minute. But in cities, which are a kind of social organism, it's the opposite. All the signs of the metabolism are fast, mouse-like. The bigger a city gets, the faster its metabolism. An interesting paradox. We're beginning to understand it."

"And when you do?"

"Maybe we can figure out how to intervene—"

Lee leaned forward from the back seat, and changed the subject, as if he couldn't bear not to be the center of attention. "Here's a stab at one of your questions, Lucita. Why architects love buildings everybody else hates."

"And then you people stick us with them, Lee."

"Yeah. And then we stick you with them. When I was in school, we'd say doctors buried their mistakes; architects grew ivy over theirs. Notice how we keep hoping the plant life will come to the rescue. Anyway, two things Mikey just said: memory and invention—"

"Which he first heard from his papi," Mikey interrupted.

"Who first heard it from one of his own teachers," Leandro went on. "Okay. Architectural energy comes from a balance between the two. If you're just doing memory, like these houses we just saw, the torpor is oppressive. Yet the new—Picasso said anything new is ugly. We have to learn what beauty is. Up until the eighteenth century, the Alps were dark and scary, just a barrier to get over, more dead than alive. Then somebody said, no, they're not dark and scary, they're sublime. By the nineteenth century, mountaineering was a transcendent experience, said to enlarge the soul. Different point of view, formulated and eventually learned. Same in the Americas. Alexander von Humboldt—well, you get it." He was animated, moving around spiritedly in his seat. She looked back: no seatbelt, arms waving. He was a Latin talker, wherever he'd grown up.

"Okay, does that mean I want everything to be novel? *Toujours l'avant garde*? Ehhhhh. You look at my buildings, they have—I hope they have, I aim at—both memory and invention, as well as a sense of place. A great building breaks through convention—it thrills us, changes what we think our culture can produce, even if we don't at first get it, even hate it."

"A taste of the *terroir*, you said."

"Yeah, I said that. Not a widely held belief in my field these days. So I design a building in Dubai and I have to think hard about it, because what's memory in Dubai? Camels? Tents? Sure, to some degree; so some elements in the building evoke tents. Inside, plenty of room to put those circular seating arrangements—pillows, chairs—that actually come from the time when men sat together in tents. Islam? Yes, and the Islamic elements found in mosques. Arabic calligraphy. Calligraphy, that's Islam's pre-eminent art. For me, written Arabic is like spoken French, a beauty that no other language has, semantics aside. In the hand of the calligrapher, they say, you can see the spiritual state of his soul. I tried it—got a guy to tutor me in Arabic script. I wasn't too bad. Probably the sad state of my soul that wouldn't let me get any better. Trade. The Arabs have always been great traders. All that. I've spent a lot of time in Andalucia, in North Africa: I *get* the Arab village. But this is the beginning of a new millennium, so we don't use Turkish tile or mud walls; we have new materials that can bear new loads, do other things too. Memory and invention."

She watched Mikey as he drove, trying to read his face, how he responded to his father's statements. He seemed to be slightly amused, slightly skeptical, but if he disagreed, he didn't contradict.

Leandro's phone interrupted. "Sorry, I've got to take this." He listened, grunting every now and then. "Okay." He slammed the clamshell shut, swore, said something in Spanish to Mikey.

Mikey said to Lucie: "Bad news. The developer's bank that was to finance one of my father's buildings in Spain may have failed."

"Has failed, Mikey, has failed."

She twisted to the back seat, saw the transformation. A moment ago, he'd been so cheerful, so eager to talk, help her understand. Now his head rested on the back of his seat, shoulders slumped, one hand covering his eyes. Below the hand was not precisely a grin, nor even a grimace, but something in between. Pain. Controlled with great effort. He was embarrassingly naked to her. She tried to summon compassion, but all she felt was mortification on his behalf—for the depth of passion in his outburst. His unwillingness, his inability, to conceal this was so disagreeable. Would he weep?

"Papi, shall we call it a day?"

His father didn't answer.

"Let's," Lucie said. "We can do this another time." They drove back to town in silence, Lucie desperate to escape the misery that flowed from the back seat. Was this news so important, or did the man just hate failure of any kind? She didn't know him well enough to figure that out. As she got out of the car, she said: "I spoke to Molloy's wife. He'll be in touch."

"Molloy?"

"For the German-speaking salon. An invitation."

"Oh. Yeah. Sure."

She was grateful to close the door behind her.

11

Before he'd taken the long European trip with Judith, Molloy had some general ideas of what he wanted to do with his new foundation, but it has always been his habit to gather information systematically. What should he know about philanthropy now? What's succeeded? What hasn't? He'd met with half a dozen experts in the field, and those conversations, which he'd hoped would help focus his work, stayed in his mind, emerged piecemeal on those dark European afternoons when Judith slept and he had his feet up, emailing, dozing, reading.

Philanthropy, he'd learned, is changing radically for many reasons. In the last two decades of the twentieth century, personal wealth increased dramatically: one well-known list had contained thirteen billionaires in 1982; now it contained nearly four hundred. With some amazement, he tells Judith that there are ten thousand families in the United States with assets of a hundred million or more. "So you're just a regular guy," she teases.

"Well, yeah. But hear me out. Most of that money is out of play. The Rockefellers and the Carnegies had this religious tradition of giving back, but my ultra-rich colleagues of the last two decades have no such tradition—you might even say it goes against their Reaganomic grain—so they sit on their assets instead."

"And what drives you?"

He stops. "I was an altar boy; what can I tell you?"

"You weren't."

"I was. Serving in mass was where I learned to keep a straight face."

"I thought it was playing cards with old Italian guys behind the barbershop."

"That too."

The new technology is also pushing philanthropy toward new rules, new leaders, a new Zeitgeist: social venture philanthropists, on-line giving, even community foundations, which allow donors to outsource their donation decisions.

Yet compared to government funding, private philanthropy is negligible. Even with his considerable resources, Molloy knows he isn't going to be able to solve the problem of world hunger—or even hunger in New Mexico, for that matter, a state with the highest food insecurity rate in the country—higher, on average, than all of Latin America. He suspects that adding more and more money to clearly defined problems isn't as effective as it was once thought to be.

So what, then, he's asked the experts, is the most effective way to spend his money? Spend to influence government policy, by example and by argument, they reply. Okay, he'll say, but what exactly does that mean? Strategy plus soul, somebody says. And what does that mean? Leverage has always appealed to him—its judicious use has got him where he is—but what does it mean in terms of philanthropy?

Early in his information gathering, one helpful conversation had taken place at New York City's University Club. Under a gilded Beaux Arts ceiling of breathtaking sumptuousness, he and a veteran professional in philanthropy could observe the weather and Fifth Avenue out of two-story-high Palladian windows. He'd felt a pang when he passed the Hallo, Berlin! cart right outside the club's front doors, knowing he'd be missing some beloved German sausages. As he gazed down at the Episcopalian soul food on his plate, he consoled himself with the thought that he'd be at the soft opening of a new restaurant that night, his friend Mark's Amuse Bouche, already generating great volumes of buzz on the foodie websites.

So he turned his attention to the woman across from him, a veteran of many prominent foundation boards. Catherine Newton was what he thought of as *echt* New Yorker—as chic and scrupulously groomed as any Parisienne, but with an incipient impatience you'd never see in a French woman. Even in normal conversation she looked pained, eyebrows knit, a kind of grimace around her mouth.

"Should the foundation be focused?" he asked her. "If so, what does focus in this case mean? Or can I successfully spread the wealth among some of the causes I've always been interested in?" He had in mind the checks he'd written while he was himself living in New York, to theater groups, for example, whose talent was far deeper than their budgets. He also meant the major New York City museums whose boards had invited him to join, and smaller opportunities that just popped up now and then, and spoke to some of his personal interests.

"You need to make the distinction between charity and philanthropy," she said briskly. "Charity is when you give to a cause that makes you feel good. Philanthropy is when you see a problem that desperately needs to be solved, and you ask yourself how, given your resources—and that includes your personal skills—you can take a significant step toward solving that problem, toward making a real difference, in the foreseeable future." He wondered how much of this was boilerplate. Or, how well she'd read him.

She leaned back in her chair, her food untouched, not because she had any opinion about its culinary pleasures, but precisely because she didn't. "You might think of dividing your resources. Put most of your money into a foundation dedicated to the problem you choose that desperately needs solving, the grand challenge. Put a smaller fraction into a kind of discretionary fund, a privy purse, that you can dole out because you've worked hard for these assets, and you're entitled to get the pleasure of some immediate gratification." A smile that was not quite a smile, implying that immediate gratification was slightly contemptible.

He arranges things this way later. Out of the privy purse, as he calls it, he funds the German-speaking salon, his annual museum board donations, and other relatively small causes that give him pleasure. Catherine Newton had been helpful if unlikable.

But a later conversation galvanized him. He'd been introduced to a historian of philanthropy, a gentle, animated social scientist who was only too pleased to help.

"Think of giving as slowly changing stages," the historian began. "It was once local, short term, face-to-face—you gave alms, let's say. That changed to patronage—you supported artists directly, you founded orphanages. It was charity. Then a hundred years ago, it got a fancy new name and became something more organized. Philanthropy." The historian tented his fingers, a signal to think. In his mind, Molloy pulled the word's etymology apart, love of mankind. Well, in his own case, not quite. Yet he was drawn to this man, whose benevolent face mixed what seemed to be a love of mankind with a love of mankind's history.

"Philanthropy. Now, philanthropy has been driven by metaphor," the historian went on. "Early in the twentieth century, when professional philanthropy—as distinct from charity—began, the driving metaphor was the germ theory of disease." To Molloy's puzzled look: "No, really. You see it in the language—'curing social ills' or 'getting to the root causes of poverty.' It was the turn of the twentieth century, biologists had just had dramatic success with getting to root causes: preventions, not cures. For the first time ever, they could plausibly think of keeping whole populations healthy instead of offering only to assist individuals. Nobody thought literal germs existed in the social body, but here was a powerful idea that thrilled the Rockefeller brothers as they were

setting up the Rockefeller Institute—you know it now as Rockefeller University."
The historian paused. "But a hundred years have passed. What's a powerful new idea for philanthropy in the twenty-first century?"

Molloy waited to be told.

"You live in Santa Fe," the historian prompted.

Molloy laughed, slightly embarrassed. "Complexity. The sciences of complexity. Of course."

The historian nodded, his Socratic success with this well-meaning plutocrat a satisfaction to him. "I don't know enough about the sciences of complexity to tell you which parts would be useful to you, but you're a smart man. You can figure that out. Or experiment—some things will work, some won't."

So all through Europe, Molloy yearned to ask Judith to play with this idea, give him some guidance. How would the ideas of complexity shape the organization of a new kind of philanthropy? But Judith made it clear that she was as far away as she could possibly be from thinking about complexity, or anything else that had preoccupied her professionally. She'd taken him through a useful tutorial, and that was all she planned to do. Well, fine; that's what led to them finally becoming lovers, and he's ever grateful for that. But it left him alone, leaves him alone still, to try to map what he knows about complexity on to what he's learning about philanthropy. He reviews and adds to his laptop notes conscientiously.

Complexity—populations of connected, diverse agents, with behaviors and actions that are interdependent. The agents adapt to each other, to outside influences, and those adaptations can unexpectedly change the entire landscape.

Philanthropy—a way of leveraging a relatively small sum of money to make big important changes.

Given that all the interesting systems on the planet—economies, ecologies, epidemics, financial systems, social networks, government agencies—are complex. Given that diverse agents—individual actors, lawmakers, clients, traders, workers in NGOs, friends, enemies, viruses—are all connected; that they interact over both space and time; that they influence each other in unpredictable ways; that they can move systems to change in nonlinear ways. Then to harness such systems—not to control them, because they aren't controllable—requires a sense of what makes them complex, what their most important attributes are.

A complex system needs to be supple and robust, and for this you have to encourage diversity—but not too much. You have to keep an eye on the long tails of the distribution of events, where low probability events can jump out, and produce large consequences. You have to be deeply aware of the interdependencies, push on the positive connections, avoid extreme efficiencies, so that diversity thrives, which encourages innovation. Extreme efficiencies can also push the system into a critical state, where a phase change can blow everything up. This is, he thinks, sharpening, giving an explicit vocabulary to ways he's practiced all his professional life.

How is an effective philanthropy to define its goals under these circumstances?

Can philanthropy be both smart and wise? Can it thrive on cooperation instead of competition? He mulls over what he's heard from Danny Hillis at the Long Now Foundation: what seems impossible in two years looks quite easy if you take a fifty-year view. The old philanthropy had been fragmented, and short term; the new philanthropy could be connected, cooperative, and patient. Someone had suggested the civil rights movement as an example: it had no business plan, no structure, and yet it was one of the most successful social movements of the twentieth century. Bottom up, yes, but with visionaries at the top who had a new kind of power, the power to achieve purpose.

As Judith slept away the European afternoons that winter, he was left alone to ponder the grand challenge that might absorb the largest part of his assets. He examined the problem in terms of physicians and research. Physicians were essential to cure an individual's disorders. But research was what allowed those physicians to act effectively in the first place.

"Fast change gets attention; slow change has power," he'd heard Stewart Brand say. A really visionary foundation could focus on the slow, powerful changes. But which ones? How to choose?

Molloy yearns for the larger vision. He wants to use his funds to seek, discover, and perhaps answer, the greatest questions that lie beneath the evident, the obvious. He wants to know how the levers of social change are pulled (but then doesn't every politician?). He's certain that to reveal those underlying questions, and to find answers to them, is the key to genuine change, and will shape the future in a way that simply pouring money into the obvious problems will not.

It might even yield deeper and wider solutions for problems no one has yet thought of.

Certainly it will leverage the foundation's assets better. On the other hand, it might squander them sadly.

Complexity as a guide, as a metaphor.

As a trap?

He ponders the idea of a think-tank, something like the Santa Fe Institute itself, except devoted to philanthropy, perhaps a kind of center for discovering deep underlying principles of social change, for testing innovations that might foster that change. Like the Institute, it has to be staffed by people with depth in the particulars of philanthropic projects, but they also must be young enough—or broadminded enough—to be willing seek out patterns beneath disparate projects; adventurous enough to try the new across disciplinary lines. With a fifty-year horizon, his foundation can become a guardian of the future. Better than a guardian—a shaper of the future.

Yet for his own peace of mind, he also knows that he has to spend effectively in the near term while he's planning for the long term. If he waits to see what might come out of a decade of research, the enterprise will freeze and his frustration will be monumental. But if he makes decisions on the first facts that come his way, the foundation will descend into chaos. Finding the right vantage—that fecund and dynamic zone called the edge of chaos?—is the real task. He begins to call his foundation, only in his mind, the Center for Innovation in Philanthropy.

He knows, but seldom lets it surface in his mind, that he yearns for this to be an even more spectacular a piece of work than his financial career has been. He might not have Carnegie's money, relatively speaking (then again he might; it occurs to him he should do the arithmetic, given inflation, taxes, and all the other changes since that time) but he sometimes imagines his name being known the way everyone knows the name of Carnegie, carved into the lintel of their branch library, attached to their symphony hall, their university, their foundation for promoting world peace. When this daydream does surface, he acknowledges its vanity, shrugs. Vanity has driven so much in the world; why not his vanity too?

Yes, of course he wants to make the world a better place, whatever that old bromide means. He'll show that money can buy justice in its widest sense, instead of only corrupting it. He wants to show them—whoever they are—that despite some major social injustices, he's climbed from nothing to something. Sometimes he thinks of the guys he went to high school with, as smart as him, but maybe not as driven, thrust by circumstances into jobs whose obituaries were already being written. Morabito, into the mills right after high school until, a decade later, the mills closed down forever. What happened to Morabito then?

Markus Lenczowiz, as bright and funny as they came, vying with Molloy for the high school Latin Prize; but down into the mines, and six years later, with a mine safety inspector having evaded his eyes, so badly injured that he was on disability the rest of his life. And the girls…oh, the girls hadn't a chance, even then. Pregnant by graduation (because they were good girls, and knew that condoms were the devil's tools) desperate for the guy to marry them—before he went into the mills, down into the mines. Or to Vietnam.

But somewhere mixed in all this is the longing to make another, a better, more memorable mark in the world than he has already. The Center for Innovation in Philanthropy might not bear his name, but other projects will. Anyway, the people who matter will know whose name belongs there.

To Judith, he sometimes lets this yearning slip out, though couched in other words. She knows what he's really saying, but to his relief, doesn't reproach him for his vanity, for his deep desire to show them. Instead, she asks, "Do you know Andrew Carnegie's history?"

"Every kid in Western Pennsylvania grows up learning that."

"Don't you think that his father's dismal failure as a cottage weaver might've had something to do with the son's ambition? That he too felt he needed to prove something?"

Molloy turns away from her, discomfited by what feels like a smallness of soul. But maybe she's right. He's long believed that the only people capable of shaking the world are the original poor boys, like him.

One night sometime later she remarks: "Here's what I tell my graduate students, my post-docs. Do something with impact. Stop the world in its tracks and put it on a different course."

"That's all?"

"That's all."

12

The lunch Molloy has with the architect, the starchitect, Leandro Torres, goes on until the waiters rattle the silverware behind them, eager to close. As they leave the restaurant, Torres walks over to a young man in a car, who gets out and will apparently follow them at a distance, bearing what looks to Molloy like a messenger bag. He's instantly alert.

Torres comes back. "My phone wrangler."

"Your what?"

"He covers the calls my office people can't handle. I have two of them. The other one's in Asia. Between them, they cover me twenty-four hours. I told him we're gonna walk, and he can follow us at a decent distance."

"This is a new one for me, Torres." Family members, a few friends, and his personal assistant have Molloy's mobile number, and that's it.

"The building trades. There's always something to be—somebody needs his hand held by *el maestro* and *el maestro* alone." Molloy has seen over lunch that Torres is one who closes his eyes for emphasis.

Thus they walk together, at first down Canyon Road from The Compound restaurant where they've eaten, then through town. They end by walking as Molloy walks every day, along Palace Avenue, with Torres interrupting himself on the grander points of architecture to comment on what they pass—the thick trees and vines of silverlace hanging over tilting stone garden walls, obstructing pedestrians. Small bridges over the unexpected branches—the laterals—of the *acequia*, Santa Fe's original irrigation ditch, which you never see at driving speed. The irony of curbs carved out so that the disabled can easily get off the curb—though the pavements themselves are wildly contorted little mountain ranges, thanks to the deep roots of the high cottonwoods that shelter the road.

"And look," Torres says, kneeling down to run his hand over the inlaid black brick of the oldest parts of the pavement, "these are way old, been here for a hundred years or more. A little mica in them—that's what gives them that glitter." Molloy crouches down beside him; has never noticed. They pass a couple of former neighborhood groceries, one such structure converted into an artist's studio, the other abandoned, waiting for its new purpose. Torres comments on the gradations of neighborhood within just a few blocks: Molloy's compound is large because it was once a rancho; but further west, toward town, the structures are much smaller, mostly hidden behind high walls, and in those thick high walls, inviting wooden doorways. "Maybe these originally belonged to the guys who worked your rancho, my friend." Between town and the small dwellings, the avenue is the Midwest: two-story houses with circular driveways, lawns ("Lawns!" Torres exclaims. "In parched Santa Fe! What were these idiots thinking of? Eh, the gentry never think"); gazebos and noble flagpoles; flower gardens. Molloy is amused and delighted; will not make this walk ever again quite so naively.

Of course Torres speaks at the salon (the phone wrangler in the back row) saying some of the things he's said to Molloy at lunch.

"If a building is to inspire, it must recast what people think they already know; it can't simply confirm what they already believe. This is the essence of great architecture: it rests in a tender balance, a co-existence, among the old Vitruvian precepts, commodity (usefulness), firmness (it has to stand up), and delight (art). It also rests in a balance between what is and what might be, comfort and challenge together. At its best, then, public architecture should be a setting for public ritual, ritual that makes of each user, for a brief moment, a larger person than he or she is in daily life. It ought to fill each one with the pride of belonging to something bigger than themselves. Public architecture should not only show us who we are, but also what we aspire to be."

At the front of the room, Torres moves slowly back and forth. An outbuilding at Molloy's compound has been converted to an intimate setting for talks like this, for chamber music concerts, even, sometimes, movies. Torres speaks with confidence, yet somehow leaving the impression that he's open to other considerations; that if someone questions his assertions, he'll understand, welcome it. Molloy already knows that this is something of a pose, but appreciates the trope.

"Architecture must be beautiful, yes, but what does beauty mean here?" Torres knits his brows, as if he's tackling a question no one has ever thought about before. Nods as the answer comes to him. "A beautiful building can't be changed except to make it less. Nothing can be added, nothing taken away. Like great art that way. Architecture—good or bad—lives in both a physical and a social space, and embodies a desire to do more than simply solve a functional problem. That's why we're concerned with its beauty. And something else. Architecture embodies power, domestic or public."

He stops, turns to his listeners as if something has just occurred to him. "It's of interest that the great monuments are almost always built early in the regime of an elite—the great pyramids, the Mayan temples, the Parthenon, Machu Picchu, even New York's twentieth century skyscrapers—because they announce the arrival, the consolidation, of new power. A great building is not one we need," he adds, quoting Louis Kahn without attribution, "a great building is one we cannot imagine doing without once we have it."

When at last he gets more personal, he speaks of how he loves materials, and always sets himself to learn their limits, which is why he engineers his own buildings—he thinks of himself as both engineer and architect. If you can always tell a Torres building, that's because it *is* a Torres building, the hand of the maker evident in every part.

The talk is a magnificent success. The questions are sharp, but friendly. His answers—like the answers he gives to prospective clients, Molloy thinks—are both satisfying and provocative. Molloy has to put an end to it so the group can break for supper.

Molloy and Torres fall into an easy friendship that Molloy, for one, hasn't felt for many decades, not since his best friend was murdered in Germany so long ago. Molloy has good friends in Santa Fe—he'd made friends with the retired moviemaker, Ron Gresham, before he even dared to approach Judith, Ron's lifelong friend. For a few days Molloy had gone to California with Ron's partner, Gabe, so he could enact an enduring adolescent dream of learning to surf. He has a regular men's lunch group, low-key and friendly, professionals who've arrived in Santa Fe to continue to work, though often on second, even third—encore—careers. He knows a few of the financial mavens at the Santa Fe Institute, and he's getting acquainted with other foundation leaders in town. But until he meets Torres, he has no one to simply call and check in with, someone to have those conversations that friends have, conversations that range from the profound to the banal, often in the same sentence.

In Torres, Molloy dares to think he might finally have found someone he can even call a close friend, someone to replace Jürgen. No, no replacing Jürgen, ever; but still, a friend. Torres loves the same art, visual or musical, that Molloy loves, for many of the same reasons—and when they aren't the same reasons, so much the more interesting. Torres is at the top of his profession worldwide, as Molloy had once been, the arcs of each profession being differently timed, differently shaped. Molloy understands that, and understands in his bones the endless sacrifices, the excruciating effort, the planning, the plotting, the risk-taking, to scramble to the top, the even harder scramble to stay there. They've both had intimate experiences of being simultaneously American and European, and those shared cultures allow them to understand much about each other implicitly. Unlike Molloy, Torres seems at ease with, and much admires his own son. Molloy hopes he can learn from that.

The lunches soon become Saturday hikes, days of fly-fishing on the Pecos, watching soccer games together as the season opens in Europe. Torres doesn't have a phone wrangler on the weekends (at least not until late Sunday when the business day has already begun in Beijing), so they're lazy days, happy days, days of pure escape and recreation in its most literal sense. The architect soon becomes a regular at the Sunday night long table, where Judith also finds him a charming companion, always welcome. "All this talk about Man United," Judith teases. "I thought you guys were into arcane political issues." When he's away, which he often is, Molloy misses him and their companionship; when Torres comes back, they resume again easily.

Only one time does this falter. Molloy reports to Judith: "Torres and I are thinking of doing the Paris-Dakar rally next year. Turns out we've both always wanted to do it, and this coming one— My love, you don't like this?"

She sighs, and for outspoken Judith, is hesitant. "Jack, I don't want you to think for a moment that becoming a married man has clipped your wings. You were already skiing the double blacks when we met. I didn't utter a peep when you took up mountain biking. But this. Paris-Dakar isn't exactly a walk in the park." Desert bandits had killed some participants a few years earlier; other participants had got lost and died of dehydration in the Sahara. "If I may say so, it took us so long to find each other." She needs to say no more. Torres, who would have teased her about her fearfulness, is firmly told to shut up. By each of them. Separately. Molloy and Torres go to Scotland and Ireland for fly-fishing instead.

The architect's son, Mikey Torres, seeks Judith out at the Santa Fe Institute, where they're colleagues. He brings his lunch into her office one day. "I'm glad your husband and my papi are getting to be such good friends."

"Well, not just my husband. I like your dad a lot too, Mikey. I had no idea he was—well, who he is, much less that he's based in Santa Fe."

"I guess he came here for us. He says a time in life when a man needs to be near his family." Mikey chews his sandwich. "He could live someplace else. Up to now, he always has. Has he mentioned to you guys if he'll stay? He was talking about building a house when he first came here, but it hasn't happened, so I'm wondering if, in the long run, he'll even stay."

Judith detects wistfulness in that. It can't be easy having an outsize father like Leandro Torres. She's surprised that father and son haven't spoken to each other about the father's future plans, that Mikey thinks he might learn something from her. For all his worldly naiveté, Mikey Torres has an admirable career of his own, is recognized internationally for the pioneering work he's doing in urban modeling, discovering the dynamics of what makes cities, those wonderfully complex systems, grow or fail, and how you can possibly intervene to make them grow more successfully, fail less fatally. That recognition isn't the same as the popular celebrity his father enjoys, but from what little she knows of Mikey, she doubts he even yearns for that kind of public acclaim.

"He's settling in, in other ways," Mikey goes on. "He's found you guys, which is great, and he seems to have a new girlfriend here."

"Ah," says Judith noncommittally, who's not only guessed that, but has had it confirmed by Molloy.

"Do you know Lucie?"

"From way back. Don't know her well, Mikey. She first came to our salon when it was more German-speaking than it is now, when Molloy was bringing in German artists and whatnot, and didn't want them to have to struggle with the language." Not that any educated German she's ever met struggles at all with English. "She's a fluent German speaker, very intelligent lady." She hesitates, then adds: "It seems an odd match, to tell you the truth. Lee is such a—well, exuberant guy, and Lucie is so, uhm, restrained. Is my impression."

"Opposites attract. Sometimes." Mikey gets up and studies her whiteboard. "So what have you and your group been up to lately?"

Judith is relieved to escape into scientific discussion. It's a fine old tradition at the Institute—you share with anyone who asks, who walks through your office door. At a place where everything is at the edge, you never know who might ask the unexpected question that will clarify, consolidate, put you on the right path toward your goal, even uncover your unexpected real goal.

When Mikey leaves her office she stares at an unproved conjecture on the board. He's admired it, wondered if it were provable. Intuitively, she believes it is, but every effort has so far ended in failure. She's used to such difficulties: she's always taken on the hard problems, and solving them has got her where she is. She trusts her gut. When she came back from the long trip in Europe with Molloy, she was rested, refreshed, alive with new problems to think about, new attacks to make on them. But this conjecture. She curses it for its stubbornness. Wonders how she can recast it so that it finally yields. Wonders if she can just get around it, and get on with proving bigger things in her long quest to define the known in science, the unknown, and the forever unknowable.

13

Molloy has two children. Stephen, a son, is in his late twenties, and Nikki, a daughter, is two years younger. Though they've been polite enough, welcomed Judith into the family, she knows that the conflicts between father and children are chronic, and will inevitably rub off on her as his partner. As not their real mother, who is dead. She has no idea what a stepmother should do, what a mother would do—the childbearing urge skipped me entirely, she once said to Molloy. "My maternal instincts are pathetically stunted, and really, I've never missed it. When some plot turns on a woman's frenzy to bear a child, it's always a sign of second-rate art—if that."

The low point between father and son surely had to be when Stephen came to Santa Fe at his father's invitation, and got himself involved with Molloy's girlfriend, Inéz, the three of them living under the same roof then. Judith had heard about this during the long European teatime talks. "She was only a placeholder for me; you seemed forever out of reach. So it wasn't some Greek tragedy. Truthfully, it wasn't a tragedy at all. Least of all for me. Certainly not for Inéz. But the proprieties must be observed. I threw them out." When he told Judith this story, he and his son had been unreconciled for almost a year. But Judith suspected from other things Molloy said that the abrasions between them were longstanding.

He'd called each of the children to tell them he was remarrying. When he and Judith came back from Europe and repeated their wedding ceremony in Santa Fe, Stephen and Nikki accepted invitations to the wedding. At the reception, Stephen made a sweet and generous toast to the newlyweds. Nikki went back to New York, but Stephen, who'd split from Inéz months earlier, has remained in Santa Fe; has a small house just off Upper Canyon that he claims he's renovating himself.

Judith makes sure that he comes to dinner regularly. He has an open invitation to their Sunday night long table, with assorted guests, and since his German is impeccable (nearly a decade in a German boarding school) he's always included in the salons. In addition she'll call him at other times during the week, just for family dinners. It's a chance for Judith and Stephen to get to know each other better, and he seems to like that, never refuses an invitation. Never, Judith notices, has other plans. But never just drops in spontaneously, either. In his own way, as formal as his father. Alone at the table, the three speak German, by now the family language, since each of them has lived in Germany at one time or another.

Yet it's at a Sunday night long table, just after father and son have gingerly reconciled, that things flare again. Stephen is one of nearly a dozen guests, yet clearly preoccupied by thumbing his palmtop in his lap throughout the meal. Molloy at first tries to overlook it; tries to conduct a conversation in spite of it; finally gives up in exasperation. To Judith, used to lively conversation over dinner, her guests eager to contribute, argue, the young man feels like a black hole at the table, drawing everything to him to destroy it. Stephen is oblivious—or maybe isn't, maybe is being deliberately provocative. He's been raised with European table manners, and knows better.

Molloy watches his son and finally speaks: "I guess you're texting the headhunter who's been after you." It's in German, presumably to spare Stephen's public humiliation, but a sufficient number of people at the table speak the language, and those who don't understand anyway. Stephen reddens, slips his device into his pocket. Dinner ends soon afterwards.

Relations between father and son have lurched on like that, but at least they're speaking; at least Stephen stays on in Santa Fe, accepts further invitations to dinner, and can be charming. A mystery, Judith thinks. She knows Molloy loves his son; she thinks Stephen loves his father, or at least admires him. But they can't seem to help dropping broken glass on each other's path.

Nikki, Molloy's daughter, has only visited them a handful of times. Much more than her brother, she has Molloy's genes all over her. "Papa!" she cried in despair once, "how could you give me this heinous hair?" Molloy's had been deeply black, now beginning to go silver, coiled tight to his head; Nikki's is shoulder length, shoulder width too, a mass of kinky black curls that won't be tamed by hat, process, or product.

Judith thought Molloy had looked hurt. "He also gave you his bone structure, gorgeous," Judith said lightly. "You thank your papa for those killer cheekbones, those eyes to jump into, those lips that drive men to madness. Right now."

Nikki had laughed at the flattery, dutifully thanked her father, and the moment had passed. Judith knows he's also endowed Nikki with his luxuriant body hair, not so attractive for a woman, and in her middle age she'll be at a specialist's, having the moustache removed.

"Is it really heinous?" he wondered to her when they were alone. She was right; he'd been hurt.

She's amused and touched by how often this titan of hers needs reassurance. "Don't be silly. It's wonderful." She rubs the top of his head affectionately. "I'll spare you why humans don't have the hair other primates have—nah, not even you, my furry missing link—and just say that tightly coiled hair on the head is optimal for both protection and heat dispersion, which is what human hair's all about. In other words, your genes did it exactly right." He smiles, perhaps a bit ashamed of his need.

For Molloy's relationship with his daughter is troubled too. She's capricious: sometimes full of affection, sometimes full of rage at him, always unpredictably. Her moodiness has always reminded him unpleasantly of her mother, his first wife, and he's loved his daughter dutifully without particularly liking her. Yet because she so resembles him physically, he's vulnerable to her, yearns for her love and approval in a way he doesn't yearn for his son's.

Judith first befriends Nikki one early summer morning when they discover each other by surprise on the west-facing terrace of the New York place. No one has thought to warn anyone; all assumed the place was empty, and so, in their sleepwear—Judith in the luxurious lingerie that Molloy loves to remove, and Nikki in a tee shirt that barely leaves her decent, no chance for polite how-do-you-do's—they meet for the first time since the wedding.

Nikki is in despair over a man who's dumped her, and Judith, no stranger to romantic oscillations, hears her out, suggests the obvious, ordinary mother's advice, that Nikki is better off without the jerk. Nikki receives this with gratitude and thoughtful solemnity. Thus begins the friendship that eventually allows Judith to say to Nikki things neither her father nor brother, nor for that matter, her friends, have the temerity to say, a return, Judith knows, for simply being willing to listen to Nikki. Judith guesses that no one has hugged this feral young woman in comfort, even in simple friendship, for years. That spiky disposition has probably repelled most romance too. Judith also concedes to herself that Nikki claims affection from her because she so resembles her father.

Nikki's appearance is one of her great dissimulations. She exudes a ferocity that must unman anyone lacking perfect self-confidence. Her eyes, even larger than her father's, dominate her face, staring out skeptically, intensely, distrustfully, from under eyebrows as thick as her father's that nearly meet over her nose. Not only do you almost forget she has a mouth until she speaks, but she habitually pulls up the top of whatever she's wearing and covers that mouth, as if to silence a heresy so potent it needs physical force to contain it. A young man approaching her would have to know that this was fear, not self-censorship.

Later that summer, perhaps three months now since Molloy and Judith have married, Molloy proposes a family vacation in Provence. Everyone agrees. It's a chance for Judith to get to know Molloy's children a little better, for them to get to know her.

The first afternoon they're all together at the villa, Nikki comes to the pool and, European style, strips off her swimsuit top, baring her full young breasts. While her brother makes no secret of his amused curiosity, Molloy studiously buries himself in his book. Judith sees all this, hides her own laughter. After a little while, Molloy sends his wife into the house, upstairs to rest, saying she's still not altogether herself, that the afternoon naps are still a good thing. He follows her a few moments later. She can't resist teasing him quietly about his sudden dedication to his book. He sighs. "The modern father simply averts his eyes from so many things."

The children stay on chaises by the pool.

"What do you think of her?" Nikki asks, rearranging herself luxuriously.

"Likeable. Quite likeable. Not what I was expecting from the Jackster. After Inéz, I thought we'd be getting, you know, a stepmother we'd have to bring up. A superannuated super-model. The usual rich guy's twentysomething muffin. Then in the second act, she falls in love with a penniless student and runs off to find real happiness in true love and poverty, leaving rich old Jackster in the lurch. Or she renounces the young guy because she's a fallen woman, and Jackster takes her back, everyone sadder but wiser. Depends on which opera. But no. She's a professional and hardly needs a rich guy in her life. A mind mate. Which for the cerebral Jackster, is the same thing as a soul mate. Too old to produce other claimants on the estate. Likeable. How old is she, anyway?"

"I asked her. She's five years older than papa. She told me she wouldn't have anything to do with him at first because she thought he was so much younger, but it only turns out to be five years."

"And that made it okay?"

"He was persistent; that's what made it okay. I like her; she's not the usual whatever. Did you see that necklace she was wearing?"

"With a big silver flower?"

"A big silver chrysanthemum. But if you looked at the petals, they were all beautifully sculpted little hands. Papa says she likes unusual jewelry. Not the dreary old diamonds and stuff. I like how chic she is."

"I'll bet she was hot back in the day."

"Stevie, she's still hot to papa. You don't really think they're napping?" She makes air quotation marks around the last word.

He props himself up on one elbow. "Speaking of hot, my, how you've grown since we used to take our baths together, little sister."

"I'm sure you have too, big brother."

"I'll show you."

Nikki makes a disgusted face, turns away.

"Little sister, I'm hot."

"Go upstairs and wank, then. Not my problem."

"And you're not hot? Those beautiful little nipples are telling a different story."

She grabs for her towel and covers herself. "You are so gross."

He collapses back laughing.

14

When Molloy had first arrived in Santa Fe, having sold his Wall Street firm at considerable gain to himself, he intended to reshape his life. He would find the right woman at last, and have time to think about some of the intellectual issues that had puzzled him, but that he'd never had the leisure to look into properly.

There were times when he spent weeks alone, or with guides, exploring the petroglyphs of the Southwest, trying to draw from them some kind of theory about meaning, significance, in visual images. It wasn't that he wanted to know what was intended by the meaning of particular petroglyphs—the cultures that had chiseled them were lost to history, and so were the intentions of those artists—but he wanted some kind of coherent theory that linked these deeply moving images to the images on his walls, his much-admired contemporary art collection.

He's still in touch with a handful of experts—anthropologists, art historians, even people in artificial intelligence, with a very practical interest in symbols— who gladly guide his reading. Among the many journals that arrive regularly at the house are *Current Anthropology*, and *AI Magazine*, but nothing he reads quite matches what he wants to think about, or answers his larger questions. (Or maybe they do, but the jargon of academic philosophy, for example, simply fatigues him, and he isn't sure that if he masters it, the payoff would be worth the effort. He's long ago decided contemporary art criticism is hardly worth wrapping fish in.)

When he'd tried raising these questions once with Nola Holliman, a Santa Fe gallery owner whose collections he admired, he failed. Either he hadn't learned to articulate his concerns very well, or maybe Nola relies solely on an innate judgment, intuition, not on theory, to keep her very successful gallery going. In any case, they spoke right past each other, at least on that issue.

So when, after a week's stay, the children have departed the Provençal villa, and the grownups don't feel obliged to tend to them, he asks Judith if she'd like to come with him to a scholarly meeting devoted to paleo-art and symbolism, a day's drive away at Grenoble. One outing he'd taken everyone on this last week was to a cave closed to the public, where they'd all been able to shiver, and gawk, at the charcoal and ocher sketches of long-gone animals by long-gone artists.

"Most experts think the cave art hereabouts is a culmination, not some fresh explosion. Art that sophisticated has to rest on a well-developed tradition. Of course no traces have yet been found of it, may never—"

"My love, go and enjoy yourself. This woman needs a little time alone."

"Was it—were they too much?"

"No. But I need to ease into family life. I need my little islands of solitude to help me along."

So regretfully, he goes alone. He hears it again: this glorious European cave art is a mature example of symbolic behavior. Such behavior, not to mention finesse, must have emerged much earlier, and not in Europe but in Africa—perhaps with language. If so, the oldest European paleo-art was created at least 70,000 years later than what he's seeing at the conference, these elaborate beads and decorated tools, dug up in Africa, that seem to be the earliest material expressions of symbols. These themselves must have come long after the first emergence of symbolic thought and communication, maybe a very long time after.

In the discussion periods, dissenters rise up passionately. Couldn't these artifacts be accidental, merely playful, of no particular symbolic meaning to their fashioners? No one can say for certain. Even more controversial, artifacts are being shown that might have been fashioned by non-humans a quarter, maybe half a million years ago. Perhaps they were made by the common ancestor of both Neanderthals and modern humans. No, others cry; these artifacts are too few and far between. If they resemble human figures, it's only coincidence. You can't infer anything from them, except that present-day humans are projecting meanings on to them. Symbolic behavior requires that the symbols have a commonly understood meaning among a group of people, that they send a message. One-offs don't count.

Matters of chronology will probably be nailed down eventually. But the scientists at this meeting are also asking each other the hardest question of all: to humans, what has been the evolutionary advantage of symbolic behavior? Why did humans develop symbols in the first place, then elaborate upon them incessantly? This is closer to what fascinates Molloy, and his attention is keen.

In a darkened auditorium, barely air conditioned, he weighs what he hears. Symbolic behavior—especially the evolution of language—would have benefited all parts of human social organization and adaptation, like group hunts, sharing food, teaching tool-making, sharing past experiences, and raising children. Graphic symbols might be the social glue that that helped early humans survive and reproduce, by expressing meanings difficult or impossible to put into words. Artistic expression, including music, might have helped insure the survival of the fittest. If so, how to prove that? The talk is heated and sometimes not entirely good-natured. Scientists at this meeting are making large intellectual bets that they know they might lose.

It invigorates him, gives him a pang, now and then, when he wishes he'd been not a financier but—well, some kind of scholar. So much of his life wasted thinking about crap. He doesn't mind being a wallflower in the breaks, watching the scientists greet each other, gather to argue further, to cement status or clamber higher. Then he happens to spot Richard Crawford, an English anthropologist to whom he's given a modest private grant to continue his work on the symbolic issues surrounding tool making. Richard hails him, wants to press on him a copy of the paper he'll deliver the following day, introduces him enthusiastically to some of his colleagues.

It's Molloy's turn to play anthropologist, with much private amusement. Crawford has obviously identified him as someone with money to give away, and that information flashes around the meeting. Molloy is suddenly the center of groups instead of hanging around silently on the perimeters. They invite him to dinner with them. He sips local wine late into the night as he hears them argue— as he watches them show off, much of it for his benefit. It's blatant opportunism, but Molloy recognizes it as ordinary human behavior. "My only legitimacy with these guys is my money," he'll say to Judith when he returns to the villa. "They're the ones who've done the real work. So if money buys me a ticket to all this, it's fine; I eat it up."

"Did it answer any of your own questions?"

"Ah." He shrugs. "One interesting talk, not quite what I was wondering, but an idea worth chewing over. Something new to me. A woman, I've got her paper with me. Ellen Dissayanake. To her, art isn't some human peacock tail, to signal a prospective mate that here lies healthy reproduction. It isn't a byproduct of a big brain that gets easily bored. She's saying instead that it's an adaptation in its own right. Given the time and resources it absorbs, it can't be just an evolutionary afterthought. It gives us great pleasure too. Stuff that gives us pleasure, like sex, is stuff that evolution doesn't want left to chance."

He has her full attention. "Go on."

"In most cultures, art's communal, not the calling of the gifted few. That kind of art summons all members of the community to join with each other, take part in a collective energy, cohere socially—something transcendent. Sort of like religion. And then she speculates that art began with the interplay between mother and baby—the visual and vocal cues, gestures. They're spontaneous, but still have a kind of formal code—repetitions, exaggerations, what have you. In other words, across cultures, mother and child communications are ritualized, with a common pace, common variations. You violate them, and things between mother and child go wrong. All this eventually—very eventually—is reflected in the arts. She concludes that artists use the tools that mothers have used everywhere, for thousands of generations."

Judith has a big, satisfied smile. "I love that. I really do. I can't think how to prove it, maybe impossible to prove, but delectably satisfying on so many levels." At that moment he understands something profound. This love of learning something new is as strong a bond between them as their physical attraction for each other. He'd seen it first the evening he'd spent with Judith at the Bosque, early in their acquaintance, when she and her old friends, Ron and Gabe, exchanged these tokens of facts, speculations, conjectures—little gifts to each other, which had moved him deeply.

This connection between him and his wife will also depend on, grow stronger with, each little intellectual provocation, each piece of unexpected knowledge, that they bring one another. It will nurture them and bind them all their days. As a young man—when he wasn't flying across the Atlantic to see his small family—he'd sequestered himself at the end of a workweek in dozens of dull hotel rooms in the second-tier cities of Europe, reading voraciously. He'd thought he was only killing time, keeping an active mind from going crazy, when in fact he was preparing for what would eventually bring him the deepest joy of his life.

As their vacation in Provence draws to a close, their evening conversations at the Provençal villa are murmured over *kir royales* in the twilight before supper, sometimes about art theory, sometimes about the children. Molloy is exasperated by his son's lack of focus, absence of ambition.

"You seem to have such high expectations for Stephen, but not for Nikki," Judith says to her husband.

"Nikki will—well, get married and have a family," he finishes sheepishly.

"Jack Molloy, if I weren't so besotted with you, I'd divorce you for that."

"What do you think?" The late summer Provençal twilight is embracing them gently, lovingly, its heavy scents of sage and lavender lulling them, insects singing, and they can almost hear the bubbles in their champagne.

"They're so different from me at that age. I was on fire. Nothing could stop me. Plus, I was living on fellowships and teaching assistantships by then. I wonder if I'd had real money. If that would've filed down my sharp teeth a little."

"I've tried very hard to make their lives as normal as...they haven't been indulged, particularly. They've heard me say *no you can't* often enough." Though it's nearly dark, she picks up his discomfort, his defensiveness.

She murmurs to soothe him. "Of course you did. But something stopped them from—oh, that's stupid. Since college, I've been surrounded by scientists. That's a tribe that, by definition, is deeply driven. The rest of the world, not so much, is it?"

"I was," he says tersely. She knows. And loves him for it. Just as he loves and admires her ambition.

So they return to Santa Fe, see Stephen often, hear from Nikki in New York less often. As time goes on, Nikki gives up making the art her father disdains, but she still moves in a circle of young New York artists, where she pours herself into playing Gypsy artiste to the hilt, exotic fashion and exaggerated makeup. Judith, also no stranger to theatrical self-presentation, enjoys this thoroughly. Yet she can't tease out of Nikki what the girl wants to do with her life besides play at Gypsy queen. How much of it is something particular about Molloy's children? How much of it is the elongated childhood that almost all Americans seem to dwell in nowadays? Judith can't say.

But the fact remains that Molloy's two children are adrift, and no one knows what to do about it, if anything can be done at all. There it has rested.

15

A few days after her conversation at the Institute with Torres's son Mikey, Judith ran into Stephen at Garcia Street Books. Though they saw each other regularly at the Sunday night long table, at the salon, even at family dinners, she hadn't seen him alone since the Provence vacation. She was charmed that, however awkwardly, he asked her to come and have coffee with him. Though she was pressed for time and would have liked to decline, she knew that some things won't wait; some opportunities present themselves once only.

Next door in the coffee house, Downtown Subscription, while she waited for him to get the drinks, she thought how long it had been since she'd had time to sit in a coffee house—not since she and Molloy had been in Europe, when she was presumably recovering from whatever had felled her. That the driven Molloy had taken all that time with her, as patient and unhurried as if he hadn't another thing in the world to do, as if she were his job—in retrospect, it astounded her. Moved her deeply. Endeared him all the more to her.

From the uninspired acrylics on the coffee house walls—Santa Fe had plenty of good art, but this wasn't it—she gazed out the French doors to the patio (an early winter day, the brilliant sunshine deceptive in its lack of warmth). In line for coffee behind Stephen, a very young mother, toting her infant, a crown of thorns tattooed around her ankle. A few tables away, a young man who got into loud yet intimate conversations with the barista, the busboy. Mostly she saw the preponderance of gray heads. At this hour, who else?

Stephen sat down with two steaming cups. Judith began to make the usual small talk, how was the house coming along, but stopped. This was his show. She watched him stir his coffee compulsively, looked for his father in his face. All there—not as sharply copied as his sister's features, in fact a softer version by far of his father, more rounded, boyishly earnest in a way his father had probably never been, but the same curly black hair (tied back in a tight ponytail), the same oversized deep black eyes, though Stephen's seemed more puzzled than guarded, as his father's had always been. The same bust-of-Adonis puffiness to his lips. He spoke at last, a low, almost inaudible voice. "You get it that my father and I don't always get along."

She nodded noncommittally.

"Maybe you can guess why?" The words were forced out slowly, a hand nervously playing with the ponytail. His father's long fingers, too. Had their mother contributed anything to these children? Her lunacy, maybe. But maybe it was only the circumstances of their childhood.

"No. Honestly, I can't. But as your dad's wife, I wouldn't exactly count as an unbiased observer." She wanted him to be at ease. "Say more."

He looked desperately uncomfortable. "Oh Jesus, Judith."

She shrugged. "Stephen, I'm not a mind reader."

"You know about the affair with Inéz?"

"Sure. In my face for some long, very painful months until your father and I got over ourselves—until I got over myself—and realized that he and I belonged together."

"Did you know that—" He sucked on his cheek, looked away, toward the coffee bar, the magazine racks "—that we'd shared Inéz for a while, my papa and me?" He looked back at her. "No, I see you didn't know that."

She'd known. It was the mention of it that embarrassed her. She tried to recover herself. "Did—at the time, were you both aware of—?"

He took a deep breath, shrugged. But still the voice was barely audible. "I've sometimes thought papa invited me here exactly to get Inéz off his hands without, what shall we say, inconveniencing himself. He knew he could count on me."

"Did he say such a thing?" Molloy had long ago in some dark afternoon teatime admitted to Judith he couldn't have said for sure.

"Speculating, Judith. I'm only speculating." She thought she'd never seen a human being look so miserable. But he seemed capable of some self-irony. On the whole, a good sign. He went on. "Papa, he's a chess player kind of guy. He always figures out all the moves ahead of time. I don't even think it's, you know, conscious—it's second nature with him." The voice dropped even further. "But this isn't about Inéz. She's history. It's—what my father knows about me. I always, I inevitably, end up wanting what he has. Well, that sounds totally Oedipal, doesn't it? Don't worry, your virtue is safe."

"Stephen, how ungentlemanly. Shall I be relieved or insulted?" She kept it light; for all his hesitation, he could be a little snot. What if she hadn't known about Inéz and the last few weeks of Inéz's stay with Molloy and Stephen? For all its tentative inquiry, too much glee in Stephen's *did you know.*

Suddenly his voice picked up considerably. "Noble lady, I like you enormously. I'll bet you were a hot thing back in the day."

She closed her eyes, resisting this insult too. "What's this conversation about?"

The voice fell again. "I'm not doing a great job of it." He looked around the room, as if for help. "Let's try again. I've never really got to know my father—he was never around when I was growing up, just too busy—too busy chasing the almighty buck. D-mark. Euro." He shrugged, as if it were an accusation he seemed not to believe himself, entirely. "When my mother got really sick, couldn't take care of us, he shipped us off to a German boarding school. To be near him." He fingered quotation marks in the air. "You know he was working in Frankfurt in those days? Please. A boarding school inside the same national boundaries isn't—isn't exactly family togetherness. Nikki and I didn't know a word of German. It was pretty awful."

"I'm sure it was. But what you call chasing the almighty buck was a man making a living, Stephen, which most of us have to do. He happened to be unusually—okay, extremely good at it. Should he have stayed home, Mr. Mom, and gone on welfare?"

"He could've made other arrangements."

"Maybe. But he didn't. Too bad." She studied him for a while in silence, at last began to muse aloud. "I'm just trying to calculate when the general myth changed from women should immolate themselves on behalf of some man—you've seen the operas—to parents should immolate themselves on behalf of their children. Kind of a crackpot cultural idea isn't it, that half the population must perennially sacrifice itself for the other half, or that one generation is compelled to sacrifice itself for the next generation? Just thinking aloud here. Let's say those myths overlapped in mid-century. Then, just as the dictum about women's sacrifice on behalf of men lost its potency, its ability to move women, just as the whole idea of the patriarchy looked so plainly ridiculous and self-serving, the idea—no, the myth—of parental sacrifice took hold instead." She sat back, thinking it over. "I wonder why. I mean, it's all bullshit, Stephen. I never bought into the idea that I was on earth to redeem some guy, and I don't think parents ought to immolate themselves for their kids. Hundreds of thousands of years where children are to be seen and not heard, and then suddenly all you hear about is children first? Weird."

"That's not what I meant." But in the silence she offered him, he didn't say what he did mean.

"Or maybe when ostentatious piety about religion—that goes way back in this country, Stephen; read Fanny Trollope on it sometime—becomes too, too tacky, ostentatious piety on behalf of your kids takes its place? Just asking." She was examining these questions with genuine interest, generating hypotheses as if she were attacking a scientific problem, almost forgetting that a needy, uncomfortable young man sat across from her. She brought herself back to the moment. "Your dad did exactly right so far as I'm concerned. You always knew he loved you. He provided for you—very nicely, apparently. He put you someplace safe and secure with consistent rules. He set a good example for you, a man with a sense of responsibility. What else do you want? What more does he owe you? Be grateful he wasn't a mining engineer and you weren't all in the Australian outback."

Stephen didn't smile, as she'd intended; he seemed a young man far too steeped in his own grievances. His expression turned impatient. "All I can tell you about my father is that he's the stiffest, most pompous, most unyielding man on the planet. You, however, must have found the other side. He actually unbends when you're around, but it ain't nothing the rest of us can do. How did you get him out of his pinstripes? Business casual! I hear you even had him wearing a beard for a while. It's a wonder he didn't go into cardiac arrest. For sure I almost did."

True, the fastidious Molloy went to work in freshly pressed khakis, shirt and sweater these days, a ski jacket when it got cold. Walked there in the bench-made shoes he loved, though a slightly more casual style than the wing tips she'd first seen him in, Wotan trotting happily at his side. Slung a messenger bag over his shoulder instead of carrying an attaché case. She'd teased him a few mornings earlier: "Sorry, but your sex appeal has really crashed. I loved it when you were all dressed up in a suit. Nothing quite like undoing a beautifully tied Windsor; opening a perfectly starched shirt." Grinning, he'd countered: "Unlacing a Victorian corset is big fun too, but you wouldn't want to walk around in one all day, right?" Then he'd colored slightly, recollecting those mornings when he got almost to the door, only to be deliciously detained. True, he'd had a beard for a while, but told her he realized shaving was a personal ceremony, a moment to center himself first thing in the day, and moreover did his best thinking when he was shaving, so the beard went.

Stephen continued. "I never heard my father laugh until he was with you. Don't think I'm making this up: I checked with Nikki, did she remember the same as me? She did. The anal Jackster could smile, chuckle in a pinch, but laugh out loud? Never."

She weighed what Stephen had said. "The anal Jackster was singing an old Pointer Sisters song in the shower this morning. 'Jump, Jump, for my Love.' Followed by 'Slow Hand.'"

"The fucking Pointer Sisters? My father knows about the Pointer Sisters?"

"You should hear him when he's channeling Hank Williams. Totally trippy to hear him sing he's nobody's sugar daddy now. Does anyone say trippy anymore?"

"My father can yodel?"

"Better than Hank. Of course he learned how in Switzerland." She sighed. "Come on, Stephen." In the silence, she could hear her husband and his Irish repertoire, how he could make her laugh with "Finnegan's Wake" ("That was a folk song?" she cried. "Who knew? Well, Joyce, I guess.").

Stephen looked up to a distance she couldn't see. His voice changed from jokiness to something more pained. "Everything he touches turns to gold—and I don't mean that literally, though you could take it that way. He made a shitload of money. He has, like, one of the great contemporary art collections, and every museum in this country and Europe will be kissing his ass to get at it. And now he's got this foundation, which of course will also be a huge success, because everything he touches is a monumental triumph, right? He even ends up with the best, the prettiest, the smartest girl at the party. If he ever made a wrong step in his life, I don't know about it."

"So much resentment in your voice, Stephen. You think your father never struggled?"

"How the hell would I know?"

"But you know he did."

"When? He's sailed through life on the S.S. Serenity, first-class cabin, and he can't begin to imagine why I don't sail that way too." He'd finished his coffee, unaccountably turned the cup upside down and splashed a final drop on a napkin.

"How much have you actually lived with your father?"

Stephen shrugged. "We were with my mother—well, my grandmother mostly—when we were little; then when my mother got sick, we were shipped off to the German boarding school. After that, college. Since then—well, not much. When we were kids, we saw him on holidays—no, to be fair, he came every weekend to the school—but he stayed in the parents' guesthouse. Sometimes a

94

hotel. It was pretty artificial, frankly." A judgment on his father yet again.

Judith thought about this, how the texture of everyday life had never happened among these three, Molloy and his children. No yelling at each other about taking too long in the bathroom, or squabbles over which TV show they'd watch, which movie they'd go to see. No wonder they were such strangers to each other. "How much do you know about your father's earlier life?"

He shrugged. "There's aunt Char; I guess she raised him. I don't know what happened to his real mother, my other grandmother. She was sick, I sort of remember that, because I was already in, like, college when she died. About the same time my own mother did, actually. Weird coincidence. But he never said much about either death."

Judith hadn't known about the coincidence of the deaths, mother and wife. She'd think that one over when she was alone. Why had Molloy put a block on his family history, at least as far as his own children were concerned? Did he mean to spare them something?

"Death," she said slowly. "A dear friend of mine died a little while back. As she was dying, she taught me a crucial lesson, which is, tell the truth whenever you can. So I hope this is tactful, though I'm more interested in truthful." But not the whole truth, not to this stunningly ignorant, aggrieved young man. "As I see it, your dad did his best to protect you from a lot of unpleasantness. Unpleasantness—forgive me for the euphemism. From a lot of heartbreak. Maybe that was a big mistake."

"Like what?"

She kept her voice as neutral as she could. "Did you know what your mother's sickness was, Stephen?"

"Like something mental, I guess. Nobody talked about it."

"Something mental. Well, yes, you could say that. She was a junkie, Stephen. Yeah, you can be a junkie in the fanciest penthouse on Riverside Drive. Started out as a post-partum breakdown after your sister was born. Maybe before that, maybe after you yourself were born. She got hooked on the drugs, never got off them. She died of an overdose." The long fingers were splayed on the table. He was hopelessly bad at hiding his shock. "You didn't know that?"

"Jesus. So is this like, payback for me telling you about Inéz?"

"Why would I need to pay you back? I thought I'd do you the favor of telling you something about your father's struggles, that golden life you think you know all about. Do you know where he grew up? He drove me past the house once.

Okay, not a sharecropper's shack or a log cabin. But next best: a steelworker's row house in a moribund little mill town in western Pennsylvania. Here was a kid who yearned down to his toes, was eminently fit, to be a scholar, a classics scholar no less, fighting his family tooth and nail, because they wanted him safely in the mills. Safely." She repeated the word and its irony, the fact, as Molloy had told her, that no one ever got off the mill floors safely. "He did that one summer, did you know that? Your father as a mill hand; doesn't that just take your breath away? His own father gone missing, mother a ghost, aunt and uncle who love him, true, but completely clueless about what this kid is, or could be. He got himself out of all that on his own hook. If he never told you about this, take it as a sign of his modesty, not his shame."

"Is this Oliver Twist story supposed to, like, make me feel better?"

"I wouldn't think so, Stephen. How could it?" She let the implications of that sink in, and was gratified to see that they had. "Just a few more things you should know about this golden life your father's led. You call him cold. Believe me, he is not a cold man. A formal man, no question. Reserved. But think about it. If he has a carapace, doesn't it figure that he was forced to grow it? By something? Oh no, I promise you, a man of deep, of extreme, passions." Tempted to say more, she stopped. "You say he invited you here, for whatever reasons. If you've served his purpose, as you seem to think, how come you're still hanging around? He gets up your nose, yet you stay."

"Where am I going to go?" he cried in real pain. "I want to be in the family. *A* family. I want to know him, Judith. My father, the eminent J. B. Molloy, pal to the central bankers of every European country and Turkey too; the ruthless Mackie Messer, who'd slice your eyes out before you even saw him coming; *Wunderkind* on two continents. But every time I see him, he's holding up a giant cue card that says SLACKER, all caps. It's hard to get past that."

"You want to be part of the family? You sat through dinner the other night way deep into your palmtop, your PDA—not quite talking on the phone, true; not quite reading a book in our faces—but about as offensive. It's not like you weren't there. It's like you were saying—well, what was that all about? It felt like a snotty little putdown of everyone at the table. Your dad had the balls to call you on it, but believe me, I was just as irritated. Some guy invited me out to dinner once. The second time he answered his phone—we were still on the appetizer course—I put fifty dollars down on the table and walked out of the restaurant. It's not like he was waiting to hear he'd cured cancer that night. Are you so eager for everyone to think of you as the family lout?"

His puffy lips stretched over his teeth, a shoulder flickered up and down, and finally he looked away.

16

She'd let her temper flare, and was sorry. She said softly, "You're a particularly fortunate young man, Stephen. You have the financial freedom to do nearly anything you want. What do you want?"

He kept on staring into the distance, silent. His phone rang, and if he was tempted to answer it, he didn't.

"No great obsession that just won't let you go? No passion to—?"

"No, Judith," he said with a world-weariness that almost made her laugh. "Judith, I'm really trying to be up front about this. My father is all those things I said—pompous, distant, an icy, judgmental man. At least to me, no matter how he is to you. But he's also a fucking hard act to follow. Were your people scientists? Did you have that little obstacle to overcome too when you started out?" More silence.

"So you want to be a financier? Financial developer, whatever they call themselves these days?"

"Please. I can hardly add two and two. I don't have my father's awesome genius for numbers, his uncanny feel for the market. Legend in his own time. As they say. And they say, and they say. No, that's not what I want. Can't I just be?" He quoted a few lines in German to her, lines she didn't recognize. "Thomas Mann, *The Magic Mountain*. It's a dream Hans Castorp has when he's listening to 'Prelude to the Afternoon of a Faun.' Hans wants to be that faun, his flute drawing from nature exquisitely colored, magical tones. That's all. A total resistance to Western demands for an active life."

"You'll settle for JAWS?"

"Jaws?"

"What my late dear friend Sophie and I used to call all the guys around Santa Fe like that. Just Another Wealthy Shithead."

He looked stung, and she was sorry. She'd heard the immense yearning in his voice. Yearning to be part of something. The family would do for a start. Then and only then, maybe the Western demands for an active life. After all, Hans Castorp didn't remain on the magic mountain forever.

"Let me ask you something. Does my presence, as your father's wife, make it better or worse?"

He looked puzzled. "It's kind of like being at the eye doctor's, where they put a lens up and say, better or worse? And you say, I don't know. Different. Better for him, I can see. He was very lonely. We really didn't see it, how much he's needed someone like you for a long time. He always seemed...totally self-sufficient. If he remarried, Nikki and I expected the usual, a dumb, perfectly shaped twentysomething we were going to have to—"

Judith laughed richly. "Your father wouldn't do that if only because it's such a dreary cliché, buddy. He is so particular about such things."

He seemed to relax a little. "Better," he finally said. "Better for us too. Because you make us see that you, at least, are a human being, not some assigned role—*die böse Stiefmutter*, the wicked stepmother. Maybe you can make us see him, that he's a human being too. With needs. Desires. Hopes. What I'm seeing is that you're the trophy wife, all right, but the Jackster's kind of trophy." To her perplexed look, he went on. "Internationally known scientist. Oh yes, that's right up the Jackster's alley. Suits him perfectly."

"You got it, bucko. One another's trophies. He got a sub-Nobel laureate and I snagged a rich, handsome young stud. The girls in the locker room are dying to know how I did it. What's that, a blush? Surely a man who poaches on his father's girlfriend can't be entirely unaware that his father has a carnal life. Stephen, for God's sake!" Behind him, she saw a young man taking them in. "Is that a friend of yours?"

Stephen turned. "No. Don't know him at all."

"Oh, good. He cruises this place for sugar daddies. He's complete trash; the last lover threw him out because he was stealing from his benefactor. The bait is, he buys the most expensive designer glasses he can, and the older guys he's looking for think that's a sign of how cool he is. He's got some totally implausible story about how he's the son of a French aristocrat mother and an American millionaire father. I sat next to him at a quite memorable dinner once, got to probe a bit. The fantasies were—well, fantasies. I looked at his boyfriend across the table and thought, you don't really believe this stuff? He's actually a young predator. Him, his victims; it's all kind of sad, really."

"Judith, I like girls."

"Nobody cares, Stephen; just a warning about some kinds of people. Boys or girls." And a way of getting past insulting each other, you and I.

"Your duty as stepmother."

"My duty as stepmother." She leaned toward him with a wicked smile. "Plus a little social sewage for your ears."

At least this time he smiled back. "Did you always know what you wanted to do with your life?"

She snorted. No one had demanded she be a mathematician. Quite the opposite. She'd had to fight her way there ferociously. The battle was still engaged. She folded her hands and looked solemn. "I ought to be able to instruct the young appropriately by saying yes, of course I knew; had absolute clarity on that. But no, God knows I hadn't a clue. I loved math and I was good at it—it was like a second language for me. I felt into it intuitively. But there were obstacles. Social in those days. Girls didn't do math. I sort of accepted that. Until I didn't." She smiled in private recollection.

"Did you struggle?"

She laughed. "Hell yes. But I gave as good as I got. A few guys walking around with one less nut than nature intended. No full castrati, though. At least not my doing."

He opened his mouth to reply to that, then couldn't.

"As your father detected in me instantly, I'm not a woman to put up with shit just because it's coming from someone with XY chromosomes. That's a shock to those who think their chromosomes entitle them. For your dad, bless him, it was a feature, not a flaw. At the same time, I love men, I really do—as a class, so to speak. I like the noises they make around the house, the rude ones as well as the polite ones. I like—well, it's one or two individuals I can do without. Like the high school trig teacher who was sure I'd cheated because how else could a girl score highest in class."

Stephen shook his head. "You're certainly nothing at all like my mother."

"I expect I'm not like anyone's mom."

They were silent again. Finally he said, "In my life, I feel as if I'm looking ahead into a really dense fog. How do you struggle against fog?"

"Why don't you sit down and talk it over with him? He's a terrific problem-solver."

"Papa, I really don't want to do anything or be anything in life. You covered enough territory for the both of us, including, God help us, the Pointer Sisters. So try and accept me as a little half-goat, lying on my back in a summer meadow, just playing my flute. Oh, I don't think so, Judith."

She smiled at that. "No. I don't think so either. But look, if Arcadia's granted to us, Stephen, it's only temporary; living humans are eventually ejected. It's not a life calling. Plus, we've usually earned it somehow." He made a face. "Well, then. You asked me to have coffee with you for a reason. Do you think I can be mediator in all this? Would you like that?"

He refused to look at her directly. "I don't know."

"Your dad's never mentioned this to me, I swear it. But I wonder if he's worried at some level that, absent a compelling mission in life, you're going to go the way of your mother in terms of—escape."

"It's possible." He swiveled on the wooden chair, looking for some kind of comfort, sitting on his hands. Around them, Santa Fe's temporarily idle—geniuses, trust-funders, and the unemployed alike—sipped their coffee, read their newspapers, engaged in earnest conversation, cruised for scores of different kinds.

"Don't let it happen. Just don't." She smacked the blond wood tabletop. "No whiny excuses. He might stand for it; I won't. How's Nikki that way?"

"Even more at risk, I think." He grinned. "Whoa, Judith, you are one tough babe. My father knew what he was doing when he hooked up with you."

Her eyes widened. He was goading her again, and she'd nearly let him. She wasn't his shrink: she was entitled to her rage, and spoke with great precision. "Hook-up? Not quite. Thanks for the coffee, Stephen. See you at dinner one of these nights. Lose the toys before you come."

He reached out, gripped her hand, pleading. "Don't go yet. I'm sorry. That was stupid. You know so much about him—"

"You could ask."

"I am asking."

"No, Stephen. Ask him."

His face collapsed. Over her washed a melancholy: he really didn't know how to go about knowing his father. Sad to say, his father didn't know how to know his son. I don't have kids, she thought desperately; how should I know? But she probably understood more than either of them. In her own behalf she heaved a sigh. She'd never yearned for children; loved and followed her demanding profession instead. This man she'd married had seemed hers alone. But behold, like everyone else who marries, she'd married a family. She'd become default den mother for Molloy's two children, something she hadn't counted on, and she doubted her ability to learn how to do that at all. Or her desire to, for that matter.

"Stephen, you haven't asked for advice, but here's some anyway, free and worth every penny. Invite your father out. Drinks, breakfast, lunch, a hike, whatever—sorry, but dinner's mine. Don't make a big deal of it; just do it. It doesn't have to have a purpose—and there you'll have to stop your dad: he's the most goal-oriented guy you'll ever meet. Tell him to chill; you just want some face time. That'll have to be goal enough for him, okay?"

He seemed doubtful. He stood up with her, looking ridiculously forlorn for a man in his late twenties with a serious education, a hefty trust fund, all his good health, and a life ahead of him. He should probably be a poet with that capacity for self-dramatization. She reached over and hugged him. "It'll be okay. Give it some time." As she waved a goodbye, she wondered what it took for a man to forgive his own father for sins real, sins imagined.

She only smiled when Molloy soon reported to her, with some puzzlement, that Stephen had called him and suggested they go have a beer somewhere. "*Sehr deutsch*," she said at last. Very German. "Enjoy yourselves."

17

Leandro Torres called Lucie Marchmont a few days after the aborted New Urbanism tour. "Sorry. People think architecture is an art. It is. It's also a business. I've got a big nut—overhead—to cover. The news was unexpected. Unwelcome. I wasn't at my best. So, never mind. Let's finish our tour."

"No," Lucie said. "But I'll meet you for drinks."

They met at the intimate bar in La Posada, a downtown hotel. The season's first fire was cheerful. Torres had clearly made some effort to dress up: a sports jacket, a freshly starched shirt open at the collar, cowboy boots instead of work boots. Still, he looked exhausted—the permanent shadows under his eyes were darker, heavier. His jowls seemed to be pulling his entire face down. She felt obliged to say something: "I'm sorry about the bad news."

"Oh, it's catastrophic," he said without a smile. "Let's not go there."

She nodded. "Well, then. Say more about needing to learn about beauty."

"No need to console me, Lucita. Sorry to be so down. My client will pull it out one way or another. Or I will. I just haven't figured out how yet. As you've heard, loans are getting hard to find. Architects aren't social engineers; they get to design only what a client can, or will, pay for."

A silence, which she allowed to stretch. "Actually, I'm interested in the beauty question." Did that sound like she was more interested in aesthetics than in his immediate problems? It was true. She hoped he missed that.

His smile was perfunctory, the eyes fully closed now. He nodded. "Where did we leave off? My memory got blitzed."

"You were saying the new is weird, sometimes ugly. We need to learn how to appreciate it, love it."

"Not all weirdness, not all ugliness, Lucita. Some things abide." His heart wasn't in it, she could see. But she resisted taking on this man's professional problems, being the sympathetic listener to a story that, a few days ago, she hadn't even known existed.

"How did you get into the field?"

An eyelid opened. "Never wanted to do anything else. I thought structuring space was an answer to—many problems. Maybe, when I was young, an answer to all problems." He looked melancholy. "I had a dreamy view of what it was all about then. The dreams get driven out by the realities." He'd ordered a second glass of wine. "Self-medication," he said as it arrived. "I'm crap company, sorry. Tell me about you."

"What? How I got into my field? It was almost accidental. As a girl, my ambitions were—ill-formed, let's say. I needed to get out of a difficult home situation. I ended up abroad. I studied law, but I wasn't cut out for public argument. Since I was bilingual—trilingual, actually—I put that to work for me instead."

"Married?"

"Once. It didn't work."

"Me too. My fault, not hers."

"But you haven't given up on women."

"Not at all, Lucita. I need their company, their friendship. The way they look. I liked your looks from the beginning. I'm an architect: looks matter to me. Then I liked your humor. I see in you a kind of sweetness I've always admired in human beings. Me, I'm an old cynic. As you get to know me, you may excuse that, at least understand it. Maybe forgive it. But it doesn't mean I don't appreciate people who are otherwise." The lazy eyes were nearly closed. "My son Mikey isn't cynical. When it comes to the real world, Mikey is almost naïve. Not almost. He *is* naïve. That's why I like my son. I mean, I love him, of course; that's only right. But I like him too."

"Then we'll get to know each other gradually. I hope I don't disappoint you. Sweetness isn't my most salient characteristic. Thanks for the drink." She made ready to leave.

He reached for her hand, both eyes wide open now. "Not too gradually, I hope."

An urgent, sharp desire for him. An old-fashioned man, she cautioned herself. He kissed her hand, his eyes never leaving hers. A man who needed to be the predator, be in control. Head raised now, the lazy eyes assessed her. "Lucie, you are so deliciously prim."

"Not so prim." She examined him, savoring the challenge, the equipoise between desire and denial. Chose at last. "All right, then."

In retrospect, Lucie thought, the three days they spent together could be plotted on a curve. It began with the slow delicious dance of seduction, followed by a frenzy that was only one part desire, another part escape. And then it plateaued. Began to decline.

She understood he wanted to bury terrible things in that frenzy; fair enough, she had things of her own to bury. She neither expected nor heard words of endearment. They got up, went out for meals mostly in silence, smiling at each other knowingly, without communicating anything save the anticipation of the return of lust. Sometimes he talked about architecture, about the buildings he had underway, some problems of design. He was constructing a large trophy hotel in Dubai, where he said he was actually dealing with Iranians. "I won't say they own Dubai, but damn near. No oil in Dubai—they make it all on trade. The Iranians are very, very good at that."

But he was also doing low-cost quality housing for Chinese workers in Shanghai, he wanted her to know. And yes, other trophy buildings elsewhere—in China, in South America. He'd just won an award for a green building. Maybe the project in Spain would find alternative financing. Almost pro bono, he was doing a community center and library in East Los Angeles.

"Really," she said in one interlude, "where are you from?"

"Born in New York, just like I said."

"But—"

"Okay, the rest of the story." The sleepy eyes seemed to fight to stay awake as he stirred through his past. "In a nutshell. My mother—ah, *mi madre*—was a very beautiful woman, a Copa showgirl, who not only caught the eye, but eventually the legal hand of my father, a big man in a small country in the Caribbean. So while I was born in New York City—because the Copa showgirl wants the best of everything, okay? including the hospital where she'll give birth to her babies—I grew up in the tropics. I was bilingual from the time I could talk. When I was eleven, there was a palace coup, and the government my father was in was overthrown. An old story in Latin American countries, right? My father had very strong connections in the U.S., but he wasn't allowed to settle here, so after a while my parents went to Spain. My little brothers went with them. I was the eldest, sent to boarding school in Connecticut. A few years later, I joined my family in Spain. An awkward time to take in an adolescent son—my mother and father were discovering in exile that they had less in common than they'd thought—so they sent me off to boarding school in Switzerland to avoid the fallout."

"When were you in Connecticut?"

He thought. "Late fifties, early sixties."

"How strange," Lucie said. "I was in Connecticut then too. Living with, I guess you'd call it a foster family. I'd had to leave my parents because—well, the coup hadn't yet taken place where we lived, but it was coming, and they worried for my safety."

Each of them knew that the other had told an abbreviated and smoothed story. He stroked her long chestnut hair that he'd so admired at the chamber music concert. "So we're both exiles, Lucita. *Desterrados*. Uprooted."

"I was an exile the moment I was born. Nothing changed."

Though she'd anticipated it over coffee at Whole Foods, was offended, wearied by it, she saw he lacked any curiosity about her.

He was interested enough to ask about her furniture, though. He lay on his back looking up at the dark wood canopied bed, the soft translucent draperies, mosquito netting against the nonexistent mosquitoes in dry Santa Fe. "Not exactly the local furniture. Where did this come from?"

"My family."

"So it's—what? Tropical?"

"British colonial, you might say. From the governor's house in Borneo."

"Borneo," he repeated softly. In silence he studied the bed, let his eyes drift over the rest of the room and its furnishings—a couple of cane-fronted chests, a mirror whose silver was growing opaque, an armchair with sinuously bent wood arms and legs. After a while, he was inspired to muse about his own parents again. "They didn't really understand what they might have been. My father had grown up in a cane-cutter's shack, would've been one himself, except he joined the army. He had a great talent for organization, for leadership. That's how he got—as high as he got. He was said to be, well, ruthless. People always say that who—anyway, at the same time, he was a scholar. No, let me say it differently; he longed to be a scholar. He longed to be thought of as a scholar," he amended. "He collected the biggest private library in our country. When I was little, he'd call me into his office late in the afternoon—I always see him in his spotless white trousers, his white shirt—and have me tell him exactly what I'd learned that day at school. Great training for the memory. We'd discuss it, whatever it was. He was very serious about it, very patient; made it seem just as important as all the other things he was doing. That library ended up at the national university.

"My mother, on the other hand. *Mi madre*." He stopped. "She kept on playing the part of beautiful woman. Beautiful thing, to be desired." He ran his finger across Lucie's cheek, up to her eyebrow, implying something, but not, Lucie guessed, that she was beautiful in his eyes. "She was much younger than my father. A young trophy wife. My God, she was beautiful. Men would stop in mid-sentence when she came into the room. That ends, eventually. That ends. A fatal flaw, I think, that she understood nothing but how to be a desirable woman. As the beauty faded, she helped it all along with alcohol, drugs. Got very coarse-looking. She was so distant, so strange, so sad. I thought that was all; that was it. My father did what all rich, formerly powerful old men do; continued to buy beautiful things, human and otherwise. She knew that. Then after she died, I was packing up her books. Think of it, I was already doing graduate work in architecture, and I looked around that room of hers. Aesthetically speaking, it was the room of a girl who'd never got past the Copa. The glitz. Crystals suspended from wall sconces. Fluted pink lampshades. Peach chiffon draperies. The mirrors, the chandeliers. It was like a rich girl's dime store. Kind of sad, actually." He made a dismissive face.

"But the books. I was stunned. I didn't even know she read, to speak of. If I thought about it, I'd have said magazine romances in between the *telenovelas*. We never talked about it. Apparently she and my father never talked about it either, even when the power—political, physical—ran out. I packed those books with a million questions in my head, couldn't figure out the pattern until finally—they were all books written in exile. A lot of the Spanish writers who'd fled Franco. Petrarch. Dante. Beckett. Nabokov. Late Solzhenitsyn. Late Mann. Conrad. She'd written in the margins of the Conrads, especially the South Seas books. My mother! My rich girl, dime store mother! She'd never let on about—anything. I missed it altogether. Well, she'd always been so private. So elusive. Especially to us, her family. I didn't know my mother. I had no idea about her. Maybe I never asked."

"Perhaps if you'd cared enough to look."

Toward the end of the second day, he began taking phone calls. At the end of the third day they were both checking their messages, apologizing perfunctorily to each other. On the morning of the fourth day, he told her he must leave.

It was as if the half-closed eyes prevented him from actually seeing her. They spoke about architecture, but never about translation; he never asked what she was doing in Connecticut at the same time he was there. Maybe he thought she'd always lived in Connecticut, except he'd asked, and learned that some of her furniture came from Borneo. The absence of curiosity was hurtful, and then laughable. She was emotionally spent, physically sore, longing for her customary equanimity, an equanimity that had been a long time coming, and was the more precious for that. All along she'd feared another exposure of his vulnerabilities like she'd seen in the car, but no, at least his troubles were under control. Above all, she feared wanting him to come back, and the disappointment if he didn't. Better—easier—not to want it.

"Until next time, then," he said at the door, leaning over for a goodbye kiss.

"Next time? Yes, we can take up getting to know each other. You might even have a question or two about me. Leave the razor. But take the toothbrush. It won't be useful for anyone else."

His face changed, a kind of recognition. "Lucita—Lucilinda." Pretty Lucie. "I was a pig, right? I'm capable of better."

She closed her door without another word.

18

Embarked on as calm and happy a private life as he's ever known, Molloy continues his information-gathering, getting finer grained. First, he calls his old friend George in New York, who'd run a famous and early hedge fund, and had then retired to spend his money well, if controversially. To George, Molloy discloses the formation of his foundation, if not quite his ambitions for it. "I haven't settled on the foundation's mission, but I need some functional advice. Don't want to be swamped by the chaos that drowns most small institutions, a rowboat in the North Atlantic. On the other hand, I don't want to create an organization that immediately falls into frozen order." He notes to himself how potent that particular metaphor has become to him.

His old friend clucks sympathetically. "Let me send you one of my best people, guy by the name of Greg Pontocorvo. You'll like talking to him. Unless you're coming this way soon?" No, he's not. He's weary with traveling, he tells his friend, and having found the right woman so late in his life, has no wish to be parted from her anymore than necessary. This is nonsense. His wife is on the road regularly, having resumed her career in international science (he goes along sometimes as consort) and he himself returns to New York City for board meetings and Knicks games (though if the Knicks don't improve soon, that particular reason for travel might end); he goes to Europe to attend more board meetings and look after some interests there. If she can, Judith is only too happy to travel with him. He just likes the sound of the phrase, the right woman, as he says it aloud.

Greg Pontocorvo arrives in Santa Fe, and they begin a series of talks.

To the young man, Molloy lays out his goals—to seek out and detect the underlying patterns, which in turn might suggest underlying problems, including the ones no one has thought about yet. He hopes to use the metaphors of complexity the same way the Rockefellers had used the metaphor of the germ theory of disease a century earlier, but he thinks he can call on the actual sciences too. Move the metaphor to model (a distinction he's learned from Judith). Do patterns in social behavior exist that mimic each other across fields, at different scales? Are such patterns the characteristic signature of natural and social systems?

Pontocorvo nods slowly, takes dense notes.

"I got to complexity sciences through my business interests, but this approach could change the way philanthropy's done, make it much more effective. With a complexity point of view, you look through multiple lenses. You use techniques that hold across many disciplines, techniques of great generality that have shown themselves useful in a bunch of situations. Solve a particular problem and, if you've got the wit to see it, you've solved a whole class of them. I want this new foundation to identify and support people who work at that deep level of problem solving. This won't be a halfway house for philosophers—I want people who've been neck deep in the enterprise, and can see the possibilities of generalizing."

"You have a place like that right up the hill here."

Molloy says smoothly: "I can support the Institute at a modest level, and I do, but my wife's on the faculty, and she feels uncomfortable with any suggestions of quid pro quo." Judith has put it much more strongly: "How would I ever know that you weren't just buying my presence, my position there?"

When Molloy is convinced that Pontocorvo gets the big issues, he allows the discussion to turn to nuts-and-bolts.

"You'll be active in this foundation? Live donors—active donors—are different from deceased ones." Molloy merely nods; yes, active. "You want to spend everything while you're alive—giving while living?" Molloy wants impact soon, but also to build something to last beyond his lifetime. "Your family will be involved?"

"Not in the foreseeable future. My wife would be terrific, but for now she has other interests. At some point my children might like to participate, but not just yet."

"It's a good thing to get them involved now, if only in a small way. A great learning experience." Molloy's silence says no. Not yet. Pontocorvo shrugs, goes on: "I worked at other foundations before I worked for George, so I know that how the donor made his money matters. You're a financial guy. You're used to making fast decisions; you have strong feelings about purpose; you're willing to adapt to new ideas. You'll give your people lots of room for autonomy, initiative." Molloy feels as if his palm is being read, to hear next that he'll eat what he kills. "Whereas I once worked for a donor who'd made his money in retail, wanted to kick the tires, was very much hands-on."

"A micromanager?"

Pontocorvo smiles. "Maybe it had to do with the difference between moving into an existing organization, instead of being there from the beginning, like I've been with George. Your managers, your program officers, even your trustees will be there from the beginning. They'll get to do a lot of shaping."

Molloy sighs. "The first thing they'd better get is continuous shape-shifting. This is how it is in the twenty-first century. Also, I'm for evidence-based work. Show me the numbers and I'll show you the money." He makes a face. "Enough clichés for now."

They move on to intervention points. One foundation Pontocorvo once worked for intended to help education, but most such money was wasted—lots of money, not lots of payoff. No one knew this for sure; there was little accountability, and the means of measuring effectiveness were primitive.

But one of the program managers had suggested supporting a debating team at an inner city high school—paying a coach, supplying books, transportation to debates. The payoff from that was startlingly good. Modest amounts of money, and the kids were learning to speak effectively, to be competitive someplace besides a basketball court (in fact to bring those competitive instincts in to debating). They debated—and won—at some of the most selective high schools in the state; had been national champions a few times. They loved it. Every member of that team (and by now the program had been underway for a decade) had gone on to college, to successful careers. Greg couldn't say what the equivalent in Molloy's world was of the debating team, but the example was telling. Look for intervention points, points of high leverage.

"In complexity, it's not quite like that," Molloy counters. "The intervention points might be elusive. You've got to look at many more things—how you define your goals and outcomes, interdependencies, connections, especially the ones that enhance responsiveness; you want to cut the connections that limit responsiveness."

Pontocorvo is clearly stimulated by thinking this new way.

The following day, they move back to the basics of organizational issues. Molloy learns that foundations generally are old-fashioned, very hierarchical, not at all what he's used to in finance. The flatness, the nimbleness, of financial organizations ought to be adapted to the philanthropic world, he says. Pontocorvo agrees. Foundation program officers traditionally wait for applicants, act as gatekeepers, filters, choosing among them. A modern foundation would instead get smart, gifted program officers to go out and seek new opportunities.

Molloy is alert. "How do you finger talent in philanthropy?"

"In finance, you hired young people on the basis of talent and promise, not knowledge or a track record." Molloy nods; that's how he got his start. "So what makes a good foundation staffer? Here's one piece of advice. Hire generalists, not experts. Most foundations ignore that. Easy to see why. Big problems like education reform, climate change, poverty reduction, are intricate. It's tempting to hire experienced program officers for these fields, and, hey, that's not stupid— you really don't want to have grantees dealing with a guy who has to learn on the job. He could take years to get up to speed on, say, the dreary saga of immigration reform, or the relationships and rivalries among human rights or environmental groups. Whereas someone with knowledge, experience, and a network of relationships will hit the ground running."

"But?" Molloy thinks he knows the answer, waits for Pontocorvo.

"Specialists have their own obvious drawbacks. They don't always get the big picture, a larger context about public policy or social change that's essential to making an impact. They may not know how to manage people, or how to translate their theories into programs that can make a difference in the real world. Worst of all, they can be too close to the field. To a fresh perspective, that's fatal."

"In other words, strong views about the particulars aren't necessarily good. A point of view is."

"Exactly."

Molloy is swiftly mapping this on to his own ideas for a visionary foundation. "But generalists have their downside too."

"Mirror image of the expert. But a good generalist, with wide knowledge, wide experience, can approach a new issue with a fresh perspective. They know how to transfer techniques, take lessons from one area to another. They know how the world works, how interdependent the elements of social ecosystems are. How to locate an issue or a field in that broader landscape and make the necessary connections. Still, you ought to know that in philanthropy, hiring the specialist is the way it's done. You might not be able to get away from it."

"Happy to say I know a handful of such generalists," Molloy replies, "but what I really want are young people."

"You want both—some old hands and a lot of young generalists. Not just any generalists. For all the talk about how a liberal education prepares you for anything, sometimes all it prepares you for is a specialty in the medieval epic."

"Who should I be looking for, then?"

"People who can winnow broad quantities of information and data, and make judgments that they understand will have consequences for everyone: those included, and those left out. People who pick up quickly on patterns that aren't apparent to everyone else. At the same time, they need to be sensitive that their judgments will have an impact on public debate and policy."

"Good traders," Molloy says thoughtfully.

"Sure. Only you won't be able to pay them the money good traders make."

"Some have already made money enough, and are looking to do something different with their lives. A few of those."

"Journalists. Great pickings with the consolidations and job shrinkage. Journalists are expected to come up to speed in a new area, even a new language, and learn the key players and issues in a matter of months. You might be able to pluck some plums."

"How do I find these people?"

"Begin with a very open mind. Expose yourself to tons of experiences that won't pay off, just for the one that will—brilliantly. No choice in this game but to kiss a lot of frogs. Keep a close eye on young people. Scout the schools. Look for just the right mix of enthusiasm and skepticism. You want passion enough so the person is a strong and effective advocate. They've gotta be able to take their own side in a fight. But they also need a sharp critical faculty, the ability to raise the right questions and see through the hype. If they can't do that, if they can't honestly present the risks and dangers, along with the promise and potential, they won't have the credibility they need to make a case. Won't acquire the confidence that a good program officer needs."

"What the complexity people call unfocused search." To Pontocorvo's questioning look: "As distinct from focused search, which is later. An immune system can't prepare for every germ that comes along; an ant colony can't predict the future. So the system does some random searching, finds something that seems to work, allocates more resources to whatever that something is. But the system doesn't stop exploring new possibilities. It gathers new information—this germ is conquered by this particular lymphocyte, or here's a good source of ant chow—and exploits that information so it can adapt. You see a fine interplay between focused and unfocused processes. Getting that right—again and again— means success." This is straight Judith Greenwood, straight Santa Fe Institute, but since the words say exactly what his intuition has always told him, he's happy to repeat them. He looks inquiringly, somewhat skeptically, at the man across from him. "That's all?"

Greg Pontocorvo takes in Molloy's expression. "That's all."

19

Pontocorvo comes home to dinner and meets Judith. "Pontocorvo," she says, savoring his surname. "Ravensbridge. How beautiful."

"Just a name that drives receptionists up the wall." But he's flattered, and pleased she's part of the discussion that continues. Over drinks before dinner, Molloy tells his wife what he's learned during the day, reading from well-fleshed notes on his ever-present yellow pad, which later, Judith knows, he'll transfer to his laptop. Pontocorvo nods, correcting sometimes; listening with pleasure to hear his ideas amplified and recast into something Molloy is aiming at.

"How should the foundation identify grantees?" Judith asks.

"A central question," Pontocorvo says. "I've told your husband, he has to decide if he's going to practice a kind of curated, don't-call-us-we'll-call-you strategy, or something more open, like requests for proposals. Tried-and-true, both approaches. But in both there's—what shall I say?—an exclusionary mentality that thrives. Both tend to favor Eastern seaboard institutions. In American philanthropy, there's an embarrassing lack of racial, gender and class diversity. So most grants go to the folks who know how to get grants. If you could find a different way, you might evade that problem."

"That old stuff isn't going to work for this foundation," Molloy says decisively. "Not in the long run. In the long run, I'd like to make a revolution. You're familiar with the work on diversity?"

Pontocorvo isn't entirely sure.

Judith says, "Some of the best work has been done by people associated with the Santa Fe Institute. Pretty results, really counter-intuitive." She means that diversity of teams in problem solving isn't just a politically correct idea, but that, in good organizations, diversity delivers better, more effective solutions than homogeneity. Worse news, to those devoted to excellence, a diverse population of problem-solvers, each with a different weak approach, will outperform a single agent with a strong approach.

"So, you'll aim for diversity. Small example: a friend who chairs the board of a settlement house in New York City told me the other day that their new executive director, their first Hispano, suggested that maybe their web site should be bilingual. She was mortified. Twenty years on the board, and she'd never thought of putting the web site into Spanish. Well, neither had anyone else on that board, I said. But you know? This settlement house is in Spanish Harlem."

Judith has no desire whatever to participate in Molloy's foundation, as advisor or as grantee. But the discussion stimulates her. One evening a few months earlier, she'd been complaining yet again about the tedium of writing grant proposals. Her husband had murmured diffidently: "We really have enough to support your research in any style you want." She was shocked by the idea. It seemed an unfair advantage, somehow; almost illicit. "Don't be silly," he said. "Priestley, Darwin—they were independently wealthy, supported their own work. Do as well as them, and no one will object."

She caught her breath. "Sorry, my love, but I'm not as smart as Priestley or Darwin. I need to go through the usual channels to hold on to my already shredded credibility. Of course, I could always suck up to kings and princes, the way Leibniz did. How did von Humboldt raise money?"

"I'm acquainted with a prince who'd welcome—"

"That particular prince gets all he can handle."

Molloy laughed, shrugged. Keep it in mind.

So though she has no wish to participate, she's nevertheless taken by the issues, as she always is when somebody suggests that the old way isn't working but a new way might—if only that new way could be found. She says to Pontocorvo: "By now it's second nature for me to wonder what might lie under the surface. I want to know where the deep patterns are, how viewing events in different frameworks offers important—vital—insights into their functions. I'm always looking for the different timescales you get with the variables in a complex system. The squirrel timescales are the most obvious, but also the most negligible. The slow-moving scales—barely noticeable in human time—are the ones whose shifts cause the big changes in any complex system. Above all, I know how new structures serve as the raw material for further analysis, further inquiry. I admit it, I'm hooked."

Molloy turns to her hopefully. "Well, then—"

"Oh no, my love. Oh, no. Your baby, yours alone."

As they get to dessert and coffee, Judith says, "Okay, we've hired these smart, diverse program officers. Now. How do they go about finding their opposite number in their field of interest? What I'm saying is, how do they find the best, the most innovative of the emerging leaders and even organizations that need support? How does the foundation turn its people into talent scouts?"

"Same way your husband hired them. Unfocused search, eventually focused search." Greg Pontocorvo likes to use the new terms he's learning. "They keep their eyes wide open, they expose themselves to endless possibilities." He turns to Molloy. "You, as the president, or head, or chairman of the board, or whatever you're going to be, you have an interesting role to play. Your role is to be intellectual leader. You need to get up in the morning and think about how to advance the field. You want to learn constantly, and share that knowledge. You want to have a point of view to advance without being doctrinaire. You've got to ask tough questions of program directors and others down the line, sharpen the case for any grant. But if you're overturning recommendations, blocking them, or micromanaging them, then something's wrong. You need a strong sense of political and social context, not a tunnel view about a particular issue. If you, or one of your key program people, don't have that, you can't graft it on. Impossible to make up for a deficit in curiosity, in vision." Molloy nods. He understands that part very well.

"One more thing," Judith adds. "The Institute was founded by some silverbacks—three Nobel laureates, and a handful of sub-Nobel laureates. That gave it instant credibility. I think this foundation, or this institute, or whatever it's going to be, will need that too." Both Molloy and Pontocorvo are making notes.

"I'm playing with names," Molloy says. "Right now, I like the Center for Innovative Philanthropy."

She smiles at him. "Not bad. Not bad at all."

Greg Pontocorvo comes to dinner several nights, partly because Molloy has taken to the younger man warmly, and partly to check Judith's impressions, that Pontocorvo is as smart as he seems. Judith concurs. "Greg is saying in his own terms what we think about up at the Institute. But be careful," she says to her husband privately. "I don't know what counts for smart in that field."

"Smart is smart," Molloy replies.

"I like how he raises odd questions."

"You would."

"Build in your rotation," Pontocorvo advises the last day. "The Ford Foundation's program officers serve for six years, then leave the foundation, or move to another position with a different area and set of grantees. This built-in refreshment allows for a lot of flexibility. I've already told you about hiring young people, but I'd like to say a word about older people too. I'll bet Santa Fe is awash with retirees who could be incredibly valuable to you. They don't need to be on your board. Give them other ways to serve, opportunities for social entrepreneurship in the last decades of work and life. This is an encore career for you. Other people can contribute with such things too."

By now they've covered much ground. Pontocorvo is adamant that the so-called support staff should be in on all aspects of a grant from the start. "This is not your usual back office," he says firmly. "You want their expertise, and you want them to get satisfaction and pride knowing that their work serves an important social goal. They'll work even better for you. Let them figure out how to do the audacious things you want to do, not tell you why it can't possibly be done. You'll be handling the investments?"

Molloy will, along with a small group of people who can fit around the kitchen table, the micro-firm.

"Then that's another job you don't have to worry about. But if you want this foundation to outlast you, make plans for the eventual transfer of investments."

"When I'm the deceased donor?" Molloy says wryly.

"When you're the deceased donor."

As they're saying goodbye, Pontocorvo has some concluding advice. "Never believe you're as smart and wise as your grantees and grant-seekers say you are. Stay open. Create a questioning culture. At George's, we change strategies every few years. We don't change our top-level purpose or our goals, but we change our strategies. The world changes. We gotta, too. Think about sabbaticals. Good people need some sustained time, well beyond vacations, to relax and refresh themselves. My first sabbatical, I used it to see things from the point of view of one of our grantees, a group that helped prisoners re-enter the world. What I saw helped me see that organization's weaknesses as well as its strengths, and put me, then a program officer, in a position to be more helpful over time. Find out who needs a Spanish-language web site, so to speak."

They stand beside the car that will take Pontocorvo to the airport. "In fact, that kind of crossover is enlightening. Try sitting on the board of some small nonprofit. Listen to their budget review, feel into your gut the consequences if a grant doesn't come through. Get a glimpse of the thoughtless, arrogant and inconsistent ways so many foundations deal with grant seekers. It'll make you a better grant maker when you go back to work the next morning."

"I've done a little of that," Molloy says. "I think I know what you mean."

After Pontocorvo leaves, Molloy calls his friend George. "What do I owe you?"

"Nothing," George says cheerfully. "Maybe you can return the favor some day. Or pass it on. Did you offer him a job?"

"Of course not."

"Would you be interested in him?"

"I'd love someone like him."

George wheezes into the phone. "Greg has a very good young woman as his assistant. She's ready for more responsibility. Greg's ready to move on. To have something of his own. In other words, you have my permission, if that's what you're waiting for."

"You're sure?" George is sure. "What do you pay him?"

"I can't promise you he'd leave New York. Which would also be fine by me. I'm not looking to get rid of him. It's just a good time for him, if he wants it. And with the girl, I won't be hung out to dry."

Molloy comes home and reads to Judith from his notes what he's learned the last day. "And," Molloy adds, "if I can get him, I think he'd be a very good public face for the foundation. Young. Presentable. Enthusiastic. Eloquent. He already has all the connections I don't have, don't want—the associations for philanthropists, the forums, the roundtables."

"Still think you can stay under the radar?"

"Can and will. You really don't want to know the downside of public exposure for someone like me. Only it wouldn't be just me. You too. Us. We don't want to have to hire more protection."

She exhales. Life with Jack Molloy is financially comfortable, but so near to normal that she sometimes forgets the wealth issues. They've agreed from the beginning that they'd rather do most things for themselves than give up the privacy necessary to keep a substantial staff in the house. They'd rather stay in superb hotels than buy more houses. She changes the subject. "So, my love. An encore career. One of several for you. I wish for you the success in philanthropy that you've had first, as financier and then—an encore—as a caregiver."

"Caregiver? Ah, yes." This woman he loves, her deep passions, intellectual and otherwise, alive in her merry eyes, by now engraved forever on her face; captured in her quick gestures, her incisive talk; all so different from what he's thought of as the tentativeness of ordinary women. Altogether distinct from the high pitch of hysteria that a woman—his first wife—had once thrust ruinously into his life. Very different too from that utterly depleted state where he'd later found Judith, coaxed her back from. He drops his eyes modestly. "Caregiver. I'll take credit for that."

"You should. And now?"

"I'll make an offer to Greg Pontocorvo, and see what happens. I know how it has been done. I want to invent how it *will* be done."

II

Strange Attractors

1

Torres called Lucie occasionally over the winter. He'd leave generic messages: he was calling from the airport in Dubai, en route to Beijing. He hoped all was well. He thought of her. So long, Lucita. No number where she might call him, though she wouldn't have. It was probably on his card, but she'd put that away, determined to resist searching for him on the Web.

The messages perturbed her unpleasantly, and she did her best to bury that perturbation. She translated contracts and articles of incorporation assiduously, and spent some decidedly unmagical evenings with Rick the hydrologist. In mid-January, Torres was back in Santa Fe and called her.

"I don't think so," Lucie said. "All that ego is wearing, tedious—excessively tedious. I do hope you'll take that in the spirit intended."

He whistled softly.

"You see. I am not sweet."

"I had that coming." A silence. She hadn't hung up on him, and he was encouraged to keep trying. "Give me another chance, Lucilinda. I think this has possibilities. Something good for us both. Train me. I can learn." Slowly, he persuaded her to have dinner with him on neutral territory, and they met at Geronimo on Canyon Road, whose austere décor was the direct opposite of its rich food. It was also an easy walk from each of their houses.

"What's this all about?" she hissed across the starched white tablecloth.

He smiled. It's about sex. If it isn't about money, it's about sex, always. But he knew better than to say that. "It's about the apology I owe you, Lucie. It's about how I, at least, think that this could be quite lovely if we let it. I could explain why we started off on the wrong foot—but I'm not insensitive to the use of the personal pronoun, so let's put that off. Let's talk about you."

She looked at the ceiling in exasperation. "I am not a goddam performing seal."

He reached for her hand. "No, you're not. You're a beautiful woman, a woman with great spirit, and I want to know all about you. We have some chemistry. You know this kind of chemistry doesn't just happen. Right now it's only chemistry—"

"Lust," she interrupted.

"Lust," he agreed cheerfully. "Lust at first sight. That's a very good foundation, Lucilinda. If you allow it, we can go on from there. Let's build on that good foundation."

She didn't reply, but waited with him until he'd settled the bill. The cold weather was brutal, and the checkroom attendant brought out his hat, and a swirling knee-length black cape that he threw around his shoulders.

"What's all this?"

"Spanish architect get-up." He adjusted his hat, black felt with a wide flat brim, a low cylindrical crown; she'd seen something like it on gauchos. "Córdoban hat, except I have mine made in Seville. And a horseman's cape."

"I thought I recognized that."

"It's what the clients expect from a Spanish architect." For a moment his accent had grown decidedly more Spanish, the final consonants disappearing, the vowels lush. "And if it reminds them just a little, on the edge of consciousness, of Frank Lloyd Wright, that's okay too. You ride?"

"Once upon a time, I did show jumping, dressage. You?"

"Every Spanish gentleman rides. Well, then. We must—"

"No," Lucie said. "No. I don't ride anymore."

But it was the case that he walked her up Camino San Miguel to her small house on Talaya Hill, followed her inside, and eventually made the most careful, mindful and prolonged love he had ever made to a woman, murmuring her name a thousand times, a thousand different ways, a term of endearment in its own right.

"Lucita," he whispered as they lay resting. "*Lucida*. In Spanish that means magnificent, it means perceptive. You were well named, *cariña*."

Eventually he pattered across the tiles to the horseman's cloak, flung on to a living room chair, and fished out a package for her, insisted she open it. Inside was a pair of pale yellow silk slippers, lavishly embroidered with little beads, the toes turned up absurdly. They fit her feet perfectly. She was charmed, puzzled.

"From the souk in Dubai. As I was making love to your beautiful feet last time, I measured them too. For me, all in a day's work." He was pleased with her pleasure in them, how she stretched her pretty legs up to see her feet, turning them this way and that to admire his gift.

"And more." He'd stopped at the fine chocolate shop in Sena Plaza, Todos Santos, and picked up two large chocolates in the shape of human eyes, covered in gold foil, edible *ex votos*.

"How nice, but—"

"I missed your name-day in December, Lucie. So here's a present, a little late. Santa Lucia was martyred by having her eyes put out. Or, another legend says, having dedicated herself to our Lord, she wanted so much to remain virgin that, when a suitor admired her eyes, she put them out herself and sent them to him. These are her symbols."

She examined the golden eyes. "I'm not sure I'm even entitled to a saint's day. We've been Church of England since Henry the Eighth. Given what happened to poor old Santa Lucia, maybe it's just as well." But with delicacy she unwrapped one of the golden eyes, broke off a piece and put it into Leandro's mouth, kissed him gently in thanks.

They lay in a sweaty afterglow, biting into small sweet apples grown in one of the sheltered valleys north of Santa Fe, putting pieces of those into each other's mouth too. He rolled over, held her tightly to him. "Now please talk. Please tell me," he said softly to her hair. "You will tell me how a woman so passionate is nevertheless so frozen deep inside."

"Is that how it seems?"

"Lucita. The passion—oh, my. We just had such a demonstration. But—" he released her, took her face in his hands "—you guard yourself so carefully. Don't be afraid of me, Lucita."

She smiled. "No, Lee—Leandro. Your full name is so nice. Not now. But I like it that you want to know. My passion? Don't take it seriously. It was only the hat and the cape—like Zorro making love to me. Your clients must swoon."

"Of course. That's the point. Would you like to commission a signature building?"

"You'd reduce my carbon footprint?"

"By the cubic acre. Beautiful lady, I'll transform you into a carbon sink. People will pester you to buy credits."

"You'd design me a building as irresistible as your hat, your cape?"

He only laughed. "Now look. I come with an invitation to dinner. Mikey and his wife would like to have us over tomorrow night, and—"

"So sorry. I have plans."

He seemed genuinely perplexed, as if it had never occurred to him she had a life without him. "Really?" Studying her face, he said, "Do you see someone else?"

"Astonishing though it must be to you, Leandro the Magnificent, I do."

"Well, who?"

"Really, Leandro, it's none of your business."

"No, I want to know." He became indignant. "Who else uses that razor? These most convenient condoms? Who is he? What does he do?"

"His name is Rick, and he's a hydrologist. A very decent man."

He fell back on the bed, laughing merrily. "Oh, my God. An engineer. Lucie, an engineer knows everything about one thing. An architect knows something about everything. A woman like you deserves an architect, not an engineer." Spat out with infinite contempt. "Tell me what you talk about—aquifers? How deep to drill a well? Senior and junior water rights? A decent hydrologist. Oh, my God."

"Leandro, you really are a pig."

"All the better to hunt *las trufas, señora.*"

She lay alone after he went home, thinking about passion. About passion she'd learned very, very early. When nothing else in her life worked, passion always had. James. Her refuge, her joy. Her guide. Her first, her enduring lover. A colonial experience, it seemed now. He was master; she was willing, even grateful, colony. Though she later had her liberation, the old days seemed preferable in many ways.

She got up, got dressed, meaning not to dwell on James any longer. How vivid it was all these years later, how strange that each new lover evoked James—in comparison, or in contrast. To distract herself, to erase the ghost of James, which sometimes came to her as a deeply pleasant visitation, sometimes not so pleasant, she began at last to search the Web for Leandro Torres.

An easy search; many, many hits. Known worldwide. Expected to win the Pritzker Prize soon, whatever that was. The sites came up in half a dozen languages. "He translates," one critic had written, "the beauty of Latino magic realism into structures of grace and surprise. Torres's work could aptly be described as credible magic." She laughed out loud, not knowing whether she laughed at the preposterous rhetoric of architectural criticism, or Anglo obtuseness (Torres was a Spaniard, *un Español*, not a Latino, idiot). Another critic spoke of Torres's deep sensitivity toward a site, his willingness to design in ways that were both complementary to a building's neighbors, its environment, yet fresh and contrarian too. He was praised for his feel for materials—he understood better than any architect practicing how materials meet and give meaning to each other; and he understood the structure of his materials as if he'd invented them himself. He was praised for the drama of his structures. "To walk into a Torres building is to discover anew the profound magic of darkness and light." He was praised for his psychological penetration, how he understood the rich symbolic meaning of bridges and gateways. The magic architect. The magic lover. Well, well. The biography was as he'd said: born in New York City, a childhood abroad, educated at Berkeley and MIT.

His renown was unexpected, unwelcome, and depressed her deeply. Such a man would have a woman in every branch office. Whatever drew him to her could only be a kind of temporary delusion that imbued her with allure she knew she didn't, in fact, have. When the delusion dissolved, so would his interest.

She sat back from her keyboard almost breathless with despair, with grief. Then came rage: how could he do this to her? Pick her up, pet her, make so much of her; famous architect toys briefly with obscure translator. The cramped dimensions of her life threatened to close in on her yet again. Translator! Even her words weren't her own. Hardworking, competent, yes. But so what? A compliant scullery maid, seduced away from scouring the pots and pans, the work of others, by the handsome aristocrat upstairs, who'd soon drop her, go back upstairs. How could she have let this happen?

Tears stung and outraged her. He wasn't even here and he was making her cry! In despair, she summoned what had always served her so well, a carefully constructed self-protection. Futility. She wept without restraint, not just for a man who'd touched her, who'd teased her with the possible design of lifting her to some plane she'd long ago given up on, but for all the things that had gone wrong, one after another, and always would, all her life.

2

Yet they continued to see each other that winter when Torres was in town. One night, they'd finished dinner, got a little tight on the wine. He'd asked her once more for her story and Lucie looked at him skeptically. "You want my story? It doesn't fit into the usual categories. Don't try to force it."

"Lucilinda, I promise." Leandro Torres took her hand, stared into her eyes with what he hoped was a look of concern, genuine interest, animated with desire.

She was silent for a long time before she began.

When she lets herself remember, she sees them coming for her in the schoolyard, early afternoon, the sunlight softened by the high dense canopy of the trees. Mimin, her nanny, graceful in her long wrapped cotton skirt, walks toward her, wiping a tear from her right eye. Lucie sees the gold bangles on Mimin's wrist flash in the sun. Or maybe this is only how Lucie likes to remember it. "Come, my darling," Mimin says, holding out her hand. Her treacherous hand. "You will be safe."

She'd understood for a year or more that she was not safe. She'd be curled up on the cushions of the rattan sofa, an open book before her, pretending not to listen, not to understand, as her parents murmured in code (the servants) over languorous cocktails late every afternoon—the insurrections, the bloody Communists, the possibility of children being kidnapped, held hostage. The child was wise and could break the code easily, even if those who'd learned English as a second, or third, or fourth language could not. Later she thought, who's to say they couldn't? If a ten-year-old understood, why not an adult, seething under the colonial boot, placed in the governor's residence to spy?

She took Mimin's hand, climbed into the back of the car. "But this isn't the way home," she observed, slightly puzzled.

"Be a good girl, my darling. Your mummy and daddy want you to be safe."

The capital city was still severely damaged, first from the Japanese, and then from the Allies. They were driving along the waterfront, past buildings still in ruins. Lucie looked away toward the sea, so much more beautiful, a deep aquamarine. The plane waited at the airport, propellers already turning, and she climbed up the aluminum stairs, her nanny's hand still guiding her. But the woman stepped back, crying openly now. "Do as you're told, my darling, be a good girl for me. For your mummy and daddy. Be a brave little soldier, my darling. Don't cry. Someone will meet you when—when the journey is finished."

She didn't know for certain where she flew. She tried to piece it together later, thinking maybe first to Singapore, maybe as far as Hong Kong. Another crown colony. The men who met her were unused to children; they'd brought a teddy bear, which she was much too old for, and when she asked for books instead, they looked at each other, mystified. What would a ten-year-old daughter of a colonial governor read? It was too late now to remember whether the men were Asian or English, or anything else. They were only men in suits. Another plane, the journey so long she slept deeply. A kind stewardess, an American, showed her where the loo was, made sure she got some extra treats. An extra blanket: she was still in her school uniform, tropical weight. She felt as if she traveled for days, being handed off from one stewardess to another, the light outside the windows going from day to night in no pattern she understood. They put down in one plane and took off in another from island airports, the eternal sea below them. She wondered how it would be to plunge into that sea, all the way to its cold unknown bottom.

When she reached the end of her journey in New York City, the uniform had long lost its starch. She'd cried after all, but only when the lights were down so no one could see. As she came down the plane's steps, the cold air attacked like a ravenous animal, and she hugged her thin arms to her body to protect herself.

"I'm Uncle James!" a man boomed at her, and a woman held her, kissed her wetly: "I'm Aunt Evelyn. You're going to live with us, darling, and be safe and happy once more!"

"Where are my mummy and daddy? Where's Mimin?"

"Mummy and daddy are still in Borneo, you dear little thing. They sent you here to be safe and happy. You'll be safe and happy with us. You'll have a new sister. You'll have your own horsie, won't that be nice? Your daddy told Uncle James you ride."

Horsie? She hadn't used such a word since she left the nursery. She was faintly repelled by their enthusiasm, their extreme and troubling words of affection. Not yet. Not yet, please. She was concerned that she'd be obliged to reciprocate these extreme emotions—or be found wanting. A pleasant perfume came out of the woman's fur coat. The girl thought of the animals in the tropical forest. Where she lived—at home—humans didn't wear animal fur except at special ceremonies. Somebody put a coat on her that fit well, and politely she said thank you. "She's just a bit smaller than Grace; she can have Grace's old things," the woman said with satisfaction.

"When we get home, we'll telephone them to tell them you're safe. You can tell them yourself." More words about Uncle James and her father arranging all this at their London club for her sake, to keep her safe, talk at a volume that embarrassed her. She'd been brought up to believe that loud voices were common. Vulgar. "They should've told her more," the woman said to her husband. She turned back to Lucie. "Do you know about the bad Communists, dear? How they wanted to kidnap you and hold you for—ransom, I guess. We're keeping you safe from all that. We're saving you. Nobody will hurt you here."

The girl fell asleep in the car, one part fatigue, one part fear, one part a deep desire to escape whatever all this was. She only awakened when she felt the car slowing, heard gravel under the tires. They'd reached a big brick house, much grander than the governor's residence in Borneo. To the girl it looked English, something from the frontispiece of *Jane Eyre*. A servant—she knew it was a servant, because the woman wore black with a white pinafore, introduced herself only as "Mary," and not as Mrs. So-and-So—took her hand and led her to a pretty room. "May I talk to mummy and daddy?" the girl asked politely, thinking of the promise in the car.

"I think they'll be sending a cable. They didn't know when to book the call, because they weren't sure when you'd arrive. Never mind, honey. You have a good sleep, and in the morning you'll meet Grace and the two of you will be great friends, won't you?"

Lucie lay in a bed at last, under a thick down comforter. From the open window she breathed the freezing air, thought it might shred her lungs. She'd lie in this bed for many nights to come, reciting to herself the names of the birds of home—hornbills, eagles, herons, kingfishers, birds that chattered all through the night, unlike the birds here that didn't awaken until dawn. She'd call to mind how the cicadas sounded, how she used to envy the native children, who were allowed to chase them with little nets on sticks. When she looked back, she'd feel as if a great curtain dropped suddenly, splitting her life into two parts: what had been, and what was to come.

In the morning she met Grace for the first time. Grace was taller, heavier, grabbed her and kissed her forcefully, without affection. Lucie would have preferred to shake hands.

This was the beginning. Did she want to tell the rest?

"This was how I came to Connecticut. I don't think I want to talk more about it now."

Leandro poured them each more wine. "Things about your story remind me of mine."

She turned to him wearily. "Doubtless, Leandro. Doubtless." Her face spoke her scorn. He understood, and turned his head from it. Suddenly she said, "I'll tell you some of the rest. This is the part you mustn't try to force into preconceptions."

He nodded, eager to be forgiven; leaned close to hear her low voice.

"From the time I was thirteen, my foster father, James, and I were lovers. When—when damage was seen, therapists without imagination assumed the obvious. First I had a private therapist, and then they put me in group therapy, where I had to listen to girls who talked about the coercion. Waiting helplessly for the...night intruder to open the bedroom door, pull back the covers, climb into bed, force himself on her. The complicity of older women. How they turned their heads away. It wasn't like that for us, for James and me. We became lovers slowly..."

"You were thirteen? That's not so slow. That's not only illicit; it's illegal. Not to say repulsive."

"Listen to me, Leandro. From James came the only kindness, the only affection, the only sense that I might be worth something to somebody else in the world, that I was going to know...for many years."

"Until?"

She brushed aside his question. "No, the—the preparation, the foreplay, so to speak—took place earlier. We only became real lovers when I was thirteen. Don't look so piously shocked. All over the world, thirteen-year-old girls are given to men. Younger. Always were. Probably always will be. It's a fine old tradition," she added icily. "And you should know—you should know this. At least I was prepared. At thirteen I was begging for—what shall we say, union with him, for a real consummation. It had taken a year of—" she hesitated, searching for words, "well, a year for him to prepare me. I was so very, very prepared." Then with ferocity: "I've never regretted it. It was thrilling. It was thrilling in every possible way. The father who'd abandoned me, the lover who loved me, and fulfilled me, the future husband who'd protect and defend me, all rolled up into one delicious, ecstatic, illicit—yes, oh yes, illicit; that was so much part of it—magnificent experience." She picked out the words carefully, the voice of the translator there.

She looked away. "To know that intensity again would be—altogether wonderful. But imagine trying to say this to a circle of women who'd each been raped by fathers or brothers or uncles or stepfathers. Brutally abused by older men. Imagine. I couldn't. No one forced me into James's bed. In his arms was the only place I was safe. I loved being in his arms. They wanted to tell me he exploited me. No. He loved me. That wasn't where the damage lay. I've never even told anyone this—this much."

Torres rose from the table in rage. "Jesus, I could kill that bastard."

"James is long ago dead. A riding accident. It broke his neck."

He exhaled. "If the damage wasn't this, where did it come from?"

Now she was silent. "Another time. Another time."

"Did his wife know?"

"Yes, in the end, I believe she did."

"Wasn't that a problem?"

"She'd told James long ago she wasn't interested in sex. It was a relief for her."

"Is that what he told you?"

"He never mentioned her to me. She was nobody, nothing to him. That had happened long before I came to live with them. In her own way, she was the one who told me."

He sat down again, scowled. "You never told your husband about this?"

"There was no husband. I say that because it's easier than explaining to people that I never married. Never will."

He shook his head, trying to clear the confusion. It horrified him that this had happened to her, but he knew instantly that what horrified him most was that she'd invited it, that she enjoyed it. That it was thrilling. That she looked back with yearning. *To know that intensity again would be altogether wonderful.* This was beyond his understanding. They got up from the table. He held her beautifully symmetrical face in his hands, studied her deep, dark eyes, her perfect mouth, then ran his hands through her hair, kissed her, began to undo her blouse. Yet even as his passion rose, her words mocked him; a suspicion crept upon him that he might be no more than a substitute for this James. Maybe the ghost of James had never disappeared, a ghost he'd always be competing with.

Sated, he fell away from her. He was obsessed by what she'd told him. If making passionate love with Lucie was a new joy for him—love made with such abandon he was left exhausted—it must be an old path for her. The whole thing seemed utterly perverse, and he felt—he couldn't help it—soiled.

3

Judith and Molloy regularly mark up the morning newspaper for each other with marginalia, even a star system—one star for an article worth reading, two stars for someone they know, three stars if an article names one of them, which sometimes happens. He'll have read it after he came back from his run; she gets to it after he's left for the office, and this day finds a huge scrawl across a two-star article on the front page of the arts section: CALL ME WHEN YOU'VE READ THIS. She understands. Leandro Torres's new library and community center in East Los Angeles have been savaged by the architectural critic of the *New York Times*.

To Judith, the article is incoherent. It first praises the "soaring" design, the "structural pyrotechnics," "tricks and sleight of hand" that make the building seem larger, hence more dramatic, than it is. But the critic goes on to accuse Torres of building "what amounts to a monument to his own virtuosity, at a time and in a place where resources are desperately scarce. Are no other branch libraries or community centers needed in this desolate piece of urban territory? Is that why Torres can get away with this neo-Alhambra, a *palacio* of overweening sculptural purity that will surely puzzle and might even intimidate the very users the structure is supposed to welcome?"

Judith can recognize nasty rhetorical tricks and sleight of hand when she sees them. The question really being posed is whether the druggies, gang members and other lowlifes of East Los Angeles can in any way appreciate such glamorous design in their midst. Do they deserve it? A subtext of slime seems to float beneath the surface of this piece, which she recognizes but cannot entirely decrypt. Whatever it is, their friend has been publicly humiliated, and she's furious on his behalf.

"What shall we do?" Molloy asks her when she calls.

"Nothing we can do, sweetheart. He's probably endured worse. You put a little piece of your heart out in the world, there's always someone dying to make hamburger out of it. Though getting chopped up in the paper of record can't be much fun. I'll call him and ask him over for dinner tonight. At least he can vent to us."

"Stephen's coming."

"Maybe a lesson for him," she says. "That just being, as he likes to put it, takes no balls at all." They say goodbye, him thinking he's married a tough cookie, but she is, as usual, right.

Judith sees Mikey at the Institute, pulls him into her office and shuts the door. "You read it?"

"*Ay dios*, I read it." His great dark liquid eyes look as if they might cry. "Papi will be pretty down for a few days. His heart was in this one—it wasn't just a rich insurance company headquarters or some Arab's toy of a hotel. He cut his fees and everything." He looks at her warily. "You don't think that guy is right?"

"Mikey, I'm no architecture critic. But I know what it is to get slammed in public for reasons having nothing to do with the stated slam. That's what I'm guessing, anyway. None of it made any sense."

"Did papi tell you that part? That this guy and he went to school together? I think there's some, like, rivalry, envy, or something."

"I'm going to call your papi and invite him over for dinner tonight. Nobody should be by himself after—such a thing. Can you and Adriana come?"

He shrugs. "It's tough to get a sitter at the last minute. But thanks for taking care of him, Judith." She guesses the last-minute sitter is the least of it. When she calls Torres, who seems grateful for the invitation, she asks him if he'd like to bring Lucie. After a slight hesitation, he says asking Lucie isn't a good idea just now. "It won't be completely intimate," she adds, "Stephen will be with us. But it's all family, Lee." All family, he repeats. And thanks her for that.

Torres is the last to arrive for dinner. Judith has expected to see him looking the worse for wear, but in fact he's better groomed, better dressed than she's ever seen him. She helps him out of his gallant horseman's cape, takes the gaucho hat, the white silk scarf. He's wearing a custom made shirt under what she recognizes as a very expensive cashmere sweater, trousers he might wear for a presentation to a client—casual and perfectly draped. How does it happen that the men she's closest to are such peacocks? For his part, Molloy understands perfectly. You pull an all-nighter and lose, then the following day you buff yourself up to the max. Torres gladly accepts Molloy's offer of a glass of wine.

"You must be pissed, friend," says Molloy.

"I am. Yeah, I am. I think of that structure as one small, maybe hopeless, gesture against California's prevailing view of private wealth, public squalor. Everything doesn't have to be shit on a string to reassure the taxpayers that nobody's squandering their precious dollars ... But to my critic, it's an ego trip. *Mierda*. I'm old enough to remember when public architecture was some of the best we had. No, I'm not. I just know that once it happened. And I'm not talking about the Acropolis. But it hasn't happened in my lifetime. Public buildings owe—public buildings must..."

"Can this human trash really appreciate the Alhambra? That got me, Lee," says Judith. Her heart goes out to him, one part of him trying to pass it off; one part so wounded.

"Yeah, I picked up on that too." He sits on the couch with elbows on his knees, twirling his wineglass so energetically that she thinks it might go flying. "The folks in that neighborhood are from Central America and from Asia, about fifty-fifty. Some of them on the public advisory committee—there *was* a public advisory committee—they were really tickled that the architect actually spoke their language. We had a good time, you know? They got it, what I was trying to do. They were born in the midst of more magnificent temples than this *capullo* can begin to imagine. The guy's a façade-ist—doesn't know anything except how a building looks from the outside—a trait he shares with nine-tenths of his fellow critics. Not a word about the interior, though maybe that's just as well. Spare us, please, how these animals will break or steal every computer the first twenty-four hours the place is open. Me, I care about how it works for people who'll actually be using it; how it relates to the street and the surrounding cityscape; maybe what effect it will eventually have in the neighborhood. *Me cago en* how it looks to magazine photographers." He looks at Judith. "That means I don't care how it looks in fancy magazines. I don't do fucking paper architecture." Now he reaches over for the wine bottle and helps himself. "Not a word about how it will float over a nine-point earthquake while everything else around it is collapsing. The building's as green as green gets, got a LEED Platinum award. Even California needs green buildings. Especially California." He stops, sighs. "*Mierda*. Do you ever wonder why you even try?"

"I could have him whacked."

"Jesus, Molloy, you probably could. But that's okay; I got enough debits on my karma."

"Just saying."

Judith appraises her husband, not sure herself if he's kidding.

"I could've slapped up a decorated shed. No distinct difference between it and a strip mall. Costs the same. I was within budget."

Stephen breaks his silence. "Why do you even try?"

"Because I'm a man." He looks at Judith. "I don't mean a guy man, *nena*. I mean what the Germans call a *Mensch*, a person in the world. You don't go along to get along. You do what you think is right, but there's always some little bastard to snipe. You've had your own issues that way, no?" She nods, wonders how he knew about a bitter vendetta a rival had waged against her.

As the evening goes on, and supper begins, Torres grows more animated. No one counts the glasses of wine he's using as balm. After supper, his feet up on the coffee table, he says very softly: "The problem is, some critics are so goddamned smart they know just what you've worried about yourself. They intuit exactly what's kept you up in the small hours, what you've fretted about, and decided you were okay with. They home in on that. They worm their way in, find it, turn it up, belly to the sunlight, let it squirm all exposed. You've already examined it and decided that—oh, fuck him and the horse he rode in on. *¡Me cago en su madre!*" I shit myself on his mother!

Judith nods slowly and knowingly through his tirade; smiles at the last of it. Molloy wonders which part of that blistering newspaper critique had phrased the misgivings Torres had privately worried about, only to find them publicly exposed. It doesn't matter. Molloy understands perfectly that almost anything novel is disdained at first. But that doesn't make Torres hurt any less. Molloy's earlier career had displayed its own form of unambiguous criticism, instant feedback: money gained, or worse, money lost. Gain or loss, a boss might have ripped him a new one, a client gone nonlinear, but no one had ever dumped on him publicly, in the country's leading newspaper, in front of strangers. He'd thought he was tough, but wonders if he's tough enough to endure the prospect of such humiliation every time he takes a risk.

He's read a little bit of the criticism of Torres's work in general. "Architectural porn," one blogger had written. "No one under seventeen should be permitted to look at these buildings without adult supervision." What the hell does that mean? Another described Torres as "one of those morally ambiguous opportunists to be found throughout architectural history, willing to compromise and fine-tune his aesthetics to serve his clients." Did that critic think Torres should choose starvation over work? Say what you would about finance, nobody expects people there to be saints. Or martyrs.

Stephen has been silent, as usual. His father glances at him, wonders if he's taking any lessons from it at all. Being a *Mensch* and engaging with the world.

Judith says, "I hear there was something personal in it."

"Yeah, somewhere along the way I must've hurt the poor guy's feelings, and it's been payback time ever since. Like all politics is local, all criticism is personal. One way or the other."

"I had one like that," Judith says. "A real son of a bitch. Just wouldn't let go. Though as a friend once said, I gave as good as I got." Her husband smiles, thinks she surely did.

Molloy opens yet another bottle of wine, and they continue drinking in the living room. For all his wine, Torres is still clear-headed. "I love that building, I really do. I poured my heart into it. It has a great strong center, beautifully organized so that people know just where they are. The whole shape of the building takes its sense from that center, and there's positive space all around it. You look carefully and you see a pattern of repetition. Not just repeat-repeat. The patterns are recursive, alternating, fun to figure out; fun to be near, deeply satisfying even if you're only responding subconsciously."

He grows a bit dreamy. "People think—somebody once guessed—that the strength of my designs comes from classical uses of classical shapes. They'd be freaked out to hear the classical shapes are from the people of the Kongo. Spelled with a K not a C. The original civilization of Zaïre, or what's it called now? The Democratic Republic of the Congo. Anyway, before it was the Belgian Congo. Most of the slaves transported to my island originated there. They hung on to that potent home religion, though a lot of it was in secret. I learned the cosmogram of the Kongo people through Santería—you know what that is—at a very young age."

Santería. His three listeners can only think of the shabby little storefront *botánicas* in Upper Manhattan; maybe headless roosters left on the front steps of the Cathedral of St. John the Divine, the odd chicken claw turning up in public parks. They don't know about a childhood spent in the company of country-girl nannies who brought the secret country ways with them into the presidential palace.

Torres goes on. "People always love what I do with light and dark—it's easier in sunny places like L.A. But I can do it anywhere. Not something you learn in architecture school: it's in my bones, in my heart and soul. I've always known how. Light is energizing; dark is restful, not scary, if it's handled right. I handle it right. When I first got to Spain, I hated the light there. It was bright and cold, like a Canaletto painting of Venice, you know?" Molloy nods, knowing exactly. "And see, both these sets of people, Central American and Asian, the people who'll use this structure, understand these ideas—call it Santería, feng shui, the mesoamerican equivalent, whatever it is—fundamentally the same. We all speak to each other without needing words. What does some *maldito yanqui* know about such things?"

He falls into silence. The wind in the cottonwoods above the house can be heard. An old Biedermeier clock that Molloy loves and brought back from Germany chimes. Wotan snores softly in front of a dying fire.

"I think I see some judicious uses of Fibonacci series in your work," Judith says quietly.

He looks up, smiles as if caught. "*¡Claro!*"

"And the golden mean."

"Why mess with success? Good enough for the Greeks, the Renaissance. You can guess that it must be speaking to something basic in the human psyche when it appears across so many cultures." Torres pours himself yet another glass of wine. "Same with the water—the way the fountain is situated. Very important; speaks profoundly to everyone. I could go on about water all night. The scale. I was so careful about the scale—just to the left is the children's library, separate from the adult library, and the kids love it, feel really at home there because it's sized to them. At the same time it's visually connected to the adult library; their designs reflect each other, different scales, but a lively interaction. The meeting rooms are actually inviting; they enclose you and your group—" he makes a giant circle with his arms. "Between the meeting rooms and the two libraries there's a little patio to sit and have a coffee. A still place. You can be peaceful there. You've had a big argument with someone in a meeting? Good, go sit in that patio and breathe the fresh air, feel the stillness, and talk it over. You need to keep your voice down because that's what people do in libraries, so you can't yell at each other the way you did in the meeting room. It's a good thing. If I could take that guy to my little patio we could talk it over—and I would separate that *gilipollas* from his stupid head and *huevos* once and for all!"

Judith laughs aloud, gets up, bends over him and gives him a hug. "It's late. I gotta go to bed. Early conference call. But the guys aren't going anywhere."

Molloy agrees he's not going anywhere. He'll be up at six to take his run regardless of when he goes to bed. Stephen smiles too; he isn't going anywhere either.

The three men settle down for more talk. Torres looks up the staircase where Judith has disappeared. "You're a lucky man, *tío.*" He turns to Stephen.

"And you, *chico*. You have a girlfriend?" Stephen shakes his head. "Why not?"

"Haven't found the right girl."

"You have to take some chances, *mi chico*. Take some risks. Great women do not hang on trees. And the great ones expect greatness themselves. So maybe start by being great, and then the rest will come." Though without understanding, they can see by his expression that a doubt about that suddenly assails him.

He sips his glass empty. "As one of my teachers, my mentors, I had one of the greats in this century's architecture, a name you'd all know—" he names the man. "But the reason I've exceeded even my teacher is strange. It's not because I'm more brilliant." He makes a self-deprecating little gesture that suggests he might indeed be more brilliant, but that's beside the point. "It's because—it's because I love the human body. My teacher was superb at design, and not bad as an engineer, but it was totally cerebral. He was afraid of human bodies. No, it's true. He despised the physical facts of humans. That they sweat and shit and piss and bleed. They get inconveniently horny. They get fearful or jealous... Or even that they can expand their souls with happiness. So he failed to understand what it was really like to be a human being inside a structure, inside a built space; that some spaces are congenial to the human animal, and some are just okay, and some are downright threatening. I feel myself so very much as a physical human inside a physical space... I know how to translate that feeling. I love the physicality of being human." He stops, lets his mind drift to Lucie, whose body he thinks he might love, and wonders if she will ever let him know, and love, her soul.

More silence. Wotan gets up and prowls restlessly. Molloy murmurs to the dog in German, lets him outside, closes the heavy door against a cold night.

"Being great doesn't sound so great tonight," Stephen finally says with a smile.

"You wouldn't want to be anything less," Torres retorts dismissively. "*Dios mío*, how much did I drink tonight?"

"You want to crash here?" Molloy says. "We've got plenty of room."

"No," says Torres. "It's an easy walk. Or el chico here can drive me home. He's a model of sober restraint. I tell you, Molloy, I don't know what this younger generation is coming to. In our day..."

"Is there anything you'd like to design that you've never been able to?" Molloy asks idly.

"Yeah. I'd like to do an airport that didn't look like it was constructed by slave labor." He laughs at his own joke, but Molloy can see that tears have come to his eyes.

Stephen has gone to the hall closet and found Torres's cape and hat. I biked, he mouths to his father, who tosses him car keys. Stephen ties the white silk scarf gently around Torres's neck, moves behind him and drapes the cape over his shoulders, finally puts the hat firmly on his head. Torres stands passively, nearly asleep on his feet. The young man puts his arm around Torres, guides him toward the front door.

Molloy watches these gestures of tender indulgence, sees the affection on his son's face, and feels a sudden jealousy he knows he should be ashamed of. He longs to say, come back after you've dropped him off and be with me. Be with me that way. But he doesn't say that.

Torres stops at the doorway. "This young man—he might have been a fine architect. He told me that he feels like what's inside his head he's putting outside into his house." Stephen looks away, embarrassed. "No, *chico*, you had it right. That's exactly what you're doing. Stephen Molloy made manifest. Some of us are just lucky enough to have heads other people actually want to live in. It's a gift." He pulls a reluctant, grinning Stephen to him and plants a wet kiss on his cheek. Molloy wonders how long it's been since he actually kissed his son.

4

Torres now resisted seeing Lucie when he came back to town between trips. He didn't question himself about this; he was acting on feelings he hardly understood. When Mikey asked how things were going, he answered evasively. Mikey clucked. "Papi, you need a girlfriend." His father answered offhandedly. "It gets harder and harder to find the right fit as time goes on. It's not that our needs are greater. It's that we become more discriminating. The sword of truth won't let it be otherwise."

Yet one night he saw Lucie at the Baja Café with another man—this Rick? someone else?—eating burritos and laughing. His sudden jealousy was poisonous, and it mortified him. His heart beat wildly, he could hardly breathe. He felt himself flushing. He wanted to sneak out without her spotting him, for he knew his rage and jealousy were humiliatingly all over his face.

After a few nights of stewing, he finally called her.

"Are you back, then?" she said coolly.

"Lucie, I've—I've come and gone a few times. I want to talk to you about it."

"I'm very busy right now. A big project to push out the door."

"Please."

But when she opened the door to him, showed him in, he was tongue-tied. Tongue-tied by shame, by his sense of having treated her unjustly, having made a moralistic judgment that he didn't admire in himself. As if he had the right to moralize. She'd asked him not to push what she told him into preconceptions, and that's exactly what he'd done. He hoped his eyes said what his tongue could not. After a while, she led him into the bedroom and they continued where they'd left off.

Later, he said: "I really need to talk about this. This—us."

"You're a friend with privileges, Leandro. Don't make it more than it is."

"Give me a moment to say something."

"Leandro. As if anything ever stopped you."

He closed his eyes. "When you told me about James, I just—just couldn't handle it, Lucie. To think of you in that situation. A girl, not even a woman yet. And you were so honest. You told me you—you enjoyed it."

"It was true, Leandro." She said it simply, gravely. "Is that so hard to believe?"

"No. No. I found it easy to believe. Such a passionate woman, Lucie. Easy to believe. I just didn't know how I felt about all that. Well, I knew. I was shocked. I was very upset. I was—"

She looked at him pointedly. "Leandro, this is tiresome. I can't unlive my life. I can't tell you what you ask, and worry unduly how you'll receive it. For once this isn't all about you." She lay back on the bed pillows, to his eyes provocatively, even though she'd modestly pulled up the bedcovers over her chest.

"No, it's not. It's not all about me."

They remained in silence. He was stupefied, that he had somehow fallen in love with—well, was utterly infatuated by, whatever it was—this beautiful distant woman who regarded him as only one of several, and ho hum. It was a novel sensation, neither pleasant nor welcome, to be merely one of the crowd. Even when the world had ignored him, he'd been driven by an overwhelming, a deeply nourishing sense of his own uniqueness, his singular gifts. But to Lucie, he was just a pleasant diversion, equivalent to, interchangeable with, Rick the Hydrologist, or whoever else crawled between these sheets. Ultimately forgettable.

Finally he began to pull on his clothes.

"I hope you enjoyed that," she said evenly, her tone low and soothing, if only she'd been voicing something he longed to hear. "I certainly did. As you saw. But Leandro, it would be helpful, you know, convenient, if you gave me more warning about when these great encounters were going to take place."

He wouldn't turn to look at her, finished buttoning his shirt, tucked it into his pants. "Did you have a schedule with James? Do you have one with the hydrologist? Do you have a free night of the week I could claim?"

She was on her knees to grab his nearby shoulder, pulled him roughly around so they faced each other. Now her voice was not even or cool, but tense, swelling in volume and anger. "What's this all about? You come in here after God knows how long; you're all over me like a crazed weasel. You have your fun, you're still all bent out of shape. What do you want from me, Leandro? Why did you start this up—start with me in the first place, and then all over again now—if all you want is an occasional jump? Who the hell do you think you are?"

He stopped, the breath knocked out of him. Sat back down on the bed. "Okay. Good. I'll tell you who I think I am. Who I am. I'll tell you how I came to Connecticut."

He was born in New York, yes, but from the hospital his mother and he flew directly to the presidential palace. His mother, the Copa showgirl with dime store tastes, had married his father a few years earlier, and though she'd understood her side of the transaction was to produce sons, start a dynasty, she hated what childbearing did to her beautiful body. She hated being pregnant in the island's eternal summer heat; she hated the way her breasts looked, distended with milk. She refused to nurse her babies, handed them over to wet-nurses and nursemaids as if it were the nineteenth century. Which, on the island, was probably about right. If you don't count, he interrupted himself, that in those days the island had more Cadillacs per capita than any other place on earth. When she stopped at the nursery to see him, it was a great occasion—she was so beautiful, so perfumed, so out of reach, so worried that somehow he'd muss her hair, or spoil her dress. In those years, he sometimes thought he dreamed her, asked his nanny if she was only make-believe. This must have made him sad, he thought later, but since he didn't know any better, since he was held close by a series of kind and loving nannies, and had as playmates not only other children in the palace but also affectionate, hulking men that he called *mis tíos*, my uncles (bodyguards he realized later), he felt mostly loved, mostly secure, mostly happy.

Above all, his father doted on him. He understood even from the earliest times that his father—always in immaculate white, a guayabera and fresh linen trousers—his father was in charge, the head of things, was deferred to by all; that from his father emanated such power that everyone acknowledged it in a thousand different ways. His father was not loved, but he was admired. Deeply feared. Behind his back the very brave (or the blasphemous) called him Elegba, which sounded Spanish to naïve ears, but in fact was the name of one of the greatest of the Santería *orisha*, gods. Elegba the trickster, the mischief-maker, the wonder worker, who darkened the good and lightened the evil; who combined within him male and female aspects in his great creativity. Elegba devoured all things, himself included; and Elegba caused all things to multiply. Elegba was also Eshu, Satan. Yet his father was the personification of coolness, of gentle generosity of character. In short, a leader. He'd risen from nowhere and led his country to become one of the most prosperous in Latin America by nearly any measure. This was why he was not called Ogún, the hard god, the god of iron.

It may be that his father knew of this epithet, Elegba. He wouldn't have objected. He was physically beautiful—in an ambiguous way, it was later said, though the old ones thought this only natural, since Elegba embodied both the masculine and the feminine. Thus the way he was rumored to enjoy the pleasures of both sexes was only natural too. He was strong: in fact, ruthless. He dealt with some of the greatest criminals in the hemisphere, and got what he wanted out of them. He had accomplished things for his country, but his means were not cool, gentle or generous.

As his father's eldest son, Leandro was privileged beyond the other children. He was permitted to play in the presidential office even when matters of state were under discussion. He stared out from under his father's desk at the grave men who murmured in low voices, came and went with papers in hand. Over the desk, a jacket would fall open to reveal a holstered pistol.

Other sons were born, but he was the eldest, the one who would grow up and be in charge too.

He and his brothers were pampered with expensive toys (he later realized) and given lessons of every kind. He had his own pony, bicycles that grew in size to match him, toy cars he could pedal around the palace gardens, luxurious clothing he hardly paid attention to, except when they were going to *el norte*, where his mother had come from, and he needed heavy woolens that he never needed at home. These he would wear for the duration of the holiday, then not see them again, because he would have outgrown them by the time the next holiday came. He had his own car (a new one each year), driver, and bodyguard from the beginning, to travel from the presidential palace, to the private residence, and out to the *finca* in the country. He spoke Spanish to his father, the courtly Castilian he learned from his tutor, different from the rough dialects he heard as he listened under his father's desk; and he spoke English with his mother. He had tutors for French, music and drawing. As he got older he was allowed to go to a small private school on the presidential grounds with other children attached to the palace. They were deferential, and he sometimes yielded to the temptation to bully them.

And yet. A layer of the island's society, its colonial aristocracy, did not welcome him. These were families with money from generations of sugar and rum, tobacco and industrialization; who sent their children abroad to Europe and the United States for education, for holidays. They lived in the luxurious suburbs of Vedado, Siboney and Miramar, in grand white houses with gardens that seemed to stretch for miles. Without needing to be told, he sensed that they despised him and his family for the rough and vulgar *arrivistes* that they were. For reasons of political tranquility, they must invite him to their children's birthday parties, but the invitations came as an obligation, not because Leandro was actually welcome in their homes. When his driver delivered him to one of the great white stucco *palacios* on certain palm-lined drives above the sea, he was received politely. But he always detected an undercurrent of hostility, of contempt, that wounded him. It came from the servants, it came from the hosts, it came from the other children who were playing the games and eating the ice cream. He was not even allowed at parties at a certain private club, because his father was a mulatto—*el mulato lindo*, the pretty mulatto—so by such standards, he failed to be fully white, fully acceptable, himself.

One afternoon, he bowed and greeted the birthday girl—a girl arrayed in the proper white tulle dress, perfect white socks and shoes, of their class—in his excellent French. Behind him, he heard her father snickering, as if a toad had suddenly started speaking the language of Racine. The deep humiliation of that moment never left him. But painful as these occasions were, he continued to accept the invitations as part of his own duties as the son of *el presidente*.

Then one Christmas when he was eleven, his uncle, his real uncle, proposed a trip to New York City to see the Christmas lights. The children, he and his brothers, his uncle's children too, were thrilled: so much more fun than the same old Christmas lights at home. But we must be quick, the uncle cried, clapping his hands. At once, tonight! The children's excitement grew: no long wait for the delicious treat, but leaving this very night! In his exhilaration, Leandro threw into a little bag the things he wished to bring with him to *el norte*, his watercolors and brushes, a block of paper; rushed to find a favorite book in the children's rooms, and instead found his old nanny, now the nanny of his little brothers. She held a carved round tray. He knew that this tray held sacred dust, dust by which she could divine the future. Part of him wanted to hug her goodbye, to feel her arms around him once more. But another part of him wanted to show how much he'd outgrown, including magic. This was the part that made him laugh at her mockingly, proud to leave such superstitions behind. She did not return his laugh.

His father calmly wished them all a good journey. He was sorry, he said, that he couldn't join them for this festive holiday, but he'd see them soon. His mother, however, rushed on board the small private plane at the last minute, also carrying a little bag of things she wouldn't let go of. Her brother-in-law, the uncle, looked disgusted. They were her finest jewels, Leandro learned much later. Once or twice, the younger boys tried to sit near her in the plane, but she pushed them away wordlessly. Leandro had learned the futility of approaching her long ago. A young maid of his mother's opened her arms to them instead.

They were experienced travelers already, these presidential children, used to airplane trips, the routine when they disembarked. People would greet them with flowers, sweets, kisses; flashbulbs would pop; they would smile and wave to the people because, as they'd been schooled, that was their duty as the children of *el presidente*.

As they prepared for landing, the flight attendant helped their mother, her maid, the aunt and uncle, to bundle them all up, the heavy shoes and socks they never needed in the tropics, the heavy sweaters and coats.

But as they climbed down the steps from the plane, something was wrong. There were flashbulbs, but no flowers, no sweets, no kisses. Policemen held back the crowd, and the faces on those people were angry, ugly. The words were ugly too. His uncle's hand, holding his, suddenly trembled—his uncle was afraid of those bad people with their ugly words and contorted faces. Then he knew he was right to be frightened himself. He wanted to cry, but he was the eldest, a man now. Eleven years old. Would someday be a leader. He heard his uncle shout in Spanish: *los niños, los niños,* the children, the children; but the crowd was contemptuous. He heard them call his mother a whore; and as for him and his little brothers, his cousins, all too young to understand but frightened enough to cry, the sons of whores. The young maid trembled. *Demonios.* Demons.

Someone with authority rushed them across the tarmac into a low building, a windowless room where they could still hear the menacing noises outside. There they stayed. He didn't know how long. Hours. The smallest boys no longer wept, but they whimpered. He dared not. Their mother smoked steadily, stared off absently, did not offer to comfort them. In his gut he felt a burning liquid that he would ever after associate with fear.

Many years later, when he examined it, doubting the power of a single night of terror to cause him so much grief, he came to believe that instead, that night he had crossed a boundary into a new world. In the old world, it had always seemed calm, sunny, happy, warm, safe. The new world was turbulent, gray, unreliable, cold, with no security whatsoever. Later yet, he would concede to himself that under the tranquility and warmth of the old world, other currents had run, malevolent and inscrutable. Menacing. Humiliating.

At last they were permitted to get into a limousine, and go to the hotel where his parents always kept a suite. For some odd reason, he remembered that the limousine was maroon. The windows were so dark you could barely see out of them, but he was too scared to look for the Christmas lights, which they'd come for. He wanted to be at home in his warm gardens, smelling the sweetness of the blossoms, playing in the sunshine. He wanted to be riding his pony, his bicycle; he wanted the reassuring bulk of *los tíos*, the sweet strong arms of *Niñera*. He wanted anything but this.

At the hotel, another crowd stood at the entrance, barely held back by the police. They'd known where the presidential party would come, and waited in the bitter cold, stamping themselves into a fury: a crowd enraged and bloodthirsty. The burning liquid bubbled up in his gut again. He would come to think of this fluid more as something animate, sharks, to be exact, *los tiburones*, roving somewhere below, ready to surface unexpectedly and destroy everything. *Los tiburones* always glided under the surface, and if he allowed himself to think about them, they could paralyze him. But more often they pushed him into effrontery, a lifelong determination to protect, to save, to avenge, that frightened young child he'd once been.

"At first I didn't understand what happened," he said to Lucie. "There'd been a coup. When my parents saw this was inevitable—and I think for much too long my father, who was shrewd about so much, refused to see the inevitable—they arranged to get me and my little brothers out of the country. My uncle took us with him, one part for family reasons: my father was his brother. One part for—I don't really know. In the coup, which took place the night of our flight, my father and his party were deposed. Most of his colleagues, most of the men loyal to him, were arrested and shot within twenty-four hours by the new government. Not a good idea to leave anyone who might pick up the pieces. Many of them were evil men; no doubt they deserved to be shot. But the new government murdered plenty of loyal patriots also, people who might have stood up to a new dictatorship. If we hadn't gone to New York that night, we'd have been slaughtered too."

"And your father?"

He hesitated, deciding what that question meant. Was his father also an evil man; did he deserve to be shot? He'd been compared with, was sometimes thought to be possessed by, one of the most powerful of the *orisha*. If the man had known that, did he believe it? That, like a god, he was invincible? Here was another of the central paradoxes of Leandro's life, one he hadn't yet unraveled and didn't expect to. So he took Lucie's question only as an invitation to say what happened next. "My father escaped to a country nearby, a country run by a friend, a fellow *presidente*, a fellow strongman, if you must know, expecting that the American government would pluck him out. He'd had very good relations with the American government. For all his sins, he was a bulwark against the Communists, my father. But my father had also set up arrangements I didn't understand until much, much later."

"Arrangements?"

"The usual. Financial arrangements. Pieces of the action of everything— sugar, banking, transportation. The casinos, of course. His partners there were— well, unsavory. As a result of these arrangements, the American government kept its distance. So his friend to whom he'd fled in good faith, in great danger for his life, this so-called friend actually held him for ransom for an entire year. The family eventually paid up. I didn't know about any of this then."

"What was happening to you?"

"My father had been transferring money out of our country for—well, for many years. Large amounts of it. In that sense, he was a complete"—he sighed, knew he must use the word—"a complete thug. I was sent to a boarding school in Connecticut, enrolled using my mother's name, the name I've used ever since. Which is how we might have overlapped inside the Nutmeg State." He'd sat half-dressed as he recounted this. Now he was chilled, pulled on his sweater, a jacket, in silence.

She watched, finally spoke. "So you know what it is to be threatened, and need comfort."

He nodded. "Yes, I know… And to be *desterrado*, torn away from everything you've ever known and loved." Sardonically: "That distant past, always so warm and golden."

"Yet you can't understand that I too was threatened, I too needed comfort."

He shrugged. He'd tried to be honest. His life was full of paradoxes. "Nothing you've told me sounds like a threat, beautiful Lucie. But maybe I haven't heard everything. The distant past for you. That tropical beginning. Was it warm and golden for you too?"

She didn't reply.

"You protect yourself always." He sighed. Maybe Lucie had her own *tiburones* she wanted to keep submerged. "*Hasta la próxima vez*, Lucilinda." Until next time. Took her hand, squeezed it gently; thought better and kissed it; let himself out.

5

Grace wanted to be her big sister. For the first few days in Connecticut, Lucie was so confused that she politely agreed to everything, or at least never protested when Grace made these declarations—that they would be sisters, best friends; that all those other girls (which other girls?) would be so jealous they'd spit. Lucie must wear this, have that, they used to be Grace's; how lucky that Lucie was so small to be able to fit into all of these things (Lucie looked at Grace dubiously, thinking that Grace was so big, so much the opposite of her name). Sweaters, as she learned to call them (not jumpers); skirts, blouses, even socks. For the summer, a swimsuit (not a bathing costume). And then, a riding habit. For the first time since she'd arrived, Lucie smiled with genuine pleasure. It was stupid that Lucie had her own room, Grace declared; Lucie should share Grace's bedroom so they could have PJ parties every night. When they took the bus to school, Lucie must sit right next to her big sister.

Lucie found Grace's keenness—was that the word?—suffocating, and wished for a little peace from all this. But as a well-bred English girl, she smiled and nodded politely. As she lay in her own bed, mercifully left, so far, in her own room, she suspected all this enthusiasm, feared it stood for something else.

Meals were a trial at once. Grace would taste and spit, throw her food, her knife and fork, her plate, across the table, against the wall. "I won't eat it! It's horrible! It's poison! You can't make me eat it!" In mortified silence, as if she were somehow responsible for this ridiculous behavior, Lucie stared down at her plate, well instructed that you ate everything put before you, no matter your opinion of it; clean your plate and think of the starving children in England. But Grace's nanny would rush to her side, comfort her, hold her; there, there; don't eat it if you don't want it, darling, while a maid appeared and cleaned up the food that was sliding down the wall, the shattered crockery. Grace would look over her nanny's shoulder with a sly smile, gauging how well the performance was playing, whether Lucie understood that it was a performance.

Lucie did, and was at first shocked. Then disgusted.

She was shocked by how Grace addressed her parents. It was unthinkable that any English girl would speak to her parents that way—in turns sullen, hectoring, hot-tempered, ever disrespectful. She couldn't even imagine what kind of punishment her parents would have meted out for this; it simply never happened. Grace gave no warning about her storms: they came suddenly, she screamed, fell on the floor sobbing hysterically, pummeled her fists into the carpet, kicked wildly; wouldn't allow herself to be picked up, comforted, until the storm was past. Lucie knew the word tantrum, but only as something she had never been permitted to have.

School was difficult for different reasons. First, Lucie's own education was considerably further along than American girls of her age, and so she was put into a higher grade than Grace, even though Grace was older. Lucie was also an excellent student, which Grace was not. Lucie had been sharply aware of unwelcoming coolness from the other girls, but once established in a different classroom, the coolness thawed as she came to be regarded as something besides an extension of Grace. She began to make some friends. But these weren't friends you could meet up with after school or Saturdays: everyone lived so far from each other, and students were delivered to the school by bus or private car. At recess, or lunch, or in the gym, the tentative friendships she began would shatter if Grace insisted on joining them.

"My mother doesn't allow me to associate with Grace Ludlow," one girl said candidly. "My mother thinks she's nuts." Lucie was torn between the loyalty she owed to her hosts, and her concurrence with that idea.

"Is she related to you?" another girl asked. They were drying off after swimming, where she was safe from Grace, who didn't like to swim. Lucie peeled off her swimsuit (not her bathing costume) and answered: "No, I'm just staying with the Ludlows for the time being."

"Your people getting divorced?" Lucie was startled, pulled her towel unconsciously to her. No one she knew got divorced. That was for film stars. Respectable people stayed married. "You don't have to be embarrassed," the girl continued. "See Alexandra Milton over there? Her mother's been divorced so many times she's lost count." Everyone laughed. "Better than Marcie Griffin's mother, who doesn't even bother to get married anymore. They say." More laughter.

"No. My country isn't safe at the moment."

"Noooo, my country isn't safe at the moment," came the mimicking echo of her accent.

"Cut it out, Barb. Lucie's accent is darling. Leave her alone." And so Lucie was saved for the moment.

Lucie stared furtively at each girl in class when she had the chance—she'd never known people whose parents got divorced.

She soon discovered that if she stayed after school for sports or clubs, there was a late bus. It let her evade Grace politely, since Grace did no sports, belonged to no clubs. In the spring Lucie would find an even better escape—the stables.

She also discovered that her accent was an unexpected asset. Everyone told her they loved the brave little Brits, and sympathized with what they'd gone through during the war. But Lucie realized it was more than that—for all the talk about equality and democracy, American snobbism was oddly biased in favor of anyone who spoke the way she did. Girls would invite her to supper at their homes so parents could ask silly questions, just to hear her speak. She acquiesced. In some ways, she thought later, she exploited it.

One day, Aunt Evelyn said quietly, "I know you'll understand this word to the wise, Lucie. When somebody kindly invites you to supper, please ask if the invitation includes your big sister Grace. If it doesn't, it might be nicer if you declined, very politely, of course. It hurts Grace's feelings to be left out, and I know you wouldn't want to hurt her feelings, would you? I know I can depend on you. There's a good girl."

On one of the first mild days of spring, she got off the late bus one afternoon with an urgent need to pee. She ran to the front door, only to find it was locked. Never mind, she could hold it until she got to the back door. But that too was locked, a door that was always open to grocery deliveries, the servants, workmen. Desperate, she pounded on the stout back door, but no one opened it; somehow no one was there. At last she ran to the bushes beside the shed, and barely pulled her panties down in time.

At supper that evening, it was, as usual, just the three of them—Uncle James was working late in the city as he always did. But as Lucie took her place at the table, she glanced at Grace, who had a new look on her face, mocking, almost triumphant. By now Lucie could read these warnings in Grace's transparent face, a signal that Grace had made mischief, and Lucie would be sorry. Aunt Evelyn cleared her throat, made a small loop in her pearl necklace, adjusted the collar of her blouse, and looked very uncomfortable. "Lucie dear, there's a very unpleasant matter we must take up. I've been told—never mind who told me—that you went to the bathroom outside in the shrubbery. Can this possibly be, Lucie?"

Lucie looked at the woman, and then at the smirking Grace, and understood it all at once. "Yes, I did, Aunt Evelyn. Both doors were locked. I—I had to go." Unlike her own mother, Aunt Evelyn treated the servants as if they were deaf, and Lucie was humiliated in front of the serving maid, who could hardly wait to go into the kitchen and report this further.

"The back door is always open," Aunt Evelyn said firmly. "Always. This is nothing but an alibi, Lucie." Lucie had thought only cowboys and detectives used the word alibi. "It sounds to me as if some of those filthy jungle habits of yours need to be corrected. We don't behave that way in Civilization." As Aunt Evelyn said it, Civilization always had an initial capital. "You must never, ever succumb to that again; I don't care if fifty doors are locked. Even if, by some chance, both doors were locked, a lady plans her powder room visits, and is never caught short. Never. That's a word to the wise." Lucie put her head down in shame—not the shame that Aunt Evelyn thought she should feel, but the shame and despair of being in this terrible place at the mercy of these terrible people, with no sign that she could ever leave.

A few days later, Aunt Evelyn caught her in the upstairs hall. "I need a word with you, young lady. You simply have to be more careful about flushing the toilet. Grace tells me that twice she's found BMs in the toilet that you've carelessly left. This is not acceptable in our home. Simply not acceptable. I know you lived in primitive circumstances in Borneo, and I've told Grace we're trying to make allowances, but you must learn to operate flush toilets properly and not leave your—your leavings—for other people to find. I think the best way to convince you that I mean it is to ground you for a few days. No after-school swimming for a week, young lady." Not swimming was bad enough; but much worse, the invitations no longer came that had once allowed her to escape. People understood that if they invited her, they must also invite Grace. She was hobbled at the dinner table, forced to watch Grace routinely throw the tantrums that Lucie had grown accustomed to, but was still disgusted by.

Just a few days earlier, when they'd visited Manhattan, Grace had been thwarted in something minor—Lucie didn't even remember what: an ice cream cone? Going along one block instead of another?—and when her whining had failed to get her what she wanted, Grace had thrown herself on the pavement, screaming as if she were being tortured. Passersby stopped, astonished; this was not an infant out of control but a girl on the brink of adolescence. Aunt Evelyn looked about her, her face coloring. "She didn't get her proper sleep last night," she explained to one stranger who'd stopped with her mouth agape. The excuse must have sounded silly even in Aunt Evelyn's own ears. "The city over-stimulates her," she explained to another. Lucie hung away, trying to appear as if she didn't know them. There was no escape from the humiliation. When Aunt Evelyn had inevitably capitulated to the ice cream cone or the detour, the din stopped instantly.

These outbursts disgusted Lucie, but they wearied her too. She didn't understand why Aunt Evelyn didn't see through this theatrical nonsense. She heard her own nanny in Borneo speaking firmly: Well-bred people do not make scenes. Her mother: We do not make a fuss.

A month after her grounding, she was getting into her bed one night to read. As she pulled the covers back, she saw that the bed had already been disturbed, and then understood why. A warm pile of human waste rested halfway down the bed. In disgust and rage, she ran for Aunt Evelyn. "You come here. You just come here and see what Grace did!"

Aunt Evelyn looked weary. "Girls, I can't get involved in your fights. You need to settle this between yourselves."

"No, this is—please, Aunt Evelyn!"

Aunt Evelyn got up sighing heavily, melodramatically, and followed Lucie up the stairs and across the landing to her room. "What's that dreadful odor?" She hesitated, and Lucie pulled her by the hand.

"This. This. Look at this. And it's still warm. She did it to me, to my bed. Everybody at school says she's crazy, and she is! She is!"

Grace stood at the door. "She's trying to blame me, but really, mother, it was her own accident. She's still a baby in so many ways. Poops in her bed."

Lucie turned in outrage. "Liar! Liar! Filthy girl! Liar! You ought to be in a nuthouse, a place for crazy people! You ought to be in a straitjacket! Everybody says so! You locked me out of the house when you knew I had to go! You're the one who leaves BMs in the toilet and blames me! Now this! Now this!" She burst into tears. "I want to go home. I want to go away from this horrible place."

Aunt Evelyn's lip trembled, but she said nothing. She stripped the bed awkwardly, carried the dirty sheets into the bathtub, ran the water. When the water had covered the sheets, she said neutrally, "Mary will look after this in the morning. Go to the linen closet, Lucie, and get clean sheets for your bed. You're eleven; you can make your own bed."

Lucie went downstairs again afterwards to speak to Aunt Evelyn. "You know it wasn't me. It was her. She's a demon."

The woman looked up wearily over her newspaper. "No need for that kind of superstitious talk, Lucie. I know all you girls read horror stories under the sheets at night." She took a deep breath. "I wasn't there, so I can't judge who's at fault. But let me tell you frankly. We hoped you'd be a friend to your big sister, Lucie. We brought you here to be company for her. She's a difficult girl and has had—difficult moments. We try to love Grace, we don't provoke her as you seem determined to do."

"That's very unfair!"

"We're counting on you to do your duty, Lucie. Otherwise we might just have to send you back to the Communists. I'm sure you don't want that."

Lucie understood that she was to be blamed, no matter who had done the deed, and turned away, both her sense of justice and any hope for herself crushed.

Another week passed, and on a rainy afternoon, Grace came along the hall, took her by surprise standing near the winter clothes closet, pushed her in and locked the door. Lucie screamed and pounded on the door for a moment, then gave up, sat down in the darkness, inhaling the smell of camphor that permeated the winter woolens. She knew her screaming thrilled Grace. Though there was homework she needed to do, at least she was out of Grace's way, and once it was dinnertime and everyone was at home, she'd be released. She sat against a wall, breathing the camphor in, breathing herself calm. When at last she heard footsteps in the hall, she pounded on the door. It was Uncle James who heard her, unlocked the door. "What on earth are you girls playing at?"

"It was no game," Lucie said angrily.

"You're all right, Lucie?" His concern was genuine, but she knew from sad experience that he wouldn't take sides, especially against his own daughter.

She refused to answer, ran around him and to her room, where she slammed the door, threw herself on the bed and wept. After dinner, she wrote the first letter to her parents that wasn't a polite lie.

"The situation is quite impossible here. Please send for me. Please rescue me. I think this girl will try to do something terrible to injure me."

She took the letter to school so that no interceptions would be possible, and posted it immediately. It took a month for the answer from her mother.

"Daddy and I have spoken on the telephone to Uncle James and Aunt Evelyn, a frightfully *dear* proposition, as you need only imagine, all the way from Borneo to Connecticut. It isn't something we can afford every day!!! They are quite certain that you and Grace are having the kind of difficult but ordinary moments any girls your age will, it's only a matter of time before things straighten themselves out and you'll be best of chums. At your age things loom much larger than they really are. Please try not to dramatize!!! In any case, you cannot come back here. The Communists kidnapped an aide's daughter not a few weeks ago for ransom, the government has strongly forbidden paying ransoms to terrorists, and no one knows where the girl is or what might have befallen her, though I think you can *imagine* the worst!!!! Once you yield to these savages and pay a ransom, you'll never hear the end of it. Her parents are extremely upset, but of course as loyal subjects of Her Majesty they support the government's reasoning. You can understand the government's point of view perfectly. Daddy and I support it *altogether* of course. It is our *duty*. But this is what we've saved you from. Bear this in mind and one good turn deserves another, do your duty too by showing your gratitude by being a good girl for Aunt Evelyn and Uncle James. Be good, my darling, God bless you and keep you,

Love Mummy and Daddy."

No one would ever save her. She ran up the staircase, across the landing to her room, locked the door, threw herself on to her bed, and wept yet again. What would come next? What would this demon do to her?

In the second year she was with them, as the spring came around again, she had a new escape. The "horsie" she'd been promised was a warmblood, originally bought for Grace, who had no talent for, or interest in, riding. Lucie had just begun to learn jumping in Borneo, and was pleased to hear that Mucho was trained to jump.

But when the Hungarian trainer at the club saw them working together, he spoke to Uncle James. "That girl has talent. A great natural seat. Great poise. She could do hunting and jumping, eventing, but for dressage, my opinion is she'd be outstanding. She knows how to listen to her horse. Better, how to speak to it. My view is, let her begin with Mucho, see how it goes, and then get her something better."

Uncle James reported this conversation at the dinner table that night, enthusiastic about the idea himself, since he was working in the city less, and just beginning to train as a show judge. For the first time since she'd arrived in America, Lucie felt noticed as something besides a nuisance. She listened to Uncle James's praise gratefully, vowed in her heart to be as good as he hoped.

Best of all, the club—the stable and the ring—were an escape from home and the dreadful Grace. The more time Lucie spent there, the more people she met. From groomsmen to club members, people treated her kindly, people who were interested in her development as a horsewoman, even admired her accomplishments. Like the parents of her schoolmates, these people also invited her to dinner. If she must regretfully decline these invitations, at least she could stay away longer to muck out Mucho's stable, though the stable hands were supposed to do that. Anything to put off going home.

Everything in dressage was different from jumping. Her saddle, the bridle, the bit, the very way she sat on horseback. Lucie learned the changes easily and stylishly. She sometimes noticed people gathered outside the ring to watch her and the Hungarian trainer working. Sometimes she saw Uncle James in consultation with the trainer, getting a few pointers himself, he told her cheerfully. If she'd been nervous at first, she soon learned to feel at ease with Mucho, even pleased with how she felt on his back, tall, graceful, at one with this magnificent creature, who was beginning to respond sensitively to her, just as she was learning to be more subtle in her instructions to him.

Then in late spring, another invitation came, this time not merely to dinner, but to join the Welches, a family that stabled its horses at the club. They wanted her to join them in a trip to Saratoga, where work in dressage took place alongside the famous summer races. Aunt Evelyn asked pointedly: "Is the invitation only for you, Lucie? Doesn't it include Grace?" Uncle James snorted. "Grace doesn't ride, and this is all about riding." He seemed very pleased with the idea. "These are important people, very influential. If the Welches want her with them, she couldn't learn from better people." Gratefully, Lucie joined the Welches, their horses, their dogs, their goofy high school age sons, for July and August of that year.

In the hard work of learning, in the deep sleep that outdoor exercise gave her, she was relaxed and happy for the first time since she'd left Borneo. Uncle James sometimes came up on weekends, quietly drank his scotch, and listened to the Welches tell him how gifted Lucie was—every horse suited her; she had a superb touch with them, but she needed a better one of her own. "And such a pretty little thing she is in breeches and boots."

Martha Welch took him aside. "James, I'd like your permission to buy Lucie some proper undergarments. She's getting to be a young woman now, and the right brassiere is as important as the right breeches." She smiled prettily, and James, altogether embarrassed, pulled out his wallet and pressed cash into her hand. Martha Welch pushed it back at him. "No, it's not the money. I just don't want her to arrive home and—well, this summer she's blossomed beautifully, don't you think? Should I call Evelyn just to touch base?"

6

Lucie came back to Connecticut vowing to herself that the exuberance, the sense of wellbeing, the peace she'd felt in that magical July and August would not be tarnished, no matter what. She was shooting up and out physically—in the next six months, she added three inches to her height; had to have her clothes altered, acquire new ones. Grace, on the contrary, was oddly static. She grew a little fatter, perhaps, a little squarer, but was trapped in the asexuality of pubescence, neither girl nor boy; not adult, but no longer a child.

Aunt Evelyn took them both into her bedroom to talk about the facts of life. To Grace, this all seemed to be an enormous affront, a nasty surprise. She made faces at each fact, stuck out her tongue as if to gag. It was old news to Lucie, who'd swapped stories in the girls' locker room at school ("I think it will hurt, but it will be a good kind of hurt, right?"); who'd seen stallions and mares in the stables. Restrained from each other, but so eager. When aroused, the stallions had enormous members, and she tried to imagine what men looked like down there. What she was feeling these recent months was strange, maybe wrong, and in church she begged God to stop the strange feelings that enveloped her when she saw an aroused stallion. God understood that she didn't want to actually do it with a horse. She only wanted—she didn't know what she wanted. When the feeling persisted, she asked God if this was something He wanted—to give her some pleasure in a life that had so little. She lay in bed at night, thinking about the stallions, feeling her swelling breasts, discovering the private pleasure between her legs.

She loved being on horseback. She loved the sense of weightlessness she felt as she soared over the railings, the complete trust between herself and her mount. She loved the feeling of the horse between her legs. She practiced faithfully. She began to win prizes. At first they were only in the club, but Uncle James was pleased. Janos, he said, had suggested she was ready to enter a county competition. There she won seconds and thirds, but everyone congratulated her, told her she was a comer. She kept practicing, and knew that first prizes were within reach.

Uncle James was with her much more now. He acted as coach and trainer when Janos wasn't available. He'd sold his business, he said offhandedly (at a handsome profit, Aunt Evelyn had said, though his great-grandfather, who'd founded the firm, would be spinning in his grave). Now he could do what he'd always loved, which was to be around the stables, around the rings and courses. He knew she could take a first prize. She only had to practice. "Get a first, and you'll have a new horse," he promised.

She got the first, and got the new horse, Malko, a beautiful creature that trembled under her touch, a creature that seemed to know at once that they were a team, that together they were bound to excel.

But it was when she won the Tri-State competition at the end of her twelfth summer that things altered. She slid off her horse after the events, and into Uncle James's arms, embraced in happiness. Pressed to him, her heart pounding with the exertion and the thrill of winning, she felt for the first time a swollen human penis against her groin. She did not pull away. It gave her something to imagine at night in bed besides the ridiculous stallion fantasies.

Late one afternoon, a week or so after her big win, she was finished with practicing, and grooming Malko when Uncle James came into the stall. "Ready to come home?"

"Give me just a moment," she said with a smile.

"Leave Malko to the stable hands. Let's go."

In the car, he seemed ill at ease. He made small talk, but after a while, he turned off the road to home. "Lucie, I have some things to talk to you about, and this is the only private place we have." It was a dirt road, and he drove for another five minutes before he stopped the car. "Let's get out, shall we? Much nicer in the fresh air."

The leaves were beginning to turn, and Lucie loved the smell, a vegetable mustiness that wasn't the same but reminded her of the tropical forests at home. They walked further down the dirt road in silence. He stopped. "Lucie, you've become very dear to me. I mean, I'm so proud of what you've accomplished. Everyone is."

She smiled, murmured her thanks. She felt that a momentous thing was about to happen, felt the delicious drama of it. He faced her, his hands on her shoulders, warm even through her jacket. "Such a lovely young woman you're growing into. So beautiful, Lucie." She suddenly saw herself as a movie heroine, moved into his arms, raised her face to be kissed, felt the swelling in his crotch against her, and gasped. He pushed her away. "No, my sweet girl, oh no." But it was said softly, sadly. Strange sensations overwhelmed her, sensations that intimated pleasure, intimated doom; she could almost hear the music. She looked away in confusion, in shame at their intensity, part hunger, part anger. He took her chin and pulled her face back towards his. "Not now, but I hope someday... Lucie, what I feel for you is—is tremendous. Just tremendous. It's taking everything I have not to touch you, to kiss your beautiful lips, make love to you. Do you understand that?"

"Why not?" she suddenly cried. "Why not?"

"Beautiful Lucie, you're a child! I shouldn't even be thinking such things!"

She grabbed his hand, put it inside her jacket on her breast. "I'm no child. See? I'm no child."

He let his hand linger, and she felt for a moment his thumb and forefinger on her nipple, a pleasure that made her think she'd melt, like the Wicked Witch of the West. But he dropped his hand to his side. "God! I shouldn't even be here with you. I shouldn't even think the things I think. I shouldn't—I'm almost a father to you, Lucie. I can't be your lover. You're—you're twelve years old."

"I'll be thirteen in May."

He clicked his tongue; his head fell back. "Thank you. That certainly broke the fever." He collected himself, looked off to the distant field behind the woods. "Let's go home." He spoke sadly, not angrily.

Now she saw him looking differently at her across the dining room table. They had shared something special in that early autumn afternoon. They would glance at each other and smile for each other alone, almost conspirators against the others. Aunt Evelyn droned on in monologues nobody heard; Grace threw some half-hearted tantrums. Lucie didn't care. She only knew that Uncle James was there, and his presence changed everything. At the stables, in the ring, he was all business, speaking sharply to her when she made a mistake, praising her when she did well. She always pushed herself to the limit to do well for him. They spoke only of school and other ordinary things on the drives home.

"My God, she's lovely, isn't she?" Martha Welch said to him as they leaned on the fence, watched Lucie and Malko go through their paces one afternoon. "She'll be a heartbreaker, no doubt about it."

"Yes, she'll break hearts," he agreed. "How's Sam doing at Yale?"

"Getting more gentlemen's C's than he should. Thank God he's a legacy." And they laughed. "Will you let her come up to Saratoga again this summer, James? We loved having her, and she's no trouble. Anything but. She's like the daughter I never had."

"It's so very kind of you."

"I hope she can."

"I'll need to talk it over with Evelyn. Grace misses her very much when—"

"I suppose we could take Grace too."

"No, Martha. No, you really couldn't. Very kind of you to consider it, but Grace is—troubled. We hoped having Lucie as a kind of sister to her would make it easier for Grace. Fix things. It hasn't. Not at all. If anything... Well, we're thinking of sending Grace to a special camp in the summer. We don't know yet."

Martha Welch turned to him. "You've had your hands full with Grace, haven't you? I'm so sorry. My own boys are a handful, but they're a normal handful. Grace is—well, as you say, troubled."

Lucie had grown careless about checking her bed before she got into it, but tonight something was disturbed—Grace didn't make the bed the way the maid did, no matter how she tried. So Lucie pulled the covers back suspiciously, wondering what she'd find this night.

At first, she saw nothing, and was relieved. She was dead tired, in no mood for games. She turned off the light, climbed between the sheets. Then something sharp pricked the back of her leg. An insect bite, probably. But as she lay down fully, more sharp pricks bit her buttocks, her back, even her scalp. She screamed, jumped up, and turned on the light again. Hundreds of small shards of glass caught the light, gleamed up at her.

Her uncle burst through the door, followed by her aunt. "We heard—" James stopped himself, took it in quickly; even her aunt saw the blood seeping all over her back. "That's it, Evelyn! Jesus, that is absolutely it." Aunt Evelyn was weeping herself, trying to brush the glass out of the bedsheets, which only scattered it on to the floor, getting it underfoot. James got Lucie's pajama top off her, ran his hands down her back, searching for slivers that still remained.

Lucie was sobbing, less from the pain than from the implacable hatred it stood for. "Let me go home," she cried between sobs, "oh please, let me go home from this terrible place. She's a witch! She'll murder me!" James took her in his arms, soothed her, eventually led her to the bathroom where, under the bright bathroom lights, he could see the shards in her back, pulled them out gently, one by one. He called to his wife. "Evelyn, get me your tweezers." As she sobbed, he murmured to her. "Darling, you'll have to be still for me to get these out. It's all right, Lucie; it's all right. I'll stay with you tonight. Evelyn! Get Mary to change the goddam sheets and sweep the floor."

"Not Mary," Aunt Evelyn said weakly. "No one else should—"

"Then do it yourself. Now!"

As his wife was changing the linens, James turned Lucie around to face him. He put a towel around her shoulders, stared deep into her eyes, willing himself not to look beneath her chin at the bareness he'd already carefully covered. "I think I have all of them out, darling. If I haven't, we'll get you to a doctor tomorrow morning. I'm going to put some Mercurochrome on these. It will sting a little, but it's to keep them from getting infected." Impulsively, he hugged her to him. "Oh, lovely Lucie, I am so sorry about this. Grace is sick, you know that. She doesn't really mean to—"

Lucie pulled away from him: "She means it! She means it, Uncle James! She's going to kill me. She wants me dead!"

"No, no," he groaned, "she's sick, honey. Troubled. She needs to be in a hospital. Her mother's going to take her first thing in the morning. A hospital where she'll get well, and won't be upsetting you anymore. Upsetting any of us."

"Maybe not tomorrow morning," Evelyn hissed through the open door. "Maybe it was accidental, something that happened with the laundry. What will people think?"

"Tomorrow morning, Evelyn." A voice that brooked no argument. He turned back to Lucie and spoke softly. "And I'll stay outside your door tonight to guard you. Nothing's going to harm you anymore, sweet girl."

The next morning Lucie woke to hear Grace's screams. An epic tantrum was underway. Lucie got up, felt a shard of glass in her foot that her aunt had missed on the floor, and pulled it out with her fingernails. She went cautiously to the window, looked down to the gravel driveway. She could see that though Grace was struggling mightily, she was being forced into the back seat of the station wagon. Mary the maid was beside her, holding her; the door locked on her. Aunt Evelyn must be at the wheel. After a brief delay, the car drove off.

Lucie got dressed and went to the breakfast room. James sat at the table, and though he was reading the morning newspaper, she could see that his hands trembled slightly.

"We're on our own, sweet one. Your aunt is taking Grace to the hospital. It should've been done long ago, but we... we hoped..." He ended in futility, went back to staring at the newspaper. "You don't have to go to school today if you don't want to. It's been a shock, I'm sure."

Lucie sat down at the breakfast table, undecided if she wanted to go to school. She caught Uncle James's eye, smiled shyly at him. "It's all right."

"No, it's not all right. But what's done is done. We should've hospitalized her years ago; maybe they could've done something for her before now. But her mother wouldn't hear of it. I couldn't make her see reason. When I spoke to your father in London, I thought—we invited you here thinking that maybe a little sister would calm her. We had no idea it would be so terribly hard on you, honey. No idea at all."

Lucie slid off her chair, moved toward her foster father. "It's all right."

He shook his head. "It's not all right. How's your back? Any more glass?"

"Maybe. I feel something. Could we go upstairs into the bedroom so you can see?" So the maid wouldn't? He followed her upstairs, closed the bedroom door behind them. "Just about here." She turned her back to him, removed her blouse. "Here, under my bra. I felt it when I put my bra on." She unhooked her bra. He scrutinized her back, ran his fingers over the area she meant. "I don't think so, sweet one. I don't feel anything, see anything. Maybe just a puncture that hasn't healed over."

She turned quickly, so that his hands were inadvertently on her bare breasts. He gasped, saw what was offered to him, turned his head. "It will not be," he said decisively. "It will not be." But he had her hand, put it impulsively between his legs, breathing hard. Lucie had been reading *The Screwtape Letters* for Sunday school, and on the back of its red book cover was a drawing of the demon Screwtape with his thick, segmented tail. What was under her hand now felt just like Screwtape's tail. In her confusion she wanted to laugh out loud.

She did not laugh. And it did come to be, after a fashion. For nearly a year, she and James secretly, surreptitiously, in dark halls and in dark cars, in the basement and in deserted horse stalls, on the grass when they had ridden away together cross-country, gave each other every pleasure short of actual consummation. She made him show her Screwtape's Tail as she called it, made him let her caress it, and he showed her how to use her mouth. When she turned thirteen, he reluctantly conceded they could make love fully. It continued until she went away to college at seventeen, considered a catch for the college equestrian team. Away from the family, she thought she was tired of James now; could easily evade him. Late in the spring of her sophomore year at college, his horse refused a jump, pitched him over the rails, broke his neck, and he was dead.

She never rode again.

7

In the taxi from Heathrow to Kensington—"not the most fashionable part," her mother had written, "but we can walk to Holland Park"—Lucie Marchmont was trembling. She forced herself to take long deep breaths, inhaling into air passages so dessicated by a transatlantic flight that each breath seemed to abrade them. She felt as light as dandelion fluff, so light she might have floated across the ocean without a plane. Something utterly alien shimmered inside her, making her weightless and lightheaded too, sometimes dizzy. It was happiness. She was on the way home. A home she'd never known, but on the way home at last. Home. The word itself seemed impossible, forbidden, denied to her for so very long. Exotic, and ordinary at the same time. She'd used the word carelessly enough: I need to be home by ten. I don't want to go home yet. I'll do it on the way home.

That wasn't home. Home was that soft ineffable enclosure where you were wanted and loved; where you knew all the customs without needing to ask, be told, be reminded of irritably. You knew because you'd grown up inside that enclosure and its customs. They were you. You were them. A place, the poet said, where they had to take you in. No. That was Connecticut. Real home was a place she'd been born into and exiled from. On the way home. Tears pushed forward and stung; with great effort, she held them back. Not here, not in the taxi. There'd be time for that. When she was enclosed by home.

Ten years since she'd been ripped from Borneo and dropped in Connecticut. Ten years since she'd seen either of her parents, who, by now, had themselves been withdrawn from Borneo, an imperial sacrifice to nationalism. She wouldn't have been able to see them even now except James had left her some money. Her parents had often written to protest these last few years, sometimes sadly, sometimes matter-of-factly: as much as they yearned to see her, they didn't have the money to send for her.

Ironic that the landscape of home was so foreign. The bleak brick walls of terrace houses were unfamiliar, not at all like Connecticut, nothing like Borneo, of course. Maybe something like leaving New York City as the train made its way through Harlem, the Bronx. But even those structures had eventually grown more familiar than these outside the taxi window, yellow, gray, sometimes deepest carmine, sometimes trimmed in limestone, but always cloaked in soot accumulated since Victorian times. Bay windows—two narrows flanking a wide—probed from these block-long monolithic brick walls, blunt little teeth that might someday clamp against identical teeth across the road. All windows were carefully shrouded in lace or sheer curtains: these houses had discretion. Or maybe secrets to keep. What might have once been bombsites twenty years earlier were filled in with new structures, thrust into the orderly old rows like the lurid gold teeth of Russians in a familiar mouth of bone.

Through shopping streets, on the sides of buses, none of the brands advertised were familiar, though she knew what the shops sold, what a chandler's or a chemist's was, an old vocabulary exhumed word by word. Her heart beat faster. This was home. Home at last.

Her mother's letters had been direct: money was scarce; they'd had to "scrimp and save" since her father was retired. But Lucie wasn't prepared for the house where the taxi arrived. A narrow three-story row house, the inevitable bay windows on the first floor, smaller windows above, tiny windows at the top, stucco and limestone trim all a sooty gray. A small area in the front let light into the floor below the street, a border zone protected by an iron fence in disrepair. This set of identical houses was the most modest—the most rundown—in the street. A shock after the spacious Connecticut house. Decidedly more humble than the Governor's Residence in Borneo. It didn't matter. Small was cozy. Small was loving. She nodded, paid the driver, and pulled her suitcase out. It wouldn't matter.

A half dozen steps from the pavement up to the front door. She rang the bell—a real bell, strident and electrical, not the church-like chimes she was used to in Connecticut houses—and prayed that the happiness shimmering inside her wouldn't make her faint before the door was opened. Would her mother embrace her with a great hug, a kiss, would they push each other lovingly into a fit of weeping? Would they laugh until they cried?

Her mother opened the door. "Lucie dear. So nice to see you after all this time. Nice and punctual you are, too, aren't you?" She leaned forward to give Lucie a brief dry kiss on the cheek. "I'm just watching 'Coronation Street;' won't be a moment. Come on, then, come into the sitting room."

"Mummy—"

"Shhh!" her mother said sharply, straining to catch dialogue from the other room.

Lucie put her suitcase down in the hall and followed her mother to a small back sitting room that looked out onto a forlorn garden.

As it happened, the moment her mother wished her to wait was in fact twenty minutes until the program ended. In these twenty minutes, what began as a fine needle of doubt and disappointment broadened to a great hammer of defeat, battering inside her chest without mercy.

She was stunned, deeply hurt, that this strange elderly woman, rapt before the old-fashioned television set, found more meaning in a televised performance than in a reunion with her only child. For a few minutes, Lucie told herself it was British understatement; British reserve; the Brits did not emote. She'd got used to Americans and their boisterous ways. Be generous, she told herself; it was only her mother's way of controlling something that might get out of hand.

But after ten minutes of silence, save the voices from the television, shock and hurt transformed themselves into scorn. Yes, she recognized this woman as her mother, but time had not been kind. The mother she remembered, the mother she'd dreamed of for a decade, Borneo Mother, was slender and chic, taking her late afternoon cocktails with a soigné cigarette in her hand. But this woman, London Mother, was sloppily stout—needed a better foundation garment, Aunt Evelyn would have said. She wore a dress of some unpleasantly shiny artificial fabric, patterned all over with tiny flowers, what Lucie recognized, with a year of art history behind her now, as derivative William Morris. Not a pattern any grown woman should wear. The dress buttoned up the front, and was too small, so that the spaces between the buttons gaped unflatteringly, exposing glossy underthings. Her mother's nylons were heavy, not the sheer stockings American women wore, and her heavy white summer shoes, vaguely orthopedic-looking, needed re-heeling. Her gray-brown hair would benefit from tinting (in her head Lucie heard one of Aunt Evelyn's friends say "we're all for natural when it's pretty"). Her mother's hair had not been washed for days.

This TV drama that captivated her mother. Its characters spoke with accents that Borneo Mother would've dismissed as the diction of Other Ranks. Lucie herself could barely understand the dialogue, barely follow the plot, which told her how far she'd come from things British. She surveyed the room, recognized some of the furniture from Borneo, a few curios. But the furniture had gone shabby, the upholstery actually threadbare in some places, a dull green velvet cushion with its cording separating from the seams. Though much of her parents' original furniture must have been discarded, the remaining pieces were far too big for the modest room, a sofa too grand, scuffed tables jutting dangerously out to catch limbs unaware. Then there were the curios—the masks, the statuettes. In a cramped little house on a rainy London summer afternoon, they weren't charming but bizarre.

The carpet, at least, was new: great yellow flowers with curling maroon leaves, bearing no visible relation to the green upholstery. Was it her imagination or could she actually smell that poisonous aniline? The vulgar dyes made the old furniture look even shabbier.

Into her derision she also swept herself up without pity. She'd imagined this encounter so often, the warm embrace, the sweet tears. Yes, a little awkwardness at the beginning, but then genuine family affection, her own joy at being with mummy and daddy at last, the laughter as they caught up. How should she speak of Connecticut? Be evasive, be polite: so very kind of the Ludlows to take me in like a daughter; well, yes; their own girl was troubled, eventually needed hospitalization. The first two years of college had been wonderful. The secret life with James must remain secret, of course. Possibly she and mummy would grow closer as time went by, and she could confide a little bit. Nothing lost then if she revealed that James had left her a bit of money toward her college expenses. All this had been planned, dialogue imagined, revised, rehearsed, improved upon.

Yet here was the reality. A blowzy middle-aged woman enthralled by the television. Mortified by her own expectations, Lucie could have wept, but these would be very different from the joyous tears she'd held back in the taxi.

The ride in from Heathrow had been long, and Lucie needed to use the toilet. Finally, she ventured an interruption. "May I wash up?"

"Shhhh! Upstairs to the landing, first door on the right. Can't miss it." Her mother did not turn to look at her.

In the bathroom, damp and chilly even in this summer afternoon, accusatory fingers of mildew stretched down from the ceiling. The wallpaper was peeling. At the cracked mirror, inexorable recognition. A woman without a country. A woman without a family. A woman without a home. A woman without love. Raw need erupted: she so desperately wanted the warmth of a mother's hand, holding her, sheltering her, reassuring her. She leaned against the basin. Could she rush back down the stairs and demand her birthright? Would that shatter the indifference of this stranger in front of the TV? Could she fall on her knees, beg for recognition? For love? Would that move this stranger to take pity on her at least?

Humiliation. Did she want such a thing from this terrible woman? Whatever had shimmered inside an hour ago was gone. Now in her chest lay a heavy, inert black mass.

The program had ended when she returned to the sitting room. Her mother jumped up, as if aware she might have been more hospitable. But she kept her distance, a warning to Lucie that intimacy was not welcome. Not possible.

"Let's see you now, darling." The smile was forced, animated by shame. Badly maintained, ugly teeth. Lucie had grown used to American dental care and though she hadn't seen that many Brits, was always shocked by their bad teeth. Now her mother's. "What a beauty you've become, Lucie. Fancy that! Of course you always were a pretty little thing, but now you're a real beauty. Daddy will be back from his club in just a few minutes—he knows better than to interrupt 'Corrie'—and we'll all have tea, shall we? How was the journey? How's America? Are they all rich as Croesus and twice as common? We love the Yanks, but they're really not our kind when all's said and done, are they?"

Lucie did not answer. The frozen black mass inside her was grief, a crushing distress, the beginning of a kind of icy anger. None of this was her kind either.

"How long do you expect to be in London?" In London. Not here. Not at home. Lucie had hoped to stay for days, perhaps weeks, forever, if all went well.

"I'm just on my way to—Paris." A destination fished out of the air, out of the Balzac she'd read, out of the Picasso she'd seen in her college sophomore classrooms.

"Oh, the French," her mother said dismissively. "Rude people, and between you, me, and the lamppost, not quite clean, are they now?"

Her mother's face was a fine network of wrinkles, and Lucie wished for a great razor to scrape that all off, peel away all time, all worry, to find the fine English camellia petal skin that must surely be lurking under this ugly mask. Find the mother she remembered. Or imagined. Borneo Mother. Not London Mother. Many years later she would realize that smoking, and easy afternoon cocktails, had done their worst. She would allow herself to guess that the ugliness also came from a different kind of toxin that had eaten at her mother from within.

She was now led upstairs to a room as dismal as the sitting room, its furniture also oversized and oppressive. "You'll be here, darling." Lucie didn't recognize it as furniture from the Governor's Residence; perhaps they'd bought it when they arrived in London. If so, then it wasn't poverty but their own ghastly taste that accounted for the dreariness of the cramped house. She was grateful that conversation was one-sided. Her mother had become a chatterer—it was enough for Lucie to nod or answer monosyllabically. She hardly needed to do even that much; her mother's questions weren't really questions at all but phrases that declared themselves as self-evident truths. If Lucie started to reply, how America had been, what college was like, her mother interrupted with a tangential remark that overran any answer. Was she so oblivious? Or indifferent to anything beyond her own preoccupations? Afraid of answers she didn't want to hear? Lucie kept a sullen silence that let her feed her rage.

Would her father change things? When he returned home an hour later, she knew he wouldn't. He was shrunken into his clothing, his shirt collar far too big for his neck, a marker for the heft he'd once possessed. He seemed seedy, necktie slightly stained and askew, shirt badly ironed, the suit threadbare in spots, definitely not fresh. He at least gave her a perfunctory hug, said she was looking very well, America agreed with her, did it? And wondered what was on for tea.

For a moment, Lucie made an effort to put aside her own feelings to offer these people pity. She tried to open her heart—this new black mass in her chest—to their steep descent, their disappointments. Her father had found himself superfluous in the foreign service, forced into early retirement on a pension that was less generous than it once seemed. A shrinking empire had no place for an ex-governor of a small and tentative British colony on a small and insignificant island. It galled him; he was sour and permanently out of sorts at the injustice of it.

"They lost all respect for us when the Japs invaded. It wouldn't have happened under the old Rajah Brooke, Sir James. He knew how to command respect. He wouldn't have let the Japs near the island. He'd have cleared them off in no time. And his nephew, Sir Charles, who inherited the Raj, had gumption too. Chinese for trade, but never politics; Malays for politics—gentlemen in their own right, even if they were Mohammedans—but couldn't trade, mustn't. Beneath them. This last one didn't know up from down. The Brookes had a private country, don't you know, and this last one, a weak twig, by Jove, gave it over to the Crown because he couldn't cope."

He was shocked by the gross ingratitude for his vital contribution to the cause of Empire. His most cherished beliefs about the grand cause of civilizing so much of the world had been mocked, not only by foreigners, but by young

Englishmen who should have known better. Why, this contribution had all but won the war by itself alone. "Would we have won against the Jerries without the New Zealanders, the Aussies, the East Indians? Of course not. The Fifth Indian won four VC's alone."

And the Yanks? Lucie wanted to ask, suddenly on America's side if only in opposition to this couple she'd had such high hopes for, and who had delivered such deep disappointment. But she kept silent, and heard how an idiotic world was going off in its headstrong way to home rule and other sentimental notions, "It's mad, of course; quite mad. They'll be begging for us back, won't they, but we won't be there. Why should we? Serves them right."

"Are you pleased to be back in London, at least?"

Her father shrugged. Her mother said she missed the servants. But she didn't miss the heat, not a bit of it. They intended to find a cottage down in Devon or Cornwall, now that things weren't working out as they'd hoped in London.

"I would have liked my books. The bird guide, for instance. You didn't keep it, then?"

"We gave it to the public library when we left," her mother said with excessive haste.

Over tea—her father was chewing strangely with ill-fitted false teeth— he looked only occasionally at Lucie as he spoke to her, as if they were on the telephone, not face to face.

"Pity about poor Ludlow's death. A young man, after all. Nice chap, very good of him and his wife to take you in. You won't be staying on for long, then, Lucie? Mummy says you're going on to Paris, then." He stared into the garden, and she knew her answer was of no particular consequence to him.

No one inquired who'd paid her way here—she supposed they thought it was the infinitely rich Ludlows of Connecticut, America, which, in a way, was true. If asked—if, as she'd once imagined, her parents might offer her money, a sacrifice they could ill afford, but anything for their only daughter—she'd planned to say she had scholarship money left over. But this wasn't going to be necessary. No one knew. No one cared. She saw that as a daughter, her presence was inconvenient to them, an irritating disruption in the life whose narrative they'd already laid down, without desire for commentary or correction. To them, she was better gone than not. Lucie considered the bedroom upstairs where she was expected to spend the night.

"Yes, on to Paris. This is only a stopover. I have to be back at Heathrow. Tonight."

"Tonight? Well, we thought you might stay a day or so, but if you must be off. Pity I changed the sheets in the spare room." She knew that her mother recognized the lie—Lucie had let herself be led up to that spare room and not protested. But each of them smiled politely. "I must be off. Thank you for tea." Which she barely touched, so appalling did it seem, the over-sugared sweets, the slightly off cream clotting in the discolored teacups. The stained tea cloth.

A taxi was summoned. What kind of goodbye could be said? When she offered only a hand to each of them, they seemed relieved. It was a species of corpse she dragged back to Heathrow that night, dead in some vital place. In later years, she seldom went back to London, and when she did, she was nearly made sick by the hot shame she felt at herself and her laughable expectations that day.

She did go on to Paris, where eventually she finished her undergraduate work at the Sorbonne Nouvelle, studying both French and German. From there she went to the Frei Universität in West Berlin for law studies. She'd planned to become an attorney, since she did very well in her schoolwork, but for no precise reason, she scaled her ambition back to being simply a notary, which in the German system, was prestigious enough. After a time, she retreated again, became a licensed interpreter and translator of court proceedings and legal documents. She would watch the attorneys in court, know she could do as well, perhaps even better; sometimes she'd murmur to one of them a legal point he'd missed. But she had no heart to engage. She had a pleasant life, she told herself, with an apartment in a leafy Berlin suburb, friends, casual lovers, and when the Wall came down, she was busier than she'd ever been. Her past receded into the infinite distance, Borneo, the United States, even that single shattering afternoon in London.

When her parents died, never having had the energy to go to Cornwall after all, she was left the house in Kensington. Its value had increased dramatically. She revisited it, tagged a few pieces of the Borneo furniture for storage, a reminder of roots she'd once had, a paradise she'd once known. As she wondered what to do with money from the house, she took a holiday in Morocco. There she heard from someone that southern Morocco reminded them very much of the area around Santa Fe, New Mexico in the United States. Why not? she asked herself. She had no real ties to Berlin. To Europe. So she drifted westward, southward.

III

Self-amplifying Instabilities

1

Judith was sitting in the sunny breakfast room, reading the *New York Times* science section, when the phone rang. It was her old friend Jill. "Are you watching TV?"

"Of course not." Watching TV during the day was like drinking during the day. Anyway, why disturb the peace of this quiet September morning with a sound track? She was luxuriating in the stillness, the sun, nibbling at her breakfast toast, sipping her tea.

"Turn it on. Something—something terrible, unbelievable, has happened. The World Trade Center Towers have been attacked. The Pentagon too. All air traffic is grounded." Jill's voice was very low, barely controlled. It seemed so far-fetched that for a moment Judith wondered if her friend had slipped off the rails.

"Turn on your TV," Jill said urgently.

Still disbelieving, Judith turned on the kitchen TV. In the horror of the reality, her first thought was her husband, who was in New York City. What was he scheduled to do today? Panicked, she couldn't remember. She dialed the Riverside Drive place nervously and got an answering machine. Dialed his mobile, got voicemail. Where was he? Wotan sensed her fear, came close to protect her from whatever it was. She felt comforted by this loyal creature. "It's Alpha Dog," she explained. "We don't know where he is."

Molloy was, it soon turned out, on the phone to her, reassuring her he was okay: he'd been doing email on the south-facing terrace toward midtown when it began. He'd seen both collisions, the smoke roiling up, a colossal cloud of destruction. His voice was strained. "But Nikki. I don't know where Nikki is. I can't get her cell—all the networks are down." Nikki had a loft in Tribeca, and didn't bother with a landline.

"Maybe she'll call here, babe. I'll let you know the moment." She sobbed. "Oh, Jack. I'm so relieved to hear your voice." Then, as always, he soothed her. Everything will be all right.

Nikki did call Santa Fe. She'd been with a friend uptown in his Harlem studio. "It's awful here, Judith. Just awful." She was crying. "I don't know what to do."

"Go right now to your papa. He's at Riverside Drive. He's frantic about you. If you can get to a landline, call him."

"Papa's here? Oh, thank God. I don't think anything's working. I'll have to walk."

"I'll call him, tell him you're okay, you're trying to get to him. Nikki—take care of yourself, honey." But when she tried to call Molloy the landlines too were clogged, and Judith could no longer get through.

She stayed by the phone for several hours, talking to friends, making an inventory of who was in town, who was not. Between her calls, calls came to her—Ron and Gabe checking on her, on where Molloy was. With relief and gratitude, she could reassure them. She called Stephen to tell him that his father and his sister were safe. Did he want to come over and be with her? He hesitated. Yes, he did. He arrived at the house, hugged her, played with Wotan for a few minutes, then settled down with some reading. "I can't watch," he said. She shook her head. Neither could she. Once she heard him murmuring into his phone, but mostly he was silent, trying to distract himself with a book.

Late in the day, another phone call came. An older couple in Santa Fe were systematically rounding up all the people whose mates, spouses, and significant others they knew were out of town and unable to get home because all air traffic had been stopped. "Come to dinner," Frances said. "At least let's be sad together." Judith asked to bring Stephen, also alone.

The Kennedys lived less than a mile from her, just off Camino Monte del Sol, but she drove herself and Stephen, both of them a little too sad and shaken to walk. As they rounded the lane where the Kennedys' house stood, her heart lifted to see a large American flag in the front window.

"Oh, wow," Stephen said softly. "What a sweet sight."

Roger Kennedy, a historian, had once been head of the National Museum of American History in Washington, so perhaps it was no surprise that the Kennedys owned such a flag. But Judith and her stepson were grateful to see it; happy, once inside the Kennedys' fine old house, to be surrounded by dear friends, who embraced each other, one by one. If the absent ones couldn't get home, this group knew they were each blessed that all their loved ones were safe, wherever they were.

As they sat down to Frances Kennedy's generous dinner, a journalist for the *New York Times*, whose husband was marooned somewhere in the Midwest, thanked the Kennedys for hanging the flag up. She looked defiantly at the group:

"I want my flag back." For decades, the stars and stripes had been seized by the most manipulative of self-proclaimed super-patriots as their symbol, and theirs alone. They draped themselves in it; they wore little flag pins on their lapels, as if someone might mistake them for being not American. Everyone at this table wanted their flag back, wanted the country back that it had once stood for: quarrelsome maybe, but not poisonously fratricidal. Dinner was cheering, comforting, and Judith was grateful to be among them.

After dinner, she drove Stephen to his house just off Upper Canyon Road. "Thanks," he said. "Thanks for today. For tonight. I'd just have sat there watching the tube like a fool."

"I needed you too," she said honestly.

"Really?" Impulsively, he leaned across and hugged her. "Ah, Judith. It's gonna be all right." She was suddenly touched by how he'd unknowingly echoed his father.

"Do you want to—would you be willing to spend the night at our house?"

She knew he hadn't slept under that roof since his father had thrown him out—him and the girlfriend they'd once shared. At last he answered. "If you need me. If you'd like the company."

"That house is a hard place for you. Maybe I shouldn't have asked."

He took a deep breath. "It's a place of great shame for me, Judith. Enormous shame."

"Oh, Stephen. Far as your father is concerned, that's past, done. He forgave you a long time ago. Hasn't he said that in plain English? God, you Molloy boys." She shook her head. "Let it be done for you too, Stevie." She called him by his nickname for the first time. Considered adding that he needed to forgive his father for whatever—but she let well enough alone. "Come and be family for me tonight, Stevie; this terrible, terrible night. Your old room is all made up. No one ever uses it. We put guests—well, somewhere else."

"I'm very glad to be family for you tonight," he said softly. She backed her car out of his driveway, and took him to the family compound.

"A wee dram before we go to sleep?" She studied him. "Is your house getting finished now?" She and Molloy had seen the wreck of a place when Stephen had first bought it; had been asked specifically not to come back and see the interior until it was finished.

"A couple of plumbing fixtures haven't yet arrived, but yeah, it's almost finished. A great learning experience. I didn't know I could do all that." He paused. "Torres came over to see it once or twice. Well, actually more than that. He likes it very much."

"That's a profound compliment. Leandro Torres isn't given to idle flattery. What are you doing with yourself, your time, now that it's almost done?"

He shrugged. "My father has—well, as I realize it now, one of the great private collections of contemporary art. He didn't need formal training in art history to do this. His instincts are spooky they're so good. I don't think he's ever sold anything he finally bought. Well, one or two pieces. Not mistakes, he says, just bought in a different place from where he is now. We always thought of it as papa's little hobby. I never thought, hey, my dad buys masterpieces. He didn't refer to his collection that way. He always got there before an artist became famous, when the work was cheap—that was part of the game. Always living artists—he wasn't interested in enriching art dealers when some poor bastard had died hungry a hundred years earlier. That's verbatim Jackster—er, my dad. So I grew up with my father's collection. Or to be more precise, when I came home to Riverside Drive from boarding school, college, there was my father's collection on the walls at home. Anyway, as time went on, I wasn't interested in being a curator or an art historian, but I thought I might go to work for one of the big auction houses. My heritage, right? God meets Mammon. I speak four languages fluently, and that's a big deal for selling art. But when the time came, I—I didn't. I came out to Santa Fe instead. I didn't, you know, need to work. My father set me up pretty well. But I was looking for something. Some instinct told me I'd find it here. Maybe."

"Funny. I came here for roughly the same reasons."

"Did you find what you were looking for, Judith?"

She spread her hands out—all this. My life with your father. "And you, Stevie?"

"I don't know yet. I've gone through stages. At first I thought, well, I just want to be. I don't have to do. The little faun, remember that? But my stepmother squashed that but good. Oh, JAWS, she says? Just Another Wealthy Shithead? Santa Fe's full of them. Thanks, Judith. Yeah, I was really crushed, but I came around to seeing you were right. So I thought okay, if I don't want for women like you, women I admire, to consider me just another wealthy shithead, what then? I guess this was the second stage. I'm doing something else now."

"Can you say what?"

He looked over her head, seemed uncomfortable. "Well, I've been taking a kind of course."

She brightened. "In what?"

"Mmm, what you might call mythology."

"Your dad loves the myths. Greek. Nordic. You name it."

"You could say he got me started." He swirled the cognac in his glass self-consciously. "Judith, I'm beating around the bush here. I'm learning about... I'm taking some lessons in Jungian psychology. Mostly for the meanings of the myths. Mostly."

"I had no idea."

He looked worried. "You don't think that's nuts? Un-scientific?"

She shook her head slowly. "Sometimes, at some levels, myth is the only way to grasp human affairs. Your father and I have come to understand each other on that level, a little bit. A love affair, a marriage, begins as an exercise in projection. He is what I need and want. I am what he needs and wants. Gradually, you peel away those projections and come to love each other in spite of them, not because of them. Your father identifies very strongly with, well, Theseus. Thinks of me as the Queen of the Amazons."

"And you?"

She laughed softly. "More like Athena, I think. Though some very major differences. I'm not all head. Tiresias maybe. Strongly male and female, and God knows, often blind. Are you taking a course at St. John's?"

"No. I have a tutor, a guide I see privately. A man who knows a great deal about myth."

"Oh, sort of a Joseph Campbell? How wonderful."

"Sort of." His eyes were alight. Encouraged, he went on. "I sometimes think this family needs a—well, a custodian, a curator. Everyone's so high-flying; everyone but me, I mean. I know that. I had to think about it. While I was fooling around with the mitre joints and plastering the walls. If I'm not the high-flyer, and I'm not—no, I'm not. But suppose I was ground control, maybe? Keep the rest of you from crashing into things? Be your safety net? Catch you when you fall? Maybe that's exactly what my destiny is. My mother was on the edge and fell off, no one to catch her. My father walks the high wire. I know he chose you because you walk the high wire too, a different one from his. Even Nikki's on the edge; the most physically daring of us, a maniac in some ways, no discipline. But with some ground control, she might be the painter she should be. I could do that. You need me."

"I hadn't thought of it that way." His face was so touchingly earnest that Judith wouldn't even let herself smile. In the last few months, it was true that a Stephen had emerged quite different from the petulant young man she'd listened to over the coffee at Downtown Subscription. She hadn't given it much thought, but now she could see that a new gravity, a maturity, had infused him. As he'd built his house, perhaps he was also building himself. She laughed. "Maybe we do need a keeper. But is that enough for you? At the end of the day, will you be content with that for yourself?"

"You have satellites, so to speak. They might need help too. Torres. There'll be others. I think maybe my task is to keep everybody in orbit. I have somebody I'm seeing—she needs some ground control too."

Judith didn't scoff. But she tried the phrase over in her mind. Ground control. *Control.* No, I don't think so.

"I wanted—mastery of something. But one of the other things I was looking for was—" he stopped, then plunged ahead, "the sacred. Not in the usual sense—I didn't want to go off and live in an ashram or something. The kind of religion I got as a kid? I certainly can't take that seriously. But just because everything around you is junk food, the hunger doesn't go away. So I began to look around. Spent some time at Upaya, but, congenial as Buddhism is, I'm not cut out to be a good Buddhist. So I began looking elsewhere. With this tutor."

Finally she said, "What set you in this direction?"

"You'll laugh. A dream. A deep dream that I still don't understand. I've had it two or three times."

"Can you share it?"

He shook his head. "No, not yet. If ever. Don't get me wrong. It wasn't a message from the universe. It was a message from me to me."

"God love you, Stevie. Let me think this one over." She stood up. "Good night, dear one. Thanks for being with the old lady. Breathing the same air. I did need you nearby tonight." She kissed his cheek and left him.

2

The first time he had the dream he woke with his pulse racing, utterly befuddled about where he was, in his own freshly plastered, still unfinished bedroom in a small house he was fixing up in Santa Fe, New Mexico. In the dream he'd stood in a grand hall among many people, hundreds, maybe, whose dress was strange, though he hardly noticed that. Like everyone else, his attention was on a queen-like figure in a long purple gown, a striking woman neither young nor old, seated on a dais at the front of the hall. Coiled beside her was an enormous serpent the size of a boa constrictor, but its scales were iridescent, blue and green, peacock colors; its wedge-shaped head altogether blue. From time to time it lifted that head, and the woman stroked it tenderly.

Someone was making an argument to this queenly figure, but whether it was in a language Stephen didn't know, or he was too far away to hear, he understood nothing. The argument ended. The hall was completely silent. The figure in purple was still. Then, on some signal he couldn't see but was sure the woman had made, the snake suddenly uncoiled itself, flew—or slithered—instantly across the floor and wrapped itself around the petitioner, brought him to the floor, crushed him slowly, methodically to death. The victim struggled, pushed in futility at the serpent's fluid body, seemed to scream. Yet all was silence. A paralyzing dread seized him, as if the serpent were compacting him instead. But he could see the victim's body, limp at last. Two attendants appeared and hurried away with it.

The serpent glided back to its mistress, who held and stroked it, leaned down to kiss its wedged head. As she bent, her long dark hair also caressed the beast.

But the snake was restless. Its deed had unsettled it, and instead of coiling beside her as before, it moved across her body, around her arms, even her neck. Now Stephen feared for her, that the snake was unsatisfied. She was serene, stroked the serpent, held its head, kissed its snub mouth, perhaps to calm it. Soon, she pushed aside her robe and offered it her breast. Stephen was horrified that the serpent would sink its fangs into that naked breast. But no, the snake seemed to suckle. Time passed, and he could see the woman's head drop back, her long black tresses moving over her shoulders, around the snake, almost snakes themselves. Her face began to go slack with desire. Now someone next to him murmured urgently: We must leave. We are not allowed to witness a sacred copulation.

He was suddenly in another, smaller room, up in a sort of gallery where he could look down upon the woman, now naked, trembling slightly, supine on a bed draped in white silk. The shimmering serpent drew near the bed, its enormous blue head lifted, swaying, its red forked tongue darting forth. She turned her head toward it, opened her arms. As it coiled around her trunk, she stroked it fiercely. Its head sought her mouth, which she opened welcomingly. When at last its tail found her vulva, she cried out in joy, writhed, held the serpent to her feverishly. At her climax, Stephen awoke.

He lay back on his soaked pillow, fearful, pulse racing, tried to calm himself. A stunning piece of theater: every detail remained vivid. But above all, he knew that from the depths of his being, he'd been sent a message, something meant to change him completely. He'd been allowed to witness the sacred copulation. In return for this cosmic privilege, he must—what?

Sometimes he willed the dream to his conscious imagination, and it came back in all its drama. But awake, having summoned it consciously, he could slow it down. He could study the languor of the woman's body, stroking the head of the coiled snake beside her as she listened to the petitioner. He could turn away from the dying victim and see that the queen was impassive, serene in her own judgment. Then the sudden grotesque death of the petitioner; the snake's restiveness afterwards, the rosy redness of the woman's areola, her own snakelike black hair, the shape of her graceful hands on the snake's shimmering scales. He could see her mouth open to the serpent's head, tongue touching tongue, her back arch in ecstasy, cushioned, embraced, penetrated by the flowing muscles, the iridescent colors. He could see the snake itself, first calm, then ferocious, until at last it was satisfied. Or she was. The whole dream aroused him deeply; it frightened him even more.

When he did not consciously will the dream, when it came again to him in deep sleep, he felt everything he'd first felt. The puzzlement. The dread. The deep fear. The sense of having been chosen for something that he must discover, and discover soon, if ever he was to know some peace himself, pursue a destiny concealed in the mists.

This dream seized, troubled, and preoccupied him. In a moment he regretted, he'd shared it with his sister, who hooted: "The serpent wants to fuck the queen? It all but has labels on it." Yet he knew that this facile interpretation was—maybe not wrong, but far from sufficient. It was certainly opposite from Hans Castorp's dream of sweet passivity. But he needed to know more to understand it fully. He was grateful that Judith hadn't laughed the night he stayed in the house with her, and told her he might like to be the family's caretaker. But he couldn't imagine sharing this strange recurring dream with her, not even when the time might come that he fully understood it.

The serpent? his tutor, his guide, had asked at the beginning. Ah well, such a rich symbol. Fundamental to nearly all mythologies. Life. Life above all. Healing. But death too. Polar opposites. Protection. Deceit. Consciousness. Rebirth. Regeneration. The re-creation of the self. Some shamans see—quite literally see—DNA as a serpent. The serpent is a long, long story. And then the queen, who both controls the serpent, a kind of goddess of wisdom, and who seeks union with it. The sacred copulation. Something you're permitted to witness.

The tutor was thoughtful.

It'll take some time to probe what that serpent meant in your particular dream, the queen, the sacred copulation. Dreams rise out of an individual consciousness, an individual set of symbols as much as from what we all share. Are you prepared to work and wait? Perhaps for a long time? Jung, for example, didn't really understand some of his own dreams for years. Can you make such a commitment?

Stephen nodded, worried that the tutor was going to dismiss him. But the man, lean and soft-voiced, an unlined face not because he'd known no sorrows but because he'd allowed himself no excess flesh, dressed always in neat faded jeans, a neat faded denim shirt, making Stephen wonder if he wore the same clothes every day, or whether he had a closetful of identical jeans and shirts, the man said: I agree that this is an important dream for you, an important message from your subconscious. Let's begin.

That summer, his house almost finished, Stephen had started to search the strange landscape of northern New Mexico for places that signified something to him. He found many that moved him, some that even spoke to him, some of them landscapes, some of them interiors, including a strange rose-colored cave in the far north that seemed almost an ancestral home.

But the place that spoke most intimately to him was called La Plaza Blanca,

The White Place. It was distant and austere. Exigent. But hiking through its hard landscape began to strip from his soul much that he saw needed to be stripped. When he left Judith the morning after he'd spent the night guarding her, keeping her company, sharing the horrors of what was to become known as 9/11, he drove north to The White Place for sorting things out.

3

Judith was at loose ends for the first few days after the attacks on the World Trade Center and the Pentagon. She tried to work, but concentration was impossible. The phone lines opened spasmodically; she could talk to her husband, hear his voice, hear what it felt like to be in Manhattan after this catastrophe—surreal, he said. Surreal in its normalcy where he was. Surreal because we know what's happened. But when the brief calls were over, when she conveyed to Stephen what she'd heard from New York, she couldn't work. On the third day, she succumbed to the great American delusion, that being on the open road is actually doing something, getting somewhere, and drove northeast on I-25, the route of the old Santa Fe Trail, through the Glorieta Pass, where an odd Civil War battle had once been fought, and lost, by the Confederacy. Over the pass, the slow descent into the flattening landscape would lead to Las Vegas, the meadows, of New Mexico, themselves foreground to the infinite horizon of the Great Plains. She was only half purposeful when she turned off the interstate to visit a structure she'd heard of, never seen, called the Dwan Light Sanctuary.

Six or seven miles north of the town of Las Vegas, she found it. She'd once read that it was the conception of artist Virginia Dwan, who collaborated with a light artist and an architect, a sanctuary for people of all beliefs. She'd always meant to visit.

The stone and stucco structure sat on a modest knoll, surrounded by tall pines, fragrant in the late summer warmth. In the nomenclature of her field, she'd have described the structure's shape as two conic sections, set one on the other. She wondered idly what architects like Torres would call it. It evoked a Navajo hogan, or a Pueblo ceremonial house, a kiva, miraculously lifted from underground. Yet unlike either of those, this structure was not meant to cover a mystic world in darkness, but instead to capture and play brilliantly with light.

Through double doors she discovered an austere white circular interior. The entrance was at the western point of the compass. At each of the other cardinal points—so fundamental to the worship ceremonies of the Pueblo Indians, who had first roamed these lands—were three apses, bays, each with candles set on simple wrought-iron stands. The north and south apses stretched from floor to ceiling, and their tall windows had six prisms embedded, three candles below each of the windows. The eastern apse that she faced as she came in was different. It suggested a kind of altar, a center of attention: no prisms in its window but a framed clear view onto the pines and the blue sky outside, at dawn perhaps, the sunrise. At this central apse, steps led from the granite floor to a kind of platform, with six candles, not three. In the sheltering ceiling of the entire chapel, skylights were also embedded with prisms, and complemented the three recessed windows in the walls.

The place was about light and numbers. How had she not known this? She sat down on the plaster bench that ran around the perimeter of the room, and began playing with the numbers. All combinations of twelve, she saw, a number profoundly rich in mathematical meaning, profoundly rich in world culture. Twelve was a composite number, the smallest number with exactly six divisors; it was a sublime number, with a perfect number of divisors, and the sum of its divisors was also a perfect number. Hadn't Ramanujan played with twelve? The hardware on the entry doors, perfect circles: twelve divided perfectly the 360 degrees of the circle, and the degrees of the angles of an equilateral triangle. Time itself was twelve's child: twelve divided the hour, the day, the solar year. The minute hand of a clock turns twelve times faster than the hour hand. Twelve-tone music was another of time's children; she thought she remembered that there were twelve major keys and twelve minor keys.

In Tibetan medicine there were twelve pulses; in Western medicine twelve cranial nerves. The twelve tribes of Israel, the twelve apostles, the twelve days of Christmas, the twelve signs of the zodiac. Where did nature leave off and human imagination begin?

The sanctuary was not silent. Each time she heard a creak, she expected someone else to join her, the author of those sounds that echoed softly through the drum-like space. Then she understood that almost imperceptibly, the prisms were moving, changing the play of light on the white walls as she watched from the bench. Their slow movement was the source of the sound, as comforting in its way as the whisper of a gentle wind.

These mobile prisms generated sudden bursts of spectrums, brilliant rainbows that splashed the white walls unexpectedly, ultraviolet shading through blues, greens, yellows, and orange to crimson red. If a certain combination of sunlight and prism came about, the spectrums might be cross-hatched with bright white lines. Sometimes the spectrums appeared in a perfect arc, rainbow-like, sometimes in a simple rectangle. Sometimes the white light appeared not only as cross-hatches but as arcs too, chastely independent of the spectrums. Hadn't Newton done something important with prisms? His statue at the entrance of Trinity College, Cambridge, had him holding a prism. It came back to her: Newton showed that white light could be transformed into the spectrum with a prism, and back again to white light with another prism.

She tried to reconstruct the beautiful mathematical calculations that had gone into achieving this tranquil yet deeply dramatic place. They would not only have taken into account the optics of the prisms, but also the path of the sun over the year. The brochure claimed starlight and moonlight had also been taken into account. Then chance, randomness, the passing of clouds over the sun, the swaying of the pine branches in the wind, decided whether a spectrum might suddenly appear on the wall.

When that was too hard to calculate in her head, she tried to imagine colors that lay beyond the edges of human perception: ultraviolet, infrared, invisible to human eyes. Three primary colors, three secondary colors, six tertiary colors: twelve again. Too bad so little of her college optics course had stuck; it seemed at the time like just another curriculum barrier to crawl over; a boring taxonomy to be memorized.

But things had changed. Optics had become sexy. Someone had recently mentioned that even the science of rainbows was poorly understood: most of the textbook explanations were incomplete or just wrong. The cognitive act that took place behind the human eye, an act that formed the continuous spectrum into bands of discrete colors—primary, secondary, tertiary—was, so far, even more mysterious.

She stopped. The scientific impulse had suddenly spent itself, seemed only the beginning of this experience. It could be a terrible habit of mind, always trying to figure things out, their reasoning, their logic, like searching on a hike for the botanical names of plants or the proper names of birds, as if this somehow captured an experience in a deeper way than just enjoying things as they came into view.

So she let herself glide into simple perception of the colors when they appeared, when they faded away. The vivid white light came and went; the virgin white wall reappeared, drab after the spectrums and the white light had dissolved. Sometimes the spectrums were elusive, shadowy, merely suggestive; sometimes their pure radiant colors were almost too much for the human eye to take in.

Shadowy or bright, they were above all evanescent—they appeared, shimmered, then dissolved at random. In exactly this lay their beauty.

Time slipped away. Perhaps she was in this magical place for one hour, two. She was undisturbed, tranquil, not only for the first time in days, but savoring a deep peace she hadn't felt for a very long time. She sent up prayers of profound gratitude (though to whom? to what? and had no answer, except to generous chance) that her husband was safe, his children too, in this terrible moment. She sent out sympathetic prayers of comfort to those who weren't so lucky, both the anguished living and the dead. She meditated in the moment. Felt herself cleansed, at peace, and drove serenely home.

4

When the elevator doors open and Nikki Molloy limps sore-footed into her childhood apartment, her father is on the southern terrace, staring grimly at the smoky turbulence rising from the devastation further downriver. The television in the study to the left plays to an empty room. She calls to him, but he's already heard the elevator open. He spins, races indoors, sweeps her into his arms and holds her close. As she remembers it later, she thinks they were both crying. They were crying in joy at being safely in each other's arms. They cried at the overwhelming thing that had happened that morning to the city they both loved. And she, at least, cried from fear and relief simultaneously.

She tries to explain where she's been, how far she's had to walk, but he doesn't care, only that she's safe beside him. He sits her down, strokes her face and hair, scrutinizes her as if he's seeing her for perhaps the first time in his life.

"I was so scared, papa," she says. "Thank God you're here." He's touched to think she still imagines he can protect her from anything. Well, anything like this. He holds her, murmurs reassurances. Finally she says she'd better shower. She's worn out, filthy, needs fresh clothes. Anything in the fridge?

When she comes down the stairs after her shower, her hair still moist, her skin lustrous, she sits down again beside him, nods toward the TV. "Anything new?" He shakes his head, nothing.

"Who did this?"

"Who indeed?" her father mutters.

"I need to tell you something." She's fidgeting beside him, and it comes out in a rush. "Papa, I was scared for myself, but also—scared for my baby."

He hits the remote and gives her his full attention.

She looks away from him. "I'm pregnant, papa. I'm pregnant."

He gasps, closes his eyes, wills himself to be gentle. That little-girl voice, telling him she's going to have a little one herself. "Oh, radish." Her childhood name.

"You aren't furious?"

"Why would I be furious?" he asks softly.

"Well, papa—you're—you like things done a certain way. A—a—bastard isn't exactly the way you like things done." Now she begins to weep. He pulls her to him yet again this strange afternoon, caresses her heaving shoulders, thinks bleakly and with shame of the portrait of him she's offering: martinet, despot, Victorian tyrant, so far from the human being he thinks he is. Or has finally allowed himself to become.

"Is there a dad?" he murmurs. "No, your old man knows the facts of life. I mean, will we have a wedding?"

She shakes her head. "I don't want that guy in my life."

"Oh, pumpkin. Oh, princess mine. Oh, dear radish." He's called her radish since she was a newborn, very red, and she'd adopted it as her own. He takes another deep breath, strokes her hair. "Even if he seems like a shit now, sometime in the future he'll want to see his own little one. He'll have that right. Probably legally. Maybe morally. If you have the baby, that guy is in your life for better or for worse." He's kissing her temple, and it comes to him how much being with Judith has relaxed him, put him in the habit of kissing, stroking.

She turns to look at him directly, eyes brimming with tears. "Can't you fix that?"

He's taken aback, shakes his head gently. "As a man who loves babies, especially his own, I wouldn't. Even if I could."

"Did you love us as babies, papa?"

He whispers. "You don't remember? How I came over almost every weekend from Germany just to be with you and Stevie? I'm on a plane in Frankfurt right after work, in New York Friday night, stay until Sunday night when I get back on the plane. Went from airport to office Monday mornings. I did that for years, honey, because I wanted to be with my kids. You were here with your grandma then, and a nanny. Mama was already too sick to take care of you."

She thinks about it. "I sort of knew all that. But not really. Most of what I remember is the boarding school in Germany. I don't remember much before then. It was hard, papa."

"I know, radish. I could see that. It just seemed like the best thing at the time. Mama was slipping faster and faster. Grandma was getting fragile. I needed you guys near me."

She's silent. The September night is falling, and the lights across the Hudson mock them with their normalcy. Both of them think how the lights might now go out forever. Surreal to be here, safe, in the quiet of their home, watching the agony only a few miles south, even if it's muted. The silence outside is unnatural. Nikki speaks. "Papa, do you think I should have this baby?"

"How can I possibly say?" He sighs tenderly. Does such a question even yield to logic? For what it's worth, he tries. "So—downside: your life is really just beginning, radish. A baby would be a tremendous change, would cut off forever some paths you might have taken as a single, childless woman. You say you don't want the dad in your life, but if you have the baby, you have the baby's dad too, sort of. And then, even with no serious financial worries, being a single mom isn't easy."

"You were a single parent."

"So I know whereof I speak." He keeps it very soft, very low, deeply afraid to sound as if he's scolding her. "Plus, a single dad with the kids is a hero. A single mom with the kids is a stupid slut who didn't know how to hold on to her man."

"I really meant—is this the beginning of war?" They gaze out the window onto the river flowing past Emerald City, a city deeply wounded. The stench from that wound has started to drift up the river on the wind, and he's cautioned her to stay inside; who knows what's in that plume? She rests beside him, his arm still around her.

"Ah, pumpkin, we don't know, do we? Judith did scenarios for some group at the Pentagon. She told me she's shocked but not surprised by this. Some of those scenarios, they have follow-ons, multiple attacks on the country. There could be more, yes."

Judith would come home from those weeklong workshops almost dazed. "I can't tell you…"

"No, of course you can't." He'd meant their classified nature, and maybe she'd meant that too.

"I've been doing this for years, Jack. It used to be almost—abstract. They do this. In retaliation, we do that. They respond that way, we counter with this. Now, it's all about real flesh and blood. Oh, Jack. The unintended consequences of love. I'm not stupid. I've often thought the big windows in my little *casita* rest on such optimistic assumptions. That life will always be secure enough for such fragile barriers to be enough—between inside and out." She looked at stout adobe walls around her. "At least whoever built this house knew enough to be scared of the Comanches." She'd put her head on his chest, deeply troubled, and he'd comforted her. "The advantage of love," she'd added softly. "Now at least I find consolation after thinking the unthinkable."

Unlike most Americans, he himself had never taken safety for granted. Was this because his parents had disappeared from his life so early—first his father, then, for all practical purposes, his mother? Or was it because he'd lived almost twenty years in West Germany during the Cold War, where the fragility of peace, the possibilities of war, were always present? Maybe it was because when he soared upward in the German business world, radicals were targeting businessmen viciously, and he had to take extraordinary precautions. So he too has been shocked by the attack on the World Trade Center and the Pentagon, but not surprised.

His daughter brings him back into the present. "No world to bring a baby into."

He laughs softly. "Radish, it never is. But people go on having them, and bringing them up and being glad they have them to love." The room is almost completely dark now except for the outside lights. A timed light goes on across the room, and he gets up to turn it off. The mayor, wearing a Yankees cap, is speaking silently on the TV screen in the study.

Her words follow him. "That's the upside, papa. Someone to love. You have Judith, now. I think you love her very much. She loves you."

He stops in the middle of the room, chooses blunt honesty. "She's the love of my life."

"And mama?"

He comes back to her, sits down beside her again, takes her hand, regards her tenderly in the semi-darkness. "Your mama. I loved your mama dearly. I can't say for sure she loved me the same." He shrugs ambiguously. "Anyway, we drifted apart. If we had lights—no, don't turn them on—you could see the wedding picture, see that I was happy that day." He knows now that he yearned to be old Stephen's son more than he yearned to be Lindy's husband, but he didn't know it at the time; has no reason to tell his daughter that.

"You were so young. Younger than me right now. Why do you still keep it out, papa? I mean, now that you're married to Judith?"

Younger as a bridegroom than his daughter is now? It disconcerts him. But she's right. "Judith thought it might upset you two to find that picture gone. It doesn't bother her. It's reality, she says."

That wasn't all she'd said. He'd also asked her if she wanted to redecorate the place, and she'd looked at him in bewilderment. "The cabbage roses on the couch getting your modernist soul down? Oh, sweetheart, I have no time for that kind of thing. That's for ladies who lunch. Plus, no sense of proprietorship about the place, nice as it is. It would be like re-doing a hotel room." Though he'd grasped what she meant, he'd still felt a little hurt. When would she decide this marriage was permanent? So the place stayed as it was, frozen in time from when some long-gone decorator had once arranged things.

"Would it have worked out? I mean, if she hadn't got sick?"

"With your mama?" He shrugs. "Maybe I loved a dream, and not a real woman. If so, for her, not so easy." Is that true? He'd often made excuses for his first wife; one more excuse hardly matters. At least let it comfort the daughter of a dead woman. "So tell me about your own dreams, my radish." For this much he knows: he and his daughter have never confided in each other before. Surrounded by devastation, surely more to come, this gross rupture in ordinary life has allowed something new. In the middle of such despair, such broad sadness, it gratifies him a little. If the next one comes and doesn't spare them, let them go having spoken openly with each other.

"My dreams?" his daughter says vaguely. "I want to be happy, papa. I don't think I've ever been happy. I know people say it's your own fault, happiness comes from inside, but I can't seem to make that happen inside. How do you get so happy, like you and Judith?"

He's pained by the simplicity of the dream, so modest, yet so commonplace as to be meaningless. How to answer? My answer is not yours.

He only says, "Lucky. Blest. What the Christians call grace. I didn't earn it or deserve it. It just came. I'm deeply grateful. Infinitely. She's—what I always hoped I might have in a partner." Doesn't think he should say deserved. "Well. The story's a little more complicated than that. You want to hear?" She nods. "Judith resisted your papa's charms for quite a while. It was hard for me. Very hard. To tell you the truth, I thought it would break my heart. Destroy me completely. We worked together. I saw her once a week. I was like a schoolboy those days—all aflutter and speechless. I admired her so much—a fine mind, a tiger, with a sweet and open heart, a wonderfully playful woman, deadly serious— so many contradictions. But no time for Jack Molloy, thank you very much. She was even involved with someone else. Well, me with someone else too, as you probably know. But I never stopped hoping, even at the worst of times. Then by chance I found her in a very weak moment. Exhausted. Drained. I more or less persuaded her I could…heal her. If she'd give me the chance. She was so out of it, so beaten down, she'd have said yes to anything. Even me. The whole thing was

193

without conditions—she didn't have to love me, she could drop me cold after I saw her through the worst of it. I was willing to take that risk. Not just for Judith. Not just for me. I thought the world needed Judith in her fullness. I thought I was the one who could bring her back. It was true. I could. I did. She had the kindness, the generosity of heart, to love me in return."

"A love story. A real love story. Papa, I wouldn't have guessed." She snuggles down closer to him.

After a longer silence he says softly, "That picture you gave me of myself earlier this afternoon. That stern, that moralistic Victorian father, ready to banish his daughter and her baby into the blizzard—" He stops, takes a breath. "Oh, dear radish, I am so profoundly sorry that you had—reasons to believe that. Good reasons. I know you did. Pumpkin, princess mine, dearest, dearest radish—" he pushes her gently away so that she can turn and look at him face to face, "I'm apologizing. I'm asking your forgiveness. I am not that guy. Not anymore, okay? I like to think I never was, but God knows the best part of me went missing for a long time."

"So Judith restored something to you too."

He nods. "Somebody else gave me back my life. What Judith has given me is a life worth living. One difference. I think eventually Judith would've found her way back. Your papa, on the other hand, was a drowning man, going down for the third time. So now I have to justify that—that rescue." He looks out the window. No traffic on the West Side Highway. Beyond it, the river, running swiftly as it always does, upstream now, the river that runs both ways, as the original Indians had called it. "Justify it if I can."

After a while, he says, "I was going to order Chinese in, but I doubt the extreme cyclists made it in to work tonight. What if your old man scrambles us some eggs?"

By now they can hear fighter planes above, an alien sound in Manhattan. "We're probably the best-protected city in the country right now," he says. At bedtime, she asks if, instead of going upstairs to his own rooms, he'd mind sleeping in the bed across from hers in her room. He's touched. He understands that she doesn't really expect her father can protect her from the next attack—the attack that must come. She only wants what all humans want, the warm animal presence of someone dear sleeping nearby. He settles down in a twin bed in a bedroom that strikes him as incongruously girlish for a woman in her twenties, all ribbons and posies, posters of rock and TV stars he can't even name except for one: a poignant picture of young Matthew Broderick as Ferris Bueller. It's a bedroom unchanged for years, since the time she was having sleepovers with her girlfriends, before she was suddenly airlifted to Germany. Her grandmother, his mother-in-law, would have overseen this just as she herself was getting ill. Maybe that's why the room seems so oddly out of joint. It's really her grandmother's sense of what's fitting for a prepubescent girl, not Nikki's own. Nikki's loft downtown doesn't look anything like this. He thinks again of Judith's quick dismissal, plain indifference, about changing things in the apartment and is saddened. Should he sell the place? Could he even sell it after today?

No, as much as he's at home in Santa Fe, he's at home here too. The river soothes him as rivers always have. After a few months in Santa Fe, this cityscape has an energizing freshness for him. Much of his history, tragic and glad, has soaked into these walls.

It's a simple Art Deco building that, even though built in the heart of the Depression, was built solidly and to last. He's got the top three floors, and while the place has many sad memories, it also has good ones. For weeks once, he'd regularly heard the sound of his downstairs neighbor's piano. Even better, he heard the sound of amateur voices singing along—old Broadway tunes, American standards. A tinkling piano in the next apartment... The phrase came to him, he wondered from where, then saw his aunt Char ironing in the dining room in the old house, the slightly dangerous, liminal smell of a flatiron on moist cotton, Frank Sinatra, Perry Como, Judy Garland on the phonograph. She sang along as she worked. He sometimes sang along too as he was doing his homework. That's how he'd memorized the lyrics of an earlier generation's music, for he loved music, any kind, and regretted that he'd never had music lessons as a kid. What he knew he'd learned later, on his own. But now he thought that Char too must have been imagining what these Tin Pan Alley songs conjured up, the impossibly glamorous life, silk top hats, slinky gowns, champagne for breakfast, love and heartbreak in old Manhattan. Maybe she actually yearned for it all, or something like it, as she ironed work shirts in a small mill town in the Monongahela Valley. He'd never thought of his aunt wanting anything more than she already had.

So he'd been envious of the piano in the downstairs apartment, wished he knew who they were, wished that he too were singing merrily with them. One night he'd worked up his courage, gone downstairs and knocked on the door. His neighbor had recognized him, rushed to apologize; everyone knew poor Mrs. Molloy was very ill. "Oh no, that's not it," he said softly. Poor Mrs. Molloy was, with drugs both self-administered and not, conked out well beyond the reach of some amateur piano playing and singing. "You sound like you're having so much fun. I wondered if anyone could join?" They'd invited him in gladly, and after that, if he was in town, he never missed a session.

But oh how those old songs could wind you up. He'd done a near-solo of "Penthouse Serenade" with them one night, a song he loved, and was singing with such feeling that the others fell silent. In mid-song it hit him that he had a grand place, a three-story penthouse, in view of the Hudson just over the drive, but no one to share the sweetness of it all. He'd stopped at the last verse, pretending he'd forgotten the words, not that he was overcome with sadness, might weep any moment. This kind of thing hit him every now and then. He could only wait for it to pass.

They were a good group, mostly people in journalism, publishing, or advertising. Their pianist had written a well-known book about the great American songs, and they all appreciated—they loved—the turns of phrases, both lyrical and musical, the sly rhymes in those old lyrics of the twenties, the thirties, the forties, some of them written just down the drive by the brothers Gershwin, or up the drive by Ellington, a crosstown bus ride away by Porter, Rodgers and Hart, later with Hammerstein, Lerner and Loewe.

After they'd finished up a song, they repeated the best of those phrases with admiration. Their pianist would replay some elegant chords he wanted them to hear anew, or listen to this, this guy knew his Bach. He wrote that one for Judy Garland, but when the widow published his song book, she deliberately omitted it. They had their favorites that they always sang, and tried a few new ones each time too. Between songs they argued about which shows the songs had come from; supplied names of composer or lyricist to one another. He'd go upstairs and fall asleep with a dopey smile, so happy did it all make him.

They would always inquire courteously about Mrs. Molloy. He'd say she was doing as well as could be expected; or eventually that she'd been moved to long-term care in Connecticut, which was a polite way of saying rehab; until one night he could tell them that she'd passed away while he was in Turkey on business. To their murmured condolences, he replied that it was a release. For whom he didn't say. Whatever grief he felt was for a dream long gone, not for the shell of a woman who'd expired for no particular reason one night, instead of some other night, five years in the past, five years in the future.

He made no friends among them and never saw them except for singing together. He later asked himself if the habit of solitude had become so fixed with him that he'd forgotten how to make friends, how to suggest drinks some evening when they weren't singing, a lunch maybe. Eventually his neighbor had moved to the country and the group had broken up. Solitude had become acute loneliness; the sadness came more and more often. Molloy deconstructed his life with the help of good ears on Central Park West, sold his firm for serious money, and decided to start again in Santa Fe, on not much more than the strength of a picture he'd seen and clipped from a trade magazine. But those nights of singing together were cherished memories for him.

His daughter whispers from the bed opposite. "Papa—uhm, I don't know if you—well, would you like a toke?"

It's the first time he's laughed all day. "Yeah, radish, I could go for that. You keep a stash here?"

"For emergencies. Most of my stuff is down in my loft."

"Afraid you can kiss that off." He inhales deeply, finally lets the smoke out. "Man, this does bring back the old days."

"You did this in the old days? You?"

"Oh, my radish. You and I have a lot to catch up on. But honey, should you be smoking in your condition?" She giggles, and he does too.

As they begin to drift off, she whispers, "Papa, do you remember how you used to sing to us when we were going to sleep? Could you do that?" Through his tears, he does.

5

She wakes first, sees him sleeping in the opposite bed, lying on his back immovably, like a knight on a medieval tomb. We are both alive, she thinks. They did not come again. At least they did not come here. Not yet. She gets up silently, so as not to disturb him, goes downstairs to the west windows to gaze out. Another beautiful day, New Jersey bathed in late summer morning sunlight. She does not open the French doors to the terrace, which overlooks the Hudson, remembering what her father said, what might be in the air. It hardly seems it could have happened. Everything seems normal. People are walking their dogs beneath the trees in Riverside Park, stopping to talk to each other. New Jersey looks the same, the new high-rises unchanged. We are their view, she thinks. Our catastrophe is their view. The river between runs imperturbably.

It did happen. It really did happen. If she painted that scene in the park, how could she show that things only look normal, but horror lies underneath? That human beings forever insist on pasting the ordinary on top of the terrifying? That what matters is underneath? Behind? In college, she's sure, she'd had to write essays about the difference between appearances and reality, but then it had been completely abstract. Now the difference strikes her like a spiritual revelation, a way of seeing the world she's never considered before. Her father, what he'd told her about himself last night: a different, a contrary reality exists behind the image of him she's always held. Her mother—that reality's too much. She'd been a child; how was she supposed to deal with all that? Still, she's shaken by this new revelation, this *insight*—she tries the word on her tongue—and wonders if it's a sign of what she must now pay attention to, that her task as an artist is to dig beneath, and somehow represent the reality, not the appearances.

She was almost through college when she discovered that her father owned a portfolio of Otto Dix etchings, *Der Krieg*, "The War," which he'd never shown her until she said she was studying Dix in an art class. "One of the few dead artists I've ever bought, but this series spoke to me," he said. "And they were very cheap. Nobody was interested then."

"You never showed these to us."

"They're not for children." He was right. At the time she'd thought they were unbearably ugly, as if Dix were deliberately making repulsive what didn't have to be so revolting, but now she reconsidered. Maybe Dix was showing the reality under appearances.

She hears noises from above: he's wakened, and goes first up to his own rooms to shower and dress, then comes back down to join her in the living room. They stand together, his arm around her shoulder, observing the peculiar normalcy of life outside, traffic on the drive, the walkers and joggers. "I'll run up to H & H and get some bagels for breakfast," he says in German. "Stay here, please. We don't know what it's like out there." He walks into the study, turns on the TV. Cameras are panning over the destruction, the smoke. He mutes it— he doesn't want to hear commentary, he tells her. The images are more than enough. Images. He's always been the image of what he called last night the Victorian father, stern, unyielding. Yet now she knows there's something else underneath, behind. She's moved by the wonder of it.

"A bialy for me, papa. Two."

When he returns from Broadway, she looks at him quizzically.

"Surreal," he says to her unasked question, still speaking German. "It's as if nothing happened. Except everyone is very quiet. Very polite. Kind to each other. Taxis are running. Some of them have American flags on their antennas. The stores have maybe half their staff. No fresh milk. We're in a state of collective disbelief. Mrs. Siegel stopped me in the lobby, and I quote, *Isn't it awful who would've done such a thing I hear you're remarried Mr. Molloy mazel tov.*" This in English.

They take their breakfast into the study to watch some more.

"I cannot," she says sadly. He nods, and turns off the TV. "Our president wants us to go out and shop."

Her father's face tells her what he thinks of that. Ground Zero. His voice rises as he switches to English: "The fucking vulgarity of it. The coarseness. The sheer vacuity. Are these people begging for the second coming of the Bolshevik Revolution?" They eat their breakfast in silence.

After a while, she gestures at the bare walls. "I miss the paintings, papa. I know why you took them to Santa Fe, and I'm sure they look great there. But I miss them." He smiles slightly in acknowledgment. "When did you first get interested in art?"

"Way back. I gave myself a trip to Europe as a college graduation present. I had a little money left over from working in college, so that's how I used it.

Nothing grand. But Jesus, I went ape-shit. I'd never seen art. Not really. There were decent museums in Pittsburgh, but going to the museum wasn't something on my radar in those days. So that summer, I saw art for the first time in my life. I was on a high the entire time from great paintings. I couldn't get enough. That was the beginning. Later, I realized you could actually buy art. The dealers told me I had an eye. Well, the dealers tell that to every customer who walks through the door. But it turns out I really do."

"When did you go to Germany?"

"First time? That summer too. But for good? I'd been working as a trader here in Manhattan for a year or so, just a beginner. A slot in my firm opened up in Frankfurt. It should've gone to a more senior guy, but I claimed I could speak German. In a schoolroom way, I could—enough to fool my American bosses—so I went to Frankfurt. There were Jewish guys in the firm who could speak German better, but Germany was still touchy for them."

"Did you like it there?"

"Loved it there. It was—" he searches for a word, and finally says, "transforming. Deeply, deeply transforming. Judith asked me the same question while we were traveling, and I can't believe it, I'd never really thought about it. Fact is, in Germany I became a completely different man. No more little hick from a mill town in western Pennsylvania. No more the potty-mouth trader—oh those boys on the trading floor from Bensonhurst and Bay Ridge knew how to swear, combinations of human parts in human orifices even I hadn't thought of, and I'd thought of plenty. Then I got to Germany, and I couldn't swear in German without laughing—for one thing, the words just don't have the taboo charge. Fuck you in the knee. How can you say that without laughing? So I cleaned up my act and became what passed for a gentleman. But I was still considered, uhm, sharp—Mackie Messer, Mac the Knife, they called me." He's smiling in recollection.

"But mama not?"

"Mama not. She never acclimated. She came back to the U.S. to have Stevie, and wouldn't come back to Germany. I was working balls against the wall those days; I didn't get how lonely it was for her. A foreign country where she didn't speak the language, no one nearby to—Jesus, you're the happiest you've ever been in your life, and you can't see it, you don't know, why somebody else isn't happy. You see how hard it is to be happy, radish? It seems like such a simple thing. It's not.

"Then your mama's own father, the grandfather Stevie is named for, he'd got out of Eastern Europe by the skin of his teeth just as the Nazis were closing in. I'm sure that didn't help in terms of how she felt about being in Germany. She had a very hard time with the post-partum blues after Stevie was born. I could hardly believe the change in her. She was a beautiful, beautiful woman, and she looked absolutely wasted after a few months. That was the beginning of the end for her."

"But I was born later on."

He's silent.

"Was I the last straw for her, papa?"

"No, princess, no. She'd already gone over. None of us knew it."

"But wait—you were commuting back and forth to New York from Frankfurt every weekend? What kind of social life did you have?"

He raises his eyebrows, sighs. "I had a close friend. You've probably heard me mention him—Jürgen—and we played a lot of football—soccer. After work. We were co-captains of an amateur team. We won our league championship. That was my social life. Jürgen was murdered by some idiot teenager who thought she was striking a blow for the working classes."

"Oh, papa. I didn't know."

"It was all the rage in Germany just then, kill a capitalist. You had to be very, very careful. Jürgen let her into the house because she was a friend of the family. He never dreamed..." He falls silent.

"No women?" she ventures slyly.

He shakes his head. "I lived like a monk for, well, nearly two decades. Sweet girl, you're a grownup, going to have a baby of your own, so I'll tell you that it wasn't me keeping to the straight and narrow out of moral conviction. It was—well, I just lost interest."

"Oh, papa."

"You close down a major part of human life like that, and a lot of other things close down too. You don't even recognize it. Madame Genius says it has to do with the oxytocin hormone ceasing to—"

"Madame Genius?"

"Judith. No oxytocin. That accounts for the Victorian papa you expected when you told me you're going to have a baby. Again, I am so very sorry." She takes his proffered hand affectionately for a moment, then moves away from him to the window. "Papa, what should I do? Should I have it? I'm only two months along. It's still possible—not to have it."

He shakes his head and smiles. "No advice from me, my radish. How could I? But talk it out. Tell me how you feel." He knows Nikki's situation and the catastrophe outside are incommensurate, but this one at least they can pretend to deal with.

"Sometimes I think I must have this baby. It's wrong to destroy life."

"It's not quite a life yet, no matter what the dogma says. It's potentially a life. But your life—that's a real life. It has claims too."

"Sometimes I think I need something, someone, to love. Something all mine." The urgency in her voice surprises even her. "Do I sound hysterical, papa? I don't think I am. Exactly."

He comes up beside her, murmurs. "It wouldn't be all yours. All your responsibility for a while, but not yours exclusively. It would love others. Human beings form many attachments. It could turn around and blame you for everything bad that's ever happened in its life. You'd understand the mistakes you've made. That is, if you were lucky. And scrupulously honest with yourself. But you couldn't count on your child understanding."

"I don't know," she says, burdened. "I just don't know."

And so they speak into the second night. They see a candlelight vigil forming spontaneously in the park below, and go down to join. She weeps uncontrollably, and her father holds her close. But when they get back to the apartment, she feels confident enough to let him go upstairs and sleep in his own room.

On the third day after, the city is coming alive defiantly. Shops are being restocked. Miraculously, firemen are pulled alive out of an SUV that was buried under rubble, and it gives an enormous lift to the collective New York psyche. The flags are now everywhere. They walk down to the theater district, get tickets, and see a play. The theater is only half full, but the actors are brilliant in defiance. In another two days they're permitted to fly, and he insists she come back to Santa Fe with him. Her Tribeca loft is inaccessible; everything south of Fourteenth Street is closed off. She should come home. Santa Fe is not home, she wants to say. In fact, it's a strange landscape, peopled with strangers. But he's right about the loft, so she agrees.

"I'm sorry to go," she says to him as the suitcases gather in the front hall. She takes his hand, which has become newly familiar. "These have been such good days with you, papa. I feel as if I never knew you until now. It's so nice to hear you laugh." She stops. She senses he's answered all her questions honestly if not always fully. It's all right. He knows what she doesn't really want to hear, at least not yet. She's told herself that when she wants to know everything, then and only then can she be a real artist. "So wrong, when so much has been lost, so much destroyed. Maybe the city itself forever. How can we recover from this? How do I dare to be happy? Yet for me it's been—a happy time."

He stops counting bags and hugs her. "Magic. Let's hold on to it, my radish, princess mine."

As the plane comes to a halt on the Santa Fe tarmac, and the steps are lowered, he sprints down them so fast that Nikki thinks he's fallen. As she gets to the open door, she realizes he's racing to his wife, who has an ecstatically happy dog on a leash. He seizes Judith, kisses her hungrily.

Nikki stands at the door, stunned. More knowledge is newly hers. First, that through her father's life runs a current of rapture she's never suspected, private but crucial. It will always prevent her from knowing him as well as she imagined in these last days. She also knows that such rapture is absent from her own life. Finally, she senses that these last days of sweet comradeship have been an event come once in a lifetime, and will never come again. The desolation of that truth shrivels her heart.

6

Judith had loved Molloy's Santa Fe house from the moment she stepped into it as a guest at his first dinner party in Santa Fe. It was a while longer before she understood—admitted to herself—that she loved the man who created it. The house had once been a rancho, on the outskirts of the village called Santa Fe, though by now it was well inside Santa Fe's historical district. It had been fortified in early days with high surrounding walls to meet the threat of hostile Indian raids, and the original property line had run down to the Santa Fe River. But these days a public road cut them off from the river, and what were formerly ranch outbuildings had become their separate home offices, a library, an entertainment room, a home gym, and guest quarters. The entire compound was still enclosed by much of the original adobe wall, which meant that each spring and fall, a crew must come around and hand-plaster the damage from the summer rains, the winter snows, else the walls would melt away. Molloy didn't mind that expense at all: he'd wander out to watch the workmen at this ancient process, and thought he was doing the world a favor by supporting them before the skill died out completely.

Some earlier owner had done the major part of the remodeling and refurbishing, but had been intelligent enough to allow the bones of the buildings to remain, chaste and simple. Inside the structures, the interior walls were hand-plastered and whitewashed, and the great pine beams beneath the roof, the *vigas*, were topped with cedar twigs in an elaborate herringbone style. Thus to enter the house after it had been closed for a week, sometimes even for a day, was to be greeted by the scent of fragrant woods that hung in the air like a benevolent incense.

Houses like this originally had small windows, to keep out the winter cold and protect against the summer heat, but this house had gradually been opened up, with French doors and larger modern insulated windows. Its ceilings had been raised (and its traditional dirt insulation in the roof removed and replaced with modern materials). Even in the hottest month of the summer, June before the monsoons came, no air conditioning was ever needed. This wasn't just a matter of new window technology: the house sat under tall cottonwoods that drank thirstily from the nearby river, and shaded the house all summer. The original dirt and oxblood floors had given way to *saltillo* tiles, which covered a new radiant heating system, but the rounded corner fireplaces that originally heated the rooms remained, and were often used in the winter for cheer, if not for warmth. Thus the house remembered its origins while it sheltered its present inhabitants generously.

To these austere walls Molloy had added paintings from his collection of contemporary, mostly European art. He had much more art in storage, and his curator would arrive each month to change the paintings, so no one ever took a piece of art for granted. Scattered about the floors were Navajo and early Rio Grande rugs of a quality that most people would these days hang on walls, but which Molloy liked underfoot. In the upstairs rooms some Turkish rugs could be found, equally precious and rare, collected when Molloy did business in Turkey, but he felt the same way about them: they were on the floor. He'd added simple furniture, leather-upholstered sofas and chairs, the aim comfort more than elegance, and old farm tables from Mexico, deeply polished.

As his new wife, Judith had surprised herself by wanting no major changes. She was as contentedly at home in the house as she was with the man. She'd brought a few pieces she loved from her own house, and these lived harmoniously side by side with Molloy's art.

Molloy had long ago claimed the former rancho's stable as his office; her own was the former sheep shed. Of course these structures had been significantly remodeled and rewired. As they remarked to each other, everything important came by email or messaging, seldom by landline, and hardly ever by snailmail.

So one Saturday afternoon toward the end of September when the phone console lights up, Judith can see it's Molloy's line being called, and pays no further attention. After a while her husband comes over from his office and knocks at her door. She pulls the earbuds from her new iPod out of her ears, a present from him, complete with a playlist. "I love this gadget, Jack. When will it be released? The kids would love one."

He smiles briefly in acknowledgment, is again solemn. "I just got a phone call. My love, Pete's gone."

She gasps. That gallant thirteen-year-old who's suffered so long and so bravely from leukemia. "Nola called you?" Nola, the art dealer, who has been a good friend to each of them.

He nods. "She's at the hospital. She wants me to meet her at home."

"Well, of course. Let's go."

His solemnity turns to distinct discomfort. "She asked that it just be me. She said as a father myself—"

For a moment Judith is puzzled: grief is grief, and she's suffered plenty of her own. Then she begins to smile. "Jack, don't tell me Nola's one of the fallen?"

He doesn't answer, simply drops his eyes.

She leans back in her chair with a great grin on her face. "Every time I walk into a room full of Santa Fe women, I play this game in my head: which one of these women did my husband, in his monumental, his legendary, his priapic bachelorhood *not* bonk? It never occurred to me to consider married ones too."

"It was—different with Nola."

"No doubt," she hoots. She sees the pain on his face, gets up from her desk, puts her hands on his shoulders. "Go comfort her. It's an awful thing. Call me when you can. If I'm not home, it's because I've gone over to tell Alijo." The dead boy's best friend, and also Judith's protégé.

"You know—" He pulls her to him, buries his face beside her neck. "No one but you. Ever. This life. Former lives. Future lives."

"I know. Of course I know. Go do your good deed, my love. Just be sure there's enough left over for me. Because I plan to claim it as soon as you get home."

At that he has to laugh himself.

He'd met Nola the same night he met Judith, at the first dinner party he'd been invited to in Santa Fe. He'd also met her husband then, who struck him as off, wrong, somehow. He'd thought Ernie was a bit of a crackpot, an opinion that Judith has subsequently confirmed. Nola, on the other hand, has run one of Santa Fe's best art galleries—a notable thing in a city that, depending on how you calculate, is either the third or the fifth biggest art market in the country. When he learned that Nola's only child was suffering from leukemia, he'd wanted to help this brave lady somehow, but she'd shaken her head. No help possible. So they've stayed friends (though he evades Ernie as much as he can) and he and Nola confine themselves to talking about art. Except for one afternoon when, in a moment of great emotional weakness, he let himself make love to her. Or to be precise, she hungrily seduced him. He wasn't yet married—to his sorrow, he was hardly on speaking terms with Judith—but he didn't have a second thought about cuckolding that yob, Ernie. It was a sweet moment, nothing to make a federal case out of.

He lets himself through the gate, goes along the path. Nola's garden is gone to late September seed in what he thinks of as a magnificently decadent way. At this altitude, decadence happens early. The sumac, that hasn't come into leaf until late May, starts changing color in mid-August. The leaves of the horse chestnut trees in the pretty garden at El Zaguán on Canyon Road are turning brown before Labor Day. Autumn flowers at sea level—chrysanthemums, asters, other sorts of daisies—have by September here come and gone. A reminder, he often tells himself, that at seven thousand feet, Santa Fe is in the mountains, not just the desert.

Her front door is ajar, and he lets himself in, calls her name softly. She's seated alone in the shadowed living room, curiously erect, almost perched, on the edge of the couch, yet looking more gaunt and horror-stricken than he's ever seen her. To be that thin doesn't become her, and before his eyes she seems to shrink behind her enormous spectacles. She rises and lets him take her hand, then throws herself into his arms. But doesn't weep. "Thank God you're here. I'm tapped out, Molloy. Just tapped out."

"Of course you are. Of course." He knows. "Where's Ernie?"

"Who the fuck knows? Backpacking in the San Juans. Or so he claimed."

"Was this unexpected?"

"No. Not really. We could see he was losing. We were losing. It was just a question of when. Well, when was an hour ago."

And still her husband, Pete's father, had decided to go backpacking in the San Juans? His contempt for the jerk is boundless.

"Did Pete—suffer much at the end?"

"No. Drugged to the gills, thank God."

"Were you there?"

She looks up at him piteously. "Of course I was there. Where else would I be?" She'd closed her gallery months earlier, though he knows she still keeps up the lease, that she thinks of re-opening it one day after—after the death of her only child.

He sits her down and sits next to her, his arm around her thin shoulders, trying to imagine if it were one of his own. He'd be crazed with grief. "What can I do?"

"Nothing, of course," she whispers. "As usual, this is mine."

"Have you eaten anything?" She shakes her head. He goes into the kitchen to see what's possible. Packages of ramen soup, cans of tuna fish. Some cheese. He puts water on to boil.

He returns to her, speaks softly. "I'm making you some soup. You need something now. Want some tea too?"

She looks up at him in raw pain. "What I wanted was an end to all this. Now I have it."

"Nola, come on. No one's to blame. Everyone did their best—you, the docs, Pete above all." He doesn't mention her husband.

"Does Judith know you're here?"

"Of course. She sends her love."

"Does she know—does she know about the excellent adventure?"

"Not in so many words." And only a few minutes since.

"And still she let you come."

He thinks about how to answer that. "Judith knows she can be confident of my love."

"I wish you both well, sweetie, you know that. I'm just bone-deep envious is all."

"Maybe now that the pressure's off, Ernie will—will come around."

"I've started divorce proceedings, Molloy. I wish I'd done it years ago. Maybe then when you arrived in Santa Fe..."

He wants to shatter illusions as gently as possible. He sits beside her, takes her hand, searches her stricken face. "Dear Nola. I once told you I'd come to Santa Fe in pursuit of a woman. Remember that?"

"Of course. The afternoon of the excellent adventure. I wondered who she was."

"It was Judith."

She exhales. Almost snorts. "I didn't know you knew her before."

"I didn't. I'd seen her picture in a trade magazine. Sounds idiotic, I know. Molloy as fanboy. I wasn't sure I wanted her in particular. But I wanted someone like her. I wanted to be where women like that could be found. I met her right away, and there was never anyone else for me, not really."

Nola pulls her hand away, covers her face. Finally she looks up, to somewhere over his shoulder. "I should have known. Let me tell you this, Molloy.

That afternoon we spent together—the recollection of that sustained me through some very difficult times."

No answer to that. It saddens him to think that what's been a barely remembered afternoon's pleasant diversion for him has become so significant to her, might have become part of her fantasies. An afternoon when they were both so stressed, and he'd confided in her as he'd confided in no one up to then... which had led to love-making. The phone rings and he reaches over to answer it. "No, a friend of the family." He listens longer, takes down a number. "We'll get back to you."

She gazes at him expectantly.

"The hospital. They'd like to know what arrangements have been made."

"Arrangements?" She shrugs. "The Episcopal church, I guess. We're not exactly regular church-goers, but I know they'll do it right, no kitsch about angels being wafted to heaven, and suffer the little children. Though my little child suffered." She weeps a little, pulls off her very smudged glasses, wipes them uselessly, meditates on the practicalities. "Just the *Book of Common Prayer*."

"I'll make the calls. You finish the soup and go lie down."

But she doesn't lie down. She slumps in the corner of the couch, watches as he phones systematically—the church, the funeral home, the hospital, until he can tell her that all is arranged, the service to be in two days. "Unless you've got people coming from out of town. Then they said they could delay it a day or two."

"No," she says wearily. "No one from out of town. And maybe in two days his father will have come down from the San Juans."

"Isn't he carrying a phone?"

She shrugs.

"Are you living apart? Is there somewhere I can leave a message?"

"Call the church back and ask for three days. Ernie should be back by then. If not, not."

"Eat your soup. You need that right now."

She stirs it with her spoon. "You must have had a good dad. You're such a born father, Molloy. A born caregiver."

"I doubt my kids would agree."

"But I know what you did for Judith. That trip to Europe. She told me."

"Of course. I love her." He doesn't want to pursue that. "My daughter's with us now. She came back with me after the World Trade Center attack." No one has yet learned to call it simply 9/11. "My son's been living in town for a while, you know that. It makes the dinner table very lively." He stops, realizes how cruel that must sound to a woman whose only child has just died.

"I'll bet."

He stands up, annoyed at himself, sad for her. "I'm going now, Nola. Try and get some rest. Let the machine take your calls, okay? I'll come by later on to see how it's going."

She stands up with him. "Thanks, Molloy. You were very kind to do this. I wanted to see you without Judith just now. Bring her back when you come again. I mean, if she's willing to come."

"Of course she's willing. She went over to Alijo's house so she's the one to tell him."

"She's very good," Nola says politely. Loyal and generous to those she loves, Molloy thinks. Otherwise not to be crossed. Nola reaches over to kiss his cheek, changes her mind, grasps his head and kisses him on the lips, long and lingering. He doesn't push her away. She's the one who finally steps back. "Good bye, dear friend."

7

The funeral is just as Nola hoped, moving but without sentimentality. Her husband Ernie has come down from the mountains after all, and they sit alone in the front right pew of the small fieldstone Episcopal church, a neo-Gothic oddity sandwiched into Santa Fe's pueblo-revival buildings, and stare fixedly at the draped casket before them. They do not touch each other. Molloy is in a pew across the aisle and behind; watches Ernie, contemptuous of the history of his behavior, contemptuous of the man's so-called scientific research (an opinion he's borrowed from Judith, who can be trusted in such matters). When he'd first met Ernie, he'd thought the man had the face of a fanatic.

Beneath his feet, Molloy can feel the organ vibrate the wooden floor, and he looks away from Ernie to the stained glass windows, meager, amateurish things to a man who has spent much of his adult life in Germany. When those fail to distract him, he stares ahead, above the draped casket, to the altarpiece, wondering if a seven-part altarpiece is a septych. Heptaptych. He'll have to ask that word maven, his wife. Then it comes to him: a polyptych. You can stop being specific after three or four panels. He hears the church's bells above. Oddly, he can also hear bells from the cathedral half a mile away. He wonders what Catholic holy day is taking place today that the bells should be dueling; can't think of one; decides it's another funeral.

He's grateful for Judith's warm presence beside him, her hand. On her other side is Alijo, the dead boy's best friend, pushing out of boyhood into manhood. Alijo has Judith's other hand. Beside the boy, Molloy's children, Nikki and Stephen. Alijo's parents are just behind; Ron Gresham and his partner Gabe Sullivan; all of them Nola's friends, really, except for Maya Sinclair, who sweeps conspicuously up the red-carpeted center aisle of the church before the service begins and gives Ernie a fierce hug, a handclasp to Nola. It crosses Molloy's mind that Maya and Ernie might have something going. It'd be so like Ernie. So like Maya. He suppresses a smile; looks around to distract himself again. A varied collection of people from the arts are there—some of them artists Nola has represented, some her clients; a few people from the sciences. Including the archaeologist Benito Jiménez.

As the priest intones the old words of the ceremony, it's lost on no one that this funeral service in late September is not only for a boy who has finally succumbed to a fatal disease, but is also a service that might mark and give comfort for the terrible thing that has so recently happened across the continent. Nola has requested the King James Version of the scriptures, and so the words resonate with Judith's own childhood memories, familiar and comforting.

"For none of us liveth to himself," says the priest, "and no man dieth to himself." Molloy thinks that words like this are what he said to his daughter about the baby she expects. He looks at his wife, whose eyes embrace his. They have shared death. They share life. They will eventually share death again, they know.

"O God," the priest continues, "whose beloved Son did take little children into his arms and bless them: Give us grace, we beseech thee, to entrust this child Peter to thy never-failing care and love, and bring us all to thy heavenly kingdom; through the same thy Son Jesus Christ our Lord, who liveth and reigneth with thee and the Holy Spirit, one God, now and for ever."

Nola has asked Molloy to read from the lectern some verses from Lamentations, traditional in the Episcopal service for the dead, but he needs to keep prodigious control of himself to finish the old words. What he reads aloud is about the pain of individual loss, but he knows the context of those words assigned to him. He's looked at them ahead of time, has read what came before and after, only to realize that this book of the Bible is a lament for a destroyed city. It begins:

How lonely sits the city
that once was full of people!
How like a widow she has become,
she that was great among the nations!
She that was a princess among the provinces
has become a vassal.

Ron Gresham follows him, reads the Twenty-Third Psalm, but with self-control is less successful. Everyone has loved the irrepressible Pete, but the weight of the early September event amplifies grief. When the congregation joins in the Lord's Prayer, it's over. There will be no graveside service. Pete will be cremated.

Molloy has arranged that the funeral reception be at their house, walking distance from the church, and moves about the brick courtyard outside, inviting people, giving them directions.

Judith sees him inviting Benito. It must be faced sooner or later. She hasn't seen Benito since she'd gently, sadly turned down his marriage proposal—it seems so very long ago—at the Santuario. Her husband comes back to her, and they walk silently hand in hand, leading a small procession along Palace Avenue.

If most of the houses along this road are hidden by high adobe walls, Judith nevertheless knows the history that has gone on inside many of the houses they pass—the wealthy surgeon who arrived in Santa Fe and made such a social splash, until it was discovered that he was dealing in the illegal trade of ancient artifacts. The woman who was on one of Santa Fe's most prestigious arts boards until she had an indiscreet affair with a fellow-board member, was divorced on account of it by her husband, and could no longer afford her share of board-member contributions. The distinguished lawyer caught in an FBI sting for downloading child pornography. The rich and complicated web that underlies the peaceful appearance of these houses: the same stories could be told almost anywhere. But Santa Fe is so small, its population of wealthy Anglos so intimately known to each other, that the stories are mortar to the bricks.

At the house they stand as hosts beside the bereaved parents, and greet people warmly, solemnly. Molloy thinks he might add homicide to the list of his own many sins when he hears Ernie greet the guests jocularly, tell them how glad he is to see them—though not necessarily, Ernie hastens to say in his fatuous way, under these circumstances. How, Molloy will ask Judith later, and not for the first time, had a lovely woman like Nola ever found a life with such a jerk?

Benito stands at the doorway, removing his perfectly creased Montecristi hat. Judith sees at once that he's taken from an old work sombrero the beaded Apache hatband she once gave him, and put it on this splendid thing instead. He's faultlessly tailored: open blue shirt under a casual camel hair jacket, light wool trousers, tooled boots. Perhaps his expression is slightly more skeptical than it used to be.

He'd attract attention in any crowd with that arrogant conquistador carriage, those amused violet eyes not at all hidden behind his rimless glasses—these days, as his hair has silvered, the vividness of his eyes seems preternatural. With the very public history of him and Judith as a couple, he's a cynosure: people are compelled to watch.

He nods gravely to Ernie, embraces Nola, stops in front of Judith.

His arms folded over his chest, he seems to study her with scholarly, almost judicial detachment. His eyes linger on the uncommonly modest pearls at her throat—uncommon for her—and the well-tailored somber gray dress. Perhaps he's remembering that dress with more striking jewelry ("Women my age can't wear dinky jewelry"); perhaps he's remembering other times when she wore that dress. At last he unfolds his arms, cradles the hat under his left arm, takes her hand, and leans to whisper in her ear. "*Felicidades, querida.* All my best wishes to you both." His scent—a combination of who he is naturally, and a subtle lime aftershave—makes her gasp. He shakes Molloy's hand silently and moves away. Judith follows him with her eyes, and Molloy watches her watching. "It's never easy, is it?" she says to her husband softly. "No," he agrees, "it never is."

Molloy had once fought a battle with Benito over a dinner table, so polite, so oblique, that no one else at that table even perceived they were going *mano a mano*. Molloy lost, and they both understood that. It might only have been the circumstances then, for eventually Molloy won the war. But like most men who fight to the kill, the memory of the earlier loss remains. He hasn't forgiven Benito.

After the reception, when people have finally said their goodbyes, they sit alone with Nikki and Stephen, picking at the leftovers for supper, talking softly about the funeral. "All bells and smells," says Stephen. "You'd hardly know it was Protestant." "Who was the Hispanic guy?" Nikki asks. "The older guy in the cowboy hat, the boots? He was *so* fucking hot!" Judith studies a painting on the distant wall. Molloy says, "Judith's old boyfriend." Nikki hoots. "Whoa, Judith! *Yes!*" Judith can only smile. "A very distinguished archaeologist, sweetheart."

As they're getting ready for bed that night, Molloy says to Judith: "Any regrets?"

She laughs. "He's certainly just as snackable as ever, isn't he? Or as your daughter put it—well, never mind. You always hope your ex will get morbidly fat, bald as a bubble, and lose every tooth in his head from the sheer tragedy of it all, but—oh, Jack! I think you're serious."

"I could've sworn I heard his charger pawing the ground outside, both of them ready to spirit you away as soon as—he's so fucking hot! Well, shit." He's just taken off his shirt, and throws it angrily on the floor. "My children were born for the sole purpose of tormenting me." She wants to laugh and he sees it. "Fine, laugh. Why aren't you charming me with the etymology of buffoon?"

"I could. From the Latin *buffer*, bursts of air; then Italian, *buffo*, bursts of laughter, hence buffoon. Oh, Jack." She pulls him by the hand to their bed, gazes at him searchingly. "Oh, Jack. Benito knew before I did that I belonged to you. Really. The last summer we were together, he proposed to me—I mean formally, practically down on one knee. We were at the Santuario at Chimayó. I never told you this because—well, I just never did. When I said no, gently as I could, he said he'd just consulted some mystic at the Abiquiú morada, a student of his mother's, who told him I was lost to him already. Benito guessed why. Me, I couldn't. He already knew my heart was yours when I didn't. Not then. Not until much later. Your wife is supremely obtuse about certain personal issues, as you very well know."

He closes his eyes, exhales. "Sorry. Forgive me."

"Stop it, you luscious thing." As they're dozing off, she says, "Poor Nola. God but Ernie is an asshole, isn't he?"

He comes partially awake. "She's started divorce proceedings, I forgot to say. She told me when I went over to see her right after Pete died."

"Good luck to her. She's not a woman used to being alone."

"You were alone for years, my love." He yawns. "Well, more or less. Give or take a lover or two. Or ten." He kisses her goodnight again, and realizes he's kissed tears on her face, but tonight doesn't want to know why.

She wasn't sure herself. As he breathed deeply and steadily, a little snore now and then, she retired into the deepest corners of her soul to meditate on it. Yes, for that which was lost—her dear friend Sophie, dead now these three years; for the sweetness of romance with Benito, dead itself too. For the grief that would overwhelm her when the time came to face her husband's death—far better she should go first, but she wasn't precisely eager for that either.

Yet something more. Maybe worse. She might have talked about it with Sophie, dead and gone, but with no one else.

A few days earlier she'd been looking at some of her old papers, breakthrough work she'd done in her thirties, some of the work she was best known for. She'd been reviewing because she was due to receive a major prize for it from one of the professional societies. When they'd informed her, she'd said to Molloy: "Twenty years ago! Well, better late than never." But first to her puzzlement, and then to her total mortification, she could barely follow the proofs. She'd laughed with her husband that night. "God, I was so smart in my thirties! Not only could I barely follow that proof I did back in the day; I couldn't even reconstruct the reasoning that led me to it. I'm really losing it, Jack." He'd teased her about brain rot from too much sex. "It creeps up on you so slowly you don't even notice it. You have to trip back into the past to get it—like looking at an old photo or something. Old research papers. Who knew?"

But there was a profounder loss. She was grieving maybe not yet the death, but possibly the dying, of her creative self, the engine that had driven her forward and eventually to the top in a man's field. Driven her forward and eventually to the top—the only top she was interested in then—of the world. It might already be dead, and anything she felt might only be vestigial momentum. If this was so, she thought, if she was on her way to becoming mere intellectual den mother of her scientific group, she'd have to learn new skills, perfect old ones, forget others. If. Yes, she felt sorry for herself. Worse, she hadn't any idea what she would do instead. Do next. She longed to talk it over with Molloy, but he might be the last person she could tell. This power, as much as anything, maybe more than anything, was what had drawn him to her in the first place, and now held him.

He was excessively proud of her intellectual achievements. The previous June she'd received an honorary degree, and he'd actually pulled out his camera to capture her in her academic gown. He'd sat proudly through the ceremony, sorry, he'd told her, that she wouldn't be required to make a speech, must only bend to have the doctor's hood draped over her shoulders. He'd even beamed as people called him Mr. Greenwood. They still had disputes over whether she'd use her doctor title. "It's only a Ph.D. in mathematics, for God's sake. Anyway, I'd be embarrassed in front of my friends. It's just not done, Jack." "You earned it. It signals your accomplishments." "Doesn't matter. It's just not done in the United States. I know, I know; in Germany…"

For all his wealth, he'd have preferred that path for himself. Or so he seemed to think. She'd been amused when she first realized this, told him often that the certifications were only the beginning. The whole issue was fraught for him. Yes, he'd got a college degree, but from some rinky-dink church-related school in western Pennsylvania which, at some level, mortified him. His real education had come when he moved to work in Europe, and for the most part, he'd done it all himself. He had an agile mind, a ravenous curiosity, read everything and retained it, made unexpected connections, all the signs of a serious thinker. But Mackie Messer as dogged research scientist, as patient scholar? It was an endearing delusion he entertained about himself.

So she was the designated family intellectual, and she wondered—she worried—that losing that creativity would diminish her in his eyes. While he wasn't the kind of man who'd keep a poptart on the side—Nikki was refreshing her vocabulary very nicely, she thought tangentially—she didn't want his love, even his constancy, to have any part of pity, of duty.

Hadn't she gone through this with the whole physical thing? For all his sentimental talk about the inevitability, the fatedness, of their marriage, she believed that if she hadn't been so vulnerable, so indifferent to almost everything when he took her to Europe, she'd never have allowed this nearly perfect specimen of manhood to view unclothed the beginnings of her inevitable physical ruin. Unknowingly—she supposed—he'd pushed her past that foolish shame by finding the happiest, most loving delight in her flesh that she'd ever enjoyed: honoring it, praising it, lusting after it constantly. Nothing fed desire more than being desired by someone desirable. As a result, they'd still arrive late but flushed and loose for dinner parties, show times, restaurant reservations. Or excuse themselves early. Before Nikki had arrived, they were given to spontaneous bursts of affection in the afternoon, despite unforgiving daylight.

But Judith never forgot the five years' difference in their ages, already a pity; and knew men had a further advantage—they aged so well. So fucking hot, Nikki had ingenuously gushed about her stepmother's old sweetheart. If the girl had any idea what an accomplished lover Benito was, she'd have leaped on this hot handsome stranger, and her father's misery would be multiplied unto wretchedness. So Judith and her husband had, for now, solved the problem of physical decline.

But a decline in her intellect. It wasn't incipient Alzheimer's or anything like it (an optimistic assumption, Judith granted to herself) but it was the perceptible diminution of that tremendous power that had propelled her all her professional life. In this, her identity was deeply bound up. In this, so was her husband's esteem. She lay beside him and remembered arguing early in their marriage about the necessity for a cook: "You leave the soufflés to her; your job is to do great science." Great science. If this diagnosis, this sense of losing it, was right, there'd be no more grand and startling theorems proved, world-shaking algorithms devised. She'd be lucky to coach—as she'd already told herself—for a few more years. But damn it all, at least she'd coach a winning team.

8

Two weeks after Pete Holliman's funeral, Molloy scans his daily schedule, surprised to see an annotation after the name of an appointment. Jerry McCarthy, private family matter. Wally (for Guadalupe) would already have vetted this man, screened out the importunate with heartbreaking family crises, or the occasional lunatics who found the front door—the foundation is not for that—so it puzzles him. He forgets all about it until Wally shows Jerry McCarthy in.

Then he knows immediately.

Before him stands an older version of himself, white-haired, flesh gone slightly slack (Molloy is still a much-teased fanatic about keeping fit), decently but not expensively dressed. Black Irish like you, Jackie, his aunt had once said. From the inside out, he feels himself begin to shatter. He's grateful to be seated, and summons a self-control he hasn't needed to practice for years, not since he was managing the fortunes of the German dukes and princelings in his days in Frankfurt.

"My name is—"

Molloy taps his schedule. "Jerry McCarthy."

"Yes. Maybe I don't need to tell you—"

He appraises the man in a long silence. "No, I don't think you do. But tell me anyway."

"I'm your father."

Molloy says nothing. Jerry McCarthy is also composed, modest yet not self-effacing, sensitive to the gravity of the situation. Every nerve in Molloy's body is on high alert. Waiting. Waiting for what? His pulse pounds in his temples. He wonders if he might pass out. Wotan sits up in his corner, preternaturally alert.

"Char always said I'd be proud to know you." A small smile; nothing hail-fellow-well-met.

"Char said?" The aunt who'd raised him, who, these days, lives in comfortable dotage in Florida.

"We didn't always stay in touch. But she knew how to find me. I was never so far away."

Molloy hears these words, unsure what to make of them. "Say more."

The older man's composure might be slipping. "Oh, Jackie. Where to begin?"

Molloy remains impassive, gives him no help.

Uninvited, Jerry McCarthy searches shakily for his seat like an old man. Does not settle back. Molloy feels his heart rate climb even higher. He will master it. Master himself.

Jerry McCarthy looks around the office, as if hoping words will emerge from the walls to help him speak. Looks at the dog and clicks his tongue. Comes back to Molloy. "It's been a long time."

"A lifetime."

"Your mother and I—" A tenderness about that phrase goes straight to Molloy's gut. He's never heard that phrase spoken by anyone. He waits for Jerry McCarthy to continue. "Your mother and I had a shotgun marriage, did you know that?" No, of course he hasn't known that. The news rakes him painfully. For his past. For his future. He has a pregnant daughter at home without a husband in sight.

Jerry McCarthy is going on. "I loved your mother, I really did, the way we love a woman in our youth, our young manhood, but—you grew up in the Mon Valley, Jack; you know how suffocating it was. You got yourself out." He pauses. "Even worse then." Don't compare us, Molloy thinks, feeling the first signs that his shock, the turbulence this man has set off inside him, is coalescing into a mighty rage. Don't you dare compare us. But he's well practiced in keeping his face unreadable. "I tried to get her to come with me, even to Pittsburgh, but she wouldn't do it, just wouldn't. So I upped and left. Simple as that."

"Simple as that. You knew you left a son?"

"Not a son, then, Jackie, just a—"

Molloy cuts him off with a gesture. "And then?"

"Pitt had offered me a scholarship. It turned out that I was pretty good at some things. I went on to do graduate work, got a Ph.D. Ended up teaching at a small college in Lancaster. A professor. I never had any money to send—I had family of my own by then, and—"

"Jesus. Why are you here?" After all these years, he doesn't add. The dog hears the rage in his voice and stands up, tail down, ears back.

"I'm hoping for your mercy, Jackie." Another long silence. "I've had a modestly successful life, Jackie, with a good wife, and kids—you have a half-brother and two sisters, Jackie. Nice people, good people, honorable people. You'd be proud to know them. I'm given to understand they'd be proud to know you."

"Tell my assistant where you're staying, and how long you'll be there."

"Jackie—"

In an even, perfectly controlled voice, Molloy says, "Please get your ass out of here, Jerry McCarthy, before I kill you."

Judith gets a message: Cm home asap. As it happens, she's been working at home, not at the Institute, and waits for him to arrive from his office on foot, a journey of fifteen minutes. Such messages will come from time to time, usually a coded erotic summons, and she's ever pleased to oblige. With Nikki around, afternoon delights are limited, but Nikki and her brother have gone down to Walter De Maria's Lightning Field in southern New Mexico for a few days. When she hears the front gate open, she leaves her study to greet him, understands at once that Eros is the farthest thing from his mind.

He strides ahead of her into the main house, the living room, his face pale, haggard. "I hardly know what to say." She waits, imagining horrors about his children, a car accident, a death, anything. He's begun to shake. She's never seen him like this. He looks at her strangely.

"It seems," he says slowly, "I have a progenitor."

His face is distorted. He's spent a lifetime controlling it, and he tries even yet, until he no longer can, bursts into wracking sobs, covers his face with both hands. She rushes to him, this flesh of her flesh, bone of her bone—words that had only been poetic once upon a time, that are embodied now—this man whom she loves with a passion she could not have thought possible. She holds him fast, his sobs convulsing them both. She's terrified.

At last he calms. But the voice is strained, uncertain. "My father came to the office today." He's half-laughing, grimacing, still unsure of where he'll go next, how he feels.

"Your father? How do you know?"

"My love, it was my father. It could only have been my father."

"Where is he now? What does he want?"

"At his hotel. I don't know what he wants."

"After all these years? Five decades? Half a century?" She does not say fraud, which is what she thinks. Though Molloy had been extremely discreet about his wealth for years, the foundation has made it known. A clever con man might make such a claim.

She soothes him, hands on his shoulders, his face, his arms, murmurs to him; finally leads him upstairs to their bedroom, where they make tender, solemn love after all, comforting each other in this terrible moment, reminding each other silently that they're alive, and that in life, pain and pleasure braid each other. Afterwards, she strokes his cheek. "Tell me what happened."

As she hears the story, she wonders how she's never detected this terrible wound in him. A father gone forever before he was born, a mother so devastated with depression that she was no mother to him; but—the practical aunt Charlotte, the jolly uncle Jack, who raised him: he was not orphaned. Uncle Jack, for whom Molloy had been named, is long dead, but she's met Char many times; they get along well because they both love Jack Molloy deeply, and whatever their differences, that alone makes them affectionate with each other.

"So Char's known all this time?"

He lies on his back, staring at the ceiling. "I could kill her. I mean, it was just two nights ago we were on the phone. She could've told me."

"Char must've had her reasons. We can deal with that after a while. Question is, what now?"

He turns to her with a look so wounded, so forlorn, that she thinks he might weep again. "I want to know him. Is that stupid, or what?"

"Of course you do. Of course you do. Let's have him here for a meal or something. I think a restaurant would be, you know."

"If that's what you want."

Beside him as he phones, she holds his hand.

"Jerry. We need to talk. I wasn't quite myself this afternoon. Yeah, a shock. Anyway, my wife and I would like to have you here for dinner. Your wife? Yes, your wife too." After the call, he goes to the bathroom to retch.

When Jerry McCarthy escorts his wife through the front door, Judith knows there's no mistake. He's eerily her husband to the last inch, twenty years older. Even the gait is the same. Whether handouts are involved remains to be seen.

They settle on opposite couches, husband next to wife, wife holding each husband's hand. Judith sees it's a hard moment not just for father and son, but also for the women who love them. Jerry McCarthy glances around approvingly at the house, simple but elegant in the best of Santa Fe style. He barely covers surprised awkwardness when a maid (just our part-time cook, Judith wants to say) serves wine. Judith sees too that no one holds back. Even her usually abstemious husband has taken a full glass and is beginning on it greedily. Good thing for everyone.

Look at the paintings if you want to know your son, she longs to say. He bought those when nobody knew who those contemporary masters were. When they were not yet masters. Look at the books on the shelves. Your son is—so much. She's impatient with herself. She's his wife, not his advocate. But how much she wants him to be admired, appreciated, by this unlikely stranger. Who should know what he's missed all these years.

Molloy speaks only with his eyes. You have something to say to me?

Jerry McCarthy retells his story. "I was an ordinary, raunchy kid. Your mother and I had been high school sweethearts, and I can honestly say I loved your mother—Giselle here knows that—how you love when you're seventeen, which is passionately, but not always wisely." His diction is the professor's. "When she told me she was pregnant, I said okay, we'll get married. But I'd just won a scholarship to Pitt. If I had to stay in the Mon Valley, I thought I'd kill myself. Literally. Not fit. Not fit at all for the mills. So very grateful for the chance to get out of there. Be somebody. This was going to ruin everything. Everything I hoped for. Dreamed of. Your dreams are passionate then too, if not always wise. I said to your mother, let me go to Pitt. Other people with families go to college; we'll make it work. This last chance for escape—it had only just appeared—was starting to dissolve on me."

"Just a moment. Did you actually get married?" Molloy leans toward him almost threateningly.

The older man smiles, a face more mobile than his son's, a life that never needed the kind of self-protection his son has needed. "Are you legitimate, Jackie? I told you earlier today—a shotgun marriage. Yeah, you're legitimate. My name was Jerry Molloy then." Of course he's seen the name, needed his birth certificate when he first applied for a driver's license, a passport, for the various documents that have permitted him to live the life he's lived. He's wondered about and mostly dismissed a phantom called Jerry Molloy from his mind forever.

Judith gazes at her husband with infinite pity, grateful that Jerry Molloy, or McCarthy, or whatever he is, has answered the question of legitimacy to her husband's satisfaction. It's an odd revelation to her that he even cares, but obviously he does, deeply. But then he's the one who'd insisted on a legal marriage himself.

"No, she didn't want to go up to Pittsburgh. She didn't want me to go either. Her brother Jack could get me a place in the mills, and why didn't I do that? I couldn't, Jackie—I just couldn't. It was life or death to me."

Molloy slumps back on the couch, eyes closed, expels his breath. He knows.

The timbre of Jerry McCarthy's voice is so close to her husband's that Judith wonders if, on the phone, she might even be able to tell them apart.

"At Pitt I discovered I was—good, you know, very good actually, in the classics, of all things. I already knew about Latin, thanks to the fathers. In college, I learned to love Greek too. Who'd think a kid raised in a mill town would take to Latin and Greek like a duck to water?"

"Who indeed?" Molloy says, his own Latin still impressive, if not what it had once been. Judith, beside him, knows all this, intuits his thoughts. This isn't new: willingly or not, they've read each other's minds from the earliest times. But they haven't until now begun to take possession of each other's pain.

"I got a Ph.D. from Penn. I guess by that time I'd changed my name. Your mother and I had got a quiet divorce—she called it an annulment, but it was a divorce. I married Giselle and took the first job I could, teaching classics in Lancaster."

"*Amo, amas, amat*," says Molloy softly. His father stares, but says nothing. Eventually Molloy asks, "The name change?"

"I am not proud of this," says the older man decisively, getting ready to make an answer he's probably rehearsed, "but I didn't come here to lie. Your mother was after me for child support. I just couldn't swing it. Graduate student, assistant professor—this is subsisting, not living. I just couldn't swing it, son. I wish I could've. I should've. I couldn't. Conflicting duties."

"Read all about it in the *Nicomachean Ethics*." Disgust taints Molloy's voice.

"*Ta Ethika*. Dedicated to Aristotle's son, Nichomachus." Jerry McCarthy stares at his son, puzzled that he knows such a thing.

"Aristotle had a son? And even dedicated an important work to him? Nothing like family feeling," Molloy says.

Jerry McCarthy chooses to ignore the blade in that. "When I finally had a little spare cash, I got in touch with Char. You were already in college, and Char said, essentially, butt out. You didn't need me, and neither did she. So another few years went by, and I thought, I want to know my son. I cannot make him whole, but for myself, I want to know my son. Looks like he isn't a beer-and-a-shot guy either. Char told me you were married, you'd gone to work in Germany, and by the way, keep on butting out."

"She can be tough." Molloy agrees. The four of them sink into their own thoughts. Judith is grateful that nobody feels obliged to break the silence with twaddle.

However, Annamarie, part-time cook, full-time ceramicist, eventually does break the silence to tell them dinner is ready, and they fill the moment with getting to the table, seating themselves, passing dishes to one another.

Judith had first seen Molloy at another dinner table; had sat at this and other dinner tables during difficult times; had subsequently been joyful hostess to their friends, their guests, at this same table. But surely no dinner like this has ever taken place here before, she thinks. (She'd only heard about the night, one dinnertime, when he threw out Stephen and Inéz. If Judith had been a superstitious person, she might have smudged the whole room to get rid of all that, but she wasn't, and the room's shadows were left to cleanse themselves.)

More wine. Good thing. In other circumstances, the women might have made small talk to ease things, but this is an evening for father and son, and the women keep silent, let the men grope for themselves.

"Maybe I should have written first. Maybe I should have let Char pave the way."

"Maybe. This is very hard for me." Judith can see his hands, anxious to drum on the table, being held still by his well-practiced self-control. They eat. In Molloy's case, push food around on the plate. "Who was your Latin teacher?"

Jerry McCarthy smiles. "An old charlatan by the name of Father Joachim. We called him Father Yokkie. Was he still teaching by the time you got to St. Joseph's?"

Molloy nods. Judith watches him warily, knowing that this Father Yokkie had played a large role in Molloy's life, a large but mostly failed role as a substitute father. Molloy is apparently not going to say more about that. Jerry McCarthy takes it up again. "Sound in his Latin, though. Old Father Yokkie set me up pretty well." Molloy nods again.

Silence. The women look at each other. "Odd thing," Jerry McCarthy finally says. "When the first Negro colleges got started, classics scholars considered it a duty to leave their Ivy League colleges up north for a year or so and go down south to teach at them. So in the late nineteenth century, you had the incongruity of Pullman porters being able to read and quote Tacitus, Virgil."

More silence.

Molloy puts down his fork and looks at his father full in the face. Matter of factly, he begins. "Your honesty deserves my honesty. I really do want to kill you. Crush you with my bare hands. I mean that most literally. My rage at you is unspeakable." He looks away, breathes himself calm again, but Judith senses the self-control cannot last. "I've read Aeschylus too, Jerry." He's breathing deeply. "At the same time—at the same time, I want to know you." Molloy pauses; appeals to Judith for strength. "Maybe love you."

His voice rises suddenly. "God knows I want to be made whole. I need it. I needed it more in the past, but I still need it." He turns to Judith, pleads silently again with her for something, turns back to his father, resumes softly now. "You cannot know how our lives have paralleled one another's. You've found me in a deeply happy marriage with a woman I idolize. But it wasn't always like that. Yet I was there for that other, that first woman. I provided for her. She and our children did not want, thanks to me. I was there for my kids. At some—no, considerable— self-sacrifice. My life has not been modestly successful. It has been a goddam bravura performance, a chef d'oeuvre, a masterpiece, no help from anyone. Do you detect *arête*, pride, excellence? You bet your ass, Jerry. Classical Greek virtue: no Christian humility in sight. Please do not address me as son."

Judith knows this voice, so even, so quiet, so utterly honest, pulled from the man's deepest self. So devastating if you're on the receiving end, which she had once been, and deserved it then. Though he admires the Stoics, can practice detachment most of the time, he's capable of standing up and, in a cold rage she can recognize, picking up the carving knife on the table beside him and planting it into his father's breast. She doubts he will, because he's also a master at calculating consequences. But she knows that eruption has come from the heart. It's time for a gentle intervention, and she turns to Jerry's wife.

"Giselle, this can't be easy for you either."

Jerry's wife, rounded with years and Lancaster shoo-fly pie, seems grateful. "No. No, it isn't. It never has been. Not because I was jealous of Jerry's first family. He's a most loving man, and never gave me a moment's doubt that he loved us. But the human heart is big, and loves—much. Each time Jerry worked himself up to talk to Char, he came away from that just a little sadder, more broken-hearted.

This has eaten at him for a long time. He needs to make whatever rectification he can. Reconciliation."

"Why now?" Molloy says suddenly.

His father looks hopeful. "Char said—Char said you were happy enough now to be merciful."

"Let's call it a day," Molloy says. He looks exhausted. "Go home, Jerry. I'll be in touch. Or not."

9

Molloy has a Saturday hike scheduled with Leandro Torres, and they take off for the trails leading to Penitente Peak. Two weeks earlier the aspens had been lavishly gold, orange and red. Now they're going bare, the lingering leaves are a drab and depressing gray-brown. This will be the last hike before ski season. The onset of winter has always made Molloy slightly melancholy, and long ago he imagined learning to ski would help make the winter more bearable. It does, slightly.

From the Winsor Trail they reach a gate, where they follow the Raven's Ridge Trail along a fence that marks the national forest, then break out above the tree line. En route, Torres bubbles, as always, about projects and puzzles, in this case a hospital a colleague has designed, where outpatients must drag themselves from station to station for distances that would be nothing to a healthy person, but that are almost insurmountable if you're ill.

"Total stupidity, Molloy. Question is, who's at fault? The architect? The people who run the hospital and have embodied the bureaucracy this way? They could've misled the architect. Or, the architect might have done it right, and then the bureaucrats took over. But see, a good design has to be flexible, yet at the same time, it's got to impose rational behavior on the bureaucrats no matter what they really want, in their stupid, thoughtless way, to do. And then, the stuff they put in these places, my friend (my fren'). The equipment, the furnishings, they're giving off phthalates—Jesus that's hard to say for a nonnative speaker— formaldehyde, God alone knows what else. You get endocrine disruption from the air you breathe, the plastics in the IV bags. A hospital is no place to be sick. And then gardens." They've stopped at a high meadow. "Anybody would know from common sense that gardens are something that contribute to good health. But no, the bean counters said a few decades ago, show me the data. It's taken a few years for evidence, but we have it. Gardens make you feel better. Therefore they help you heal. Therefore you get out of the hospital faster and better, music to the ears of bean counters. So we get to have gardens in hospitals again. Now, evidence-based architecture is pretty interesting, let me tell you."

Molloy, usually happy to talk about these issues, only grunts. They move along a rocky trail and Wotan bounds ahead, always returning to make sure Alpha Dog is present and safe.

After a while, Torres continues. "And then there's the World Trade Center. Buildings go down, then buildings must go up."

"A business op?" Molloy asks, more neutrally than he feels.

"Well, not a business op only."

"That's a relief."

"Someone's going to do it. Why not me? It should be me. I build to pay back for what was destroyed. Don't make me feel—ah, I forgot you were there."

Molloy stops, turns around to face Torres. "I was there. I didn't know all three thousand of the folks who went down, but I knew more than I would've wanted." Not friends but acquaintances, living flesh-and-blood humans he'd joked with, played poker with, done deals with. He'd spent a lot of time on the phone, asking and tracing.

After they ramble for a couple of miles in silence, Torres speaks. "My friend, you seem *un poco triste* today. Is everything okay?"

"Let's sit." They've stopped on a bare grassy ridge and the wind is strong. Just the winter coming, Molloy is tempted to say. "*Un poco triste*, you think? Ready to do a major dive into clinical depression, that's what. Believe me, been there, know the symptoms, and fuck-all, it isn't my fault!"

Torres stretches out against a boulder, his hands behind his head. "Tell me, my friend."

Molloy remains standing, calls his dog to his side. "*Hier*, Wotan!"

"I swear to God, Molloy, when I hear you command that dog in German, I have to wonder if I'll make it to the Swiss border in one piece."

But Molloy is in no mood for jokes. He once had such a friend as Torres, and in deep despair, had failed to open his heart. That friend and his love had been torn away from him by violent death, and Molloy had ever yearned to go back in time, replay it all. Why? Not so much for consolation as for—being understood. Maybe consolation too. Older now, having known more pain, having practiced a little more self-disclosure, he begins.

"Backstory first. My father left my mother before I was born. Just disappeared. I never heard from him, she got nothing from him. She was—deeply depressed, I guess. In our family, we didn't recognize that as a disorder, though everyone seems to have suffered from it. My aunt and uncle brought me up—they took my mother and me in, when I think about it. Well, yeah. I don't know. I never lived anywhere else. My uncle's been dead for years, my mother died a while back—Kathleen Aherne Molloy, unmourned, unmissed; one of those anonymous lives of no consequence to anyone, sad to say. But my aunt, the one who really was mother to me, we're still close. She's down in Florida, we talk to each other once or twice a week. It seems—it seems that over all these years she's been in touch on and off with my natural father. She kept him from coming near me when he actually wanted to see me—he says—maybe for good reasons. I can think of times when I'd have killed him without a second thought. Now I only talk about it. To him, Torres, *to him*." He turns to his friend, his disbelief still apparent. "Three days ago this bastard showed up for the first time in my life. I was speechless. I've made my living keeping my cool, and this old man just devastated me."

Torres exhales loudly. "What did he want?"

"To rectify. To reconcile. To make me whole." The bitterness rises in Molloy's throat. "As if."

"Is he down-and-out? In need?"

"I don't think so. Not obviously. He brought his wife. She seemed okay. The hardest thing—oh, who the hell knows what the hardest thing is? One hard thing was, as he began to tell me about his life, it was my own life being laid out for me. I could connect the dots. Families. They never let go of you, do they?"

Torres snorts in agreement.

Molloy finally squats on his haunches, not yet able to sit. He looks at his friend, camouflaged in big hat, oversize glasses to keep the high altitude glare at a minimum. He's dressed the same way, and is grateful to be half-hidden. "My aunt Char! Where did she get off, not letting him near me? What kind of betrayal is that? Is that even remotely forgivable? Standing between a father and a son? She couldn't know how much I yearned for a dad, a—a dad. A dad." He'd looked desperately for substitutes, who'd failed him; feels close to tears again. Sits down now on the ground, hand buried deep in Wotan's coat.

Torres seems skeptical. "Well, there's some bullshit here. You aren't exactly obscure, my friend. Twenty seconds on a search engine would have turned you up anytime in the last ten years."

Molloy concedes that. "Maybe he used Char as a shield. An alibi. He wouldn't see me until he got the go-ahead from her. I don't know." He sighs. "For the record, two kinds of bullshit. I'm perfectly capable of finding, and finding out about, people. I had a whole file on Judith before I ever met her, before I ever moved to Santa Fe. Yeah, really. So I could've found him. If I'd thought he was alive. I actually thought he was dead. Otherwise he'd have come looking for me, wouldn't he? That's what I thought. Or maybe I was just afraid I'd unearth him in some trailer park in Alabama. At best."

"So you can't blame your aunt, can you? Though it would be interesting to know why she stood in the way." Torres picks up a small pinecone, brought here by some critter, since they've left the pines far below, flings it not far with its badminton-bird lightness. "Fathers," he says quietly. "They are us. We are them." After a while: "Do you want reconciliation with him? Is he a bad guy? Or, like so many of us with odd fathers, did you prefer to keep the dreams separate from reality? Can you forgive him?"

"No." Silence. "I don't know."

"An absent father is so much easier to shape, to believe in, to love, than a present father, there with all his faults and shortcomings and failures. I see that in my own family—I can't say Mikey exactly idealized me when I wasn't here, but with me in his face day in, day out, here in Santa Fe, it isn't as smooth as I could've hoped."

"And your own father?"

Torres's sleepy eyes open and he sits forward, a dismissive gesture with one arm. "That's a story. How much do you know?"

"History. Not your story."

"You know who he was, then?"

"Yeah."

"The history. My reality. Two different stories, it's true." He pulls water out of his day-pack and drinks.

"What happened to all the money?"

Torres seems taken aback for a moment, shrugs. "Cut to the chase, why don't you, Molloy? Okay. My mami was the last of the big spenders. Rolls Royces every year in all the colors they came in. Solid gold telephones. Solid gold plumbing fixtures. It puts my teeth on edge just to say it. My little brothers were into every way there was to spend—gambling, drugs, women who spent it for them. But really, most of it was stolen all over again by my father's goons. A family talent for extreme waste."

"You?"

He nods. "Sure. There's money for me in Switzerland. I've never touched it. Hardly ever. Well, only when I was really, really desperate, and I admit it, yes, yes, yes, there were such times. What am I going to do, Molloy, give it back to the present regime? How stupid would that be? Christ. That's why it's still in Switzerland."

Molloy grunts, his head aching with ethical questions he has no answers to. Thinks about the tangled web of his own family. He turns to Torres, as if to relieve him, equal him, in sorrows. "Then there's my daughter. I told you she's carrying a child. Correction. She *was* carrying a child. She told us she and her brother were going down to the Lightning Field for a few days—"

"Oh, very nice," Torres says approvingly.

"Not so nice. It turned out she was getting an abortion. Torres, my heart was wide open to her. I didn't rant when she told me she was pregnant with no dad in sight. I didn't tell her to do it, not to do it, even when she asked. I don't know why she felt she had to sneak away. The common sense part of me is glad she got the abortion. She's very, very young, younger than her years. But you know what else I thought? I thought, that kid could've been me. That could've been my own mother." He's about to bawl. Won't let it happen; pulls himself together. "So yes, melancholy. Just a bit."

"It wasn't you," Torres says brusquely. "You're here, left to suffer on in this vale of tears. Oh, come on, man, it's the World Trade Center. We're all running on empty. Did I tell you I was coming through Bangkok last week and there on the riverbank was a big banner, in English yet, so we should all understand: Osama bin Laden Rules. It made me so fucking mad I wanted to belt somebody, and then very, very sad. Because—well, never mind why because. Will your daughter stay on with you?"

"No, she's going back to New York. She can stay in our place uptown til she can get to her loft downtown. But I wish she wasn't leaving. I've actually had four at the dinner table most nights, Torres. It's been—well, very nice. Your kids have their own lives, I know that. But I loved it while it lasted. We've never really lived together, all of us, for very long. In fact, never at all. I was away in Germany when they were little, though I'd see them most weekends. Then when their mother couldn't look after them, I brought them to Germany, but it was for boarding school. Then they went away to college. We always did holidays together, but that's not the same thing."

"What do they think of their new grandpa?"

"They don't know. I haven't told them."

Torres whistles and says nothing.

"Christ, it's cold. Ready to turn around?"

Molloy drives Nikki to the airport a few days later. He takes the by-pass route, so they can talk a little without all the ugly commercial distractions of Cerrillos and Airport Roads. He wants her to see and remember the real desert, the Jemez range before them, the Sangre de Cristos behind them; not the spiritual and aesthetic desert Cerrillos and Airport Roads seem to represent. "I'm so very sorry you're going, my radish."

"Papa, I don't belong here. It's not my—just not my place."

"Are you willing to tell me why you kept it to yourself, that you weren't going to the Lightning Field?"

"I guess I was afraid you'd try to talk me out of it."

"Did I give you any hint that's how I felt?"

She's slow to answer. "Not really. But I could imagine."

"How could you imagine? Truth is, I didn't know how I felt, which is why I kept quiet."

"And then—you and Judith. You seem so, I don't know, like, totally self-contained. Self-sufficient."

"You mean we love each other? Yeah, we do." He'd thought his daughter might like to see love up close. It didn't occur to him that she might feel excluded.

"That dance the other night." Molloy and Judith have been taking tango lessons, and after dinner one night, got up to practice. He thought the children were laughing, even impressed. "She wraps her leg around yours—"

"*El gancho*? It's just a step. We need to practice to keep from landing each other on the floor."

Nikki shrugs. "It just summed up—how very close you are. Like, how it takes two to tango. But not three, papa. Or four."

Molloy feels simultaneous despair and irritation. What do his children want from him? Eternal and exclusive devotion? "Nicole, I wish you were staying. I understand that your life is in Manhattan, and I don't question that, but I wish you were staying. But if you tell me it's my domestic arrangements that are driving you out, I really must object. Judith has welcomed you. It isn't just politeness; she enjoys your company. I think she might need a daughter as much as you need a mother, and it could've worked out that way."

Nikki is sniffling in the seat next to him now, and he wonders if he should pull over and comfort her. He keeps on driving.

"When you call me Nicole, I know you're mad at me."

"Oh please, radish, I'm not mad." He is, actually. He knows he can't win. He's had a headache for days with all the crap that's coming down on him.

"Papa, listen to me. It wasn't easy deciding about the abortion, but I decided. Give me some credit. You never give me credit for anything. You—" The pitch of her voice is rising, getting shrill.

His headache pounds in his skull, one part stress, one part very unpleasant memories of fights with his first wife, Lindy, who also claimed that he never gave her credit for anything. He pulls out a piece of paper from his shirt pocket that he's prepared earlier; speaks with more calmness than he actually feels. "This is the guy I saw when my life was crashing in fifty different directions. He's on Central Park West. I don't even know if he's still practicing. He could be retired by now. But he's very good. He doesn't just diagnose and medicate. He really helps you to understand what your problems are all about. He may not take you because I've been his patient, but he'll be able to recommend somebody who practices the same way he does. Do it. A good investment."

"A shrink? You went to see a shrink?"

They're pulling into the parking lot at the small Santa Fe airport. He stops the car, lets his temper deflate silently, undoes his seatbelt, turns and brushes her cheek. "Who am I to you, radish? Your papa has toked up in his day. Your papa has been unhappy enough—no, desperate enough—to see a shrink, and it did him a world of good. Your papa found love that he might not have been open to without the help of that shrink, and now dances the tango. Your papa has made a lot of mistakes, but he's done a few things right, and loving you is one of them. He's real. Okay?"

She flings herself into his arms, sobbing. Molloy embraces her, smells her sweet womanliness, exhales. It might not be so bad to have all that hysteria on the opposite coast after all.

When he sees Judith later that day, he hugs her spontaneously. "Did I tell you today why I love you? For your blessed rationality, my love, that's why."

"Such a relief. I was sure it was my body."

"And your body too," he says happily, grabbing her ass with both hands.

"The rationality is bounded, you know."

"Hmm?"

She has a teasing lilt to her voice. "All human rationality is bounded. We mean to be rational, make rational decisions, but our boundaries stop us—what we don't or can't know; what can't be known. That's why diversity of viewpoints is so great—no single person can represent, learn about, predict the world, and so solve problems. A very powerful idea, bounded rationality. It won my old friend, Herb Simon, a Nobel Prize once. Of course the notion of rationality has become more complicated. So has the idea of bounded. But Herb would've been okay with that. He knew science never stands still. My incisive intellect?"

"Mmm, that too." He pushes her away, takes her in with genuine joy on his face. "And because—because you're so gloriously peaceful. Nikki goes all hysterical on me, and thanks to you, I've completely forgotten what that's like, how it drove me nuts with her mother. I love, I cherish, I prize your equanimity."

"My life is perfect; why shouldn't I be equanimable or whatever the word is?"

"Is it?"

"As close to perfect as it comes, big guy. As close as it comes." She adds: "But, talk about bounded rationality. Even when life is perfect, it's fucking hard, isn't it?"

10

A week or so later, Molloy and Leandro Torres have stopped fishing, and are stretched out on the bank of the Pecos River to eat lunch. Even at this altitude, much lower than the ski basin, it will soon be too cold to fish, but for now, the sun is comforting. Wotan snoozes under a tree. Molloy looks at his beer can as if he's been accidentally reminded, though in fact he's thought of nothing else all day. "My kid invited me out for a beer last night."

"Very nice," says Torres, who's been chewing slowly on his sandwich. "Did you have a good time?"

"We've had some rough times in the past. We're both trying to get past them. This isn't the first time he's invited me. It was nice. Until we got around to what he wants to do with his life."

"Ah," Torres says. "You have different ideas? Him and you?"

"Different like, I think he ought to do something. He doesn't feel the compulsion. He doesn't say it in so many words, but I know he thinks I'm a meddling, overbearing asshole."

Torres laughs so hard he starts to choke. "Please. You'll have to do the Heimlich on me. Yeah, well, you probably are a meddling, overbearing asshole. Get a job, longhair. Remember that?"

Molloy remembers. He'd had hair down his back in college. "What are you saying, Torres? That I'm turning into my uncle Jack?" He smiles slightly at the thought. "Easy for you to say. Your son's gainfully employed, has an actual career. Your daughter's a loving stay-at-home mom who managed to find a guy who could afford to let that happen. How did you do it?"

"My ex-wife, Angustias, gets the credit for bringing up the kids. I wasn't around unless I was between jobs, which can happen from time to time—like most of the time—when you're a young architect, just starting out. You're still busting your balls for some other architect. It wasn't so easy. It's not easy now. Mikey and I are not exactly in the same field, but it's very close. He's an urbanist; he muses about how cities work. Or so he tells me. These abstractions, these computer models." Torres dismisses them with his hand. "As much to do with the real way cities work as playing with erector sets has to do with buildings. In other words, a faint family resemblance. Where are the politicians with their hands out, who 'lose' your building permit application until those grasping little claws are filled? Where are the union so-called leaders dedicated to making your life even harder than it already is? And oh, here's the list of phantoms we want on the job, guys who don't show up but get paid anyway. Here's the non-union guys we'll be glad to have you hire, because they're our non-union guys. Where are the clients who keep changing their minds, and then don't get it, no, they're totally stunned and screaming bloody murder when they've caused their costs to double?

"Mikey says these are—I have to think of the word—yeah, epi-phenomena. He's after the essence. He wants to show all these same people how, if they do it right, according to his models, it will cost less and look and work better. And oh yes, be greener. He thinks he can figure out just how big cities should be, and not bigger. What the tipping point is between working and not working. I gotta say, they're the big questions. Whether he can find the answers is something else. He knows I think a lot of what he's after is shit, but he thinks a lot of what I do is shit too. It makes for stimulating family discussions. We only call each other *capullo* three times an hour."

"*Capullo?*"

"Spanish for dickhead."

Molloy laughs. "I should add that to my repertoire. At least you have something to insult each other about. Conversation more or less died after Stephen and I agreed to disagree on *The Magic Mountain*."

"The place? Or the book?"

"The book. A character in it. Doesn't matter."

"You couldn't move on to sports? How's Barça gonna do this year? How about them Knicks? Just kidding, my friend, just kidding. Especially about them Knicks. Tell me, does your son have to work? Or did you give him an allowance?"

"A lifetime allowance, as it happens. A trust fund. In ten years it'll even increase. I didn't want them to be old when they came into their money; let them enjoy it. And I kind of cast it in stone so I couldn't change my mind if one of them became a religious fanatic, or married someone I couldn't stand. But my kids know that's all they're getting. Everything else goes to the foundation."

"*Dios mío*, trust-fund hippies. My kids will hate your kids on principle. Well, then. Why should he work?"

"Thanks, Torres. That's his view of things too."

"I'm not saying he doesn't need a purpose. Every man needs a purpose. But work? Okay, I'm lucky; my work is my passion. It drives me crazy, I'll say it. No more than five times a week I seriously consider what it would be like to just stop—walk away and fish like this for the rest of my life. I get so fucking weary of it all. So angry—I could shit myself about it. *Me cago*, Molloy, another one for you. I spend one-tenth of my time doing what I really love, which is designing great structures, and nine-tenths of my time worrying about how I'm going to meet my monthly overhead. But that's the price I pay for my passion. And you, you couldn't sit home watching TV all day either, for God's sake. You need your foundation as much as the world needs it. You couldn't even fish fulltime, though that's a good way to spend today, isn't it?"

Molloy doesn't answer.

"Molloy, what's a father supposed to do? He provides for his family, he protects them. He keeps *mamacita* happy with what she likes best, and he carves the Thanksgiving turkey. The rest is up to fate."

Molloy has been looking at the stream, not at Torres. He pulls a small fly out of his kit, begins to tie it to his line.

"Nothing biting now, friend. What did the kids say about their new grandpa?"

Molloy stops tying but does not look up. "I still haven't told them. When did you tell your son about his grandfather?"

"Not until he needed to know. But this isn't comparable. Unfortunately I had something to hide."

"In the end, you didn't hide it."

Torres snorts. "In the end, I couldn't. No way I could make it easy for him. He'd thought—we'd let him think—we were refugees, sure, from a revolution. He didn't need know his grandpa was the biggest thug in Latin America. Up until that time, of course. Later on, government thugs in other countries exceeded even my papi. But you. What's stopping you from telling Stephen about his new grandpa?"

"I don't know how I feel about his new grandpa myself." He rubs his cheek, finally looks up at Torres. "So tell me about your own father. Your story."

"Oh, God. You finished with that brew?"

"You see?"

"No, it isn't because—okay, okay. The world knows my father as the kind of guy who was tight with the very worst of American criminals—they could do anything in my country—to my country—as long as he had a piece of the action. I mean anything. The syndicate owned all the entertainment—gambling, prostitution. That's pennies, by the way; you can't make any money on prostitution. It's a loss leader, it brings in the customers. They owned the banks; they owned the newspapers; almost everything else. He was turning his country, our country, the people's country, into a criminal state—for criminals, run by criminals. Including my papi. If it didn't happen by persuasion, by bribery, no question, he used force. He had no political enemies because he eradicated them. Eradicated them? What a sanitary word! He murdered them, Molloy. Or had them murdered, which to the blindfold eyes of justice, is the same thing. As this was happening, he was also the darling of the CIA because he was so vehemently anti-Communist. That counted for everything with the CIA in those days. Shit on the peasants who were getting reamed."

Torres stops, having delivered himself in a tone so dispassionate it's meant to play down the extremity of what he's really saying. Molloy guesses he must have said it in other circumstances, and feels a rush of pity for him, burdened with such a sad legacy. He also thinks again about the money. Torres works very hard for every penny he makes, often frets about meeting his overhead.

"Your papi realized—a lot of money."

"Yeah. For sure."

"I can see why you don't want to give it back to the present regime. But—"

"But what?"

They sit in silence. Torres is thinking over many things. His voice becomes his own again. "He was two things even to his own countrymen. The first time he held office, he instituted many reforms—public education, fair labor laws, stuff like that—you wouldn't believe it. When at last he lost an election, he stepped down peaceably, acquiesced to the will of the people. That was when he was known as the good president. The second time he took office—it was difficult, just after the Second World War...the sugar market was collapsing because the war had caused people to grow their own. Sugar beets in Europe. Corn sugar in the U.S. Things might have fallen apart anyway with the dependence on so few crops. My father was—badly advised. Became greedy. Saw it was now or never." He shakes his head.

"But to me, my father was a completely different person from who he was to the rest of the world. I can see him in his white linen suits, spotless and pressed always. He'd have a seizure to see the way I sometimes throw myself together. To me he was infinitely kind. He was gentle. Firm, you know? But gentle. Fair. Of all things, fair. He loved books. His collection was so good the national university finally appropriated it. He was only a cane-cutter's son. No reason why he should love learning like that, but he did. Most men of action don't have time for contemplation. He wrote a couple of books himself afterwards, in exile, including his memoirs. Self-published, because who would—? So we had books together. I was in boarding school most of the time, first the U.S., then Switzerland. But I'd come home on holidays, back to Spain, and we'd talk, mainly about books. He always wrote to me when I was in school—absurdly formal letters for a father to a son, so old-school, like Cervantes. Always signed I remain your affectionate father, always hoping for your continued excellent health, then his whole name. He had such a haphazard formal education himself, I don't know where he learned that. All those years in exile. He had a lot of time to read. To learn."

"Did you know he loved you?"

Torres shrugs. "Yes, of course he loved me. He was my papi. We still used the Latino term, even when he was living in Madrid. He stood up for me, you know? I'm just about to start university and oh my God, here's Greetings from the draft board—I'm still an American citizen, because I was born in New York City, and even worse, I'm scheduled to go to Berkeley that fall. Vietnam? I have no quarrel with these poor people. Why don't the Americans just go home? You want to rout out communists? Rout them out ninety miles away, not nine thousand miles away. So he called a lawyer friend who knew his way around. His advice was, just give up my U.S. citizenship, be a Spaniard, and solve the whole problem. Well, no, I didn't want that. But I didn't want to go napalm the Vietnamese, or die in some rice paddy either. I don't know. I suppose money changed hands. I got a permanent deferment.

"He was so very proud of my work. First, what I achieved in school, and then when I began practicing. I'm sorry he didn't live to see how far I actually got. Yes, he loved me and I loved him. He was a model father. I admired him as a dad, you know? Kind, fair, fun to be with, always had my back. Much easier to be with than my mother, who was a piece of work, believe me."

"When did you find out about what he—what he did in his day job?"

"Pretty soon. My little brothers and I had a rough time of it getting away, and I had to use my mother's name in school. I still use it, as you know. For a while I'd defend this guy everyone badmouthed so much. You shouldn't believe his political enemies. They spread lies about him. Look what's replaced him, even worse. That kind of thing. After a while I just shut up. After a much longer while. I began to see that it wasn't just his political enemies. Regular historians had a lot to say too. So to this day, I live with the paradox. My papi, who I loved, and who I wanted to be like, in terms of the father he was to me. And then there's my father the historical figure, who was a thieving, murdering, sonofabitch, a brute, no other word for it. Ran a thugocracy. He destroyed so much. And maybe because of that, I must build. Cheap psychology, hey?"

"And Mikey?"

"For Mikey it's all ancient history, thank God. Maybe he thinks I'm making it up, a little self-aggrandizement. We were once important people. *Mierda*. We don't dwell on it. I think he believes each of us begins with a *tabula rasa*, the sins of the fathers have nothing to do with the sons. Maybe believing it makes it so." Torres shrugs. "At least Mikey doesn't get the old cronies coming around saying, come back, *mío*." He's fallen into a parody of a Spanish accent. "With your name, head a new govermin for the people who loved your papi. And I say politely, thanks, I'm an architect, not a politician. Because I don't want to offend these old boys and their hopeless, loony dream of a comeback. No, *mijo*, you could build great buildings there, no hassles from the govermin, in fact the govermin would gladly pay for them. My own Brasília? I say, and they say *sí, sí*, your own Brasília, and the irony goes right by them. You want a cigar, my friend?"

Molloy's been smiling at the picture of Torres and the old cabal. "*Mamacita* wouldn't let me near her for days if I did."

"Ah. Is she worried about your health?"

"No. She hates the smell."

"But Molloy. Your papi is just a nice, respectable professor of classical studies at a nice, respectable liberal arts college. What's the problem?"

"I don't know if I want him in my life, my kids' lives, after all this time."

Torres thinks this over. "You want to punish him."

Molloy is silent for a long time. He stares off to the tips of the Ponderosa pines high above, the violet New Mexico sky. He hears the river running gently. "Yeah. Yeah, I want to punish him."

"My papi is long dead, but I can tell you, if he came back tomorrow, I'd open my arms wide and cry with happiness. But look. Why don't you tell Stephen, even your Nikki, and they could work it out together."

Now Molloy looks at his friend, and doesn't hide his misgivings. "Can't you picture my long-lost father and my mostly lost son as allies against me? That's why not."

"Why do you think they'd be allies against you? That's paranoid, if you don't mind me saying so, friend." Torres draws on his cigar and blows the smoke out into the pristine wilderness. Wotan looks up and twitches his nose with something like disapproval. "Look, Stephen's going to find out about it sooner or later anyway. More better he should hear it from you. You should tell him."

"Yeah, well, everything's more better than what I'm doing, ain't it?" Molloy begins to pull on his waders again. "Fly fishing was always my escape, my meditation. I've done it all over, some really weird places. In storage I have this funny collection of creels I traded for all over the world. They're beautiful—everybody, every region, does them differently. Most of the time I couldn't even speak the guy's language, but we'd recognize each other, both fishermen, and pretty soon we were sign-languaging the trade. Ehhh, once a trader. Styrofoam coolers might work better, but no poetry in them. No sign of the human hand. Those creels belong in the Folk Art Museum. I should donate them."

Torres glances skeptically at Molloy's high-tech gear, which does not include anything like a wicker creel, much less a Styrofoam cooler. "So now you're saying you bring your troubles here too."

"Yeah. Yeah, I bring my troubles here too. I always brought them here. But here they went away, at least for a little while. Now they won't even go away." He wades into the river and casts, a pretty gesture in its economy and skill.

Torres calls after him, "Like I said, nothing biting out there by now." The architect remains on the bank, finishing his cigar, watching his friend, who soon hooks and nets a beautiful brown trout after all, by far the biggest of the day. Torres can see his smile under the shadow of his hat.

As Molloy scrambles on to the riverbank, he says: "You coming for dinner? Annamarie does trout beautifully."

"Thanks, but I've got a dinner date."

"The lovely Lucie? Sorry, not my business."

"Not the lovely Lucie," Torres concedes. "Not the lovely Lucie."

"Well, whoever she is, bring her over. Between this and what's in the freezer, we've got enough here for the four of us. Judith would love to see you." And the new woman has got to be an improvement over icy Lucie.

"Ah, I hardly know this lady. Thanks anyway."

Before Annamarie serves the fish he's caught, Molloy calls his aunt in Florida. "Char? Jerry McCarthy paid me a visit."

"And hello to you too. Did he, now?"

"Char, don't—you knew he was alive? You knew where he was all these years?"

Silence.

"Why did you hide that? Why did you keep us apart?"

"If Jerry Molloy or McCarthy or whatever he calls himself these days told you the truth, it was me who said to get in touch with you."

"He said that."

"Three cheers for him."

"Char, why now? If I'd known earlier I had a dad, my whole life might have been different."

"You had a dad. Your uncle adored you."

"Char, this isn't to be ungrateful for everything you and uncle Jack did for me, it's just—well, your biological father is—" He searches for the word, is interrupted.

"Your biological father didn't have the common decency God gives a flea. Oh yes, very good at the Latin and Greek, I hear, though the news hasn't reached me he's at Harvard. You were ours, Jackie. We loved you; we raised you. And we kept your mom alongside. You really think you'd have been better off with a guy who didn't think twice about running off and abandoning you? Not to mention your pregnant mother? A guy who didn't see the light until you were in college? That's the first time he got in touch, though in the early days, your mother was after him for child support. That's when he took a powder, changed his name. By the time you were in college—I won't say that's when all the hard work was over, because for your uncle Jack and me, it wasn't hard work. You were the light of our lives. You still are. Who's he? He pokes your mom in the back seat of a car one night and therefore gets credit for you? I don't think so. Jerry Molloy, McCarthy, never thought once about anything but himself."

"He didn't cover himself with glory, God knows. But now…"

"Glad you see it. When your uncle Jack was alive, if that guy had dared show up, he'd have got your uncle's Remington thirty-oh-six smack dab in his puss. Your mom was Jack's sister, so your uncle had two very good reasons for blasting this deadbeat to kingdom come. Okay, when Jerry finally decided he could surface, he'd call me about once a year, and I'd say not yet, not yet. You were ours, damn his eyes, not his. We couldn't have our own, your uncle and I, and we felt like the good lord had given us a very precious gift. After your uncle passed, and oh, he loved you, Jackie. He didn't always understand you, I know that; but believe you me, he loved you to pieces. He thought the sun shone out of your you-know-what. Anyway, I began to think that maybe you and your natural— what did you call him, your biological father—should know about each other. You never talked about him after you were a little boy, but it didn't take no crystal ball to know you thought about him. Not always kindly. You're a good man, Jackie. You always have been. But every once in a while, a bitterness would jump out of you that was pretty shocking. I knew it was about him. So after a while I told him you'd gone to Germany. You were married. Maybe at that point, you had Stevie on the way. I told him not to expect a warm welcome if he tried seeing you then."

She takes a breath. "But why was he waiting for my permission, for God's sake? A real man would've taken matters into his own hands. Not just then, but much sooner. After Lindy died—and Jackie, say what you will, that was a blessing—you were frankly a mess. The mouth on you sometimes!" She laughs, and he does too. "When you threw everything over to go to Santa Fe, I thought, oh boy, is this more of the same? The state of you then. And then you married Judith, God bless her, and you're a different guy. No—you're the happy little tyke I always loved, heart as big as all outdoors. Even your kids say they've never heard you laugh like you laugh these days. So I told him—"

"I was happy enough to be merciful."

"Oh yeah, that's what I told him. And as far as I'm concerned, mercy's the most he can expect."

"Char, if I'd known him, maybe I would've been at the Latin and Greek myself. A professor."

"Yeah? Well, you'd have ended up at Harvard, trust me on that one."

He laughs again, feels a great rush of affection. "I love you, you know that."

"I know. But it wouldn't have entered your mind to say that in plain English before you got married to Judith."

He sighs theatrically. "Damn, woman. I get on the phone ready to tear you limb from limb for keeping this all from me for so long, and what happens? I realize how much I love you. What a steady force, what a rock you've been in my life. God bless, Char. I owe you everything." They're both sniffling. "Come see us, Char. Stevie's here now. I'll send a plane for you. In fact, why don't you give up Florida and move here?"

"I love that, I'll send a plane for you. When we were sitting on the front porch of Spring Street, who'd have thought that one day little Jackie Molloy, buried in his comic books, would be sending planes for his old auntie? My friends are thrilled when their kids send tickets."

"The heroin, Judith calls it. She says if she'd known what private jets were like, she'd have married me much sooner. I think she's kidding. Or maybe it's all that holds my marriage together."

"Jackie, shame! I was at the wedding; seen her dozens of times since." A slight exaggeration, Molloy thinks, though Char has indeed visited Santa Fe from time to time, and he and Judith have dropped in on her in Boca Raton. "That woman is crazy for you. More than we could say for Miss Lindy, her and her fecking notions of herself, her airs, but let's not go there. Look, the altitude really doesn't agree with me, or I just might come. I'm sure Santa Fe has old ladies I could talk to. I bet some of them even speak English. And you know, fifteen years in Florida, my Spanish isn't so bad." They both laugh. "That's you. You are genuinely a family man at heart. You love having all your family around you. That's why—well, maybe you and Jerry can come to some kind of peace. For your sake, and your sake alone, I hope so. I don't give a flying fuck about him."

"The mouth on you, Char." And they laugh again together.

"I hear he has other kids."

"He does. I haven't met any of them."

"What are your own kids thinking about this new, so-to-speak grandpa?"

He hesitates. "I haven't told them, Char. I don't know how I feel about all this myself."

"Listen to your old auntie. It's going to come out sooner or later. Don't wait too long."

"Yeah." He wonders if he can tell her why he still hesitates. He wonders if he knows himself. "Yeah."

11

With Judith these nights over dinner, Molloy is uncharacteristically fretful. He seems continuously torn between talking about what preoccupies him and burying it, something to forget, a nightmare not to revisit. She studies his face, a taut mask when she'd first met him four years ago, softened now: the folds from his nose to the corners of his mouth deep, very deep; the jawline going just a little bit soft. She's humanized him. Maybe she's only aged him. She puts down her fork, smiles sympathetically. "Molloy, my love. What is it? No, I know what it is. What will you do?"

He covers his eyes with one hand. Looks up, brings both fists down on the table where the glasses and silver jump. "Babe, I have such a rage inside. I had no idea it was still there. I can barely control it. It's killing me." He beseeches her so helplessly, she gasps. This man, never helpless in his life. Or so she'd once thought. "Char thinks I'm happy enough to be merciful? I wish."

"Aren't you happy?"

"Happiest I've ever been in my life," he says grimly. "Everything with us—everything with us is—perfect." He sits back in his chair, surveys the table. He sighs, as if he were making a confession. "As you said, even when life's perfect, it's fucking hard." He's thoughtful. "Sometimes, before people are coming over for dinner, I walk into the dining room and just stand there, looking at the table. A freshly set table is so...elegant. So promising. Waiting for the guests. The meal to begin. It's set. Everything that means, to be set. All my life I wanted that. I never could with Lindy. Hardly ever did it by myself. Never could have it until now. It matters to me to be a good host. Have people at my table."

"You do it just right. 'Liberality without display,' as Jane Austen put it."

"Did she?" His frown fades; he actually looks pleased.

"Maybe the *Spannfergel* feast was a bit over the top." She's teasing him about flying in a dozen dressed German suckling piglets, along with a Bavarian chef and his assistants to roast them.

"Hey, it was New Year's. A new century. A new millennium. Attention must be paid. Anyway, you can't abide American pork anymore than I can." He gazes at her attentively, lovingly. "You make everything possible. I'm so happy I almost want to—well, to say grace before the meal starts. Grace. Thanks. But you know. Who to?"

She shakes her head. "It's ours together. What we've managed together. Host, the receiver of strangers. Hospitality, hostel, hospital, even hostage—it has an odd set of derivations."

He thinks that over. "Here in our house, I'm a happy man. A deeply happy man. Grateful for it. But this. This. I have no goddam idea what to do."

"Nobody can say. But take it from a person known to be stiff-necked: all it does is give you a pain in the neck."

At least he smiles. He can't remember if he'd accused her to her face or only thought it, back in the days when she was being so stiff-necked.

"In ten years," she adds, "well, think how you'll feel in ten years if you haven't somehow pursued this. If you've closed the door. Think how you feel about Stephen."

"My God, the Molloy boys have quite a record in the father-son business, don't they?" It's a pained sarcasm.

Judith puts a hand on one of those clenched fists. "Call your father, my love. Tell him you'd like to meet, and then you go to him. You go to him. He made the first move, and it cost him, I'm sure. Reciprocate."

He nods, conceding. "But please come with me. I can't do this by myself."

Judith and Molloy stand in front of his father's house, a small, well-tended place, built when European-style cottages with mullioned windows and gabled roofs had seemed the ultimate in old-world aspirations, old-world solidity, evoking nostalgia and comfort for so many who had passed through eastern Pennsylvania's factories, en route to their graves. On the dark front porch, furniture is covered with green canvas shrouds for the winter. Incongruously, that porch also has two Greek columns supporting its roof—Doric? Judith doesn't know. Surely the mix of architectural styles—one part stagecraft witch's hut, one part aspirational classic—must be grating on her husband's fine aesthetics. She watches him taking it all in, so small, so cramped: if he'd grown up here, would its just-so comfort with its just-so scale have stunted him, lulled him, prevented him from the life he's made instead? Bravura performances need not only high energy, but deep incentives.

Jerry and Giselle McCarthy have heard the car; stand in the doorway to welcome them, a kind of living greeting card. An awkward moment, where Jerry wants to embrace Molloy, but he stubbornly offers only his hand. Jerry accepts the hand, passes over the affront silently. The women embrace briefly.

The living room's scale seems even more diminutive than the house's exterior. On top of the TV are family pictures, and Molloy walks over to inspect them. Jerry follows him. "That's Betsy, our eldest. She's a nurse, like her mom. That next to her is David. He's following in his old man's footsteps, just got tenure at Penn. Summers, he supervises a dig on the Lebanese-Syrian border. Not the safest vocation he could've picked, but what can you do? That's Margie. Margie is our problem child. Margie hasn't quite found herself yet and—time marches on. She worries us more than David in the Middle East, frankly. But we love each of them so dearly. I know you have kids."

"Two. My youngest, Nikki—a daughter—only bothers to communicate with me through Judith, whom, thank God, she likes." "Tolerates," Judith corrects softly, though the family together after the World Trade Center attack eased things with all of them. Nikki calls her regularly to discuss her love life, her clothes, nothing at all. Stephen has a new gravity, even if he isn't living up to his father's standards for him. "My oldest, Stephen, is—also having some trouble finding himself. Did Char tell you that their mother was ill for a long time, and then died a few years ago?"

"Char told me." In Jerry's reply, Judith hears that atavistic Celtic evasion of a yes or no.

"It affected them both more than I realized. Still, I did my best. Is there anything you don't know about me?"

"I know the externals. What you've done with your life. Well, so far." He looks over to his wife, as if he's just made a small joke and hopes for appreciation. "What you hope to do. Char called me when you and Judith married. She said that for you, this would change everything for the better. She said, I think after a while he'll be able to see you. So I, you know, hung on to that hope."

"Here I am," says Molloy, less than graciously.

"Jack, why don't you and I go into my study and leave the ladies to visit for a while?"

Molloy looks unhappily at his wife, but follows his father into a small side room that serves as a study. In silence Jerry lets him examine the spines on the bookshelves, listening to little sounds of recognition as old friends of books speak out to his son.

Molloy picks up a small volume of Epictetus. "I knew I wasn't a sage when this guy said sages are immune to misfortune. I know someone in Santa Fe who actually keeps a copy in the bathroom for reading on the throne." He doesn't say it's himself. "And Marcus Aurelius in the other bathroom."

His father nods. "Marcus Aurelius loved Epictetus, had been his student."

Molloy replaces the book, looks sidelong at his father. "It's hard to believe there's a gene for all this, Jerry."

"Yes. Hard to believe."

"I stopped doing Latin after high school, but at the time, the good fathers, as you call them, thought I'd be just right for the vocation. Straight A's in Latin and German. But one of the good fathers told me later than he damn near laughed his ass off to hear that. He could see that I—that the celibate life wasn't going to be my life. It was—what did you call him? That old humbug, Father Yokkie." Molloy moves over to a relatively large and elegant pot alone on a table. He recognizes it as a red-figured krater, a bowl for mixing water and wine, with a scene from that most grisly of trilogies, the *Oresteia*. "Jesus, Jerry. It's an exquisite piece, a museum piece, but of all the damn scenes."

"Just a family quarrel, Jack. Seduction. Betrayal. Murder. It seems the right thing to have here. So let's talk about our own family quarrel—no murders, but seductions, betrayals, abandonment. Misunderstandings."

Molloy slams the study door shut behind him, stands with his fists clenched. "Fine. You start. Why now?"

The older man replies softly. "Why now? If you're really asking why not before now, I'd say a combination of cowardice, and some worry that it was already too late. But maybe it's never too late."

"Too late. What the fuck does that mean? Where were you all these years? I was a little boy. I needed my dad. Where in the hell were you?" He moves closer to his father, but his voice has dropped. "I'm surprised you didn't hear it, Jerry. Just a quiet sound, floating over the hills and the hollows, along the runs. Maybe you thought it was only the wind in the mountain laurel. No, it wasn't very loud, you certainly could've missed it—because I didn't want to wake anybody up. It was the sound of a little kid sobbing his heart out of a night into his pillow. Because his dad was gone." Softer now: "That little boy used to believe—oh so profoundly—that if only his father knew how unhappy he was, that father would come rushing to the rescue. If that little boy just had enough faith, believed deep enough, hard enough, then his pain, his longing, would be strong enough to carry its message outside the bedroom, outside the house, outside the town, all the way to wherever his father was. And his father would hear. Would understand. Would come running. You never heard that sound? That call?"

"Jack—" Jerry McCarthy sits down slowly in an armchair. He exhales, gathering his thoughts. Molloy looks at that chair, a chair where many books have been read, annotated, translated. Where all drama has, up to now, been imaginary. "I wish they hadn't named you after that—Hibernian bogtrotter. But at least it's my last name."

Molloy's temper flares. "That Hibernian bogtrotter. You actually make me miss Jack Aherne, Jerry. Carrying his first name is, God knows, a small enough gift for a man who fed me, clothed me, and kept a roof over my head for eighteen years. Which is infinitely more than my sire could be bothered to do." Now he moves toward the older man, leans over the armchair, both hands on its back, his face inches away from his father's.

Jerry McCarthy drops his head, covers his face with his hands for a moment, looks up. "I am ashamed of that. Deeply ashamed."

"Are you, then?" Molloy hears the Irish coming back into his voice, the locutions of his uncle.

"Yes. Yes, I am. But—"

"You're ashamed, then, are you? So what?" He's shouting, and he can see Jerry McCarthy is afraid. He likes that. Jerry McCarthy has admitted his shame, and deserves to be afraid, too. But Molloy drops his voice again. "Where were you when I was that little kid on third base, ready to come in and score one at the bottom of the ninth, a little hero, don't you know, and I told myself that this time my dad will be at home plate, pick me up as I slide in, and he'll hug me, praise me, I know he will, because I heard a voice in the crowd that's my dad's own, cheering for me. That's when I would've forgiven you. That's when I needed you."

Jerry McCarthy looks deflated. "Let's try and reason this out, my friend."

"I was thirteen when President Kennedy was shot. That's when I knew you were dead. A sign, I thought, from God. It's really my dad who's dead. Everyone grieved the president, oh, me too. But me, I also walked around for a week numb with the secret knowledge that the president's death was a sign that my own dad was really, really dead. You reason that one out, Jerry."

Molloy steps back, sees the older man take a breath of relief. Realizes he's been bullying this man. He folds his arms across his chest, tries to make his voice reasonable. "Let me ask you something, Jerry McCarthy. Jerry Molloy. Would you have come looking for me if I was the steelworker I was meant to be, you left me to be? Though by now I'd have been out of work, collecting unemployment for the last, what? Fifteen years since the Braddock Works closed? Counting the days until social security? Would you? Would you have come looking if I had some crap disease, lungs, nerves, ruined bones, the usual legacy of the mills? Would you? No, Jerry, I don't think so. You've come looking because I made something of myself, just wouldn't let your neglect, your indifference, stop me. As an old bookie used to say to me, everybody wants to back a winner. Okay, here I am."

"You're very harsh, Jack. Maybe with good cause. But looking for you has nothing to do with that. I'm proud of what you've accomplished. I think I'll be proud of everything you're going to accomplish." He smiles slightly, ingratiatingly. "Maybe, in some way, the hard times you had as a kid helped form that iron will of yours, but—"

Molloy throws up his arms, spins away from him. "Oh you fucking do not get any credit in any way whatsoever for what or who I am. In no way whatsoever."

Jerry McCarthy smiles somewhat more broadly. "Well, I hear something of myself, my young self, in that."

Molloy turns, looks at him over his shoulder. "Your young self? I'm fifty-one, Jerry. No youngster. A guy who's seen the world and knows which way the wind blows. Especially when it blows from a shitpile." Molloy is breathing hard, puts a hand on the Greek krater, runs his fingertips around its rim, fingertips that radiate rage.

The older man watches this uneasily.

Molloy's chest is heaving, but his voice is soft again, as he gazes at the krater. "You really don't know me if you think this—beautiful thing is in any danger from me. Yeah, there might've been such a time. Lucky for you, my destructive days are over. Leave it to me in your will, Jerry. A token of, what did you call it? A family quarrel. Seduction. Betrayal." He drops his hand from the pot, but imprisons his father in a glare of such intensity that the older man trembles slightly.

His father closes his eyes for a moment, perhaps hoping this will break the withering condemnation he's trapped in. "But—listen to me, Jack. Nothing to do with taking credit, or wanting—anything from you. It's me. It's me. My own need to know you, to have you as part of my life. To be forgiven. Above all, I hope for that. That you can find it in your heart to forgive me. It would take a very great weight—not the entire weight. I'll always be ashamed and sorry for what I did, I'll always regret—sharply, deeply—what we've missed over the years—but it would take a very great weight off my heart if my son could forgive me."

"No."

"You won't forgive me?"

"Never. Simple as that."

"I understand your anger—"

"You don't understand a fucking thing."

"I think I understand your anger, and no one can blame you for it. I'm asking—I'm hoping—you'll go past that anger and let us know each other. Maybe forgiveness will come."

"Let us know each other," Molloy says mockingly. "I'm an old trader, Jerry. What have you got to show me?"

12

When Molloy slams the study door, Judith and Giselle look at each other helplessly. As voices rise and fall, the women are silent, both trying to eavesdrop on this clash, its intimacies. At one point Judith queries Giselle silently: whose voice was that? Giselle shrugs.

"Does he have a temper, your Jack?"

"No, I wouldn't say that. He's self-controlled to a fault. But nothing like this has—I have no experience."

"How do you want it to turn out?"

Judith is surprised. "Do I even know? And if I know, am I entitled to an opinion? Jack and I have been ridiculously happy with each other these past few years. To go on like that forever would be heavenly. But this has thrown everything off-kilter. I had no idea how important this was for him. No idea at all. You think you know a man." She does know him. And yet. "You?"

"I want it to turn out okay. I want these two pigheaded guys to love each other. This has eaten at Jerry ever since I've known him. Not in any major devouring way, you understand, but always in the background, always in a way that said get this settled, clear up this unfinished business. We talked about bringing Jackie here when he was a youngster, bringing him up with his half-sibs. Char wouldn't hear of it. We weren't about to go to law."

"Jack with a brother and sisters. How sad. I think he'd have loved that. Why did Char stand in the way?"

"I've often asked myself. The easy answer is plain old jealousy. She adores her Jackie, and, you know, isn't shy about taking credit, loud and long, for everything he's achieved. She's entitled—she's the one who wiped his bottom and nursed him through the chicken pox. Some absentee father horning in on all that limelight? But that's the easy answer, and Char, from what I've heard, is not a simple woman. I can tell you Jerry set store by what she said. He could've found Jack before this—maybe even found him at college, or whatever. But again and again, Char said not yet, so he didn't." Giselle shrugs. Turns to some distant place. "I have to tell you, Judith, it ate him up."

The voices in the study continue, audible but impossible to understand.

"What kind of nurse are you?"

"A damn good one," Giselle laughs. "A hospice nurse. A woman of sorrow and acquainted with grief, let's say."

"Death," Judith says. "Doesn't that get you down?"

"Some folks burn out. For me, to help individuals through that last journey—I feel very lucky. It's never good to see people in intractable pain, and you can't always help them—then you do want to curse and weep. But I've been doing this for twenty years, and I'm grateful to have work that's so satisfying. Thanks to Jerry, I can quote the Greeks to them, who of course had it all down thousands of years ago. In my line I see lots of people with unfinished business. My Jerry and your Jack, they need to finish this—business." She pauses. No voices can be heard from behind the closed door. "You're a scientist, Jerry says."

"Technically, an applied mathematician. Nothing as practical as what you do. I worry about proving formal limits to science. What's known. What can be known. What's forever unknowable. I don't seem to be very close to my overall goal, but sometimes the theorems that come out of that work have all kinds of interesting applications in various fields of science, in mathematical finance. So I can keep my head up, even if I'm falling short on the big, the main job." She snorts. "That sounds so irrelevant just now."

"Maybe not so irrelevant. Char told Jerry that you were the best thing that's ever happened to Jack."

"Did she? That's touching. Very." Judith pauses. "I tell Jack just about every day that he's the best thing that ever happened to me." Most of the time he even believes me.

"Good for you. People don't think about saying such things out loud until it's too late."

"No, if anything, I worry that we—we congratulate ourselves for having found each other in a way that verges on, well, hubris. It's tempting fate, I sometimes think."

"No hubris. It's a gift, and it's only right to express our gratitude."

"Let me tell you—Jack doesn't know this. My biggest fear, Giselle. Something will take this man away from me, and what follows will be simply unendurable. Much worse than if I'd never had him to love. It all came over me one night after the funeral of a child, a boy in Santa Fe whose parents we know. I'm lying in bed weeping about the inevitable, and Jack thinks I'm weeping about an ex-boyfriend who showed up at the funeral. He was asleep before I could explain, and later..." She shrugged. "It never seemed the right time to bring it up again. It's morbid, the way I hear time's winged chariot and all that. I'm slightly older than him, so maybe we'll beat the odds. Maybe I'll go first. You can understand how happy I was to see Jerry healthy and vital, to know there were no dread diseases lurking in the DNA to pop up and devastate us. Not that other things can't, but."

"You've got many years yet, Judith. Squeeze everything you can from them. Quality is as good as quantity. In some ways." Then she observes: "You're deeply in love."

Judith groans. "Such a moon-June phrase. I wouldn't put it that way. But I guess so."

"How did you—how do you—feel about Jerry showing up?"

"I want the best for Jack. Let him come to love his father. Discover something about himself through this that he didn't know. Be made whole, as he said. I never knew he felt—not whole. Let it heal a wound I never knew existed."

Didn't she? Sometimes, when he was deeply asleep, some fierce guard finally let down, he'd cry out, from an occluded depth of fear and anger that demanded recognition. It would yank her out of her own sleep, and she'd put a hand on him, calm him. He never woke up. Was this its source? "It may not happen. Jack is, well, suffering in ways I never saw before. Even when we were having troubles between us, before we were married, he's like, well, too bad; a pity not a tragedy. This is much more profound."

"A wound for them both. But I agree, Jack's is the worst, by far. How did such a sensitive man ever become such a financial heavyweight?"

Judith shakes her head. "He was very good at it, not very happy at it. Never really felt it was his world. Was slightly ashamed of it, to tell you the truth." She knows he'd come back from Germany permanently thinking that at last he'd be at home, only to discover that in his absence, a financial culture he scorned had grown out of control. Its short-sighted self-regard sickened him He even thought about returning to Germany, living there permanently. The words he used to Judith: Vulgar. Coarse. Crude. Pusillanimous. They betrayed a bitterness about it that implied, continues to imply, something much deeper.

Giselle seems to invite candor, and Judith goes on. "My first thought when Jerry showed up was, well, protective. How do you know he's really your father?

Jack Molloy's not a poor man. I could imagine some fraud, some con man—but then I saw Jerry and I knew this was no fraud."

Giselle nods. "You're a sensible woman. My God, but he looks like Jerry did at that age. It was a shock to me, I'll tell you. When did Jerry and Giselle get old?" She smiles, thinking about that; looks at the closed door. "What the fuck are they doing in there? Would you like some more coffee?"

"No, I—"

The study door opens. Molloy comes out, face unreadable; his father follows him. "My love, Jerry and I are going to a football game. Can you find your way back to the hotel okay?"

American football? It erupts in her mind, luckily not to her lips. You who love European football and find the American stuff so boring? "Not to worry, I'll use the GPS. Same way we got here."

In the generic hotel room, a room that claims to be non-smoking and yet smells somehow of stale smoke, disinfectant, she crawls under the dreary covers—a moment to ponder why dreary is thought to be soothing to hotel guests, hospital patients—and falls asleep in the dark and chilly late autumn afternoon. When she wakes he's standing beside the bed, unbuckling his belt. She asks what time it is; he only grunts. No grave and solemn or sweet and tender love this time; an animal frenzy—from frustration? Rage? Relief?

After, he falls away from her without a word.

"Whoa. Did your team win, then?"

"Was that a victory lap? Not quite." He buries his head beside hers. "I can't forgive him. I just can't. After all those years. All that struggle. Not a word of support, of praise. Of love. A father should make you larger, better, than you are in life. Fill you with—with the pride of accomplishment, belonging." He lifts his head, whispers fiercely: "I am my own goddam father. I invented myself."

She's stopped. He's never said this in so many words.

Fundamentally a formal man, as she'd said to Stephen; a man who'd once taken easily to living in Germany, a formal society. He'd probably have been just as happy in Japan. A society with boundaries suited him, boundaries that were explicit, acknowledged, agreed upon. Though boundaries he could, and sometimes did, willfully violate.

Yet she's also come to know that his life can be described as a series of concentric circles. The formalities—always dominant, always courteous, usually somber if not downright grave—are for others, which is why he sometimes strikes people as slightly pompous. Inside a small group of friends, he's easygoing and relaxed, jokey, though that group is intimately small. With her alone, he's something entirely different—he sings to her, makes up silly nicknames for her—beloved goddess, which morphs into BG, along with the German version, *geliebte Göttin*, Queen of the Amazons, The Divine Sublime, and Seven Precious Ingredients. Alone in the shower he also sings. Broadway songs, old German drinking songs, songs from *Die Dreigroschenoper* or the Grateful Dead, the Pointer Sisters. Sometimes it's utter nonsense, chirruping and trilling, a sign of his contentment. She loves to overhear that, calls him, this tall, athletic, luxuriantly hirsute man, her little bird. Intimately, he's a riotously passionate man. Yet she knows there are parts of him he hasn't exposed, not to her, not to anyone. Maybe never will.

He exhales. "Wisdom says I need to forgive him for my own sake. But I can't. I just can't. Not now." He flings himself back on the pillow and stares upward. "I can like him. I have to like him; he's a likable guy. But forgive him? Love him? Be his son? No."

She moves over, rests her head in the dip between his shoulder and chest, unconsciously licks a bit of his generous pelt, and has never felt sadder. Unfamiliar to her: pain on his behalf, but something like his pain too, unmediated, as if some invisible nerve stretches between them, a transfer point. Flesh of her flesh. She strokes him as if he were a beloved animal.

On that first family vacation in Provence, Molloy had hoisted himself out of the pool after doing laps one afternoon, and Judith gasped with pleasure. With the water sheeting down his trunk, plastering his hair to his skin, he seemed like some magnificently sleek water creature. His daughter had also seen this. "Papa should have that back waxed at least. It's so disgusting." "No," Judith had said quietly, "Oh, no." In bed that night, she told him how she'd seen him. "You looked so splendid I nearly embarrassed you in front of your children." "You do know the way to a man's heart is through his ego," he murmured happily. She thought then and has thought since of the old saying, that the children of lovers are orphans. Molloy's have been orphaned twice over, though the first time had little to do with love.

"Could we just walk away from this, make believe it never happened?" This to a man who deludes himself about nothing.

"Yeah, right."

"There's no rush. Take your time."

He gazes at her sadly. *"Festina lente.* The maxim, not the rock group. Make haste slowly." She lies beside him, pondering his sadness, pondering the many nuances of sexual congress: urgent animal passion, of course; but also play. Consolation. Comfort. Rage. Forgetfulness. Duty. Contrition. Forgiveness. Absolution.

They return to Santa Fe, welcomed ecstatically by Wotan, take up their routine lives. Sometimes late in the evening, she catches him staring off into space, and she's bolder now, intrudes: "What are you thinking of, love?"

"Nothing," he usually says. But one night he answers: "Meno's question. Can you tell me, oh Socrates—is excellence, *arête*, something that can be taught? Or does it come by practice? Or is it neither teaching nor practice that gives it to a man, but natural aptitude or something else?"

The odd things this man has committed to memory. She smiles in spite of herself, knows the question he's really asking. "Socrates answered?"

"Old Soc dodged the question. We can't really define excellence, *arête*, he said, so who knows if it can be taught. There was even something about the unknowable in that dialogue, but in the days I was reading Plato, the unknowable wasn't a topic of gripping interest to me, so I don't remember the details. Maybe we should re-read it together."

He's uncharacteristically melancholy, and while seeing friends, and work at his foundation cheers him, at home he slips into sadness, and she doesn't know how to lift it from him. "It's interesting," she tries in another of those quiet evenings, "how in classical mythology, sons and fathers are always being separated and then reunited, and recognize each other with joy. I'm thinking of, um, Theseus here, who found his father after wandering and doing great deeds."

"Theseus? That didn't end well, my love. His stepmother, Medea, tried to poison him. His father eventually threw himself off the cliffs, thinking his son hadn't returned alive from Crete. Does Giselle look menacing? If I don't somehow respond, will my father—? Please." A tender smile, but withal, sad.

On a different occasion she probes again, and he says: "Just being nostalgic for the past I should've had."

She wonders, but cannot be sure, if resolving this would somehow open the way to his own reconciliation with his son. She knows enough not to bring that up. A few late afternoon beers, but friction between them lingers. Molloy fails to understand, is impatient with, what he sees as his son's inertia, and for all the skill he has at concealing his feelings from investors, clients, all the people he has had to conceal himself from all his life, he cannot—he won't—conceal himself from his son. True, by the time he was Stephen's age, Molloy had in fact done great deeds and would do many more, but he overlooks that it was forced on him, a necessity he has spared his son from. Does he blame himself for what he thinks is Stephen's problem? She ponders what he'd whispered to her in that dreary hotel room in Lancaster, what he thought fathers should be to their sons, and wonders why he won't—can't—be those things to his own son. Fathers. Sons. He isn't on the best of terms with his daughter, for that matter.

What's the answer? She loves her tranquil life with him alone, and would not be sorry for the rest of it to go away. *Et ego in Arcadia.*

IV

Orthogonal Patterns

1

"You're friends with Molloy." It was a statement from his cousin, not a question.

"That's right. We get along just fine," Torres said to his cousin, his landlord, the archaeologist Benito Jiménez, who seemed to have no thought of vacating the premises anytime soon. Which were his, so his right to remain, Torres reminded himself. It wasn't as if they'd signed anything formal. Benito had presumably come for the funeral of Nola Holliman's son in late September. A month had passed, and cousin Benito was still crashing in the second bedroom. Maybe Benito was trying to tell him something, that it was time to build his own house, or at least get out of Benito's. The Arizona research job would come to an end in December and Benito probably wanted to come back to Santa Fe. "There were some differences between you and Molloy, I take it," Torres said.

"A woman."

"Well, yeah. I didn't think his foundation had turned down your most recent grant proposal." He was being deliberately provocative, and wasn't sure why, but his cousin didn't seem to notice. Benito was in such a morose mood that he noticed nothing but his own grievances.

"I knew Judith for so long. Money's the last thing I'd think would attract her. But what else can it be? The guy is such an uptight prick."

"Oh, *mi primo*. Straight talk is sometimes a favor, all right? Those two are so hot for each other that you go home and jerk off just relieve the tension after being with them." It was cruel. But his loyalties were to his friend Molloy, not to this cousin several times removed.

Benito sucked at his teeth nervously, was breathing hard. "He was hanging out with this *puta* last thing I knew. Then I heard his son hooked up with the *puta*, and the papa threw them both out. Nice people."

"Is that what they say?" Torres said. "People are so unkind. People don't know shit. Not that being hot for each other is the be-all and end-all of a relationship, but it's a nice foundation to build on."

"And you?"

"I see a woman here in town from time to time. Lucie Marchmont. It's pretty casual. You know her?" He was surprised at himself, how convincing he could be about that pretty casual.

"Don't know her well. She always seemed like a sweet, decent woman. A translator or something? Well, so. You're settling in." Benito was getting a grip on himself.

"The place—your place—is very comfortable." A silence, and Torres began to feel a variety of emotions. That Benito wanted his place back. Why else hadn't he gone back to Tucson? That he didn't want to give Benito his place back. That he had to, whether he wanted to or not. He took it head-on. "I'm on the road a lot, but I could move in with Mikey's family if you want your place back. I mean, I thought you just came in for this boy's funeral, but if you'd like to move back permanently."

"I don't know. I've been at the Ark the last few days—"

"The Ark?"

"The Archaeological Institute. I had an appointment there for almost fifteen years before I went to Arizona. They'd like me back. I'd like to come back, yeah." The violet eyes were taking the room in hungrily, a place those sensitive eyes had composed years ago.

This hunger of Benito's was less a surprise to Torres than the acute realization of how much he didn't want to give the place up. "I've been traveling light. It won't be hard to move on." In fact, it would be. He'd grown fond of Benito's little house, which, he had to admit, had been put together with some taste. Okay, he said to himself as he watched Benito survey the old house, its dark and crooked rooms, its folk art, its low ceilings, its coziness. It was time to move into a place of his own. Every architect he knew built a house of his own, usually his first structure. Torres had never done that, living in city apartments or on the road.

Maybe he should think of moving out of Santa Fe altogether. Where would he go? Back to one of the big cities, New York, Madrid, L.A.? The idea depressed him. He realized that he'd grown comfortable in the little town of Santa Fe—and he'd hardly seen the surrounding countryside yet, which everyone told him was well worth exploring. What little of that he'd seen was from the passenger seat of Molloy's car when they were on their way to fish or hike. Traveling from here was a big drag, but traveling was a drag from anywhere these days. Anyway, the calendar was relentless, an ominous reminder that he wouldn't always be on the road. This would be a fine place to end up, a town the right size, a comforting

Spanish heritage, with some serious sophistication—opera, chamber music, art. Pleasant weather. A lot of good people. If most of them had come here from somewhere else, so had he, and so what?

The people. He wanted to feed the connection with Mikey and his family. Plus, he'd grown accustomed to having a good friend in Molloy, maybe the first close friend he'd ever had, certainly the first close friend in his maturity. Something might yet happen with Lucie. He didn't want to blow that off so easily.

The truth was, he conceded, that he felt at home for the first time he could remember. No. He could remember. The first time since he'd left the island forty years ago. He'd come to like the feeling very much. It soothed, even sometimes blotted out, a constant anxiety that he'd felt everywhere else, that he'd assumed was a lifetime companion. He hardly thought about *los tiburones* anymore, though he knew they always glided silently, hidden from view.

"It wouldn't be until after Christmas. I've gotta wind up the contract in Arizona," his cousin said.

This unwelcome cousin, landlord, reality check, irritated him. "I don't suppose you'd consider selling?"

"If you like the place that much, I'm flattered, but no. It's not for sale."

Torres nodded. So Benito went back to Tucson with the understanding that Leandro Torres would vacate the house right after Christmas.

2

Stephen Molloy turned gratefully to his tutor that year. He spent many hours with this man, trying to understand the strange dream about the snake and the queen. His tutor's unwillingness to assign any single meaning—any easy meaning—to the dream gave him confidence that he'd chosen a wise guide for his quest, a quest he sensed went far beyond the interpretation of a single dream. Whatever else it meant, the dream had been a sign of the need to begin.

He did his assigned readings in mythology, and then in psychology, readings that invited him to interpret the dream—and some subsequent dreams—in a series of different ways. His tutor had said that the serpent in mythology had many different meanings, and the point of their exercise together was to find the meanings that mattered to Stephen, not some one-size-fits-all vulgarization of what was indisputably a significant eruption from his subconscious.

Stephen began the analysis by noting that his father's wife, an eminent mathematician, was often called "the queen." It had been her nickname when she was a teenager in Germany; a friend here in Santa Fe, who'd known her then, still called her *die Königin Judit*, Queen Judith, a joke. But still. His father called her, simply, beloved goddess, in English and in German.

"So maybe she's that figure." Stephen said to his tutor.

Perhaps. Karl Friedrich Gauss called mathematics the queen of the sciences. Suppose she is that figure. What do you think she might stand for?

"That I want my father's wife? For her age, an attractive woman, but—"

Perhaps it isn't sexual at all. Or that's only one aspect. Could it be something else, something more?

"That I want what my father has, regardless?"

But what's that? What do you think drew your father to her in the first place?

"She's very accomplished. Internationally famous for what she does. I picture her with big ambitions when she was a young woman, and now she's fulfilled them. She's very important in her world."

A kind of queen.

"Professionally speaking, a kind of queen. I hadn't thought of that. So he must have loved this part. I know he doesn't understand her work completely, though he's pretty smart himself. So maybe there's also a kind of mystery about her that he'll never quite get."

Does the figure in your dream strike you as somewhat cruel? The petitioner, the pleader, doesn't have a chance. She dispatches him quickly.

"Maybe it isn't cruel. Maybe he deserved to be dispatched. Maybe this was third strike and he's out. Maybe she doesn't suffer fools gladly. I can never really hear what he's saying. I don't even see him very clearly. He's just there. I think it's all about how she employs the serpent."

As executioner. As part of the sacred copulation.

"The sacred copulation. I never even heard that phrase until I heard it in my dream."

An old idea. Widespread in ancient times. Sacred prostitutes were found in Phoenicia, in the temples of Babylon and Ur, in Greece, even in some parts of pre-Christian Europe. The earthly embodiments of the great goddess, the feminine principle, of life itself. They offered themselves to men as exemplars of divine sexual joy. Important members of the community. The sacred copulation energized the mystery cults of classical Greece. The Roman lupercalia was a time of sacred orgy—sacred to the goddess Juno. There's even a Jewish tradition, expressing the relationship between God and his people in erotic terms. Some early Christian examples, too, but these were suppressed. Many eastern examples—Hindu, Chinese. But you saw all that in your reading. What did you take from it?

"For one thing, that the sacred copulation is meant to unite the sacred and the profane in deep ways. Our animal selves and our spiritual selves. The sacred copulation is supposed to be a way to attain a higher spirituality. It's also supposed to ensure fertility and the well-being of the people."

You sound doubtful.

"I'm just giving back what I've read. The whole thing's a weird concept to me."

Why weird?

"I grew up with the usual Western ideas about the profanity of the body, the holiness of the soul and mind, ne'er the twain shall meet."

But your readings suggest a different way of approaching that paradox?

"My readings. My dreams."

Maybe we should leave the sacred copulation for now, and think about the role of the executioner. Is he merely an agent?

"I don't know. In this dream, he's under the woman's control, does her bidding. In that sense, he's only her agent. This is a public death. A lot of us are standing around witnessing it. Maybe the victim is a martyr in that sense. But the executioner himself. Itself. Is the snake also sacred, carrying out an obligation, an act of violence, on behalf of all society? Like those Aztec priests who opened living human chests, ripped out beating hearts to offer to the gods on behalf of all the Aztec people? Like the guys who wielded the axe, or dropped the guillotine? Or is the snake just a flunkey? Just following orders? If it's only a flunkey, it's damned at the same time, then, isn't it? Is it an agent when it participates in the sacred copulation? Does it have a will of its own? Or is it only following the woman's orders again? I don't know. This doesn't seem to be going anywhere helpful."

My great-uncle was a bookbinder in London, a very fine one. He was once called to Windsor Castle to bind some of the books in the private collection. He discovered that the royal executioners were a hereditary group—special families known for their finesse as executioners. Royal houses used to bid for them, the way team owners bid these days for baseball players. It was difficult to do the job well. I digress. Forgive me. We'll come back to the sacred executioner after a while. But for now, let's consider the figure of the serpent generally, and then here, specifically. That might illuminate things.

"I liked getting beyond the usual Judeo-Christian idea of the serpent as evil, the incarnation of Satan, and thus temptation and sin. In other cultures, the serpent takes much more nuanced roles. Often positive roles. It can stand for the creative life force. Because it looks like a phallus, I guess. Then, since the serpent can shed its skin, it seems to be reborn—a symbol of regeneration, like you said. The serpent is often the repository of wisdom, too. It even symbolizes immortality, why they're wound around the caduceus, the staff sacred to healers."

Yes. Go on.

"But the thing that struck me the most was the serpent as a means to unite with the godhead. The mystical marriage between human and god. The sacred copulation, yes?"

Yes. Sometimes. But you've decided that this female figure is already divine, so why would she need to unite with the godhead? More important, why are you a witness? You say most people are forbidden to witness the sacred copulation.

"She's a queen. She's a goddess, true. The snake does her bidding, so it's her agent, her executioner. Her lover. But maybe it's her connection with the masculine principle. As a goddess, she's only half the equation, the female principle. There's got to be a god, some yang, in there somewhere, for balance. And I'm allowed to be a witness because there's some major lesson here for me; something my inner soul is trying to tell the everyday conscious me who'd overlook it otherwise. Look, I think this is possibly about the marriage between my father and his wife, and my task is to, well, serve it, take care of it, somehow."

Go on.

"You sound doubtful. Are you telling me that it's really me? That I want, I need, a queen of my own? That I want that connection with the godhead?"

Not for me to say. Describe the gallery where you find yourself witnessing the sacred copulation. Are you alone?

"No. There's maybe four or five of us, all men, watching. It's very solemn, not the least salacious, at least not at first. The gallery itself is—well, it reminds me of pictures I've seen of the Old Globe Theater in London: balconies on three sides of the walls; it's from there I'm witnessing the production below."

A theatrical spectacle?

"Yes, exactly. It's solemn but it's hugely—"

Arousing?

"Yes, arousing. Sometimes I consciously call that dream back just for the pleasure of it."

The attack on the World Trade Center and the Pentagon interrupted their studies for several weeks, and Stephen reported to his tutor that his sister had re-entered his life.

"If I have any dreams about her, I suppress them. She's very difficult for me."

How is that?

"When we were kids, we were everything to each other—when our father was away; when our mother was also, in her way, gone. Nikki and I had no one but each other. Maybe we became too dependent on each other."

Meaning?

"Since she got here, no, even before that, I was reading about the mythology of sisters and brothers. How sometimes they want to murder each other, how sometimes they want to, well, mate with each other."

Does this resonate?

"Oh, God. Yes. Yes, it does. A few summers ago, in Provence, we had a family vacation. One afternoon, she lay down next to me at the swimming pool. She was topless. It's European to do that, but it nearly fucking drove me nuts. She'd already happened to quote *Die Walküre*—not about the brother and sister who are lovers, but…in fact, a nasty crack directed at my father, comparing his hairiness to Alberich, the evil elf, the dwarf. I knew my father and his new wife were enjoying themselves upstairs in their bedroom. That was…provocative enough. The heat of the summer afternoon. The birds. The air was so heavy with the scent of lavender growing nearby. Heavy. Sexy. Lavender and something else that went directly to the brain. Nikki's nakedness. I wanted her in the worst way. My own sister."

And?

"Nothing happened. I kind of hinted about it to her, but she took offense. Rightly so. But see, we'd come closer to it when we were younger. Too uptight to do anything more than some teasing, tongue kissing, a little groping. We look a lot alike. We both look like our father, everybody says so, and yeah, I can see it. So to join with each other—oh Jesus, I don't even want to go there."

Family connections are complicated.

"No shit."

What else did you find when you looked at the myths of brother-sister lovers?

"There are lots of them. It's the privilege of divinities, of royal houses. In the myths, sometimes it's just the expected thing. Other times it ends badly. But I'd say the key thing is, it's another world. It distances the brother-sister lovers from this world, puts them somewhere else. But my sister arrived in Santa Fe two months pregnant, very much in this world. She says she isn't even sure who the father is. Right after she got here, she decided on an abortion. Sad to say, it was the right thing. Nikki isn't ready to be a mother. She's very fragile. Have I told you about that?"

Yes. And where are you in all this?

"Confused. I arranged for the abortion, took care of her afterwards. I'd take care of her as long as she wants. She could stay with me if she didn't want to stay with my father and his wife. But she went back to New York. Luckily, things are going very well with Daniella. It may be the only thing that is going well in my life. But right now, it's enough. It's wonderful. I connect things going well with Daniella with finishing my house. This phase of it at least. One of my father's friends is a well-known architect, maybe you know of him, Leandro Torres?"

Indeed.

"He likes my house a lot. He told me I could've been an architect myself."

Does that appeal to you?

"I don't know. I'd have to go back to school. Start from scratch. I haven't even completed my house. Just the first stage. I'll add on to it as time goes on. When I understand more."

3

Molloy is hiking at Tent Rocks with his friend—Judith's oldest friend—the filmmaker Ron Gresham. It's a hike only for spring or fall: in the summer the sun can fell you, and in the winter the snows are too high. They've already pushed it, hiking this late in the fall, almost the winter, but no storms are forecast. Molloy usually likes roaming among the strange volcanic formations of Tent Rocks, high outcroppings shaped like *horno* ovens in the pueblos, smooth and conical, though scaled for a race of giants. Sometimes they remind him of medieval jousting tents, tall and narrow; sometimes he thinks of the stone beehive huts that ancient Irish monks once inhabited. The hoodoos, the large rocks that cap many of them like party hats, usually strike him as nature's charming prank. Today he barely notices them.

He usually likes the ramble up the narrow canyon, looking out for the petroglyphs, feeling the rocks close in slowly until both shoulders are brushing against the red walls as he makes his way upward; the colors, ranging from lilac below to rich red higher, to the impossible blue sky above, all of them stopping him, to gaze with pleasure.

But today he likes it less. The walls of the slot canyon seem claustrophobic. Like a Serra sculpture, he thinks; calculated to evoke unease, apprehension. For a hundred feet above his head, their strata narrate a history of millions of years past, erupting volcanoes, flying tuff, howling storms, continuing catastrophes, B-movie special effects. Today these walls seem not a scenic wonder but a menace.

He tells himself it's because getting here requires a forty-mile drive from Santa Fe, but yields only a few miles of hiking, so it's a big investment for such a brief hike. He tells himself it's because he misses his dog. Dogs are prohibited from this area, but even if Wotan could accompany him, he'd have to carry his own water in a pannier on his back. Or harder, Molloy would have to carry water for them both. Most important, Wotan doesn't have a proper fear of snakes, and must be leashed. He tells himself he's got the blues because Judith is out of town, and he always has the blues when she goes away. Thus he picks the day apart irritably.

But he's comfortable with Ron, who is not a chatterer; who appreciates the value of simply walking together in silence. When they speak it could just as easily be English or German. Like Judith, Ron spent his adolescence in Germany and is fluent. Ron has always cherished Judith, understood from the beginning that Molloy and Judith were right for each other, and did his best to bring it about. Against Judith's stubborn resistance.

At the top of the canyon they scramble for a few dozen feet, then rest on the mesa, nibbling on sports bars, taking in the 360° views, the tent rocks below them now, Cochiti Lake blunt and unsubtle as reservoir lakes in the desert always are. The Sangres to the east, the Jemez range to the west, Sandia Peak to the south, and in the distant north, the San Juans in Colorado.

Ron breaks their silence. "*Wie geht's Königin Judit?*" How's Queen Judith doing?

"Fine. Fine as always. In Seattle for a meeting right now."

Ron skips a rock across the mesa surface, watches it disappear into the void. "With all due respect, Molloy, I'm picking up something that says she's not doing completely fine."

Molloy turns to Ron and scrutinizes his face, hidden in the shade of a wide-brimmed hat, his eyes invisible behind dark sunglasses. Ron has known Judith since they were fourteen or fifteen. His opinion counts for something. "Meaning what?"

"I won't say I read her like a book, because I can't. She's deceptive in ways I can't always tell. Or maybe I make assumptions I shouldn't." Ron's dark glasses survey him dispassionately.

Molloy feels his gut begin to churn. "She confides in you. She always has. Her health? Something I'd better know?"

Ron shakes his head, smiles slightly. "Health. That's always the first worry at our age, isn't it? No, she doesn't confide in me. Well, not much since she became a married lady. I don't think it's her health. But I've known Queen Judith forever, and—I don't know. I'm picking up on something."

"Ron, we're fine. We're just fine. Believe me." Molloy looks off to the north, where the sawtooth mountains bite into an indigo sky. He sighs. "Well, not everything's fine. But it's my problem, not hers." Reluctantly he gives Ron the brief version of the story of his father.

Ron simply nods. And then after some thought, "She might not see it that way. If it's your problem, it's hers too."

Molloy exhales. "And I still haven't told my kids."

Ron whistles. Molloy shrinks a little bit. How many people know now? Judith, of course. The McCarthys themselves. Have they told their kids? His half-brother and sisters? Char. Torres. Now Ron. Everyone but his own kids. He feels a rush of shame, knows this must be faced. The longer he puts it off, the larger, more unwieldy it grows. He resents Jerry McCarthy for this too.

"Any advice?"

"Not from me. I lost a father when I came out. I don't know if he's dead or alive, and don't care. My mother and I always kept in touch, but she's been gone these twenty years. How could a father do that to his son? If I had a kid, it would take a lot more than his sexual orientation to stop me from loving him. But Jesus, my father was in the movie business. It's not like he never saw a gay man in his life. But I come out, he freaks, and that's that. Maybe some issues with his own sexuality. Who the hell knows?"

"Sorry. I didn't know that." Molloy falls into silence, listens to the wind, watches the raptors wheel above them. "Nobody teaches you how to be a father. Not all of us are so good at it."

Ron snorts scornfully. "If that's what's worrying the queen, you can fix things. Fix things up for yourself, and she'll be fine too."

They start back down through the canyon, and Molloy feels as if he's carrying the striated stones of these walls upon his back. The mantra from his trading days comes back to him: Where can I fail? Where are the places I can fail? So many.

He calls Stephen as soon as he gets home, invites him to dinner. "Annamarie's making—well, I don't know what; it'll be good." That morning she'd promised him a favorite dinner. "Do I mope when she's away?" "You mope, Mr. Molloy." "Ain't no sunshine when she's gone. How about when I'm away— does she mope?" Annamarie had smiled. "Never ask a question if you're not sure you'll like the answer."

His son says, "I thought Judith was in Seattle."

"Yeah, she is. Can you stand having dinner with just me?"

Stephen laughs. "I'll bring a bone for *der Hund*."

Molloy disconnects, wonders what Judith has wondered to him: why doesn't Stephen ever have other plans? Wonders whether he and his son will have anything to talk about.

Annamarie tonight serves a proper autumn supper: a rich onion soup, salad, cheese, and fruit, which she knows is one of Molloy's favorite meals. Molloy understands that this too is part of the effort to cheer him up in Judith's absence, and is touched. Once Annamarie's straightened up the kitchen, she leaves as always. If it's just family, she'll find the dinner dishes in the dishwasher the next morning. With guests, who require their hosts' attention, the dishes are left on the table overnight for her to clear the next day. As soon as she starts her car, Stephen interrupts whatever he and his father have been talking about. "What's up, papa?"

Molloy stalls. "Up?"

Stephen could have asked sooner; he and his father have been speaking German to each other, not a language Annamarie knows. But her absence makes intimate conversation seem safer. "This is the first time you've invited me. Invitations always come from Judith."

That can't be possible, Molloy thinks. But maybe so. He wipes his mouth clumsily with a napkin, and can't think of any way to phrase this except plainly. "A few weeks ago, my father—your grandfather—showed up in my life."

Stephen sits back, disbelief on his face. *"Nicht zu glauben. Keine Scheisse?"* Unbelievable. No shit?

His father looks dubious about this American loan translation into German, shrugs, concedes. *"Keine Scheisse."*

"What brought this on? What kept him away all these years? What's he like?"

His father shrugs. "Likable enough, I guess. A professor of classics at some small school in Pennsylvania. A wife and three kids, my generation, my half-sibs; half-aunts and uncles to you, or something like that. Why now? Who knows? Wanted to evade child-support for a long time." Molloy pauses. "Which he did, in every sense of that term."

His son gazes at him thoughtfully. "How do you feel about all this?"

"I don't know. Well, yeah, actually, I do. In a rage. Can't forgive him."

"You were how old when he split?"

"I wasn't even born yet."

"Then blow him off, papa. Fuck him."

"Just like that?"

"Does aunt Char know?"

Molloy takes his time peeling a pear. "That's kind of interesting. Yeah, Char's known where he was all these years, more or less. It was Char who told him no, he couldn't see me; then finally yes, he could. My aunt the gatekeeper.

She isn't exactly smitten with him. The only reason she told him it might be okay is—in her words, at long last I'm happy enough to be merciful."

"Are you?"

"I'm happy with Judith, you know that. Happy enough to be merciful to a father who never did shit for me? That I don't know."

"Did you tell Nikki?"

"No, not yet."

"Would you like me to tell her?"

How has his son become the peacemaker, the bridge-builder, the smoother of difficulties in the family? "No, I think it should come from me. But thanks, Stevie. Thanks for even offering."

Stephen is hesitant. "She can be all cap-locks all the time. A handful."

For once Molloy doesn't calculate, plunges ahead. "I gave her the name of a shrink before she went back to New York, did she tell you that?"

Stephen nods. Brother and sister seem to have no secrets.

"Is she seeing him? Or anyone? Or do the health privacy laws forbid me knowing that?" This last is more sarcastic than he'd intended, and he's instantly sorry. What he wants to remember is the days just after 9/11, when they were human to each other.

But his son answers gently. "She's seeing someone, papa. Will it make the pain less? Can't tell yet."

"Whose pain? Dealing with your sister is like dealing with one big unsheathed nerve. You never know when you're going to touch the wrong part and get a shock for your blunder." He knows he's blaming Nikki for the misery he feels about his father.

Stephen strokes Wotan's head next to him beneath the table. No one is allowed to give the dog treats at the table, a rule Molloy made, but breaks himself regularly. "I went with her once or twice to a session with the guy she's seeing. I don't think it's the same guy you saw. I think your guy evaluated her, recommended a specialist." I think your guy evaluated her... To his father, this is a level of detail that says Stephen knows all about it, never mind I think. "Anyway, this specialist said—and I was there with Nikki when he said it—that she was born without, well, she can't seem to regulate her emotions. She overreacts; her enthusiasms are excessive; her downers way too down. But the worst thing is, she's always frightened of being left, abandoned. Eats at her endlessly. That's why she abandons us first."

"Oh, she is the drama queen. So is she bi-polar or what?"

"No, not bi-polar. It's something else. Hear me, papa. She gets hurt at the slightest thing. She genuinely doesn't understand that she has to share someone's attention, share someone's love, with other people. Yours, mine. Even Judith's. Look, Nikki's truly in pain, papa. We want to dismiss it, think it's drama-queening, because it comes across so over the top, so selfish. So manipulative. But that pain is really there. To be loving with her even when she's at her most unlovable..." He shrugs. "Maybe it helps. It's a disease, a disorder. She's on anti-depressants, but I don't know how much they help. So she's trying to learn how to regulate herself."

He's known none of this. "Did this doctor happen to say it was genetic, or what?"

"Could be. Either. Both. Not hereditary, but familial, said the doc." Stephen smiles. "How's that for complete bullshit? Maybe a smooth and stable family life might have kept it all in check. She did well at boarding school, you know that? The routine, the totally clear expectations. She wouldn't tell you that, only what a nightmare it was. In fact, it was very good for her. Outside school, beyond the school boundaries, the structure came apart—"

"With a mother like hers." He closes his eyes, listening to the bitterness in his own voice. "And a father. Jesus. At the airport she's telling me she can't possibly feel welcome here because it so happens I love my wife, and if I love my wife, that leaves no room for her. I was upset. I thought what the fuck, doesn't the papa have any rights to joy in this family? But I tried to hide that, tried to reason with her. Knew it wasn't going anywhere. It was all such a flashback to your mother." He studies his son. "Stevie. Thank you for going with her to that session, those sessions, with—whoever she's seeing. Thank you for seeing her through the abortion. Thank you for doing everything I don't seem to be able to do."

Stephen smiles slightly, nods. "She's not ready to be a mom. It would've made things even harder."

"Did you say that to her?"

"Oh, no; of course not. I just sat there and listened, let her figure it out for herself. Then it was not—easy, but easier."

Molloy reaches across the dinner table and takes his son's hand. "Thank you. Thank you for blessing this family with—who you are."

Stephen stares down at his cheese and fruit, too embarrassed return his father's intense gaze, as if this novel tenderness moves him beyond response. His father sees this, squeezes his hand, and lets go.

After a while, they get up from the table, sit down in front of the fire. Wotan settles beside Molloy and dozes. It's cold out, and the wind is harsh. A few weeks earlier, it seemed as if the cottonwoods along the Santa Fe River and above this house had absorbed the snows of winter, the male rains of the summer, the underground sources beneath, and miraculously transmuted those waters into magnificent fountains of gold, spraying over the road that follows the river, East Alameda. It's a sight that made Santa Feans stop in awe. But then, as if such tender gold can tarnish, they suddenly went drab. Tonight the trees will release the last of those drab leaves and start their own long sleep. Storms will thrash in the nearby mountains to the east. No night to be out if you can help it.

Stephen says, "I smelled snow when I was coming over tonight. *Unfreundliches Wetter. Ganz unfreundliches.*" Unfriendly weather, as the German weather forecasts have it. Completely unfriendly.

His father nods, and they keep silent, each man lost in his own thoughts.

After a while, Stephen says, "Papa, how do you feel about me meeting my new grandpa?"

"Do you want to?"

Stephen has thought it over. "Yes, I do. I won't if you're opposed, but I'd like that. Our family is—so small. You, me, Nikki, Char. Judith of course, but she's yours, not ours, not really."

Molloy can't help the irritation in his voice. "What is it with you kids? Some stranger swans up to the table at the last minute to claim the grandpa seat and he's yours in a way Judith isn't? Forgive me if I just don't get that." He suddenly remembers Ron's warning on the mesa top this morning. Something is eating at the queen. Let it be only this.

"Papa, don't. That just came out wrong. Judith—God knows Judith is very special. She asked me to stay here, keep her company, sort of guard her, I guess, the night of 9/11. Imagine guarding that fierce lady. Imagine that she thought she needed it, wanted it. But she did, she wanted my company. She said it was part of being family. I loved her for that; I was touched. It was the first time since—I stayed in my old room. Weird." Stephen stops. "I'd have loved Judith if only because she loves you and makes you happy. I'm learning to love Judith for her own sake alone. Grand lady. But I'd like to meet my grandfather. It might explain some things."

Wotan's ears have gone up at the tone of Molloy's voice. Molloy stares at the fire, sorting his feelings. "Explain some things? Like what?" Stephen declines to answer, and anyway, Molloy's mind has darted elsewhere. "What's the matter with me? The last few years with Judith have been the happiest of my life. That's saying less than you'd think. Happiness was mighty elusive these past few decades." He stops. "Jesus, Molloy, such a whine. Let's try that again. By any measure, I have recently been a happy man. Now this bastard comes in and upsets everything. I resent it, that's all."

Stephen speaks carefully. "Would you consider it disloyal if we—we wanted to get to know him?"

His father waves the question away without answering it.

"Do you feel you owe him anything?" Stephen persists.

"Nothing. He poked my mother in the back seat of a car one night—to quote your great aunt Char—and that was the full extent of his paternal legacy."

"What do you think he owes you?"

"Nothing he can ever repay. Nothing. Ever."

"Why do you think he came here, then?"

"I don't know. Nine-eleven, maybe. It cracked open the frozen seas in everyone, didn't it? You go to work one day in an utterly routine way. Maybe you haven't had enough sleep. You're getting your first coffee of the morning. You're looking at the stuff on your screen you gotta take care of today. The next thing— you know for certain you're going to die in half an hour, and you must choose between roasting to death or jumping out of a window. All this out of a clear blue sky. No warning. I can't get my head around it, and neither can anyone else. But, we think, it could happen to me too. Tomorrow. The next day. Just as I'm sitting down to an ordinary day. Twenty-four hours later people plastering my picture on telephone poles, missing. Milling around the morgue, says a friend who lives nearby. So what have I been putting off? Meeting a son face to face I never knew— but know all about? He tracked me over the years, through Char. Maybe other ways too. But that son is a perverse kind of guy, a skeptic, and wonders, oh yeah? If I'd been—less than what I've turned out to be, would he have come looking? Where was he when he was needed? And who needs him now?"

The fire is dying, and Stephen gets up to put another few logs on it, stir it to life again.

Molloy groans softly. "Stevie, Stevie. I don't like these words. I don't like the man who's speaking these words. Judith says being stiff-necked just gives you a pain in the neck." He puts his hands over his eyes to stop the throbbing. "I wish this hadn't happened until—" He stops. "Go make friends with him, Stevie. I won't stop you. And I'll call Nikki in the morning and tell her."

"Papa, this doesn't have to be so hard." More silence, except for the wind, the fire crackling, Wotan sighing in his sleep. "Did you ever look for him?"

Molloy thinks about that—his hopes raised that he was genuinely understood by the old priest who taught him German and Latin, only to be dashed. The love, near-idolization of his father-in-law in his first marriage, who then suddenly died. A small number of other older men he's looked to and been disappointed by. Slowly he nods. "In some ways, never stopped. You're always looking for a father when you've lost him so early in your life. I used to have conversations with him in my head when I was nine, ten, eleven. I'd forgotten all about that until I started seeing Ross, the shrink I recommended to Nikki." Molloy sighs. "I don't know. I did know my uncle Jack, kind as he was, was not my father. Even if they gave me his name. He was like the furniture—comfortable, sturdy, always there. That sounds ungrateful, what with all he did for me. Housed me, fed me, clothed me til I left home. I first picked up a hunting rifle with my uncle. He taught me how to fish. I learned my way around a workbench from him. I owe him a lot. I loved him, Stevie, but in some fundamental way, we never connected. He was not my father. Not the father I imagined for myself. Snotty as that sounds." He shifts uncomfortably, suddenly remembering his uncle at his first wedding. The bride's family had invited sophisticated guests from the New York art world; his uncle was from the steel mills of western Pennsylvania. Molloy had been embarrassed. Then ashamed. And ashamed for being so. "You lost a mother," he says to his son. "Do you ever look for her?"

"I was already in college when she died. It's not the same. But yeah, in some ways I think I look for her. Or for the mother I wanted instead of the one I had."

And I long for the past I wanted. Instead of the one I had. After a moment he says to his son: "But I never actually sent out the dogs for my father, you know what I'm saying? It wouldn't have been hard to find him, name change and all. But I didn't. Now he's come to me anyway." He's in pain, having learned to know himself better than he once did. "Do you know the Delphic precepts, Stevie? Let's see if I can recite them. As a child, learn good manners. As a young man learn to control your passions. In middle age be just. I'm trying to be just, son." He exhales wearily. "Stevie, what I'm dealing with is a crippling case of envy. I envy my own father because he did just what he wanted to do in life, and wasn't stopped by any worries about collateral damage. I envy my wife because she did the same, and is so fucking good at it that she's a scientific star, lives for her work, lets me come along for the ride. I love her for it too; you understand that. She loves me. But I envy her. And I envy my son because he never had my struggles." He stops, then goes ahead, his voice dropping to nearly a whisper. "I've been very hard on you, more for that than anything. For that, I hope you'll forgive me. Maybe you have something of your grandpa in you, Stevie. You are what you are, and you say screw the world if it doesn't love that." He looks at his son, that softened version of his own taut face, black kinky hair pulled back in a ponytail as usual. Molloy laughs gently. "At your age, mine was down to my ass."

"Your ass? Oh, the hair."

"A white kid with dreadlocks. But only for one summer. When I came back after traveling in Europe, I had to shear it off. I was on the floor of the stock exchange. No hippies allowed."

They keep silence some more until Stephen speaks at last. "My struggles aren't yours. Nothing to forgive." Another long silence. "What are the rest of the precepts?"

His father thinks for a moment. "In middle age be just. In old age give good advice. Then die without regret."

"Did you—" Stephen starts to ask, but Molloy's phone rings.

"Excuse me, let me take this. Judith said she'd call tonight." He glances at the caller ID. "No. Lucie Marchmont. Ehhh, icy Lucie can wait." Puts the phone down. But the mood's broken. Stephen says he needs to be moving along, thanks for dinner. And everything. They embrace, pat each other on the back in the way that men do who've bared some little part of their souls to each other.

"You biked? I'll run you home. It's colder than a witch's tit."

"No, papa. Thanks anyway. The ride up Canyon Road gets the cobwebs out."

"I'll call Nikki first thing tomorrow. You kids sort it out the way you feel best. Talk to him; don't talk to him; add him to your Christmas card list; your choice."

"Do you want to know?"

"Oh, yeah. I want to know. I might even…have reconciled myself by then. We can all have a big family Thanksgiving dinner together."

"Papa." Stephen is amused, admonishing.

"Pedal safely, son. You've got that reflector vest?" Stephen nods. They stand at the front door. Molloy puts his hands gently on both sides of his son's face, holding it, staring at it, this face that is almost his own, except so much younger; and softer, kinder than ever his was, at that age or any other. Thinks of the man who passed on his features to them both. "I love you, son. Let me know you. I need to know you. Can you come back tomorrow night?"

He thinks he can see tears rise in his son's eyes; feels his own throat tightening. Stephen pulls away, turns his head. "Same time? Maybe we can talk over—some more things. Give me some good advice."

His father opens the door, and a cold wind hits them, as good as winter. Stephen would go now, but Molloy stops him for a moment. "When you were little, I'd hold you on my lap to feed you. I was a family joke. I could hardly finish a sentence without stopping to kiss your little head. Your grandmother thought it was something to laugh at. I wonder why she did? Men love their babies. Well, some men. Me, I did." He hugs his son goodbye awkwardly, lets him go.

When Stephen is gone, Molloy sits down to review the evening, but his head is beginning to ache again, and he can't think. How come the only headaches he ever gets are from his family? A new definition of the sandwich generation. He calls Judith's number, gets her voicemail. "It's me. I finally told Steve about his new grandpa. He was pretty cool about it all. No drama. Well, drama, but not about that. Tomorrow, Nikki. Since that will be major drama, I'm going to take a pill and go to sleep, much as I'd love to hear your voice. Ron and I went to Tent Rocks today. He thinks—well, it can wait 'til I see you. Hope the meeting's a good one. Good night, beloved goddess. You're my everything."

4

Mikey was in front of his screen, sorting pensively through data for patterns. Every few days he found it useful to stop and think about the big questions he was trying to answer before he dived back into the details. The facts: A majority of people on Planet Earth now lived in cities. Cities. Always the great engines of innovation, of wealth creation—and also the main source of crime, pollution, and disease. This planetary crossover from mostly rural to mostly urban had profound implications for social organization, for land use, and patterns of human behavior. But what, exactly?

At his fingertips were data for hundreds of cities across the U.S., Europe, and China—inventories of gasoline stations, laundries, electrical power usage, patent awards, total wages earned—all this and more. These could be plotted against data for city populations. Underlying patterns were emerging, regardless of what era you studied, regardless of where the city was, regardless of cultures. Maybe a universal model of urban agglomeration was possible. A model whose features were shared by all cities, wherever and whenever. A grand, unified predictive theory of cities.

Urbanization was a fact. That it might be a big answer to sustainability was not yet a fact, though that looked promising. Per capita, people in cities used less energy than small town dwellers. When people moved into a city, their birthrate dropped immediately to the replacement level of 2.1 children per woman, because if children were an asset in the rural areas, they were a liability in the city. A city's density seemed to have many other environmental advantages that hadn't yet been quantified. If they could be, then urbanization would be an easy sell. Human beings loved cities—the action, the rich experiences, the opportunities. They flocked to cities gladly, despite the problems. The agrarian village was boring, stifling, and impossible now to sustain.

But—cities could fail. Where was that mysterious point, the collection of intersecting trajectories, where cities stopped succeeding, and started to fail? Where they no longer added value to society, but subtracted from it? The ruins of collapsed cities lay all over the planet. What did they have to teach?

Okay, certain features of cities grew in mismatched cycles, fast and slow, short and long. Successful cities maintained equilibrium among these cycles. But if one cycle failed to keep up with, or outstripped, the other cycles—if, say, population exceeded available food and clean water—a city failed. But how to quantify these failure points? How to predict them?

Fundamentally, he and his colleagues were looking for mathematical and predictive theories of human social organizations—in particular cities, but maybe other social organizations too, like firms—the precise way biological organisms could be described. Like organisms, cities consumed resources and energy, produced structures, created waste. The temptation to draw parallels was irresistible, had been forever. *Leviathan* by whoever it was—Hobbes? Nasty, brutish and short?—wasn't that a metaphor for society as an organism? Seventeenth, eighteenth century. Scientists and philosophers had taken it up again and again, but only at the level of metaphor. No one had been able to construct a rigorous model that worked—though policy decisions were often made as if one existed. Forget about help from the social sciences. For them it was the differences, not the similarities, that mattered in human social structures. Not generalizations, no matter how useful.

Specifics. Was there such a thing as a city's metabolic rate? If you could nail down a metabolic rate for cities, could you then predict resource demands, environmental impacts, growth trajectories?

His colleagues at the Institute had been looking at heart rates. An animal's normal healthy heartbeat was all over the map—complex variability was a hallmark of a healthy heart, and of other organs in the body, which, it turned out, spoke to each other at different oscillations. Lose complexity and variability, and you had a biomarker for physical failure. Was there something analogous in city rhythms? That was worth chewing over. Suburbs—too little complexity, too little variability, hence their failure? Maybe.

City size? In nature, elephants and mice did not have the same metabolic rate. The bigger the organism, the slower the metabolism, at predictable rates. The bigger you are, the slower your networks deliver resources to your cells, so your life runs more slowly: you live longer, grow more slowly, have fewer offspring, use energy more efficiently.

But unlike organisms, city metabolisms actually sped up as they got bigger. Elephant cities had faster metabolisms than mouse villages. With each doubling of a city's population, each inhabitant was, on average, 15% wealthier, 15% more productive, 15% more innovative—and 15% more likely to be prey to disease, or victimized by violent crime. This held regardless of where the city was, or the decade you examined the data. It was a fact with no biological counterpart. Cities created problems as they grew, but they created solutions to those problems even faster.

Biological organisms had built-in governors for size limits, but cities, it seems, did not. The population could keep growing indefinitely. Thus, as big cities got richer, rich cities got bigger. In theory, anyway. In reality, a boom was sometimes followed by a bust. Over time, all the cycles got shorter and shorter. The seeds of innovation were also the seeds of crisis, unless people made major adaptations to reset the dynamics. At some point, civilization would need the equivalent of an industrial revolution every half hour to sustain itself. Then the whole thing would collapse. Was it possible for a civilization to stop growing, maintain a developed society, without collapsing? Economists had never bothered to answer that question. They probably hadn't even thought of it.

He went to the men's room, got some coffee, found a small breakfast pastry that Adriana would not have approved of. He ambled around the coffee room eating the pastry, finished it, walked into the corridor and sauntered past open offices. The usual gestures of procrastination.

The real world. Land use problems were horrific and would only get worse. In a few decades, urban populations would more than double in the developing countries, land occupancy would triple. Would the fifteen-percent rule still hold in those cities then? How could you stabilize the human population, raise living standards, and achieve long-term balances between human needs and the planet's environmental limits? Head-breaking challenges. Opportunities, in the eyes of optimists. All the impacts were open-ended and would require continual adaptation. Environmental implications were ambiguous. More stress on natural environments in some cases; in others, emerging conditions for sustainable solutions.

It was all so very far from being worked out. But if and when it was... Here might be a path to sustainability. Optimize the size of cities, both in area and population, regardless of their outward form. Here might be a way to save the planet.

Mikey longed to find a point, a moment in a city's evolution, when deliberate intervention might lead that city into a future where open-ended innovation, and rising living standards, were compatible with the preservation of the planet. His intuition said that such a point existed, could be identified. His computer models didn't yet show it.

He went back to his own office, stared at the screen. Consider empiricals. In the United States, most old cities had been hollowed out after World War II, white citizens fleeing to the suburbs, places that required four times the energy per capita as cities—thank the car, thank heating and cooling in stand-alone dwellings. In the suburbs thirty percent of disposable income went into transportation; in the city it was less than ten percent. In the suburbs, mothers (or someone) must act as chauffeur-slaves to their children's schedules. Old people who couldn't drive were marooned. It was a social calamity, surely one reason why cities were being re-inhabited by the children and grandchildren of those who'd fled to the suburbs. Harlem, for instance, was on the verge of having a black minority, since so many non-blacks had recently moved in. So if you wanted to encourage—manage—this return to the cities, how did you do it without pushing the speed of the urban growth past sustainability?

Another problem. How did you keep the talent-exporting small cities like Pittsburgh, like Buffalo, like Cleveland, from stagnating, collapsing altogether, sucked dry by the allure of the talent-attracting big cities like New York and Los Angeles? It was almost always the young people who migrated, leaving the old behind them. As for China, despite all the legal restrictions, the migration to the cities was, at least in the short run, a big headache.

He leaned back in his chair, scratched wax out of his ears thoughtfully, stared at his computer and tried a new metaphor.

Was it useful to imagine the city as a large-scale social information engine, producing innovation and wealth (as well as waste and pollution) out of growing population, energy, and other resources? You could plainly see that as cities grew, they devoted more of their parts to innovation, forcing their citizens either to leave, or adapt with new roles and behaviors. Why did idea-based economies scale up so quickly? Was it the network of contacts people made with each other? That could probably be computed.

And then, the rest of the planet. Between the two billion humans living well, and the two billion in abject poverty, some three billion barely got along. Any political scientist could tell you that this was a recipe for disaster. Any humanitarian would deplore such a fact, and wish earnestly to change it. Yet studies of happiness showed that it hardly correlated with wealth.

He'd heard speculation that the next political organization might be a network of big cities aligned across national boundaries, running alongside the nation-states that had been the big players for so long. The cities already had connectivity with each other; they already had so many common problems and challenges that non-urban parts of their nations didn't face. Such alignments made some sense. And some argued that what looked like cesspools of poverty in the slums were really people getting out of poverty in a hurry. Maybe.

All these thoughts, stimulating, contradictory, paradoxical, wandered through his head in a disorderly way. He sipped his cooling coffee, hoping, trying, to make sense of everything, separating facts from hypotheses, reality from idealized models. Or at least trying to see what facts might polish up his models. What was he overlooking? Was there a different way of looking at the facts?

He'd spent time studying—both in person and the numbers—the informal mega-cities that were growing up spontaneously outside old, known cities: outside Mumbai, Nairobi, Lagos, Caracas, Rio, Port-au-Prince. Officially, they were illegal squatter-cities, denied sewage, water, and electricity. They lacked public spaces. Security was nearly nonexistent, the drug trade and other forms of crime flourished. Rebar, steel rods, protruded from the roofs, a sign that construction—mostly amateur—was still underway. Developers had no interest in them, or in building anything for the poor, for that matter. Property rights were obscure. Everything was under the legal radar. When earthquake or flood came, they were wrecked. But still, in these shadow cities, as they were sometimes called, a billion people on the planet lived. Their size, density, and mass were without precedent.

The life in them! Mikey had been in Rocinha, an illegal neighborhood in Rio, and rocked at two in the morning to music he hadn't heard since he was a kid, all the while scarfing down café food—café food!—while he did. No one expected to find cafés in a slum, but small businesses thrived there. So did extortionists. He'd scrambled over garbage piles in Mumbai that once would have nauseated him—they were hardly savory now—but he wanted to watch children pick up anything that was reusable, resellable; the kids recycling with a vengeance. He himself was thrilled by the liveliness of these places, the reason why a billion squatters worldwide had declared that they were never going back to their villages. They were pedestrian-friendly, produced less trash and consumed fewer resources than formal cities.

History said that, on a smaller scale, these same grim conditions had prevailed in medieval cities, especially in Europe. Nineteenth century cities had to deal with squatters too, sometimes by banishing them, as in China, or by regularizing them, as in Rio, or by shooting them, as in San Francisco. All cities faced great challenges, again and again. But the life in them, Mikey said to himself. The life in them. Too bad about the disconnect between international aid agencies and the people on the garbage piles. High-minded projects came and went, sucking up money but never succeeding. The land and legal issues were extreme, and impossibly tangled. But the life in them.

He sighed. His father was saving the world one building at a time. He always admired, sometimes loved, what his father did, but it was handwork, one-offs. Mikey had larger ambitions. He intended to find a grand unified theory of sustainability, cities and urbanization at its core. On a planet growing ever more dense with them, this would be how humans met the challenges that faced them.

He didn't have a bulletproof model yet, and if and when he did, neither he nor the rest of the team wanted to make the same mistake the global change guys had: just present the facts, and everyone will act rationally. Hah. But the exhilaration of pursuing such a goal—it got him up in the morning with joy, and kept him on his chair all day, oblivious to nearly everything around him. And damn, his coffee had got cold.

5

Mikey's phone rang, distracting him. Caller ID said St. Vincent's Hospital. The kids? Adriana? In his panic, his visceral fear, he could hardly press a button to talk. He was already praying without realizing it.

Not his children. Not his wife. His father had been picked up on I-25 and helicoptered to the emergency room. Could he come at once? "Is he alive?" he cried to the impersonal dispatcher. Alive, sir, but badly injured in an accident.

Leandro had been scheduled to go to the airport in Albuquerque this morning, very early. Black ice? Did he fall asleep at the wheel? The visceral fear spread, gripped his shoulders, his arms, as he shot down Hyde Park Road, got entangled in traffic in town, and sped out the Old Santa Fe Trail to St. Michael's Drive, to the hospital. "Stay alive for me, papi," he repeated aloud, as if saying would make it so.

His father was on a gurney, being prepared for surgery. The IVs seemed to branch out of him, as if he were growing strange flowers from his arms and trunk. Multiple fractures, including nasty breaks in the leg, shoulder, ribs; contusions; a mess. Miraculously no brain damage, so far as could be told, but anything could happen. The architect was floating in and out of consciousness, but smiled at his son, floated off again in a cloud of pain-killers. The state police had pulled him out of his overturned SUV. Luckily, he was wearing a seatbelt. Alone, so the phone wrangler had gone on ahead or hadn't left Santa Fe yet.

The accident had taken place this morning early. No one yet had a police report or any details. His father's ID hadn't been established until this afternoon. Then his New York office was called, and the office referred them to Mikey at the Institute. If Mr. Torres would have a seat, and allow Intake to fill out some forms. "Let me call my wife, please, first." Who cried out, and offered to come over, but what could she do? She'd need to find a sitter for the little one, and someone to pick the older one up after school. He promised to call when the surgery was over.

He grappled with the financial questions. "I'm sure my father is fully covered. He's a well-known architect with a big firm, a worldwide firm; many employees. He wasn't carrying a card?" But Mikey didn't know which medical plan the firm used. They should call the New York headquarters tomorrow during eastern office hours. They could try the L.A. office, still open. He sat and waited.

After a while, he called the Institute to see if he could get Judith's mobile number, but with that, got only her voicemail. The Institute receptionist had told him that Judith was at an out-of-town meeting. He wouldn't leave a message that way. He thought his father and Molloy were close, but didn't know that for certain—his father hadn't talked about his friendships much. Should he try Molloy's office anyway? Was such a call presumptuous? He imagined saying to that aloof man, my father's critical, and that strange, remote man replying, your father who? If only he could've talked to Judith. He pushed himself past his shyness, tried Molloy's office, but got another answering machine: the staff is unavailable right now, please leave a message. What time was it? After working hours. He didn't leave any message. He didn't know Molloy's private number, nor how, without Judith, he'd get it.

The flatscreen TV was going endlessly, though mercifully, without sound. Adriana had once said she feared having to wait at a hospital for a fatal diagnosis, all the while she waited, the inanities of game shows in her ears. It occurred to him that his father had once had something going with the translator, Lucie Marchmont, the woman they'd toured around Santa Fe's New Urbanism projects. Whether that was still a going concern he didn't know, but he found her business number, left a message. He thought he might throw up, and checked to see where the men's room was, just in case. Hospitals must be used to that.

He was desperate. The universe was full of people, and not one of them was available to help him. Did God also have an answering machine? Your call is important to us.

As he paced in anxious solitude, he tried to sort out his feelings. Deeply afraid above all. Yet edges of hope surrounded the fear. He'd never doubted how much he loved his father, and this moment was no exception. But he also understood that their relationship was fraught with ambivalence.

Adriana had sometimes suggested gently that Lee's arrival in Santa Fe was an opportunity for Mikey to make some peace with his father. Peace wasn't needed in the sense that they quarreled—though they often argued about professional things. But peace in that father and son needed to understand one another better. Yes, the man was larger than life, but he was still a father, a real human being, not the bloated parade balloon that appeared in the media. Not the monster Mikey saw—and sometimes fled from—in his dreams. Adriana had hinted, but did not say, that a release for Mikey from that paternal thralldom would be a very good thing. She didn't have to say any of this explicitly. He knew what she meant, and she was right. But.

As they'd rolled his father's gurney into the OR, the docs had been cautiously optimistic, but Mikey was a realist. His father might die—on the operating table or hours later. Things would forever be unsaid that should be said. He ached about that. His anxiety rose. Yet underneath, he admitted to himself, alone under the flickering TV screen, that Leandro's death might be delivery, severing once and for all the paternal domination. He'd be free. He felt a momentary guilt for wanting that. For needing it. He did not wish for his father's death, no. Couldn't release come some other way? Adriana had said he only had to walk away. Not from his father, whom she liked and he loved, but from the enthrallment. If so, he didn't know how. But release—he needed release from that overwhelming personality and its endless, often thoughtless, demands.

An hour passed, and then two. A world without papi, without Leandro Torres, was impossible to imagine. Then there were practical matters. Papi's firm. Papi's commitments, buildings already underway, buildings the firm had competed for. Who would oversee all that? Who would wind it down, if winding things down became necessary?

A nurse came out of the operating room to reassure him. Though the procedure was taking longer than expected, he shouldn't worry. So far, it was going well. A great surge of relief washed over him. He studied that surge: real, unambiguous. No, he didn't wish for his father's death. He only wished for—his own life. There was no reason why he couldn't have that. He'd had it for a little while, before Leandro burst into Santa Fe.

At the end of the third hour, a surgeon came to him. From the smile on the surgeon's face, Mikey guessed things had continued to go well. His tension ebbed again. Whatever the surgeon said to him about Leandro in the recovery room, procedures they'd had to do, repairs, problems to look out for in the future, the time it would take for recovery—none of this really registered. His inability to take it in must have shown on his face, because the surgeon switched to school Spanish.

Mikey shook his head. "*Hablo inglés*, I speak English. I'm just— overwhelmed. So very relieved. Thank you. Thank you, doctor. Do you know who my father is? I mean, not that it matters. Every life is precious to a doctor, every life is precious to itself; I know that. But my father is well-regarded, my father is internationally famous, an architect." Mikey felt himself begin to weep, pulled out a handkerchief and covered his eyes.

"Jesus! Leandro Torres!"

His eyes covered by his handkerchief, Mikey for once missed that look of recognition he'd seen so many times in the last few years, the response people had to being touched by celebrity—by more than celebrity, by a peak of human accomplishment. It was an expression that simultaneously made him proud and slightly annoyed. "Yeah, yeah. Sure," the surgeon went on. "I just didn't put two and two together. Gotta tell him how much I love his work. Last summer my wife and I saw the chapel he did in Barcelona. Brilliant work. We took pictures, even. And side by side with the work of Gaudí—every bit as innovative. In years to come, people will be making pilgrimages to your father's work the same way. Excuse the gushing, please, Mr. Torres. It was such an experience. I'm glad we could pull him through. Proud, in fact."

The surgeon sat down, put his arm around Mikey's shoulders. "Mr. Torres, your dad will be fine in the long run. Especially if he's diligent about physical therapy. The internal organs were undamaged. Brain function seems to be just fine. Well, later on, a little arthritis in that leg, maybe the shoulder. The ribs will heal. But he won't be sitting at his computer for a while. Even longer before he can get on a plane and supervise his projects. He'll be ready to come out of recovery in a little while, and then you can talk to him. Someone will come and get you."

Mikey's phone rang, and the surgeon waved: answer it, I'm outta here.

Mikey was expecting Adriana, was surprised to hear the slightly anglicized voice of Lucie Marchmont. He told her everything. "I guess you and my dad are friends, and I needed to tell his friends, you know? Do you know Molloy's number? I think they're friends too." He was irritated with himself for being so tentative. Confused, actually. Whatever the relationship between his father and Lucie was, he knew perfectly well that his father and Molloy had become good friends.

Lucie said she'd call Molloy. "Mikey, are you okay yourself?"

He exhaled. "I bet I sound clobbered. Yeah, I'm okay, just a little wrung out. More than a little."

"Do you have anyone with you? I'll call Molloy, and then I'm coming straight over."

Which is how Leandro Torres swam up from general anesthesia and found both Lucie and his son standing beside his bed. *Hola*, he said softly. *Hola, mijo. Hola*, Lucie. They went with him as he was wheeled to his room. A private room. The surgeon must have reassured Intake that Leandro Torres could pay his bills. As they left the dozing Leandro, Lucie said: "You can't drive. We don't need two car accidents. I'll take you home; your car will be fine here in the lot for a day or two."

Mikey was astonished that it was dark outside. Somehow time had warped. He didn't know whether he was more tired or hungry. "Lucie, thank you for this. Adriana would be here except for the sitter problem. I sometimes wonder what if something happened to her..."

Lucie was brisk. "It wasn't much; I'm glad I could do it for you. I left a message for Molloy, but he hasn't called back. Judith's out of town. I don't know what your father has told you about our relationship, but it's a friendship, nothing more. I won't be able to take on—well, you know."

Mikey shrugged. He wasn't even sure what Lucie was saying, and was too tired to care. "I'll see him tomorrow for a while, but that's all I can promise. I've got a pressing deadline just now."

When Mikey got to the hospital the next day, he was happy to see his father awake, eating jello. He was doing okay, his father said, but still sleeping a lot, the drugs probably. He lay back on his pillows, looking exhausted. His face was abundantly bruised, one eye mostly closed. Since his father's eyes were usually half-closed anyway, Leandro this day looked like a pirate.

"Eeeee, papi, you look like you've been through a revolution."

His father snorted. "It's just beginning. Has the office called?"

"Well, yeah. Everybody's hoping you'll get well soon, and all that."

"No, I mean about Beijing. About Dubai."

"Nobody's thinking about business right now, papi. You gotta get well."

"You'll take over for me."

"You don't need anyone to take over. It won't be long before you'll be up and around."

"There are reasons," his father said irritably. "Just do as I say. Working with the Chinese isn't like working with Westerners—they expect more and faster. Much more. Much faster. No time for farting around."

"Papi, I've got my own work to do."

"Please don't tell me your little pissant computer programs can't live without you for a few months. Just don't tell me that. We're talking serious business here. We're talking great work, great structures, great architecture. Not some hopeless, stupid, completely trivial shit you do which no one understands anyway, whatever it's supposed to prove."

Mikey stepped back, stunned. The trauma, the drugs speaking. "Papi, you need to rest. Has Lucie been in to see you? She sort of mentioned she'd come today."

His father was silent.

"Well, papi, I don't want to tire you. I'll say goodbye. Adriana and the kids send their love."

His father raised an index finger. "Alonzo knows you're the man. He'll bring you up to speed. Call Chen in Beijing. You can tell him I had an accident; he probably already knows from New York, but say you're going to be conveying my orders, no, my instructions, that I'm okay but need to rest. I want you to go to L.A., get a briefing from Preston. Then I want you on site in Beijing. Tell Preston, tell him—oh fuck, this really hurts. Get the nurse and tell her I need another shot, or pill, or whatever the hell, okay?"

Molloy stepped into the room. "Oh God," he said. He looked at Mikey in sympathy; down at his friend in anguish. Whistled. "Friend, you did quite a job on yourself. Sorry I couldn't be here sooner. I just got word an hour or so ago. How are you doing?"

"Okay, okay. I just asked Mikey—Mikey, *¡por favor!*" He suddenly groaned in pain. "*¡Ahora!*" Please! Now!

"You need a bedpan?" Molloy asked, all practicality.

"No, he's catheterized," Mikey said. "He needs pain meds. I'll get the nurse."

Molloy stood beside the bed, shaking his head. "What a mess, old friend. But you're alive, that's what matters."

"Yeah?"

"Lucie called to tell me. She didn't want to leave a message on my voicemail, so I didn't hear about this until now. I think it'll be a week or two before you're up to poking her again, but otherwise you'll be fine."

"Eventually."

"Eventually," Molloy agreed. He watched his friend's battered face as it contracted in pain, hoped the pain meds would arrive soon.

"My fucking son refuses to take over for me."

"Take over for you? You don't need anyone to take over for you. You mean your firm?"

Torres spoke through gritted teeth. "You above all people should know what it's like to get to the top and have something so fragile—" he groaned again in pain, "so fragile, so ready to break into a thousand pieces if you turn your back, you've worked your ass off for, people ready to snatch it out of your hands if you don't watch your back, and your own kid says no, I've got other plans. Not even sorry, I've got other plans."

Molloy changed the subject. "Look, when they release you, Judith and I want you to come to our place to recuperate. Annamarie will cook great things to get you back on your feet. You'll be very happy there, okay? You can't stay with your kids; they don't have the room. Anyway, you need peace and quiet. This isn't a request, Torres, not even a suggestion. It's a fact. It's the way it is. We've got wireless. You can yammer all you want at the people in your firm all over the world. We'll arrange a room for the phone wrangler."

The nurse arrived with a hypodermic. "They took him off the morphine drip too soon," she said, as if she were speaking about hospital bureaucrats. Torres was already trying to stifle his groans, and Molloy looked away, embarrassed in some vague way to see his friend so helpless. He noticed, however, that Mikey hadn't come back with the nurse.

Mikey had, in fact, gone home to eat a late dinner in his small house on Santa Fe's south side. Adriana had kept it warm for him, and though he wasn't hungry, he was doing his best to honor her efforts. "He's really pissed at me, Adri. He thinks I should just drop everything and stand in for him at Torres International LLC, AIA, whatever, and run things until he can take over again himself."

"And you said?"

"*Mierda*. What do you think I said?"

"Since he's pissed, I presume you said no."

Mikey nodded.

Adriana snorted. "Does he know about that other offer?" Mikey's reputation had grown to the point that a large international real estate planning and development company with headquarters in New York had offered him a job as chief of research, his task to synthesize and consolidate all the new work that was being done in green planning, apply the newly emerging principles of his urban research to the scores of projects the firm had underway all over the world. As deeply tempting as it was—the opportunity to see his ideas tried out in real life, not to mention the very big money the firm had offered him—he had talked it over with Adriana, and eventually said no. It was the kind of job, they agreed, that he should take when he could no longer generate the new ideas that were driving his own research right now. He never told his wife, nor anyone else, that the hardest thing to say no to was not the money, not the power. The hardest thing to say no to was the magic of living in a big city again.

"Should I have told him?"

Adriana smiled through her fatigue. "I don't know, Miguelito, *mi guapo*. Lee might have been more understanding if he'd known you were already turning down that kind of money to follow your bliss."

He stopped, a fork on the way to his mouth. "You mean he'd have more respect?"

His wife looked thoughtful. "More respect? He respects you, Mikey. Would he have matched that offer? No. Money has never driven your papi. He knows it isn't going to drive you. But the man knows the meaning of money, and it wouldn't hurt for him to know, in fact he'd be impressed, that somebody else thinks that much of you." She shrugged. "Maybe. I don't know."

"Are you saying I should've agreed to do this?"

"No, I'm not saying that at all." She laughed. "You under your papi's thumb? You as his mouthpiece? You taking the heat when things don't go according to plan? No way. A disaster. You'd be suicidal. Or homicidal. I'm very glad you said no. You keep your distance from Lee, baby. I know he's your beloved papi and all, but it's in the interest of everybody's mental health. His included. He's a survivor. The firm will survive too."

6

After five days, Leandro Torres was brought back to the compound, settled into one of the stand-alone guesthouses so he'd have some quiet, and began the slow process of recovery. Private duty nurses were engaged to get him up and around, keep him bathed and massaged. He had daily visits from a physical therapist. Annamarie was instructed to hire an assistant for all the additional cooking and housekeeping. After some thought, Molloy put Alonzo, the phone wrangler, into a hotel room closer to town and told him that after a week, he could begin to see Leandro once a day, and once a day only. Other visitors came and went.

Mikey was the first. He arrived an hour after the ambulance had brought Leandro to the compound, and wasn't surprised to find his father dozing—the pain meds did that to you, the nurse said. He was happy to see his father well taken care of, the room exceptionally pleasant, bright, and airy, with Navajo rugs on the brown tile floors, local art on the walls—bultos and retablos of various saints, and over his father's bed, a strange Queen of Heaven who looked remarkably like the late Duchess of Windsor. A piñon fire was going cheerfully in the corner kiva fireplace, more for psychological than thermal defense against the gray November day. A small table held a vase of flame-colored roses. Mikey buried his nose in them. Unlike the usual florist flowers, these had a wonderful scent. It was the kind of room Mikey thought he'd like to recover in, had he been sick. He looked at his father's sleeping figure, and then tiptoed out of the room until Leandro's ever-sleepy eyes opened alertly.

"What's happening at the office?"

Mikey stopped, turned back. "Papi, I haven't been in touch with them except to tell them you're out of the hospital and resting, recovering nicely."

"Where the fuck's Alonzo?"

"Molloy told him to stay away this week. You don't need—"

Leandro turned to the private duty nurse. "*Adelita, por favor. Mi hijo y yo tenemos que hablar un momento.*" My son and I must speak for a moment. He turned back to Mikey, continued in Spanish. "You're going to have to go to

Beijing. You need to keep an eye on Chen. Something's up there, and I don't know what it is but I don't like it. My gut tells me—"

Mikey's voice rose. "Papi, no. It ain't gonna happen. I'm not leaving Santa Fe. I've got work to do here. I'm sorry I didn't make myself clear the first time you mentioned this."

Torres rolled his eyes. "Make yourself clear? You made yourself clear, all right. I thought by now you'd have had a chance to reconsider, see where duty lies."

"Duty? Papi, my duty is to my wife and children, and to my work. I love you dearly, you know that, but I can't do your work for you."

"You won't? You refuse to do this for your own papi?" This with theatrical disbelief, the most monstrous affront he'd ever suffered.

Mikey assented silently.

"Get the fuck out, then." In English.

Mikey shrugged, nodded in resignation, and left the room. Outside the door he wondered if he should have taken Adriana's advice, told his father that this wasn't the first, even the best offer he was turning down, decided against it. When he came back subsequently, which was seldom, he always brought the children with him so that serious conversation was impossible. Adriana too came alone once. When she left, Judith saw the pretty young woman in tears. "He's being a flaming asshole," Judith said to her husband. "That sweet loving family, and all he can think of are his damn buildings?"

Molloy sighed, having had his own periods of such single-minded obsession.

Mostly Torres slept, but awake, he brooded about work and the unsatisfactory email he was getting from China, work stoppages in Dubai. But sometimes his thoughts drifted back to his childhood, the presidential palace, the *finca*, how after a couple of years of boarding school in Connecticut he'd gone to Spain to join his parents at last. He'd hardly had a chance to get accustomed to yet another new home before he was sent away again with his little brothers to boarding school in Switzerland. He could still see the streets of Madrid as they'd been then, the buildings sooty, in slummy disrepair; the low-wattage bulbs that barely lit staircases; an unreliable electrical grid anyway.

Madrid had been flash-frozen thirty years earlier (maybe before that, since he reckoned no construction, no physical rehabilitation, had taken place during the 1920s either) and if Spain had been spared World War II, nobody had repaired the damage of the Civil War. No one seemed to have the ambition to clean up the buildings, the streets. He'd never seen so many servants, not even in the old presidential palace at home. It was as if, decades earlier, an evil spell had been cast upon the land and waited to be lifted. In these memories, even the sunshine, which should have been warming, cheering, was a cold and imperious searchlight that was the very ally of the Guardia Civile. If you stood in the freezing light, they found you and demanded your *carnet de identite*. If you lingered instead in the freezing shadows, you were all the more suspect. He was in his teens by then, and Madrid's social order—its clear boundaries between *obradores*, workers, and *aristos*, the upper class, boundaries not to be challenged; its stern demarcations between women and men, between good people and bad, not to be challenged either—comforted him after the personal chaos of the last few years. Still, he knew that the rest of the world was beginning to erase those stern demarcations, sometimes slowly, sometimes disruptively.

And always beneath the comfort he took in such strict boundaries was the debilitating fear he'd felt for the first time when that presidential plane touched down at Idlewild. His perpetual little Christmas present, he called it bitterly. His father had foolishly trusted and then been held hostage for a year by a near neighbor in the Caribbean. What would happen when his father was no longer persona grata in Spain? For the sharks that cruised beneath the surface, the fear of them that geysered up regularly, told him that he could rely on no one, on nothing. Trust no one. Never forget that *los tiburones* glided perpetually, waiting. For no reason at all, by no act of their own, the whole family could suddenly be re-labeled, moved from the category of good persons to bad, with all that this implied. This was the way of such governments. He knew that now; knew his father had once headed one of the worst of them. So the flock of servants, all of them desperately poor, you could see by their rags, owed no loyalty to his parents. For a few pesetas any one of them would gladly denounce these rich foreigners they labored for unwillingly.

Later, when he came back summers as a university student and then as a newly licensed professional, he hesitated to drive his battered little car out of the city. The rebel Basques, the ETA, could easily spot license plates from Madrid, and were careless about whether they kidnapped for ransom or only murdered worthless Madrileños. Though he opened an office and for many years kept an apartment in Madrid; though he married, procreated, and buried both his parents there; though the great surge of rebuilding in the 1990s, underwritten by the EU's welcome euros, had given him some of his best opportunities as an architect, it was a fact that he was never genuinely at home in Spain.

But where was he at home? he asked himself as he drifted through drugged dreams and in and out of a haze of consciousness. Not the island where he'd spent his first eleven years. Not New York where he had his biggest office. God knows not Miami, where the stew of exiled Caribbean factions just turned his stomach. Santa Fe, where he'd come to be with his stubborn son? Nowhere. Or maybe only at home in his fears.

He'd come to an orderly household, and he liked that. Aperitifs appeared beginning at 6:00 (though Judith worried over him taking even a glass of wine when he was using such strong pain medicine) and dinner was served at 7:30. He was told his hosts often took aperitivos in their own rooms, and suspected a lively *cinq à sept.*

He didn't know the half of it. A few months after their marriage, Judith had said to Molloy: "You must visit between five and seven. That's the hour when a lady is changing from afternoon to evening clothes, and admits only her most intimate friends. Then you can go home to that hideous old hag of a scientist you married."

"Ah," said Molloy. He closed his eyes, smiled. "It was an arranged marriage."

"*Mon pauvre,*" she said. "By the two families?"

Eyes still closed. "No. By the Three Fates."

She shrugged. "Between five and seven, chilled champagne will always be ready. Your favorite music."

"But I have so many favorites."

"I'll know. Debussy or the Dead; Phish or fado. It's my job to know." He shook his head, laughing softly, and never worked late. But while Torres was with them, Molloy was always showered and into the living room in time for a glass of wine with his friend before dinner was served.

Often other guests arrived to share the meal too. Torres guessed that Molloy and Judith invited these as entertainment, distraction for him. For the first two weeks, he couldn't stay at the dinner table longer than an hour—he needed more pain pills; he needed to be back in bed. But gradually he could stay up and be sociable longer; he stopped sleeping after every meal, including breakfast, though he continued to nap late in the afternoon. The messages flew from his laptop to China, Dubai, New York, and Los Angeles, though never to his complete satisfaction. Sometimes, as he was drifting off to sleep, he'd see Molloy in silhouette leaning against the door jamb, a benign, comforting presence, silently checking on him, looking after him, wishing him well.

Late in the morning, when she was finished with her hardest work, Judith would occasionally look in on him. With her he talked about his design software. She was thoughtful. "Why don't you try a knowledge-based system? You know, an ontological model—grab those relationships, properties, all the factors that drive the design process. All that knowledge you have in your head ought to be captured in code so you can manage it better. That kind of model could set you free in ways that'll surprise you. I'll help you."

"Is this even possible?"

"Oh, I don't know," she said breezily. "Maybe we can get a joint paper out of it if it works."

Molloy's son Stephen was often at dinner. Torres had grown genuinely fond of him, perhaps because Stephen obviously admired him, wanted to know all about the practice. He wondered why he hadn't had a son like Stephen, someone he could have trusted with the responsibilities of a complex international enterprise. Stephen was mastering by hand the details of building; but he also had a surprising grasp of larger issues that Torres had quietly tested him for, with questions and answers that Stephen took as architectural discussion, but which was Torres's way of probing. He'd pushed, to discover that Stephen had majored in art history in college, which explained some things, though not others.

Lucie too would sometimes be one of these guests, charming without being the least approachable. It was only when yet another guest, a woman he hardly knew, had the sense to get up from the table the first night she was there and help him across the courtyard to his casita that he realized sadly just how distant, how elusive, in contrast, Lucie was. He'd been told that this other woman, who guessed what he needed without asking, who helped him as a matter of course, had formerly run one of the leading galleries in Santa Fe. She'd lost a young son to leukemia and divorced a ne'er-do-well husband almost simultaneously, he'd been told. He supposed that she was so instinctively helpful to him because she'd nursed her son through to his death. Furious as he was at Mikey, he knew he could not have faced his son's death.

Nola wasn't an attractive woman to him. She was too thin, too intense, perhaps too needy-looking. He longed for the lusciousness of Lucie's womanly body, but Lucie had made it clear to him that she was willing to be friendly, no more. Gave no sign that she understood he might still want what she called benefits. He wondered if he looked to her not like the hot, world-famous architect he'd once seemed, but like a beaten old man. That hurt. As he drifted in and out of sleep, he dwelled on the nights they'd spent together. When he'd exhausted his re-imaginings of their erotic pleasures, he asked himself what they talked about. She'd told him some things about herself. He'd got all weirdly huffy about it. Wasted so much time in his sanctimoniousness. Lucie, I forgive you, he wanted to say. She refused to give him the chance. Anyway, who was he to forgive anyone anything? Lucie, I'm sorry.

Nola, on the other hand, got livelier as they got to know each other, talked to him about art, admired some of the same artists he admired, had visited many of the places he'd lived, where his buildings were; asked penetrating questions about his designs and the process he'd taken to arrive at them. She occasionally came to visit during the day too, and brought him little presents, perhaps a book about an artist they'd talked about a few nights earlier, or a box of chile-laced chocolate, which he loved. Once—and he blessed her for this—a set of St. Petersburg watercolors, a selection of brushes, and a block of Arches paper. The first painting he did was of his room, which he presented to Molloy, who had it framed and hung in the very same room. "I'll get you clay when you're a little stronger," she said. "Then you can start sculpting again."

One afternoon when he was feeling better—which he recognized because he was feeling so persistently horny—even scrawny Nola looked good to him, and he asked her to sit on his bed, so he didn't have to speak so loudly—it tired him, he claimed. He then did his frank best to seduce her. How he would have consummated the act with leg brace and arm sling he wasn't quite sure, but he wasn't precisely thinking ahead. She seemed amused, but would not be lured. He lay back on his pillows in defeat, and they talked about other things.

"Tell me how you work," she said.

"Very slowly, Nola. You think all these structures of mine have popped like rabbits out of hats, but in fact I've been working on them, generating designs, since I was a kid. I always drew and sculpted. In my teens, my twenties, things got serious. Only now do I have the chance to see them come to life. That's why this accident is such a catastrophe for me. This is my moment. It will pass so quickly."

"You don't come to each site, each commission, afresh?"

"Yes, of course I do. So many things to excite the imagination. But part of my work is to recollect the issues I worked out long ago. Sometimes altogether hypothetically, before I was able to build a thing. Bring them to new opportunities if they're appropriate. But it's my life's work—my whole life's work, this process. A seed is planted in my twenties, and I have no idea what to do with it. Not until it germinates maybe thirty years later, looking very different from how it once looked. The early stuff, sketches, sculptures, grew out of the images that surrounded me in my childhood. But they've developed over time, partly in my unconscious. Partly because I've learned new techniques, I mean material techniques, to realize those early pieces and the issues they raise. Partly because a few good teachers guided me in what to look for. How to look. I might have arrived at those solutions anyway, but the guidance has saved me precious time. Do you understand that I don't do one building at a time? I'm always designing, always developing. Sometimes I have the opportunity to bring them to life."

"Which structure has given you the most trouble?"

He laughed wryly. "They all do. And they're all self-designing, autonomous, in a very important sense. Sometimes I just need to get out of the way."

"Are you thinking of problems, of issues, of structures now, here, while you're recovering?"

"All the time. Well, not when Javier, the physical therapist, is having his way with me. Then I can only think of my own poor battered body and the pain."

"Is it all right here?"

Torres exhaled. "Paradise. If Molloy told me he wanted to become my patron and let me live out my life in this *casita*, I'd hardly be able to say no. It's a beautiful place. The company is stimulating. Food and wine excellent. Like living in a renaissance palace. Why would anyone want to be anywhere else? I'd set up a studio in that little structure over there. The old chapel, I think it was."

"You don't find it all too—historic?"

"I don't hate history, Nola. I just prefer to make some of my own."

She smiled. "I know you're friends with Molloy. Do you see much of Judith?"

He was thoughtful. "They're both gone during the day, of course. I see Stephen, because he'll come over sometimes in the afternoon to keep me company, the way you do. Sometimes he stays on for dinner. Molloy and I watch sports on the weekends together. But Judith? Truthfully, I seldom see Judith except when…she has an interesting idea for my design software. She offered to help me with the coding, and once in a while she does, but she's busy with her own projects."

"That's an amazing love match."

"Something to envy. Do you know my cousin, her old boyfriend?"

Nola nodded. "Benito's coming back to town after Christmas. I've always liked your cousin. *Muy simpático.*"

"He isn't yet over his broken heart."

"Who is?" Nola said sadly.

Molloy discovers something about his wife. One night when she fails to arrive punctually for aperitifs, he calls her phone, realizes he's woken her up. She's at her little house on the goat path, and promises to come home at once. That night, in their rooms, he probes a little.

"How much time do you spend at the old *casita?*"

"Oh, it's a quiet place to work. I don't usually fall asleep there, though."

"My love, is the invalid's presence a bit much for you?"

She smiles. "Not the invalid. I like Lee; you know that. But the invalid's retinue is something else. Huge, noisy, and non-stop. Alonzo with the phone messages. The medical people. FedEx. His social visitors. If one of the ladies who waits on him doesn't start putting out for him pretty soon, I expect we'll be having housecalls from the local bordello. I don't blame him. It must be incredibly boring being cooped up all day. Then this morning in the middle of all the usual, Marshal drove his van into the compound and began unloading pictures with a couple of his helpers. Time for the monthly change, get out the drills, the ladders. When Bethany arrived to do the books, I just lost it."

"You're in retreat."

She nods.

"We could cancel Thanksgiving and just go away by ourselves." They've long ago made plans to rent a chalet in Colorado where Stephen and Nikki will join them skiing for the long weekend.

"No, no. Let's not disappoint the children. I've heard Stephen mention a couple of times how much he's looking forward to this. He even hinted he's bringing someone, maybe. But if you and I could go a few days earlier, or stay on a few days after they left..." She turns to him gravely. "Jack, I miss you so."

He grabs her to him. "Oh, my dear love. Whatever you want. Why didn't you say something sooner?"

7

They get in a few runs before the lifts close, then go down the mountain to a nearby hotel for dinner. The music is deafening, talk of any kind impossible. They leave after the starter course and drive back to their chalet, a log cabin palazzo that in its scale, and self-contradictions of mock simplicity and extreme luxury, of pretend intimacy and total impersonality, is vulgar enough to make them both laugh.

"Olde Scottish Hunting Lodge décor. Olde Scottish humbug. Maybe I better re-do the New York place after all," Judith says.

"I wish you would," he says with a grin, and gets a fire going. He settles down beside her on the couch. "Damn, skiing turns me into a zombie after dinner. Anytime you want, I'm ready for the rack. Sorry that bringing Torres to the house turned out to be a problem for you. I didn't mean for it to drive you to your little house. I really wasn't thinking."

"Let me just say—oh, let me say so many things. One thing is, don't apologize about Lee. One of the million things I love about you is your sheltering soul. I love, I admire, how you take care of things—of me. I've never had that. I never even thought I'd like it. Turns out I love it. I was just watching you light the fire, thinking of that, thinking of how you fashion such a benevolent nest around me. Cosset me. So when you extend your sheltering soul to your children, to your friends, well, it's only natural. It happens I have an unusual need for solitude, that's all. Luckily, there are places I can go for it."

He yawns happily. "I'm forgiven?"

"Nothing to forgive. But my love, before you nod off entirely, there's something else I've wanted to talk to you about."

He comes awake abruptly, pulls her to him and kisses her temple.

"Actually, I haven't wanted to talk about it, but here we go. You like it about me that I earn my living by my brains."

"A delightful gratification to me," he murmurs.

"Jack, that moment a few months ago, where I couldn't even follow the proofs that I did in my thirties—it really scared the hell out of me. I don't mean I'm teetering on the edge of Alzheimer's or anything. At least not for a while yet.

But that—" she hesitates, searching for a word "—creativity that I relied on all my life. I used to surf it. It seemed inexhaustible. When I gave a talk, I'd always end with the open questions I was hoping someone in the audience would solve. Guys would say quietly afterwards, I save the best open questions for my students. I'd say—with an arrogance that now takes my breath away—there's always more where that came from. But now? There isn't more. If it's not altogether gone, it's sure as hell drying up." She stops. He says nothing. "I know I can fake it for a few more years. Guide the post-docs, do committee work, maybe even mine some of the old stuff. But the originality, that great impulse of creativity that never let me down. It's all but gone."

"How do you feel about that?"

"Two ways. In one way, glad to lay the burden down. Relieved. Let the youngsters do it; that's what youngsters are for. In another way—well, I hardly know how to say this." She takes a deep breath. "I wonder about you—whether this will make a difference between us. No, I don't wonder; it's absolutely eating me. I couldn't blame you if it did, but—"

"Judith. Oh, Judith." He watches her with a look that's only partly amused. "What do you reckon the half-life of your intelligence is?"

"What?"

"You know—how long will it take you to lose half of what you had when we married? Two weeks? Two years? Ten years?"

"Be serious."

"I am. Ten years?"

"Let's say for argument's sake—"

"Fine, and you lose half of that ten years later? And then ten years after that? Dear, sweet woman, we'll both be into senility by the time our trajectories cross. If they ever do. I can't believe you've given this a moment's thought." He laughs softly, shakes his head. "Do you really think I love you for your advanced degrees? Judith my love, what do you take me for?" He sees tears in her eyes and kisses each eyelid; relief on her face. "An evening for true confessions. When I sold my firm—well, I let it go for a bunch of reasons. For one thing, I was in hot pursuit of some bluestocking babe in Santa Fe, New Mexico, and I didn't even know her yet. All I had was a newspaper clipping." He sees she smiles. "Couldn't do that from Manhattan, could I?" His voice lowers. "A life that was nothing but making money—it repelled me. Always repelled me, but now I had enough to do something about it. Unlike a certain snooty Santa Fe bluestocking babe, I thought having a comfy cushion wasn't such a bad thing—"

"Jack, don't."

"You can be embarrassed about that for the rest of your life, okay?" He squeezes her to him. "But listen. The whole financial world was passing me by. At least I got programmed trading, even if I couldn't write the algos myself. I can even understand the new, new thing, high frequency trading, they call it, where my program is a fraction of a second faster than yours, and I clean up on the arbitrage. I can't do it, maybe, but I get it. But Jesus, there are products out there that just defy my understanding. Real shit is being sliced and diced and mixed with quality stuff, in the hopes that the quality stuff makes the shit stop stinking. I don't think it will, but I'm in a tiny minority. I'm just too dumb to get it. Credit default swaps. Cat bonds. Derivatives this, derivatives that. The Dow is a roller coaster, the dips are worse than ever, like when the dot-com bubble popped last spring, and now 9/11. But the world keeps spinning.

"This old man keeps thinking the whole thing's gonna come crashing down to stay, hello 1929. It's the lowest in years, but it isn't yet the Great Depression, and all the sages say nah, that's impossible. It is? Then the brave new financial world is beyond me. Poor old Jack Molloy better step off, because this is no country for old men. So I park our assets—ours, the foundation's—in the grownup equivalent of postal savings accounts, and if it isn't on growth hormones, it ain't gonna go away, either. And oh yeah, I'm doing a little shorting, because why not? During the dot-com fiasco, I shorted a bunch and cleaned up. My gut knew the laws of arithmetic hadn't been repealed, no matter what the talking heads were saying about the New Economy. But, see, on the whole, it isn't a world I could play in now. Am I sorry? Sure. My vanity has taken a major hit. In the days of big swinging dicks, I was one of the biggest; I took chances that if they'd gone south would have landed me in cement boots in the Hudson. Or the Rhine. Or both. My creditors, my clients, could've taken turns." He pauses. "So I've moved on to other things. And I sleep nights."

He can hear her breathing, finishes up. "My love, I'm happy to talk about this more. Talk about you. About me. But tonight I've just got to go to sleep. I can't even face the hot tub. Did you decide which of these major bedrooms, or ballrooms, or whatever they are, is ours?"

When Judith skis to the chalet late the next afternoon, she sees happily that Annamarie has arrived, along with Wotan, and provisions for the long holiday weekend. Another four-wheel-drive is parked nearby, Stephen's. He'd told them he was driving up; when he arrived depended on the weather.

Wotan greets her with delight, and she stops to scratch his furry head. "*Platz*, Wotan, *platz*! Delirious animal, wait until Alpha Dog gets here. Then you can be demented with happiness. He's still on the slopes," she adds to Annamarie.

"No, he's soaking in the hot tub," Annamarie says.

"How did you leave Mr. Torres?"

"All things considered, he's fine. I let Heather go for the weekend because Mr. Torres said he was going to spend it with Mrs. Holliman."

"Mrs. Holliman? Not Lucie Marchmont? Well, well." And she and Annamarie share a knowing smile. "Talking about art, I guess. Stephen?"

"They're getting changed, hoping to get a run in before the lifts close."

"They?"

"He brought a friend. Daniella. Sorry, I don't remember her last name." Another shared smile. "Oh, and Miss Molloy called. She's in Denver, but the rental people told her I-70 is very congested, so she might not make it in time for dinner."

Nikki Molloy does make it in time for dinner, and takes everyone by surprise with her appearance. The black hair that forever stood straight out from her head has been shorn into a striking cut that frames her face, emphasizing even more its fine bones. She's in New York City black, and to Judith's eye, has lost some weight. Nikki has never been plump, and Judith finds the weight loss a little worrisome. She only says to her husband how very beautiful Nikki looks now. Molloy agrees. "An amazing transformation. My little girl has grown up."

Nikki is up the next morning to take a few runs with her father. On the lift he says pleasantly, "You look better than ever."

She nods her thanks. "How do you like Daniella?"

"She seems—very nice. We've hardly had a chance to talk. They only arrived yesterday."

"Stevie had another girlfriend before her, did you know that?" Molloy did not know that, doesn't know if he wants to know much of anything about his children's love lives. "She was a post-doc at the Institute. She dumped him because in her eyes, he was JAWS."

"Jaws?" Then Molloy remembers. Just Another Wealthy Shithead. The Santa Fe curse. Judith had once thought him so.

"I told him he was trying too hard to replicate his papa's Judith." Molloy clears his throat, says nothing, grateful for the goggles that hide most of his face.

"He was really bummed about Sonia. The post-doc. Luckily he met Daniella when they were together on some project to re-plaster an old building in Santa Fe. It's a kind of volunteer group that helps restore historic buildings. Torres got him started on that. Daniella's doing a residency at UNM's hospital. It's amazing she got the entire Thanksgiving weekend off. She must have been working 24/7 for months to get that."

"And you, radish? How is it for you?" her father asks on the next ride up.

"Bad news for you, papa. I'm painting again."

"Why is that bad news? I'm glad you're doing what you love."

"You were pretty brutal about my other work, frankly. Anyway, after 9/11, I realized, I knew, that I wanted to try—do something else. Capture, express, the truth underneath ordinary appearances. Unfortunately, as you know, that truth can be very ugly."

He declines to comment on any of that. "How's it going?"

"It's hard, papa. Very hard. I'm not sure I'm getting it right at all. But that's what I'm doing." They're at the top of the lift, and part, which leaves Molloy to think about what his daughter has said as he skis alone down the mountain. He skis alone because Nikki is the most serious and accomplished skier in the family. If she wants to—and today she seems to want to—she can leave them all behind, flying out of sight as gracefully as a bird, swooping over moguls and ridges with infinite mastery.

In fact, Nikki has cut off and gone back to the house, which is well up the slope. She finds Judith, her brother and his new girlfriend still sitting around the breakfast table. "Slugs! Papa and I have already done two runs." She calls to Annamarie. "What time is dinner?" From the kitchen, Annamarie says: "Four o'clock, sort of. The lifts will be closed by then. Didn't want to cut into anybody's ski time."

"I should get going." Judith stands up.

"We're thinking of going back to bed," says Stephen. "Daniella's exhausted."

"All I ask is that you be up for dinner," Judith says. "You can't imagine how much your dad has looked forward to this, the whole family around the Thanksgiving table. It means the world to him. So be here."

Molloy has looked forward to it inordinately. As he takes in the table that night, he's gratified beyond his fondest expectations. His son is apparently in a relationship that matters to him. His daughter seems more serene, and indeed more beautiful with her closely cropped hair, than he's ever seen her. His wife, the dear love of his life, teases him gently and lovingly in ways the family appreciates, and is always ardent enough in private to arouse him from the catatonic state he falls into after a hard day of skiing. He'd been amused and a little puzzled by her worry that things would change between them if her professional fervor declined. Doesn't she understand his love for her is the simplest and most straightforward thing about him? No, not true; it isn't. But tonight when they're alone, he'll remove those doubts. Find ways to reassure her. He's hers, come what might, and knows it. She should know that too.

For a brief, morbid moment he considers what might have happened if he'd lost one of these in the twin towers. He feels a rush of gratitude that, unlike many families, they are together, intact. In some recess of his mind, he feels a kind of accounting taking place—he has been bereft for so long in so many ways: maybe the universe is compensating him at last. At the perimeters his father sometimes appears, ghostlike, but when he allows himself to think about that, he wonders if Judith isn't right, that he should simply walk away. Who would know? Who would care? Who is this man to the people around this table, his own family? He pushes it even further away and falls into the family banter, at times feels misty at the joy of it all. He has waited so long for this.

Later, he hears Nikki arguing good-naturedly with her brother: "The pole plant is the first part of the new turn, even if you haven't started the turn yet. And you really don't get up front enough on your boots, dude. That's why you can't ski as fast as I can. Ski second, eat snow."

"We may snowboard tomorrow," Stephen says, eyeing his father, who hates snowboarders, who's promised to hang up his skis once and for all when the last slopes open completely to them.

"Hooligans, the lot of them," Molloy says mildly.

"Papa, you'd have been snowboarding at our age too. Don't be so old school." This from Nikki.

"Is he old-school purist, or just retro?" Stephen teases.

"Classic," says his wife. "You know what they say: date the snowboarder, marry the skier."

Molloy shrugs in mock defeat, sits back and absorbs the wonder of this dinner.

He hears Judith patiently explaining Zeno's paradox to the young people. "Achilles and the tortoise are in a downhill race," she says. "Achilles takes pity on the tortoise and gives him a hundred meter head start. So Achilles and the tortoise begin, and pretty soon, Achilles reaches the point where the tortoise started. But since the gun went off, the tortoise has been moving too, very slowly, to be sure: a tortoise on skis is a spectacle—he's gone about ten meters, let's say."

"Guns in ancient Greece?" Daniella asks mischievously.

Judith laughs. "Okay, since the flag dropped. But Achilles must now do those ten meters. Meanwhile, the tortoise has moved slowly on again. Achilles has to reach the next point where the tortoise was. Okay, but the tortoise has again moved on. In short, whenever Achilles reaches the point where the tortoise has just been, there's further to go. Logically speaking, Achilles can never catch up with the tortoise—"

"You call that logic?" one of them cries.

"Why didn't they just set up a race and see for themselves?" Molloy asks.

"A tortoise on skis?" Stephen asks. "You can already see the problems there."

Judith answers. "Well, okay. It was originally a footrace. Not much skiing in ancient Greece. But for a mathematician a simple empirical test doesn't work. At some point, you've got to take quantum physics into account, and those distances are so small, measurement would be pointless. Uncertainty looms. Children, it's no secret I adore your papa, even if his mathematics is pre-Cambrian—" he protests with a wounded cry "—and his knowledge of physics is about on par with a fourteenth century peasant." The children roar; even Molloy has to laugh. Quantum physics eludes him. "No, hear me out. If you want to make an exact mathematical formulation, and you lack the right tools, the whole thing is a mathematical paradox. Mathematicians went nuts trying to solve it. You could do it in terms of a discrete sequence of values, but getting at the continuum—the nineteenth century French mathematician Cauchy finally—be quiet, you ignorant brats, and listen to me—"

"Have some more wine, Judith," Stephen says soothingly.

They get up a game of Texas Hold 'Em after dinner, with Judith claiming she plays so seldom that she needs a crib sheet for what the cards mean. "Three of a kind is three of the same number, or the same suit?" Groans all around the table. Further groans when the chips are finally counted, and she's won—not by much, but she's won. Cries of "Hustler! Swindler!"

"Never underestimate a New York girl," she says, laughing.

"Or a Santa Fe mathematician," her husband says fondly.

But the day after Thanksgiving, a major storm threatens, and Stephen and Daniella decide they'd better go. Daniella must be back in Albuquerque by

Sunday afternoon, and can't risk being trapped in Colorado by a blizzard. Molloy calls the county airport. If they leave within the next couple of hours, they can be sure of getting away. He insists the couple fly to Albuquerque by air taxi. He'll get Stephen's car back to Santa Fe after the storm passes.

"Mr. Molloy, I'm so glad you understand," Daniella says gratefully.

He's charmed by her, her freckles, her ponytail, the fact that this child is nearly a full-fledged surgeon. "Molloy, my dear. Everyone just calls me Molloy. Actually it's very nice to have someone in the family with some professional urgency."

She colors at his assumption that she's part of the family already, which Stephen covers up with officious suitcase business. Molloy himself will drive them to the airport.

The house is suddenly quiet. Even Annamarie has the day off and has gone snowboarding with friends in Vail. "Shall we take a few runs ourselves?" Judith says to Nikki, and they go out. They soon lose track of each other—Judith is a good skier, but all the Molloys are superb, and Nikki soon leaves her behind. On her third run, as she skis past the house, she sees that Molloy has come back. She turns sharply, nearly falls, but gets to the front door in one piece.

"I saw you were back, babe. They get off okay?"

He nods. "I waited until takeoff."

"I won't ask you how much this is costing."

He grins. "Good. Don't."

"It was worth it, whatever it was. I never saw you happier than last night at dinner."

"Yeah, you have. But I was a deeply happy man; it's true. Nikki still out?"

"You all ski like bats out of hell. I feel thoroughly intimidated."

"Queen Judith? Madame Genius? Intimidated? I don't think so. Nikki was skiing almost before she could walk. In high school, she was captain of the ski team. Nothing like regularly skiing the Alps to get you ready for anything. She even wanted to take up ski jumping. I drew the line." He looks pensive. "That was a different Nikki. Maybe that one is coming back, do you think? She seems calmer." He moves toward her, kisses her, feels lovingly for her bottom.

"Perhaps behind the bedroom door before we go any further," she murmurs.

8

Judith puts together supper that night out of the Thanksgiving leftovers, and the three of them sit down. "Good runs?" her father asks Nikki.

"Super. Didn't you go out after you took Stevie and Daniella to the airport?"

"The old people decided to stay home and rest." Nikki nods too knowingly for Judith's comfort.

"We'll ski together tomorrow," Molloy says. "Judith claims we intimidate her."

"Well, you do," Judith protests. Nikki laughs, seems the most relaxed Judith can remember. "Tell me about your new work."

Nikki hesitates, looks at her father, then back to Judith. "The reality under appearances? It's not an original idea, but it's got hold of me just now, so I'm trying to do that. I see the reality. I see it all the time. Sometimes I can't see anything else, and I want to scream at people, look at this! But finding the right language is—very difficult."

Judith nods. "Mathematics is like that. You want to find the reality under appearances, express it somehow. You don't want to confuse special cases with general cases."

"Special cases," Nikki says thoughtfully. "They're reality too."

Later, Molloy will recall and study those brief conversations doggedly, trying to pick out portents, the telling detail, hidden meanings, which might foreshadow what was to come. Sometimes he thinks he can. Most of the time, not.

Nikki leaves on the Tuesday after Thanksgiving. She's flying commercial, and not eager to get to the airport until the holiday mobs have finally gone away. She kisses them each goodbye, an unusual expression of affection with her. She holds her father's hand for a long moment before she gets into her car. "I've never forgotten our time together after 9/11. It meant everything to me."

"And to me, princess mine. I love you. May the work go well." He bends to kiss her and they embrace for a long time. She squeezes his hand, blows another kiss to Judith, and drives off.

Annamarie piles Wotan into her car, along with cooking implements that she'd brought, convinced that no rental kitchen is ever properly equipped; tells them what she's left in the freezer for them; promises to take a day or two off after she's checked on Mr. Torres. "It's not Manhattan," Judith says. "He can't just order in."

Now is the time Molloy has promised his wife, time alone, time together.

They sleep late, ski together, read aloud to each other, and make love exuberantly. She won't allow him to answer his phone, look at messages. "It reminds me of those lovely months in Europe," she says happily. "Except you're not curing me of anything."

"No, if anyone needs a rest, it's me. You really don't care if I don't shave?"

"Even better, don't shower either. Yum."

"Perverted woman. How I love you."

They drive Stephen's car home themselves. They shuttle their own rental car to the county airport, then begin the drive to Santa Fe, from I-70 into Leadville, and down the long road home. The highways have been miraculously plowed, and they drive effortlessly alongside the Arkansas River, into the San Luis Valley, straight down the hypnotic gunbarrel of Highway 284; finally across the border into New Mexico, one more hour to home. They share the driving. What makes the time fly is her insistence that they listen to a dramatic reading of *Paradise Lost*. "The theology drives me batty," she says, "not to mention the misogyny. But oh, the poetry." He's never known the poem, and has to agree. Passages move him deeply. And from time to time, when Milton's first couple express their love for each other, Judith reaches across for Molloy's hand—or finds his reaching for hers already.

"Let's talk about free will sometime," he says when they stop for coffee in Alamosa.

"We shall, we shall; I will it," Judith laughs. "But today I'm charmed by the love poetry. Don't you love how Eve doesn't want to hear the story of the creation from the angel Raphael? She wants to hear it from her sweetie, because *he, she knew, would intermix/ Grateful digressions, and solve high dispute/ With conjugal caresses; from his lips/ Not words alone pleased her.* See? Eve knew."

When they get home to an ecstatic welcome from Wotan, she still won't let him listen to phone messages. "Let's make the holiday last just a few hours more. Everything can wait until tomorrow." So Molloy gets a fire going; they stretch out on the couches at a right angle to each other, where they usually read evenings, drink a rare nightcap, and review the holiday contentedly.

"How do you feel, having a ready-made family?" he asks.

"It's quite lovely. A gift, really. All the joys of having youngsters around, and I didn't have to bring them up. Your kids are great company."

"It wasn't always so. But this week seems to say the storms might be past. My radish all grownup competence. Stevie with a beautiful new love interest. I liked Daniella, didn't you? My son is a different man since he finished that house."

Stephen had kept them away until it was finished, then invited them to a small party to celebrate its completion. Judith had wandered around, admiring how he'd kept the integrity of the old place, its sweet original coziness, and yet opened it up so that light poured in from every direction through skylights and clerestory windows. From every room French doors invited you to step outside, yet nowhere in the house did you feel unprotected. Each window framed an important view—sometimes an intimate garden, sometimes the Sangre de Cristo mountains looming in the east, sometimes a view west to Santa Fe itself, the Jemez in the far distance. Stephen shared his father's refined aesthetic, but didn't collect the same artists as his father—instead of the contemporary German and American painters his father loved, he had bultos, carved and painted statues of saints, by the best of local santeros, and rich weavings from local textile artists that were underfoot, or that softened the contours of furniture. She'd gone into the study and stood beside the bookshelves, scanning titles in English, German, French, thinking idly that somewhere here must be the Thomas Mann he'd once quoted to her. Her stepson joined her in the study, gave her a friendly kiss on the cheek.

Like everyone else, she congratulated him, congratulations he accepted without false modesty. "It was a big project. If I'd known what I was getting myself into, I'm not sure I'd even have started it, but...I started it. I finished it. Every corner I look into—I think, I did that. I put those roof beams up—well, yeah, with a little help, of course. I subcontracted out parts of it, but when I did that, I learned alongside the guy who was plumbing or wiring. I was designer, general contractor, foreman, and flunky. I struggled with those damn windows, but jeez, aren't they great? You like the views? I'd plan, bash out some computer code to visualize those plans, think about it, revise, revise again. Then plunge ahead to make something real, something concrete." He was leaning against a bookcase as he said these things to her quietly, almost as if just the recounting of the project tired him out.

He mused. "At a certain point in the building process, there's no going back. If you screw up, all you can do is try and compensate, improvise. But there's no going back. Do or die. So it's me. It's everything I've become. The funny thing is, though it's my creation, it's changed me too. It's all me—not my dad, maybe not even something he could do. A friend once ran the New York Marathon, and he told me that after, nothing was the same for him. Well, that's how it is with finishing my house. I feel like I could do anything now."

She repeats none of this to her husband, but simply says: "Yes, finishing the house was major. And he told me that he's studying with some teacher, some tutor..."

"Studying? What?"

"Mythology, as far as I can tell."

Molloy shrugs. He strokes a happy Wotan, sitting beside him, the dog too excited to lie down and sleep. "What about free will? You can't come away from *Paradise Lost* without figuring that it's the big question of the poem."

She nods lazily.

"The Greeks wouldn't have bought that," he says. "A hero had his foreordained fate, his destiny. He couldn't evade it. Oedipus. But so do Adam and Eve. If I get it right, Milton's God can foresee how it's all going to turn out, but claims they could've done otherwise, which is why he says they have free will."

"Free will is a crock," she says sleepily. "Okay, maybe not a crock, but very vexed. I speak as a scientist, not a philosopher. I think philosophers make a pretty argument as between causal sufficiency and causal necessity, but not tonight, luscious one. So. Up until the beginning of the twentieth century, the universe was considered by scientists to be deterministic—Jack, you don't really want to hear all this now?"

"Oh, I do!"

She rolls her eyes. "Okay. Deterministic. That is, with enough fine-grained information—which nobody could yet acquire, of course—you could predict what would happen based entirely on what had already happened. But now we know about chaos, where random events intervene—no, I can't face it." She watches him, settled in as if he were hearing a good story, a small, contented smile on his face. "You're like Eve, who'd rather hear it from Adam."

He nods.

"Okay. Another thing about free will. At the moment, not genetics, not neuroscience, not neurology nor psychiatry, not experimental psychology—none

314

of those gives us much evidence that free will exists. Our decisions and behavior seem to be largely driven by circumstances beyond our control. So scientists in these fields like to use the phrase, 'the perception of free will.' If you ask how there can be a perception of free will without free will actually existing, neuroscientists will tell you that we humans have all sorts of heuristics, illusions that get us through the world. Unitary ideas of the self, for instance. Or perception mechanisms. Music, which is a bunch of discrete notes, seems to our ears to be a continuous melody. Anyway, these have very little basis in actual physiology."

"So Milton's God had foreknowledge of what would happen with Eve, the serpent, and Adam because it was inevitable?"

"It was, but—to put it another way, let's just say if you're going to take credit for building that great fortune of yours, you've got to take responsibility for the bad things you do too. To quote somebody or other, explanation is not exculpation. You're still responsible."

She swallows the last of the evening cognac. "Oh, Jack. Who the hell knows? I looked at some experiments in psychology, for instance, that seemed so very primitive, even using the newest imaging techniques. I'd say we're a long way from understanding what the facts are about human free will. Then there's the whole Stuart Kauffman point of view, that the universe is both law-based and lawless. It's impossible to pre-state, let alone predict, all that will happen. Therefore reason alone is an insufficient guide to living our lives forward. There's Edward Lorenz's view—he's Mister Butterfly Effect—that you may as well believe in free will because if you do, it's an important and responsible way to live your life, and if it doesn't exist, if you had no choice except to believe in it, you're no worse off."

Molloy bursts out laughing. "Like Pascal's Wager. You may as well believe in God, because if there's no deity, nothing lost; if there is one, you've saved yourself a certain amount of hellfire. The priests at school used to say that. I could demolish the argument by the time I was fourteen." He finishes his drink. "What do you think?"

"About free will? I'd guess it's much more nuanced than any of these points of view. These are caricatures. I haven't thought much about it, to tell you the truth. Stay tuned."

He's smiling at her affectionately as he shakes his head, no, not all clear, but blows her a kiss. "Heaven's last, best gift. That's why, that's how, I fell in love with you. Remember that night, oh, that fucking gruesome night after Zozobra, when you gave me a little talk about why you loved mathematics, how you felt it was the language of God? I was already head-over-heels, and that just plunged me to a whole new level of mouth-breathing adoration. I loved you so much all over again that night." He means the night of a strange annual festival in Santa Fe, where an enormous effigy is ritually burned, and where, that night, they'd got separated from the people they'd come with, found each other, spoken honestly to each other for the first time.

She sits up. "You did? I clearly recall inviting you in for a long-overdue night of extreme lust, and you just shrugged and said thanks, but no thanks. I can't say I felt very loved. No, I was in complete despair—with myself for being so stupid, with you for being so stubborn, with—"

"Me stubborn? Oh, my beloved stiff-necked wife." He sighs happily. "Water under the bridge." He looks out the window. "A light just went on in Torres's casita. Wonder where he was?"

"In his condition, not far."

"Maybe he and Mikey have kissed and made up, and Mikey brought him home."

"Let's hope. All the world should be happy and loving tonight. Come to bed, Jack. From your lips not words alone please me."

9

Leandro Torres spent Thanksgiving Day with Nola Holliman. It was only the two of them, and he appreciated how she went about looking after him without fuss, without nonsense. When he said so, she shrugged. "Years of experience, caring for an invalid." He hadn't meant to bring up her dead son, and was sorry.

Dinner was simple—an allusion to Thanksgiving rather than the traditional meal with all the trimmings—but he was grateful for that: convalescence was bloating him alarmingly. He knew he should have been with Mikey and his family, but no invitation had been offered, and he was too proud to call and ask for one. He guessed—rather, he hoped—that they assumed he was spending the holiday with Molloy and his family. They couldn't have known that Molloy and his family had longstanding plans to ski in Colorado, an outing he'd have been welcome to join, except that he couldn't travel such a distance. Molloy had asked Annamarie's assistant to be there to cook for the invalid, but he would still be alone. When Nola learned all this, she insisted on fetching him to her house. He realized that she too would have been alone.

Astutely, she asked less about his work than about his design philosophy. "All my work has been one long project," he began. "Different facets of a single central work, with a single central concept."

"Which is?"

"Well, that's difficult to say simply." He watched her open a bottle of champagne expertly. Though he'd thought she was unattractively scrawny, he found himself entertaining a fling with Nola. "My wife used to say she kept me around only because I could open champagne bottles. I suppose she finally learned."

"Alone, we learn to do lots of things we never thought we could do. How much say do your clients have in the process?"

"They choose me in the first place because something I've done appeals to them, and of course they set the budgets. We collaborate, my clients and I. I think of them the way I think of the site—as a given, part of the setting for problem-solving."

"Do you ever use designs you worked out for someone else, but couldn't somehow use?"

He looked puzzled. "You mean pull stuff out of a drawer? No, not really. Not in that sense. Sometimes I've been developing something over a long period that just fits a given project. But with an architect, practical considerations are always there. My hardest challenge is to balance between the unconscious impulses of the creative life, and the practical, more rational forces—constraints—in everyday life."

"Where does the creative life come from?"

"Ah, that's the adventure. When you're open to it, you get ideas from books, from paintings, from music. You imitate, you absorb; you see somebody has set themselves a problem like yours, and solved it in a musical movement, a series of paintings, even a single canvas. You think, ah, for my problem that might also apply."

"Have some more champagne," she said. "We're having duck breasts, and they're best if they cook slowly. More tender that way. It could be an hour. Hope you're not starving."

No, I sear them quick, like steak, he started to protest, then shut up. He shifted, unable to be completely comfortable, though the pain was much less; he needed fewer pain pills. "So you're moving along on intuition, and you think, ah, this will do it, this will solve the problem. Then suddenly a path opens up you didn't expect, hadn't thought of. So you ask yourself, should I take this new path, or should I continue on the way I'd planned? Sometimes one's appropriate, sometimes the other. You hope you've made the right choice."

"Life itself is like that, isn't it?"

He nodded. "When the unexpected comes your way, you can't follow your preconceived plan blindly. But that new path might be something for later. For another design. The solution to another problem. You finally have to decide. Each case is something new. Sometimes you have the solution in your mind—I want this to happen—and sometimes you discover the solution as you're going along." He swallowed the last champagne in his glass, and allowed her to refill it. "Thanks. You're a very attractive woman, Nola. I don't think you'll be alone for long." He was warming to something beyond her appearance, which was still skeletal.

"Don't you? I don't want to be together with someone just—for the company."

He nodded. "But it so often turns out that the great love of our life is impossible."

She looked for his grin. He was completely serious. "So we settle for company? Well, companionship?"

"It's not so bad, companionship." Now he grinned, opened his sleepy eyes wider. "Nola, I may be incapacitated, but I would very much like to make love to you. Without my crutches, and this stupid sling, I would come over beside you and begin by stroking your hair, perhaps kissing that beautiful earlobe. At least I don't use a walker anymore, so you wouldn't feel like your grandpa was trying to put the moves on you."

She looked at him with amused interest. "And then?"

"Well, it would depend. If you didn't turn me away, if it felt as if you might welcome me, I'd remove your glasses and kiss your lovely mouth. I'd give you a kiss that would tell us whether we should go on. That's what I'd do."

"Our duck is almost ready." She got up from the couch.

"Don't you think it's ironic that a guy who, for the first eleven years of his life, had a brand-new car every year, along with a driver and a guard, now all but wrecks his career in a car accident?" He watched to see how much she knew about him, his background. But she only shrugged, smiled. She knew nothing. Or everything.

Across the candles she asked him more about his work. Who had influenced him?

"My teachers, of course. Not all of them, but one or two. Profound influences. I had a man at Berkeley who changed the way I looked at things. Humanized my designs. So much of architecture is about—well, God knows what it's about, besides some guy's ego. But he taught me that structures are for humans to inhabit, to find comfort in, to be exalted by. They aren't fine art alone. To be successful, they need to accommodate a million years of human evolution. This is delicious, sweetheart. You were so kind even to think of me."

"Do you like the wine?"

"Ribera del Duero. Fine Spanish wine. How could I not? May I kiss the cook?"

"I'll take the word for the deed."

He shrugged in comical defeat. "People have this romantic view of inspiration. The muse breathes into the artist, and ¡mira!, the idea is born, like Athena from the forehead of Zeus. That's nonsense. The idea comes, you welcome it, but you think about it too. You add things slowly, carefully; remove them if necessary. You push that idea to its limits, testing it, maybe even skeptical of it, can it prove itself? Contemporary architecture is full of great flashes that never got developed. Instant form. Sometimes even a bunch of great flashes, instant forms, yoked together, juxtaposed and standing there, waiting to be admired. Most critics don't see that; they see only the novelty, woo hoo, terrific. My buildings are great—I don't mind using that word, Nola—because they're developed form. I really push on the development."

"Were you successful from the beginning? I don't mean successful in an economic, a worldly sense—do your early designs show this?"

"Interesting question. No, I don't think so. An architect is like a plant or a tree. He grows slowly over time, even if people aren't there to witness that growth. If a tree grows with no one to watch it grow? We look like we sprang—do you say sprang in English?—fully formed, but no, it's been a progressive development, slow, sometimes painful. Very painful. Humiliating sometimes. It takes faith at the beginning, because there are no works to speak of."

She helped him back to the living room, where they drank coffee, slowly finished the wine. "What a clever woman you are, Nola, forcing me to talk about myself so we can't follow our inclinations. I like clever women. I like them a lot."

She looked away, and whether she was amused or exasperated he couldn't tell. "And chance?" she asked. "What role does chance play in your design process?"

"Accidents, chance, it all happens. It's part of being inventive. But you have to know when to incorporate those chance happenings, and when to discard them. All accidents aren't equally important—they need some heft to be worth adopting. The work is going to stand for a very long time. The building will be used by human beings, who will feel right in it or not. It doesn't matter if they can say why; they'll just know. Your colleagues will bring critical analysis to bear. You want to succeed in both those ways, but you want the whole to somehow be better than the sum of its parts, the mystery to remain."

They fell silent. She got up, stirred up the fire. "Are you comfortable? Can I get you anything?"

"Right now? Very comfortable. The pain pills—I don't take as many as I used to. Healing, I guess. Nola, come and sit beside me."

She sat down pointedly in the opposite chair. "Why didn't you spend today with Mikey and his family?"

His face showed his surprise. "The simple answer is I wasn't invited. Mikey and I had a very painful disagreement." He stopped, fiddled with his coffee cup.

"I'm sorry to hear that. What nature, may I ask?"

"Yeah, sure. No secret. I wanted him to take over my firm while I was down and out. He—well, he refused. I said some things maybe I shouldn't have said, about the worth of my work compared to the worth of his. He took offense."

Nola's eyes opened wide behind her glasses. She thought this over. "You must be able to supervise things by now."

"Nola, no telephone or email can substitute for being there yourself. I have some very ambitious people in my firm. I value their ambition. That's partly why I hired them. But I also know they'd like nothing better than to use my name without the inconvenience of having to answer to me. That's why I'm usually on the road so much. I'm protecting my newborn buildings. I'm protecting myself."

"You make it all sound so Machiavellian."

"I grew up in a political family."

She looked interested. "Is that right? No artists, just politicians?"

"What I learned in my family has been very useful."

She smiled, unwilling to press it. "Lee, you're beginning to look tired. I'm going to take you home. Back to Molloy's."

"You're very fond of them, aren't you? Molloy. And Judith."

"They've been good friends. Molloy especially, when my boy was so sick, and after he died. It was a terrible time, a catastrophic time for me. I was going through a divorce from Pete's father. Pete had been sick with leukemia for a while, and then the death…I didn't think I'd altogether survive. Molloy just— took care of things for me, and I'll always be grateful." She was thoughtful, then brightened. "I'm thinking of reopening my gallery. Maybe in the spring. Be ready for the summer season."

"*Bueno. Muy bueno.* If I can help at all—"

"*No, gracias. No puedes ayudarme. Pero gracias.*" No, thank you. You can't help me. But thank you.

"May I come and see you again, Nola? I haven't had a talk like this for a long time. It made me very happy to talk about these things with someone who understands. Who cares."

"Yes," she said distractedly, politely. "Yes, of course. We'll do this again sometime."

"I'm an old wreck; I know it. Even before the accident. But I can still talk."

"We'll do this again sometime."

"Let me come again tomorrow night. I only want to talk to someone who really understands art."

She sighed. She guessed he was lonely. She was lonely herself. Thus when Molloy and Judith arrived back in Santa Fe nearly a week later, and saw the light come on in Torres's *casita*, it was from Nola's that Torres had come, where he'd again spent an evening talking in front of the fire.

10

The flight from Denver International was delayed, and delayed yet again. By the time Nikki arrived in New York City, she was exhausted. Through the car service window, she gazed on a cold and silent city, looking itself exhausted, surely grateful for having survived another night, awaiting the dawn. A light snow had fallen, was already nearly gone. So different from the deep embracing snows of the Rockies. What if, she thought, the attack had come in the winter instead of that glorious September morning? What if people had stumbled out of the Twin Towers only to freeze? But then in weather like that, would the impact have been so great? Yes, at least as great: the papers were always full of stories of houses that burned in the winter, some Bronx horror. The fire hoses froze, and victims sometimes didn't make it afterwards.

The doorman helped bring in her baggage, including her new skis and boots; sent the porter up with them to put them safely in the apartment's foyer. The porter offered to put them anywhere in the apartment, but she just waved for him to leave them beside the front door. He said good night. "Or good morning," he amended jocularly. She smiled weakly, wanting desperately to be left alone.

It was morning only by the clock. The darkness was deep and still. She turned off the light the porter had turned on, and without even taking off her parka, dropped to a couch, staring out over the western terrace to the park, the Hudson, New Jersey beyond. A lone helicopter clattered up the air space of the river, breaking the silence brutally, part of the vigil the city always kept now. People had said they hated living on edge like this since September. She was smart enough to shut up about it, that living on this edge gave her a rush. It seemed she'd come by that from both sides of the family. She summoned up the family photograph on a table across from her; in this darkness she could see it only in her mind's eye. All of them on the ski slopes somewhere. She'd been— what? Eight or so? Stevie ten in that case. Her mother's smile was fixed, artificial. Her father was barely smiling. Grim-looking, come to think of it. Prophetic, for both of them.

She'd never really understood her mother, so alternately distant and smothering, depending on what drugs had come her mother's way. Feared her sometimes. Been exasperated by her most of the time. But drugs—that was the edge her mother had chosen. And fallen off. As she now knew, her father chose different edges but was always at the edge; had not fallen off once. Yet. So they were a family of risk-takers, extremists. Just like Stevie said.

The skis, leaning upright against the wall in their case, slipped and fell; startled her. New skis and boots. She had perfectly good ones at her loft—but there they remained. When she'd been allowed down there to sort and retrieve stuff, she'd forgotten them. How stuff weighed you down. Papa had that one right. That was the beauty of skiing. It was only you yourself, just enough clothing to keep you warm, just enough equipment to let you fly. It was all you needed.

In her mind she re-did some of the best runs she'd taken this last week, tried to recapture the freedom she'd felt, the sense of flying, of release at last. Skiing was reality without appearances. Release from things. All things.

She reviewed the family. Stevie, trying too hard with Daniella, his horniness permeating, nearly suffocating the room. Daniella didn't seem to mind, probably ate it up. She knew about the earlier failures, Inéz, Sonia. Maybe he'd found his mate at last. He'd told her he felt called upon to be the family caretaker—that this family was so strange in its needs, its trials so extreme, that it required taking care of as a family. It needed someone who stood outside, yet was within it, to smooth and soothe when the going got rough. Which it always must for such a collection of outliers.

"Papa, so extreme in every way," he'd said. "Judith, a high-flying scientist who, paradoxically, needs the ultimate in gentle care and feeding to keep that wind under her wings. She doesn't know that, but she does. The marriage itself, an entity in its own right. They need each other, but you could imagine, since the need is so strong, deep, so intimate, that they're in the best position to be very bad for each other. You, Nicolina. You need care too." Don't even think about it, she'd said, knowing it was a lie even as she said it, for this conversation reminded her of how he'd taken care of her after the abortion. "Their close friends, like Torres. He's part of it. Char, of course. Even Opa, the new grandpa. I picture the ensemble as a very beautiful but delicate work of art. Lots of moving parts. Sometimes it needs curating. Sometimes it needs conservation. Sometimes it needs restoration." She'd snorted: That's hardly a fulltime calling. He'd agreed. He'd also been engaged in a spiritual search for a while, he mentioned vaguely. Part of why he'd come to understand his role in the family. She told him he'd been in Santa Fe too long, was falling into Santa Fe woo-woo all around. "It's the air, the altitude," he laughed, not at all offended.

She thought of her father. His wife. The marriage an entity in its own right, Stevie had said. Sure. All but groping each other every chance they got. No, completely proper on the surface, affectionate but proper. She couldn't help it if she was unwillingly seeing the reality under the appearances. She'd been cursed with X-ray vision like—was it Superman? The whole Colorado house alive with such animal lustiness, contagious, that she'd had to do herself at night for relief. She could do herself now just remembering it.

The erotic ties in her family were strange and strong. Stevie and her father had been tied sexually—had shared—that woman, that Inéz. Stevie had tried to do it again, with a young woman so very much like a younger Judith that he might as well have published his infatuation in the *New York Times*. And Stevie had once wanted her. That afternoon in Provence, he had totally wanted to do her. "And I wanted him," she'd told the doctor, "but I couldn't cross that line. I made believe it was disgusting, but I think about it a lot." The doctor had not seemed shocked but had responded mildly, "Do you have other fantasies you think are inappropriate?"

"These are not fantasies!" she cried. "This is the reality under appearances!"

But was it? Sometimes the whole set of ties seemed a ridiculous figment of her own brain fevers. She didn't know. The meds changed everything. They confused appearances and reality. What she called the brain fever was coming on again; she could sense it. One major reality: everyone mated at last except her. And each mate had stepped between her and a man she loved, her father, her brother. Each new mate had put up a barrier that Nikki could not cross; each had taken up space in a heart that might have been hers. The tears gathered in her eyes.

Was this crazy, or what? Did she take her meds at the Denver airport? She didn't remember. She'd first calculated the time, thought she'd be taking them over Iowa; then departure was delayed a second time. Had she done the calculations right? Had she done them at all? The early signals said the headache would be bad. Because she hadn't taken her meds, or because she hadn't slept? Or something else?

Oh for the lightness, the freedom, the release of skiing. No brain fever there. Just bend and lean with the fall line. See a ridge coming, and beyond it, only sky. Give yourself over. Fly and plunge, then dance, carve your way down.

Everyone said she was fearless on the slopes, but that was wrong. The fear was very great, a black hole of madness, just waiting, taunting her, even if she told no one. But jumping into the fear was the ultimate rush—that plunge, her guts being pulled down and out of her. That utter surrender to the dark fear. Do with me what you will, I am so yours. Take me, yes. *So* yours. Rapture.

She got up and unlocked the terrace door. Outside it was very cold, but no wind, like on the slopes. The cold did nothing to stop her head, cool the brain fever, which was getting bad. Soon, she knew, unbearable. Across the river, New Jersey's lights shimmered. Above, the clouds had scudded east after the snow, and she could see the stars. No moon. Delicious darkness. She climbed nimbly on to the terrace railing, supremely confident as she balanced on its top, surveying north to the lurid greenish lights of the George Washington Bridge cables, its amber roadway lights, south to the fool's gold of Lower Manhattan, sweeping across to the Jersey Palisades. All these lights themselves a sign of confidence too: no cowardly blackouts for New York City, no matter what the terrorists threatened. Directly below her, Riverside Drive was monochrome and deserted. Across the drive, patches of snow on the park grounds gleamed out of the darkness. Beyond, between the branches of the bare trees, the Hudson's waters shimmered. Occasional flashes of headlights showed that the West Side Highway wasn't completely deserted, but few people wanted to be out at this hour. The stillness was sweet, comforting, swaddling. She breathed the winter air in deeply.

Her heart began to beat rapidly, her breath was hard to keep. The fear. It had slithered up the wall below her, lapped at her feet, her ankles, her thighs, with tiny kisses. It taunted her, wooed her, begged and commanded her. She understood. Here was her missing mate, if only she'd reach out to it. Here was rapture. Knees slightly bent, ankles properly flexed, she pushed her shins to the front of her boots, and launched herself; surrendered to the fear with open arms, ecstatically let it take her once and for all.

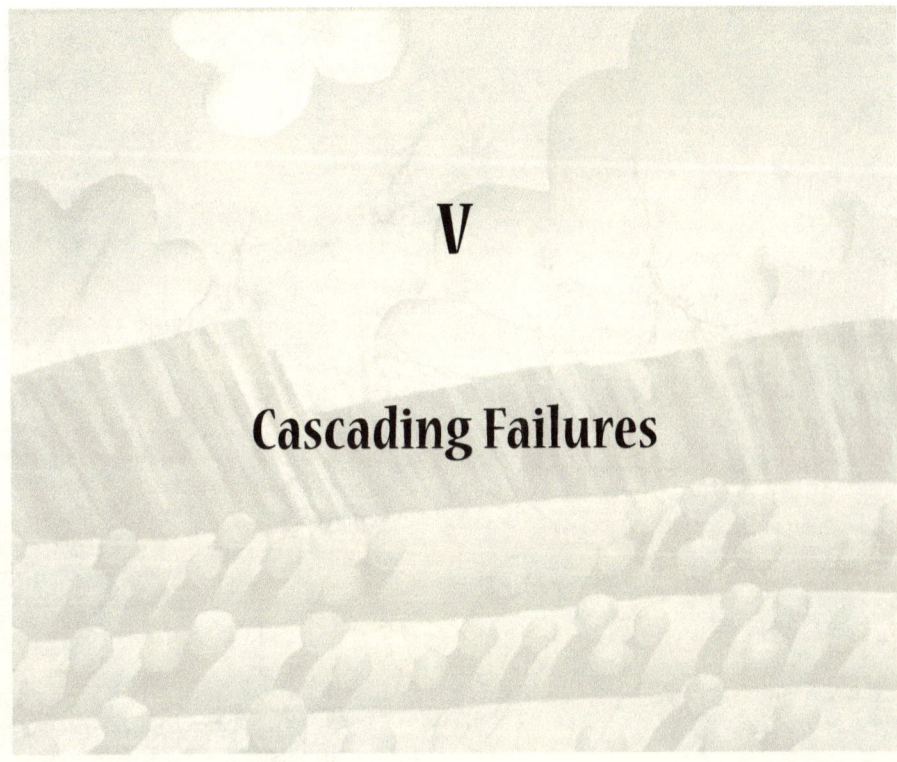

V

Cascading Failures

1

Nikki Molloy's suicide has devastated her father, though that devastation isn't apparent right away. He, Judith and Stephen fly to New York immediately, where he takes charge, deals with the details crisply, settles estate matters with lawyers promptly and competently. Only once Judith finds him on the west terrace, holding on to the railing, staring out to the wintry void where Nikki had ended her life. He turns and looks at her, shakes his head, says nothing.

He finds his daughter's mobile phone, and though Stephen offers to do it, himself calls every number on the contact list, asks them to attend a memorial service for Nikki at their home, and to tell anyone else who might wish to attend. The responses are awkward, tongue-tied—which he understands is one part their shock, one part the novelty of death at their age. He's decided against involving the church—Nikki was never a serious churchgoer. Even if doctrine has got round to conceding that a suicide victim is not necessarily in his or her right mind, not entirely culpable, he doesn't need to hear anything about sacramental difficulties. He's comforted, almost pleased, to see that the living room fills, that the crowd flows into the dining room, that Nikki has had a wide circle of friends, or anyway, acquaintances, young people who push toward the family, introduce themselves, offer their sympathies. Stephen knows many of them, and hugs persons who, to his father, are strangers. Molloy wonders which, if any of them, had been the father of her child. If the guy is in this crowd, he might not even have known he was a potential father.

Stephen has already suggested to his father that he conduct the service for his sister, and Molloy has agreed. Stephen opens the memorial with a brief word of thanks to everyone for coming, talks about wanting to celebrate, not mourn, his sister's life; speaks of her hopes for her art, which now would not be realized. "My sister and I were very close," he says simply, "but there's no way I can tell you what impulse of pain, what unbearable soreness, drove her to end her life." He stops to compose himself. "For those of us who loved her, she lives in our hearts forever. My father's wife, Nikki's and my stepmother, Judith Greenwood, knew Nikki well too, and would like to say a few words."

No, Judith thinks sadly, I did not know her well. With time, maybe; but I did not know her well. I thought that the time was long for learning to know her. It wasn't. Nevertheless, she picks up on a phrase of Stephen's to begin. "How do any of us live, except in the hearts of those who love us? And so we think that when we die—or at least when the people who have loved us die—our traces must disappear. This is not so. The fact that we've lived, the fact of our life, has changed the whole of life itself, in a direction so slight we might not be capable of detecting it. Yet change life we have. The ancients thought of this process as a cycle. But a cycle implies that we return eventually to the same place. I can tell you as a scientist that we do not come back to the same place. Not quite. A certain scientific view would argue that each human life has changed the very shape and direction of all human life, sometimes only in an infinitesimally small way. But always a change. Sometimes the perturbation is not so small. Regardless, life without each individual's contribution would not be the life we know. Life would go on, life will go on, but it would be different—perhaps quite different—without each individual's contribution. I dearly wish Nikki had been able to fulfill her promise as an artist. I don't celebrate that. I grieve for it. That art would have been as strange and wonderful as Nikki herself was. Yet by the simple fact of her brief existence here, she's pushed our lives to a different, unpredictable, and because she was Nikki, surely richer place. If Nikki has left us a message, it might be this: that life generates enormous creativity by the terms of its very existence, and for that alone, life is sacred. Therefore it deserves, it demands, our reverence. We also understand that in creativity is destruction. This too we must come to terms with. To understand this is to honor Nikki in the best way possible. Nikki also showed us that life, generative life, is always on the edge. For Nikki, this edge was an exhilarating place—you could see that in her skiing, a place to push as fast and hard as she could. Which was very fast, very hard. We owe her thanks for showing us that exhilaration, for forcing us to recognize that, from that edge, we shall each fall someday. Even those of us who never dreamed that, simply by living, we were doing something edgy." She pauses, looked at her husband to see how he's doing. His eyes are closed, his face a mask, his arms folded across his chest.

"Meanwhile, we're called upon to push—as hard and as fast as we can, at whatever our purpose is in this place that we inhabit, called planet Earth. Farewell, Nikki, and thank you." She shrugs, looks at Stephen, who takes her hand, spontaneously hugs her. He turns to his father, seated near the front of the group in an armchair. "Papa?"

Molloy suddenly appears hollowed out. He shakes his head. He's planned to talk, but cannot. Both his wife and his son see the abrupt change in him. Now, in the finality of this memorial service, all he's done to hold himself together can be seen to fray. He'd planned to reminisce a little about Nikki, and then say what the family had done in memoriam, but he can't speak. Judith grasps this, asks Stephen for permission to say one more word. "Our family has set up in Nikki's name the Nicole Molloy Fellowship, at Columbia's School of the Arts, where Nikki was once a student, and where many of you probably first met her. It's our small way of honoring her and creating a niche for future Nikki Molloys. Thank you again for coming to honor Nikki this last time. Please join us for some refreshments behind you."

The children—they seem like children—in their purple or green hair, their facial hardware, their torn jeans, press up to them, mumble repeated introductions, nervously tell little stories about knowing Nikki, even loving her. Many of them speak so quickly that Judith can barely understand them. She wonders what makes this generation feel so rushed. In her confusion, sometimes she only smiles, murmurs her thanks. As individuals step back into the group, she can see them relieved at last to be able to consult their phones. At least they've waited to the end for that. She watches Stephen, who'd confessed to her only a few months ago that he wanted to be the family caretaker. How does he feel now about this first great—failed—test, piled upon his grief?

But more than Stephen, she watches her husband warily. He's going through the motions, shaking hands, nodding, sometimes murmuring platitudes, but at least he's managing that. Only she knows when he slips away upstairs to the top floor of the apartment. With equal discretion she follows, to be with him in his grief.

By the time she comes downstairs again, the last of the guests have gone. Stephen sits in the same armchair his father had occupied earlier, staring off into space.

"You okay?"

He shrugs. "Papa?"

"He's sleeping now. I think it's the first time since we got here. Have you decided when you'll go back?"

He looks weary. "Pretty soon. I need my sweetie."

She smiles, puts a hand on his shoulder. "It'll be good for you to be together."

"Daniella said—when we were going home after Thanksgiving, Daniella said that Nikki seemed almost feral to her."

"Feral. I think I've used that word about Nikki myself."

"It seemed off the mark to me, but if you saw it too."

"Like those trapped wild animals who gnaw off a leg rather than stay trapped. Maybe that's what this is all about. We couldn't spring the trap for her."

"Maybe we were the trap."

"Oh, Stevie. Don't blame yourself, whatever you do. We don't know what was going on in Nikki's mind. We don't know—anything."

His daylong composure finally dissolves, and tears come. She holds him, crying herself a little, because it is all so inexplicable, so immensely sad, and so alien.

She wants to assure him that no caretaker in the world could have prevented this, but she doesn't know that. Anyway, none of them has prevented it. It's to their everlasting sorrow. Perhaps their shame.

2

Nikki's suicide changed things again. Stephen did not see his tutor for several months. When he returned to his studies at last, he told his tutor that the world had changed for him completely.

"My sister gone. It feels so—unreal. Incredible in the literal sense. I'm having a hard time dealing with it. Very hard. Headache she was, but I loved her. I miss her unbelievably. My father is totally—well, unreachable. It's as if Nikki sensed we were slowly finding each other, my dad and me, and stepped between us in the only way she knew how."

How do you mean?

"My dad and I were really beginning to connect. I owe big thanks to his wife for that. She's—well, she had—humanized him in lots of good ways. He was open to me in ways he never had been before. And then—this."

Can you at least share your grief with him?

"Not very well. He's—he's very depressed. Gone away from us all. He still gets up and goes to work, but at home, he's so far inside himself you can't touch him. It must be hellish for Judith. She's not reaching him either. Here's a dream. I'm walking in the desert—the high mountain desert. I'm following ruts in the sand, this is some kind of road or trail, but it's definitely the desert, like around La Plaza Blanca, The White Place. I spend a lot of time there; did I ever tell you? It's kind of a power spot for me. Ah, I'm sorry. I know you don't like those New Age terms, Santa Fe woo-woo. You're right, of course. I should be more specific. I wouldn't say it comforts me—it's too severe for that. It's a place that energizes me. Clarifies me. Its whiteness is so different from the red desert around here. The landscape speaks to me in ways I can't quite describe. I love how it's signed, formed, by water ancient and water recent, though never a drop in sight.

"Anyway, I see two figures coming toward me, way far away. At first I think they're dressed Arab style, long flowing robes, and think, wow, weird; this is New Mexico, not Saudi Arabia. Though there's a mosque near La Plaza Blanca, you know that. These two figures are moving among the towers of stone there. But when they get close to me I see these robes aren't—well, the first thing to say about them is that the robes are draped over their faces. I can't tell who they are, even what sex they are."

Do they seem menacing?

"Definitely menacing. Yes. But I feel as if I know them too. If only they'd lift the veils that cover their faces. But I'm afraid. I stop. I let them come to me instead of going to them."

Are they gesturing to you?

"No. Just moving along the trail toward me, among those stone towers, closer and closer. Utter silence. The White Place is always silent, and they don't make any noise either. Now I see their robes better. They float, they drape, they're something like the statues you see of Greeks or Romans in their togas, but—the material is very rich, patterned—not loud, but not the pure white you see in classical statues. I don't know anything about cloth, but these are very rich, very sumptuous. Maybe gold thread running through them. The veils are all part of the same robe. I think if they come near I can see through the cloth, see who they are. I won't even have to offend them by pulling at the veils."

And can you see who they are?

"No. The veils are completely opaque."

Go on.

"I'm really scared. I want to reach out to them, but I'm afraid if I do, they'll take me with them, and I don't want to go in that direction. I very much don't want to go with them."

What happens?

"They kind of float past me in silence. I keep walking. I'm relieved to get past them. It's up a big hill, a ridge, I guess. It's hard going. The ground isn't just sandy; it's also very rocky, an incredible variety of colored rocks on the white sand. Thrown off by ancient volcanoes, I guess. It's hot. I'm thirsty. I get to the top and there's a big treeless bowl below, white sand, dunes across the way; puffy white New Mexico clouds in the blue, blue sky. It isn't the White Place anymore; it's White Sands, down south. I see another figure, a single figure this time, much farther away, down in this bowl. I can't tell whether it's male or female, but at least it isn't draped—it might even be naked. As I stand there watching, it begins to rise off the desert floor very slowly. Levitates. It's very calm. Its head is slightly to one side, watching, maybe looking for something important. I think it might be dead. It rises slowly into the sky. That's my dream."

Much to consider here.

"Leandro Torres had a terrible car accident; maybe you read about it in the *New Mexican*. He came to stay with my father and Judith to recover. He was there for a few weeks until my sister died. He wanted to leave, thought he'd be intruding. His landlord already wanted to take back the place where he used to live, so he moved out from our family compound into a crummy little condo in a hurry. I go over and see him sometimes in the afternoon. We talk. He finally asked if I'd be interested in being his temporary assistant, his eyes and ears and executor while he was recovering. He has all kinds of technical assistants, project architects, even two people who do nothing but field his phone calls—those guys work twelve hour stretches, covering him in pretty much every time zone. This isn't what he needs. He needs someone with the ability to see past the day-to-day stuff, to see the kinds of things he himself would see. He likes it that I'm fluent in four languages, but I can't think why—I don't speak Arabic or Chinese, where he's got some big projects going. He'd first asked his son, who had no interest. But this would be good for me. I could tell whether the profession really was for me. Good for him, in that I could carry out some of the supervision he couldn't do himself. Win-win. I said I'd think it over. And as I was thinking it over, Nikki took her life, and I cannot—think of anything."

If your sister hadn't died, do you think this might have appealed to you?

"I don't know. I hadn't decided. On the one hand yes—a role of some responsibility. A way of trying a path I might take. On the other hand—maybe this isn't the responsibility I should be taking on. I originally started studying with you to understand the sacred copulation dream. From the beginning I felt this dream was a profoundly important message from one deep part of myself to the other, where my responsibilities lie."

In dreams begin responsibilities.

"What?"

A poem. Look at it sometime. Say more about responsibilities.

"We have, in my family, two generations that I know of who've evaded—their responsibilities. This is unfinished business for me, for two generations before me."

Could you say a bit more? About these two generations, I mean.

"When my grandmother was carrying the baby that would be my father, my grandfather just up and walked out on her. Never did anything about his responsibilities. This guy has just shown up in my father's life, by the way, wants to be friends—a father—after all this time. My dad's skeptical, didn't exactly welcome him with open arms. 'Everybody wants to back a winner,' my dad says. Now, with Nikki gone, my dad in such bad shape, my grandfather—that's such a strange word for me to say—will have to grab a number, get in line. My own mother—well, basically walked out on her children, my sister and me. I can see now that my father has been deeply, gravely injured by how his father deserted him. His absence. He never said so until this guy showed up, but now, well, it's pretty clear to me. Nikki and I—we suffered from our mother's absence. So maybe there lie my responsibilities, to my family. And then there's Daniella. She's the first woman I think I could have a life with. First woman ever. It's not that we see each other all that much, with her residency, but if I started flying around the world for Torres, we'd never see each other. This relationship needs nourishing. This is what I was wrestling with when Torres offered me a position. Then Nikki died, and everything changed."

You don't think such a job, such a position for you, is appropriate now?

"No. Not now. My family needs me more."

Do you feel your father shirked his responsibilities?

"Funny, when I was younger—yeah, I did. I resented him not being there to play baseball with me, or whatever idiotic idea I had about fathers and sons. I see now that he didn't shirk his responsibilities at all. Without us, he'd have lived his life very differently. I never understood that until Judith opened my eyes to it. A bit brutally, but that's my stepmother. A no-nonsense lady. Daniella's something like her that way. I should also say that thanks to my father, thanks to the money he made when he was younger, well, he gave me the freedom to do what I want. To choose to take responsibility. Or not."

And what do you think these dreams are saying about all of this?

"Where to begin?"

Start with the White Place. I've never been there.

"Smack in the middle of all the New Mexico red sandstone, this place is white. Tuff, gypsum, I don't know what. Hence the name. An oddity, geologically speaking. Visually speaking. It isn't in any sense a comforting place. No trees, some low scrub, cholla, stuff like that. Well, maybe a few stunted cottonwoods. What catches your eye first are three major stone outcroppings, hill-sized, each apart from the others. The first, the smallest, is red and angry, pointed, sticking out of the ground like some red shark's fin. Nearby a larger one—I'm talking maybe sixty or seventy feet high—is white, very smooth. At first I used to think this one looked like a ramparts of a medieval European castle. Then I thought no, these are like grouped Asian garden lanterns—the formation is columnar, and most of those columns have odd caps that look like pagoda tops. They're classic hoodoos. But recently I've been thinking these columns are like a group of people, standing together in—what? Fear? Solidarity? Menace? Worship? 'The Burghers of Calais.' It changes, depending on what mood I've brought to the White Place. Anyway, these are the formations that Georgia O'Keeffe often painted. You can see why. They're very striking. Evocative.

"But lately I've been staring at, maybe meditating on, the third outcropping. Again, seventy or more feet high. But not at all smooth—needles. Spires. Have you seen the cathedral Gaudí did in Barcelona, Sagrada Familia? I'm reminded of that. But here's a difference: these spires in the White Place look as if they're cobwebbed. As if they've been asleep, under a spell, for a very long time, and no one has come by to dust them. And because it's a magic place, the cobwebs themselves have turned to stone."

What is it about this particular formation?

"I like how these strange stone cobwebs remind me of bigger webs—social webs, the World Wide Web, biological webs, the web of the human brain—vital to human existence. Maybe it's a lesson in branching. We can go so many different ways, and each way takes us someplace completely different. Or maybe—I sometimes wonder if these stand for a kind of yearning in me that's been dormant for a long, long time. I come away from the White Place, from that particular outcropping, with my mind clear but churning. That's a good thing."

I see. And the two hooded figures? What do they suggest to you? Who might they be?

"Hooded figures could mean monks to me. Wanderers. Seekers. Pilgrims. It's at the White Place, which in real life has all sorts of religious groups nearby—Presbyterians, Muslims, Catholics, of course. Christ in the Desert Monastery isn't too far away. I sit and meditate at the Upaya Center sometimes. Religion—well, a spiritual thing—seems to be pressing down on me. But these figures might be something else. Death? They scared me. If it's death, why two of them? Is one my sister? Did I think she'd force me into death, like hers?"

And the other?

"I don't know. Me? An aspect of myself? With my sister?"

So you pass these figures by; you evade them somehow; arrive at the ridge top, and look down into the valley, the bowl. Who's the figure down there?"

"It could be my father, all but dead to us these days. In levitating, he's escaping. It could be—well, it could be me, struggling to achieve—I don't know, transcendence."

You told me about the architect's accident, and his job offer to you, which you feel you cannot take, as soon as you finished telling me about this dream.

"Yeah. Yeah, I did."

Do you see a connection?

"I don't know."

Think about all this.

"I do. So help me, I do. Constantly."

3

As something like spring pushed through the high desert on gusty winds, kicking up dust devils in every direction, as snowy days alternated with sudden warmth, Leandro Torres was beginning to hobble, if not quite walk. His Western hemisphere telephone wrangler had taken up semi-permanent residence in Santa Fe, and his colleagues now flew in to consult with him. Nevertheless, on warm days he sometimes liked to have Nola drive him out to the country so he could sketch. He liked her tranquility, he told her; the phone wrangler disrupted his concentration; his colleagues were—some vague insult lingered on his tongue but remained unspoken. On these sketching excursions he could seldom sit for more than an hour, and even before an hour was up, she often had to take him back to his rented condo, a place she'd found for him in a hurry when he felt intrusive at Molloy's. At least at home he could sometimes paint. He was depressed, in pain, and felt as if he were witness to a slow-motion wreck of his career.

He complained to Nola as projects seemed to fall apart—not about the events, because this was typical with big, complex buildings: things always went wrong and had to be put right—but about his colleagues, who were handling the crises stupidly, were refusing to do precisely as he demanded, what he knew was best. About his phone wranglers, who were helpless in the most obvious situations, but when they failed to check with him, made egregious mistakes. Above all, he complained about his son, who'd refused to be his eyes and ears and voice. Nola listened with more patience than she felt until one day, as she was driving him home after some sketching in the bleak countryside near Chimayó, she objected with uncharacteristic vehemence.

"I would give a great deal—everything—to see my own son alive doing anything—anything he pleased. Jack Molloy surely feels the same way about his daughter. Stop this. Stop this at once. Your grievance is trivial."

He was taken aback, began to protest. "Nola, he's—" A rush of shame swept over him. "Nola, I must sound like a pig to you."

She nodded, her jaw clenched, her hands clutching the wheel.

He slumped back on his seat. "I've busted my goddam balls to get where

I am. This stupid accident is fucking everything." But after that, he no longer complained to her.

He'd show her his sketches, admit to himself that he was almost comically hungry for her praise. "Nice, Leandro, nice. You could've had a career as an artist instead." They each knew this wasn't true, but it pleased him to hear it from her. Praise had nourished him—he'd lived on it—all his adult life. Was that why he'd learned to compromise, to design buildings that might not have been as innovative as they once were, but that got built—and praised? Away from the firm, away from the profession, he was hearing nothing. Well, nothing but calamities.

One day at his condo she picked up sketches she hadn't seen. He'd always done landscapes, buildings, especially the adobe structures that were in the process of melting back into the earth, but these were portraits, all of one woman. "Did Lucie sit for you, Leandro?"

"No," he said, looking slightly embarrassed. "Those are from memory."

She went through them slowly, appraising them, but when she reached the nudes, she put them down. "From memory also?"

He didn't answer. In fact Lucie still sometimes came to see him, and if she was feeling in the mood, slipped into bed with him and satisfied his desires—but only because they were hers too at that moment. "I'm not into mercy fucking," she said without apology.

"But since you only come here when you're bored with the well-drilling, you must think I am," he retorted.

She smiled, shrugged, and had her way. He was ravenous for her, and when she evaded him, when she merely visited for a few minutes and brought a little cake, or a stew he could reheat, he suffered in ways he told himself were ridiculous. He yearned for her as he'd never yearned for a woman, and couldn't explain it to himself. As for when she was in the mood, he replayed these rare moments in his head, re-imagined them shamelessly when he was with Heather, the college student who'd sometimes helped out Annamarie at Molloy's, who'd taken on his shopping and housekeeping, and who cheerfully, even worshipfully, tumbled into his bed.

In the silence, holding his sketches but not looking at them, Nola seemed to be thinking of something distant in time and space.

"Nola, I'm a man. I have needs. It's usually Heather. She's just starstruck, but she'll get over that soon enough. Lucie—rarely. It's nothing," he lied.

Brought back to the present, she gazed at him. "You don't owe me explanations."

"Not explanations. It's—Nola, why can't we be lovers? It means so much to talk to you, I love talking to you, more than to anyone, you know that. If we could have something—physical too. Sometimes when we're going on about art, about architecture, I have such a longing to touch you, to hold you, to—you know. It's all part of who I am."

She observed him as if he'd proposed something odd. "I have needs too, Leandro. We all do. Not just you, implausible as that might seem. But my needs are deeper and wider than yours, and you can't satisfy them. So if I could occasionally use a bring-the-rafters-down fuck, I don't think you're capable of that for me. No offense." With that she winked, as she sometimes did, and he had no idea whether she was doing it for emphasis, or just teasing him.

A week or two later she told him she was going abroad. "What with Pete's illness, I haven't been able to travel for so very long. I need to refresh my eye, refresh my spirit. The gallery re-opening in late May, this is the only possible time. Sorry to leave you in the lurch like this, but—well, I'm sure you'll find someone else to *talk* to."

She was gone for most of March and April. He missed her. He'd get email from her occasionally, where she told him what she was seeing ("some wonderful art, some wonderful friends of Judith and Molloy") which made him sick with jealousy. Her general appraisal of the European art scene surprised him with its acuity. He'd peck out long answers, wanting to engage her somehow in art talk, in talk of any kind. But another week or more would go by before he got an answer, and then it was something different, orthogonal to his laboriously crafted attempts to engage her, though he saw those efforts automatically returned to him below her own messages. So at least she'd seen them, maybe even read them. She said that now that the ice was broken, she'd travel next in Latin America. She'd forgotten, she wrote, how exhilarating the novelty of travel was. Everyone said art was really happening in Latin America. She'd like to see for herself.

I'll go with you, we'll go together, he said to his screen, ignoring the fact that she hadn't invited him, that when he could again travel like that, it wouldn't be for pleasure. Well, maybe he could stir up some business on a trip like that. He was finally well enough to fly at least to Los Angeles, though he needed one of the phone wranglers or the limo service to get to the Albuquerque airport, and once he'd landed, needed someone from his LA office to meet him. Painstakingly, he was beginning to piece together the shattered bits of his career.

Because he too had begun to travel, Nola was already back from Europe for a few weeks when at last they saw each other again. He came to her gallery, where the opening show was being hung. "My God, you look well!" he cried, and threw his arms around her joyously. He was followed by the telephone wrangler and a photographer, who filmed the reunion with a small videocamera.

"You seem almost glad to see me, Leandro," she laughed. "Whoa, look at you, nothing but one cane. Well done, amigo. It fits right in with the Spanish caballero get-up." She looked him over fondly. "I think I saw some seriously elegant canes on eBay, or maybe it was the flea market. Silver headed kinds of things. Should I get you one to complete el conjunto?"

"¡Con gusto, señora! You'll have dinner with me tonight? I want to hear all about the trip."

She turned to watch the placement of a painting, shaking her head, no, a little to the left. "Sure," she said absently, "dinner tonight. Lose the entourage, okay?" Both members of the entourage stepped backwards, but the photographer protested.

Leandro shrugged. "He's doing a documentary on me for Spanish TV."

"On you, maybe. Not on me. Take your choice."

They went to a bistro on the Old Santa Fe Trail where the noise level covered any shyness they felt about talk after so long. When she'd finished with her opinions of the contemporary European art scene ("so much going on in Germany and England, even Spain; what's the matter with the French?"), the glorious museums she'd seen, the very fine meals she'd eaten, he said: "And did you have any bring-down-the-rafters fucks?"

She hesitated, laughed self-consciously, looked around as if an answer might be overheard. "Since you ask. Yes. I did. After the passage of time, of events, you wonder if you still want this. Whether you're even capable of it. Whether anyone else wants to—join in." She stopped, smiled happily. "The very pleasant answer is yes to all the above."

He leaned across the table. "That accounts for why you look so fabulous."

"Oh, Leandro. What a guy thing to say. A great fuck: the guy cure-all."

He leaned closer, nibbled at her hand he held. "Nola, I can give you that. I want to join in—I always have with you. I've missed you so much, dear lady. You may have to teach me some things, but I can give you that. Come home with me."

He could think of nothing but his desire for this funny, smart, skinny creature behind her big eyeglasses.

"No." She made an erotic little gesture with her tongue that, coming suddenly from the reticent Nola, nearly drove him wild. It was a calculated hesitation. "You come to my house."

And when he got to her house, they made an energetic and joyous love that was all the more so for being deferred for so long. Afterwards they lay together and he murmured, "Did it bring down the rafters, *cariña*?

"It wasn't bad." But she said it affectionately. "Leandro, let's be serious for a moment. I know that if Lucie Marchmont decides to claim you, you're hers. You'd turn from me without a second thought. Even if she's only up for a quickie, for that matter." He couldn't deny it. "Maybe you're thinking of her while you're here with me, in my bed. You'd never want to sketch my body the way you've sketched hers. My God, but those drawings were erotic things. Practically pornographic. All these months later, I can't forget them. You gave yourself away, *señor*. But this body—this body's too old, too bony, too—well, just too. But there's something you should know. I have such a man."

"Someone you met in Europe?"

"Who cares? Someone unavailable to me. Let's call him the man with the deerskin gloves."

"I think I know that painting. Tiziano. Titian. In the Louvre."

She snorted, kept a thoughtful silence for a while. "If this relationship between us continues, there'll be times when I imagine those hands with the deerskin gloves are on me, not yours. His mouth kissing me all over, not yours." She patted his groin affectionately, dropped her voice even lower. "I'll imagine it's his cock, not yours. I'll wish it. I'll sometimes wish it with all my heart." She turned to gaze at him. "In fact, I just did."

He sucked in his breath. "In love and in revenge, woman is more barbarous."

"Old Spanish saying?"

"Yeah. That old Hispanic philosopher, Friedrich Nietzsche."

She smiled, stretched herself luxuriously. "So, Leandro. I accept your conditions. Do you accept mine?"

He could say nothing, reevaluating what had just happened. What he'd thought it was. Her astringent corrective.

"You don't have to say so now. Think it over. But if we make love again, those will be the conditions. The facts."

"And do you expect—my fidelity?"

"From an old horndog like you, Leandro? Be serious. And of course you won't expect it of me. But I do expect some circumspection. Don't bring me any goddam diseases."

Now he had to laugh. "Such a practical woman, Nola. A businesswoman. No nonsense. A realist. I do love that about you." He stopped, stroked the hand in his. "I love you, Nola. Maybe not the way you—or even I—want, but I do love you. You know that?"

She seemed pleased. "No, I don't know that. But it's nice to hear."

She rose, found a robe, poured them some Armangnac, and they sipped it in silence, which she broke only after a while. "My poor Leandro. Look at those scars. Are they still tender?"

"Only a little."

"Are you and Mikey friends again?"

He squirmed, not expecting this. "You could say that. I've been over to dinner. Now that I'm up and around, and can take care of my own affairs. More or less."

"Did you actually apologize to him?"

"Not in so many words, but he knows that I—"

"Leandro. You owe it to him."

"*Quizás*. Maybe I do. You know what? His wife, Adriana, told me something. A large firm in New York—I know them well—they offered him a job a while back. Staggering amount of money. He said no, he wasn't done doing research yet. So papi's little shop never had a chance."

"What do you make of that?"

"Well, you know I'm proud of him. Proud that they valued him like that. Maybe I was wrong about his work. It must be important in ways I don't really grasp. Proud that he said no, he had another path to follow. Maybe I was a little heavy-handed."

"Maybe?" She said it in a way that felt to him unkind, but this whole evening had been full of unkind revelations, right alongside its new pleasures.

"Anyway, I love seeing *los nietos*, my grandkids, again regularly. So, to bring you completely up to date, I'm sketching out plans for a house for myself here."

She rolled over, kissed him hard on the mouth. "That's for you, Leandro. Only you, and you alone. Welcome here."

4

At first the pain is unendurable. It comes at him from every direction, an iron maiden closing around him, piercing him whichever way he turns. It fills him with a toxic mixture of fear, dread, guilt, and hopelessness. In every cell, he knows he is somehow to blame for all this. In every cell he rages at his daughter for putting him through this. In every cell he despairs. In every cell he grieves for her; grieves the loss; grieves the impossibility of changing things.

The months pass and the jabbing lessens, though sometimes he'll be attacked again, feel himself bleeding when he thought scar had begun to form. Right along with the pain, he feels something else. He's being engulfed by, sinking into, something inexorable: a sea of cold, infinitely heavy mud, rising slowly, promising eventually to suffocate him. There is, there will be, no help. "*Horridas nostrae mentis purga tenebras*," he mutters, Cleanse the horrible darknesses of our mind, not realizing he's said it aloud until Judith asks him if he's praying. "Just quoting. Saint Augustine." Her face seems to say, thank God for that; that's all I'd need.

Judith is—Judith tries. But she's had no children, has never wanted them. Wise Judith, to spare herself something like this. But it means she can never understand the intensity of the pain. She's pulling away from him in ways he sees but doesn't know how to stop. Doesn't know if he cares. At lucid moments, he knows she'll finally grow impatient, sever herself from him. That will be the very end of him. He wants to say this to her; worry it aloud; beg her to hang on. But he's ashamed of this horror he's carried into their lives, this endless waking nightmare he feels so utterly to blame for, so helpless to end. What if she refuses? He has no right to ask for anything from her, and keeps silent.

Life changes. The Sunday dinners at the long table, once such a pleasure for them both, are cancelled. The salon is not reconvened. The tango lessons cease. They seldom go out, and when they do, he knows he's so ponderously gloomy that no one dares suggest it a second time. He's just as silent at home. They lie apart in their bed, and he can hardly endure even her hand in his, let alone an embrace. The playful *cinq à septs* have gone too. He asks himself whether comfort might lead to pleasure, and that, at some level, he doesn't feel entitled to either. Would being comforted, feeling pleasure, somehow betray Nikki? He doesn't know. He often gets up in the middle of the night and slips off, driven from their bed by vivid, unbearable dreams.

"What do you do when you get up?" she asks.

"Nothing. Read. Listen to music. Sometimes I wander down to the office here in the compound."

"You're not trading again?"

"You're not trading again?" he mimics, falsetto. "You're not doing blow again? Judith, give me a break." He cannot look at her. He knows the reply was uncalled for.

"Is there—do we need the money?"

"No, of course we don't need the money." It erupts out of him unstoppably: "I need—something I know how to do, that's all. I can make money. Right now that feels like all I can do."

"And do you make money?" she asks. She's remembering, he thinks with irritation, how he'd declared he was too old, too out of it, too indifferent, for this new financial environment.

"Yeah. Yeah, I do. That part still works. The old dog can still learn a few new tricks." His impatience ends the conversation.

She'll sometimes ask how the foundation is doing. "Moving along. Getting there." He simply cannot say more. In fact, he knows that this is all that keeps him going, his dogged walk every morning to the foundation offices, his dogged work over what he's creating there.

He moves the offices—he needs to, the foundation is growing—which absorbs more energy. On the foundation's behalf, he purchases a beautiful old adobe compound a few blocks east of the plaza. It has been one of Santa Fe's best-known destination galleries for many years, with its traditional pueblo revival architecture, its verdant garden, re-circulating stream and fountains. Since the foundation's occupation there is publicly momentous, Molloy agrees for once to be interviewed by the *Santa Fe New Mexican*. No pictures of him, however.

The reporter begins unsurprisingly: No matter what good purpose the foundation claims, isn't it a pity to close this lovely old compound to the public?

He has the presence of mind to suppress what's on the tip of his tongue, that he's doing a public service to get rid of what he and Judith call Texas Art, the end-of-the-trail kitsch, the bronze children at play, intended, he supposes, to be engaging, when to his eye, they're grotesque. The purchase price has included some of these children-at-play fountains ("at about the aesthetic level of Manneken Pis" he'd said to Judith). He'd offered to pay extra to have them carted away.

But to the *New Mexican* (that will later describe him as "The reclusive John B. Molloy, the main supporter of the Center for Innovation in Philanthropy, soft-spoken, ascetic looking, with penetrating black eyes") he politely replies that some of the rooms will remain public, though visitors might find somewhat different art. Moreover, the public is always welcome to stroll through the gardens, if no foundation function is underway there. Telling Judith this story is one of the few times in months he's felt like smiling.

He considers himself lucky to have brought in a chief executive like Greg Pontocorvo, who knows what he's doing, who sits on all the boards and committees and joins the associations required for someone who heads a foundation with these kinds of assets; who can take people to lunch, to dinner, do panel discussions and all the rest; a charming but no-nonsense public face for the organization.

Only at home does the vigilant self-control fall apart. Only at home does he collapse into mute anguish. Week after week. Month after month.

Judith continues to recede from him. He once imagined her as a golden girl, sailing smoothly over the seas that hid the rusted old hulks like him. A time when he told her he desired the future, not the past. Does she ever think how much better off she was then? She sometimes mentions the book she's doing, which requires research at her own *casita*, where her library is. She's scrupulous about coming home each night for dinner, dreary as dinnertimes now must be for her. He admits to himself that he wishes she'd stay away. What once seemed the liveliness of her mind, the universality of her interests, is to him now a torment of chatter. He can barely abide it.

Stephen no longer joins them, so they often eat in near silence unless she offers pieces of gossip, or tries to explain to him what she's discovering about her own work as she gets into her manuscript. He listens silently, distractedly, hears himself saying: "I just don't understand it, and I don't think you can explain it to me in a way that I can. Sorry." He knows she hears shut up, please. Maybe that's what he means.

"It isn't as hard as what you learned in Switzerland that summer," she protests mildly. "Well, maybe it is."

"I failed to learn that, you might remember," he says testily.

She sucks her lip and goes quiet; to his relief, leaves for her *casita* to work some more.

She tries other ploys. "Have you given any more thought to those issues of representation you were mulling back when we stayed in Provence? You know, you went to that meeting of archaeologists..."

He looks up from his plate. "Not really."

"Let's push on it. Representation is a kind of encoding. Now, organisms, especially humans, encode everything. That's what happens to perceptions when they reach the brain; well, even before that, as they're picked up by the sensory nervous system. So representation must—"

"I don't think so." It takes all his self-discipline to say that without shouting. He doesn't mean that he doesn't believe her conjectures. He means that he's too weary for conversation. He wants to say that; wants to add that he appreciates her efforts all the same. But he remains silent.

She says she's taken on new responsibilities, which means she travels more. Though he knows he's worthless company, he resents this—and is, at the same time, relieved. When she's at home, he keeps her at an impervious distance.

Annamarie gives notice. He accepts it passively. Judith tells him that she'd got the young woman alone and begged her not to go. "These are hard times, but things will get back to normal." Annamarie, as Judith tells him, opens her large manga-style eyes. "Call me then, please, Ms. Greenwood. I loved working for you and Mr. Molloy in the old days. You were both so appreciative. The atmosphere in the house was so lively, so much fun. I couldn't help listening to the table talk, so stimulating. This is just—getting me down, day in, day out. I've got some money saved—you were both appreciative in a very concrete way—so I won't be taking another job for a while. This will give me time to do my own work full-time." Clearly a speech Annamarie has prepared, Judith says.

"Shall we get another cook?" he asks dully.

"Put up with my cooking for a while, and then let's see," she says. But that doesn't work—she's much too absorbed in her new book, her new responsibilities. They hire someone new; fire him shortly; hire another one, and bear with it. Luckily, the housekeeper doesn't quit.

Messages come from the outside. His aunt Char calls him and bawls him out more than once. He listens, can think of nothing to say in his own defense, only wishes to hang up. His good friend Torres calls him to remind him fish are jumping. "Maybe I can't get into the river yet. Or maybe I can get in, but not out.

But I can cast from the bank. You'd have to help me over some of the terrain." Molloy says politely that perhaps they'd better put it off until Torres is further recovered. "It ain't gonna happen then, my friend. When I can finally get on a plane, I won't have time for fishing. Maybe a match? The season starting up?" He replies that he hasn't watched sports for a while. Well, anything for a diversion? No, he says. No.

Only when Molloy disconnects does he think to ask what's happening in Torres's own life. Are buildings still rising in spite of his accident? Has the firm held together? Has Torres's son stepped in and taken over, as Torres wished, hoped? But he doesn't call back.

His wife, at least, appears at the table each evening, lies down wearily next to him each night. But his son seems to treat him like an impaired, a tedious old man, the shell of a father who might once have been lovable. He feels the pain of that too. Stephen is gone, just as they were beginning to know each other. The evening they'd spent together talking frankly to each other was to be the only one: Torres's accident had happened; the message from Lucie Marchmont telling him about the accident, had Molloy taken it, would have interrupted even that. Thereafter, at least for a while, life was too full, and seemed too happy, for quiet, candid talk. He'd taken Torres under his wing then; his wife was blooming gorgeously, her glorious laughter his great joy; his children seemed—well, far better than before. Friends came in and out of the house; the foundation was up and running, challenging him in stimulating ways. Then suddenly life is too awful for talk. For so much as breathing.

Stephen has told Judith, who tells Molloy, that Daniella has given him an ultimatum: "Four years of college, four years of medical school, another three years of residency? A romance is already pushing me to the max at this stage of my career. A guy who needs nonstop care and feeding—well, it can't be done. At least I can't do it. So pull yourself together or fuck off."

"The surgical personality. I hope she's kinder to her patients," Molloy murmurs.

"I'd have said the same thing at Daniella's age, Jack." Judith pauses. "And so would you. In effect, both of us did say that. Don't confuse my somewhat abridged paraphrase with what she actually said to him. It's been a raw thing for them both. They've been quite serious about each other. He looks after her the way you used to—me. As far as she's concerned, she's a pediatric neurosurgeon. Her task is to save thousands of children, not just comfort her lover." Whether

Daniella has said it tactfully, or verbatim as Judith reports, he can only think how tragic, how wrong it is that the real world has no time for his son's grief. It takes him longer to realize that his wife is also saying something about him.

Stephen has made his choice. For Daniella's sake, he's willed himself to get over his grief, or at least bury it. He sees little enough of her as it is, with the demands of her residency, so he permits himself to mourn only when he's alone. To achieve that simulation of calm, however, means as little contact with his father just now as he can politely manage. Molloy sees this clearly, and can't blame his son. He knows his depression seems contagious. If it isn't contagious, it certainly drives people away. He can sometimes yearn for how fine it would have been to know each other as friends, as human beings; a knowledge that surely would have enriched them both. Certainly it would have enriched him as a father. Given what he knows too well about the absence of a father in his own life, it might have enriched his son's life too. But that wistful sadness is overwhelmed by his grief for his daughter. His grief and his guilt.

Rationally, he tells himself that he could still resume that human exploration with his son; that he must; what else can be taken from this catastrophic event except seize the day? Love the ones you love? But a few attempts at frank conversation since Nikki's death have devolved into grief for a daughter, a sister. Rationality, even intimacy, seems as elusive as joy. Nikki's death has destroyed so very much.

He sometimes considers his own father, who'd lost—no, abandoned—a son, and then wanted to claim that son, and fatherhood, back. Now he understands that desire in a visceral way. A more sympathetic way. When he finally gets it together, he'll call Jerry McCarthy, start again. Yes, he will. No one should suffer that void who doesn't have to. This, at least, he can do. But not yet. Not yet.

What would he have done differently if Nikki had lived? If he'd known the outcome? Everything. Well, no. Not everything, but some things. He argues with her in long dialogues in his head, late at night. "I always loved you. Okay, I didn't always like you, but I always loved you. I busted my ass to be with you, back and forth across the Atlantic for fucking weekends, just so you'd know you had a dad. I brought you to Germany because I wanted you near me; I was your only functioning parent by then. If I didn't give up my work, which apparently some people think I should've—though how was I supposed to provide for my family by doing that? Sell life insurance in Mount Lebanon, but only during school hours? Go back onto the mill floor in Monessen?—I gave up just about everything else for you. In those days I couldn't know the universe was saving Judith for me in the future. I thought I'd never have love. That grownup love wasn't ever meant for me. I wasn't perfect, but I did my best, beloved radish, princess mine. I did my best. What more did you want from me?

Why, Nikki? Why? Were you grieving for that aborted baby? Maybe for its father? Did you tell me the truth? Maybe he wasn't just a one-night stand, he was someone you loved. Did he dump you? Did you think I'd deserted you, because I got married, had a real wife at last? Did you think your brother had abandoned you, because he was finally together with a woman he loved? Were you ashamed of something? Had that pregnancy come from a rape instead of the one-night stand you claimed? Was it self-sacrifice? Fear? Frustration? Was it, as they so delicately say, that the balance of your mind was disturbed? What? He went through the possibilities systematically, over and over. Why? Oh, my darling daughter, my radish, my princess. My goddam perpetual burden.

Sometimes he thinks of her sweet early childhood, when she babbled into his ear endlessly. He had no idea what she was talking about, nor did she need an answer; the music of her little voice washed over him, soothed, charmed, moved him profoundly with love. Harder when she grew older, and the voice changed from music to blame.

I know, he tells her, tells her ghost, that it's a disease, a disorder, just the same as if you'd broken your leg, or turned up with leukemia like Nola's boy. But no. It's different. It's insidious and wicked and corrupt, because it mimics real emotions. It makes you seem like you're behaving stupidly. It makes you seem like you're deeply—unjustly—angry with me for—everything. I try not to, but I can't help it, I respond. I get mad too. I can't help having emotions too. Fury. Impatience. Rage that you're so unfair to me. After a while, I run out of sympathy and understanding. The cycling and recycling through: it's just tedious, finally. You drove me to indifference. I can't help that, though I tried not to show it.

When at last, arguing with the dead Nikki, explaining and justifying himself, haranguing her, runs its course; when he stops fantasizing that somehow she'll reappear—like one of those Greek daughters, he doesn't remember which, destined for sacrifice, but swept away by an intervening goddess who keeps her safe—then he's left with the void, the reality that he'll forever have to supply her side of the dialogue, that she'll never argue with him again. The void is black, bottomless, with a force that sucks him irresistibly further down.

On those nights when he can't sleep he gets up and, yes, reads, as he's told Judith. But what he reads are titles on book spines. Judith's books, the titles almost incomprehensible to him. He'll reach out and touch them, think with envy, ah yes, Madame Genius, maybe you're losing your grasp, your power, but there on the shelf forever are the signs of what you once were. What you once had. Before Jack Molloy, he sometimes adds to himself bitterly, Jack Molloy being good for no woman's life, it seems. Or maybe she wouldn't have looked twice at him if she hadn't, in her own view, been over the hill, slipping downward. At the summit, she once contributed something to the world's knowledge, and all he has to show for his life is—he says the words to himself contemptuously—a high net worth. Every asshole on Wall Street is pulling down in an annual bonus what he'd once thought was a fortune. So what?

"Can I—can I take you to Europe and do for you what you once did for me?" It pains him to see how tentative she is. But all he can do is look at her. "If a few months in Europe isn't what you need, tell me what I can do instead. I owe you so much." I owe you? He has a momentary urge to argue, then shrugs. "If not for you—for us?" she goes on sweetly. He exhales slowly, but still has no answer.

During an annual checkup, when he carefully evades talking about his state of mind, he asks casually how the doc's kids are doing. The doc shrugs: they're doing fine. One's with a hedge fund, the other's with an investment bank. He's stunned; remembers when these kids were going to be scientists, or docs, like their father.

But in the last few years, the elite of Harvard and Princeton have all gone to Wall Street. He'd gone to Wall Street because he had no alternative; couldn't imagine why you'd do it if instead you could do something with lasting value. He wonders if the foundation might have to set up a rescue program for all these kids when they turn forty-five, and discover how they've squandered the prime of their lives. A high net worth is, in the long run, nothing of great value. In the long run, we are all dead.

He also has a child dead by her own hand.

Molloy's daylight assessment is that he functions all right at the foundation; work, in fact, is the one place he does function. The old warhorse. He hopes that assessment is correct. Somehow he manages with board meetings here and abroad. But evenings at home, he sinks into an untouchable sadness and anger that has so many skeins that he can't even bear to examine them, let alone untangle them. When they meet between their various professional trips, he and Judith seem to glide politely past each other. Sometimes his wife will approach him, but backs off. Whether she's practicing empathy and tact, or has simply run out of patience with him, he doesn't know. He reads and re-reads the Stoics privately, especially the well-thumbed Epictetus in the bathroom. He hasn't before noticed how many references there are to losing loved ones, a wife or a child, and what demands it makes on you to survive that.

He works at detaching himself. From everything. He knows that to the world, it makes him seem grimly cold, unfeeling. It doesn't much help the turmoil in his soul. At the worst times he feels as if he's standing in his own upright coffin, on the verge of suffocation: helpless to push open the lid, helpless to call out to Judith. Sometimes he wakes with a mighty longing for her, and takes her, but neither of them would call it making love. He wonders when he'll hear it from his wife: pull yourself together or fuck off. He almost hopes for that, hopes for a kind of tough love ultimatum that might work for him as it has for Stephen.

Something has jumped out of the long tail of events and laid waste his life. The landscape isn't just dancing, it's a grotesque funhouse, changing drastically every time he turns around. Where are the interdependencies, the positive connections, all those complexity jargon terms that he can call on?

How will he survive this himself?

And if he doesn't, so what?

5

"May I?"

Judith looked up to see her former lover standing next to the table, shadowing her from the early autumn sun.

"Of course. I'm glad you're back, Benito."

"Are you?"

"Yes, I am. Was—was it a good stay in Arizona?"

He put his tray on the table and sat down across from her. "It was okay. It was fine. I came up here today for Gluck's talk. I'm back at the Ark permanently."

"I heard." From behind her sunglasses, from under her hat, she studied Benito Jiménez, smiled. "I think you're more silvery. Of course on you, that looks even more delicious." The dead girl's assessment: so fucking hot. Molloy's jealousy after that earlier, premonitory funeral. A year ago already.

Benito too was under a hat, behind sunglasses. His voice was intimate. "*Querida*, if you'll pardon my bluntness, you look like shit. As an old friend, I think I have the right—I long ago earned the right—to speak honestly to a woman I used to love."

She looked down at the table, closed her eyes. "Things have been very difficult the last six or seven months. Going on a year." She opened her eyes to him. "Molloy's daughter took her own life just after Thanksgiving. Maybe you heard."

"I heard. I'm sorry. It must have been a real shock to—" an insult seemed poised on his tongue, but he finished "—your husband."

She removed her sunglasses, looked at him skeptically. She knew him well; had heard the unspoken insult. "That's not necessary, Benito. That's not like you."

"*Por el contrario*, it is so very much like me, *querida*. I'm not a fool." Pulled off his sunglasses, which could only intensify the intimacy between them. His deep violet eyes seemed to her hypnotic as he continued softly, but now faster. "Someone's going to insist on sitting down, sharing this table with us, so I'll make this quick. I did not used to love you, *querida*. I love you to this moment. I always will. When it gets to be too much, when you absolutely must leave this—

man—to save your soul, save your life, you come back to me. I'll be waiting." The violet eyes were filling, which alarmed her. Again he looked around, and now only whispered. "I thought you broke my heart when you married him, but I can tell you, seeing you like this is worse, much worse."

That cut short her alarm. Her endless fatigue had eroded any tolerance for language she didn't understand. "Broke your heart? What does that mean? In this context, what does that mean? It was over with us, Benito."

"How long have you been married? Two years? Three? He's aged you ten." She flinched. "He and his family are under some kind of *maldición*, evil curse. This man is killing you, *amante*. Come back to me where you belong. Me, I come without baggage. No one has cursed my family. I only love you, as I always have." He glanced around the Institute patio again, watching the people emerge from the building with their lunch trays, gauging how much time he had before someone joined them. "I know you; I know how deep your loyalties run. You'll think you should be loyal even when he's killing you. But don't let him murder you, *querida*. *Queridísima*. Come back to me, to life." He stared intently at her. "I will wait always."

She shook her head slowly, got up from the table. He called after her: "Always." She walked as calmly, and with as much self-possession as she could summon, to her office, closed the door. She saw the pain in his face. Couldn't she have been a little kinder, a little less direct? Spared him some pain? No. She had nothing left to spare anyone. She leaned against a wall where she was invisible from the common area, buried her face in her hands and sobbed.

After a while she composed herself, ran fingers through her hair, went to the ladies' room and washed her face. Ten years? Maybe so. She looked downright terminal to herself. Afternoon work had started; no one took notice of her. Back at her desk she sat as if she were deep in thought, though it was not mathematical thought.

Melodramatic as he'd been, Benito had upset her profoundly. With precision, he'd penetrated her misery; reminded her, with what she hoped was an unintended cruelty, of far more carefree days. Then offered an out. But she knew why she'd said no in the first place. Why no now. No forever. The oscillations of the last months, painful as they were, were still better than resting safely on that low peak of sweet mediocrity he offered. No, not mediocrity. Unfair to him. He'd been a good friend, an amiable lover, forbearing enough to let her roam, come back to him for comfort when she would. She was still fond of him. No, more than that, she still loved him in a way; in that way, probably always would. But bad as things were at home, she was not tempted to find refuge with him. That was not where her heart was.

Though she hadn't thought of Benito for a long time, in what seemed a strange coincidence, she and Molloy had had a terrible quarrel the night before, and Benito's name had come up. The quarrel was because she'd tried, and failed once more, to shake her husband out of the despair that had sunk him so completely in these months since Nikki had taken her life. Though he got up for work every morning and seemed to tend to the foundation with care, though he attended board meetings in New York and Europe with apparent competence, in private he was shattered. He flatly refused to see a doctor. He wouldn't consider anything pharmaceutical to ease his pain—a pain he was beginning to seem infatuated with. She had stayed away from her work last evening, wanting to talk it out, before he fled into his music.

"Jack, I only want to help. You. And me too, for that matter."

He'd snapped at her. "You can't help. Nothing can help. Sorry if it's not quite what you signed up for." The great black eyes that had once been filled with curiosity, amusement, meaning, were now lifeless.

She kept her voice even. "The way you speak to me these days. You never used to speak like that. There's such a nasty, bitter edge in your voice. Believe me, I am so deeply sorry for what happened. Devastated. For her. For you. But it'll be a year. Life goes on. Yours. And your son's. You have a son to think of too. He's grieving and could use some understanding, some compassion from his father."

"And you? What's the official schedule for grieving? If I'm not over it by then, should I assume you'll walk out on me?"

She'd been shocked. "It never entered my mind. *Our state cannot be severed, we are one/One flesh; to lose thee were to lose myself.*"

The words of the first couple when they realized they'd forfeited paradise. In a new anguish he closed his eyes, knowing that she'd deliberately called up those hours when they were so foolishly, deliriously happy, driving back from Colorado, after what each of them complacently imagined was a perfect family vacation.

She nodded. *"So dear I love him that with him all deaths/ I could endure, without him live no life. Without him, live no life,"* she repeated. "Jack. I love you like—no one else in my life, ever. But for the past few months...well, year, you haven't been exactly lovable. This is a terrible thing, horrible. But life belongs to the living. I won't be walking out, but...my life goes on too." She stopped, then added bitterly: "Bed death...us... At least when I was single, I got laid more than once a month."

He looked startled, then furious. "That shouldn't be hard to fix. I hear Señor So-Fucking-Hot is back in town. I'm sure he'd be happy to oblige. Maybe already is."

"*Du Schwein. Du übles Schwein.*" She took a moment to control rage, the pain of that, collected herself. "That's unworthy. Just unworthy. I know you're hurting. I hurt on account of that. I hurt for you. I hurt when you lash out at me. I hurt just—all the time. I'm not very good at tolerating this kind of pain, but I'm doing my best. I'd like to know that you're making an effort too, instead of sinking, wallowing—"

"What do you want from me?" It was a face on him she was seeing more and more: irritated, impatient. Someone had once told her that people appeared depressed after a divorce, but sometimes it was depression that had actually broken the marriage up.

"You could start by remembering that you and I have something important between us. It's strong. Very strong. Even resilient, I think. But not indestructible. Don't let it be destroyed by—things outside. Don't destroy it yourself."

"Give me time, I'll work it out," he said, without conviction. He did not apologize, nor reach toward her.

"You and I, we began as two half-frozen people. As close to corpses as you can come and still have pulses. Everyone knew you were—" she searched for an inoffensive word, "—well, imperturbable. You were in finance; you had to keep your cool. Everyone knew I'd do anything to evade the personal. I'm a scientist; we're not supposed to get personal. It worked fine for years. For both of us. But you were going slowly nuts, and I was famished for—for what I used to call an encounter with the divine. That's what I told Sophie before she died. That's what I was looking for in my life. So we met each other. Then—you were no longer imperturbable, and me, I finally got personal. I got my encounter with the divine, Jack. My life with you. I...thrived on it. I knew enough to be humbled... in the presence of the sacred." She was repeating words she once said in another context, but he remembered. "I don't want to go back to the old way. I can't. It wouldn't work for me anymore. I know the usual story is that you rescued me from death by ice, and I don't deny it for a moment. You did. But there's another side to that story, how your imperturbable mask began to slide, how that grim visage finally became a human face as we got to know each other. So the old way won't work for you either. But I can't keep it going—what we've got, what we once were—all alone." He'd looked pained, but hadn't replied. "Please won't you see a doctor? Some meds—"

His fury wasn't icy. "Drugs. Right. We all know what a great solution that is! Fuck off, Judith! Just fuck the hell off!"

"Okay," she cried, "who's the real Jack Molloy? The man I married, or the grim visage I'm seeing all over again? This foul-mouthed creep? Which one, Jack? Make up your mind, because I really need to know." He'd spun around and left the room.

This morning she'd thought that maybe some very hard talk between them was unavoidable. Yes, the death was shattering, but was all this really something else? Did he regret this marriage? He must say so in plain English, because painful though it would be to hear, it couldn't be more painful than what was going on now. They could part in a civilized fashion. She'd make no trouble, financial or otherwise. But even imagining such a conversation made her heart race, her stomach want to heave. She took hold of herself: she wouldn't be the first woman some big swinging dick had decided was disposable. And what would the reality be then? To see him at gallery openings, as once she'd seen him, with attractive young strangers? To see him professionally from time to time, and struggle to keep it all professional? It was unthinkable. Could she leave Santa Fe? She'd been on her way to a job in Germany when he stopped her, wooed her, offered and made with her a life she loved. She might—ah, but she was older now. Could she really take up a new job, life in a new country, at this stage of the game? He had neatly trapped her—in love. The kind of trap she'd evaded all her life. In stupid, irreversible circumstances. Damn you to hell, Jack Molloy.

And suddenly, in the kind of gruesome mockery the universe loved, here was Benito, reminding her that there was some kind of out after all. All she had to do was grasp it.

Occasionally over the next few days, she let herself imagine what it might be like to go back to Benito. What if he'd only offered a little fling? "Come and see me some afternoon, *querida*. You know the way. Just a quiet little visit, a glass of wine, maybe, you and me." Wouldn't she have been grateful for that human warmth once more, that deep affection, a man who knew her well, knew his way around her body, a man who'd give her comfort, and pleasure, for a moment at least? Comfort and pleasure, so long gone from her life. But that wasn't what he'd offered. He wanted—she conceded: he had a right to ask for—something deeper, something lasting, something permanent. Impossible. She turned away from those wandering thoughts.

She buried herself—and sometimes it felt like a literal inhumation—in her work.

The book she was embarking on wasn't to be a research monograph, the kind she'd been thrilled to do in her younger days, full of new theorems, new insights, pushing the field in new directions; work she'd felt compelled to write up. Instead, it would survey and summarize her life's work, make its implications explicit, dangle its open problems as bait for the next generation, the smart young ones. If she could puzzle out the evolution of what it meant to know, the evolution of what was considered known, she might have a better book than a mere survey and summary. But that would take some doing. She explained to Molloy what she was undertaking, and he managed a ghostly, almost indifferent smile of encouragement. She wondered if she'd said she was wearing blue not green, he'd have been any more, or less, interested.

So she traveled more, and book research meant she spent more time at her own *casita:* her library was there. He never said he missed her. After dinner, the gloom of the house usually drove her back to work at her *casita*. Yet as inviting as her old bed looked, she always forced herself to come back to Molloy late at night to sleep beside him. When Annamarie gave notice, and Judith said she'd take over this for a while, she waited for, but did not hear, that her job was to prove great theorems, not to cook soufflés. She was chronically exhausted by his endless irritation, the tension between them. Yet she held on to a forlorn hope that Molloy would somehow recognize how his pain—the way he embraced his pain—was poisoning all that was good in their lives.

One day Char called, and after a moment's brief exchange about the ordinary, Char had asked how their boy was doing. "He used to call me once or twice a week. Now I never hear from him unless I do the calling. Then he's like a zombie."

"Not so well. Not so well at all." Judith let go of the tears that were always pushing behind her eyes. "I'm sorry," she sniffed. "This is so not like me. It's been very, very hard, Char."

Char spoke sharply. "I'm going to have a word with him, set him straight."

"I don't think he's quite ready to be set straight, Char."

"He's a damn fool. Does he think he's the first father this ever happened to? Stevie called me the other night and he didn't mince words, that one. It was his sister same as Jackie's daughter. Now you're getting it in the neck too? He's a damn fool and I'm going to tell him exactly that."

"Don't, Char. Please, I beg you, don't. Give it a little while yet. Jack doesn't need more harshness in his life just now. In his soul. I—I love him so much. I can't bear for him to have more troubles."

"I'm an old lady, Judith. I don't have time to beat around the bush. He has responsibilities. He has responsibilities to you, to his son—"

"I've said that to him. At least about Stephen."

"His ma got away with this poor-little-me stuff because we didn't know any better, but anymore we do. He has responsibilities to you, honey. You're the best thing ever happened to him, and God knows you deserve better than this. He's going to wake up one of these days and find you out the door and gone. No woman needs to put up with this."

"No, Char. I'm not going anywhere. Not unless—he wants that. Unless that's his wish. But it's hard. It's goddamned hard."

It was hard, she thought, because it had once been so grand. If her husband wouldn't get help, she craved it herself.

6

Lucie Marchmont put the finishing touches on a document meant to merge a struggling American firm into the possession, the outright ownership, of a prosperous German firm. She was mindful of how subtle legal translations must be, that a misplaced comma, a misunderstood phrase in one language or the other, could cause terrible mischief. But she was pleased with this document. She'd caught more than one such potential hazard, and had found ways of phrasing in each language unambiguous expressions of intent. In working on a document such as this, that demanded not only linguistic knowledge but also knowledge of both legal systems, she had another occasion to regret not having sat for the bar exams, instead of settling for legal translator's certification. But what was done was done.

And this was done. She'd leave it for twenty-four hours before she actually sent it to the two parties, but in her heart she knew it was done.

She got up and stretched, a few twists right and left, a moment on the Feldenkrais roller to pull the knots out of her shoulders and lower back. Saw the time. Doing fine. But then, by the clock she was always doing fine, a woman never late for anything. "Of course," she sometimes remarked to friends, "By being punctual for so many people who aren't, I waste ridiculous amounts of time."

This afternoon she had an appointment with a highly recommended psychic. This was not the first alternative practitioner she'd consulted. When the medical profession had failed her, unable to diagnose her malaise, or worse, pushed by limited time to jump to foolish conclusions, she turned instead to other kinds of healers. She visited iridologists, who read her eyes. She allowed herself to be pummeled by Rolfers, and reflexologists carefully explored her feet. She dutifully gave over her date, time, and place of birth to astrologers; she lay still, but untouched, while the hands of Reiki experts hovered above her supine body. She allowed acupuncturists to penetrate her flesh with needles. Ayurvedic practitioners gave her sesame and sunflower oil to ingest.

A traditional Chinese medicine practitioner suggested the problem arose because her yin was far out of balance from her yang, thus causing "a vacuity of qi." She must beware of the Six Excesses, and he gave her medicines so unpalatable that she couldn't swallow them. An unusually small man, whose dark clinic she found oppressive, diagnosed auto-intoxication, poisons that had accumulated in her bowels, and were poisoning her. She submitted to a colonic irrigation, which was unpleasant, and of no use. She tried a *curandera's* herbs, and more herbs from a Paraguayan shaman. Strands of her hair were analyzed and found to contain an excess of mineral salts, so she must drink five quarts of water a day to dilute them. A magnetotherapist sold her a blanket with magnets embedded in it that would, he assured her, better distribute the oxygen and iron in her blood. An expert in multiple chemical sensitivities argued that low levels of ordinary household chemicals, especially perfumes, were poisoning her, and she must strip her being and her household of anything artificial, such as synthetic fabrics, petroleum products and cleansers that could eventually kill her.

Her symptoms were unpleasant and debilitating—she was chronically fatigued, and life was without savor—but she didn't think her disorder was fatal. On the contrary. The sad thing, she thought, was that people could go on suffering broken hearts for a lifetime.

Today's psychic was said to be penetrating, especially about matters of the heart. Maybe she'd have some suggestions about how to ease, if she couldn't heal, this endless ache.

Lucie drove up a steep, narrow dirt lane in the historic district, a hill so rutted that most of it must wash down to the foot of the hill during the summer rains. How you got up there in the winter with the ice and snow—well, psychics must have ways of doing this. She negotiated a tree in the middle of this narrow lane, and just beyond it, saw the house. It was very small, a cottage, and she knocked at the traditional turquoise-colored door with hesitation.

A young woman of about twenty-five opened the door. "I'm Luna. You must be Lucie. Please come in." Her smile was kind but slight. Lucie followed her inside, taking in Luna's ankle-length dress of deep green velvet, her royal blue shawl embroidered with moons and stars, her long auburn hair. Luna led her into a small sitting room, its walls crowded with rough-hewn shelves that held little figures—some six inches, some as high as a foot—that seemed artfully put together, scraps of cloth, bits of jewelry, odds and ends of bones, antlers and feathers. Though they were cylindrical and had no heads as such, each figure had a circular adornment near its top that somehow suggested a face. Luna explained: "Messengers." She paused. "They don't actually carry messages. They help you hear the messages your soul is sending to itself. Some people find them useful for meditation. You might find one that suits you."

They sat across from each other in armchairs beside a corner fireplace that burned piñon. On the hearth were small bones, bones of birds, Lucie guessed, certainly the feathers among them were from birds—ravens, owls, a bright red feather from a flicker. A skeleton of a small snake. Between the two chairs, a low table was covered in a richly colored scarlet and blue tribal rug.

Now Lucie saw that the woman facing her wasn't twenty-five, probably closer to forty-five, but with an unusually glowing skin that made her seem younger. She wore heavy wrought silver rings on each finger, even her thumbs, and a great silver necklace, whose pendant was a crescent moon, rested between her breasts. The smile on Luna's face was still slight, but definitely kind. She drew the moon-embroidered shawl around her shoulders fastidiously, settled herself in her chair. "How can I help you, Lucie?"

"I don't know if you can." Lucie looked away from those penetrating green eyes, around at the room, its multiple textiles thrown over couches and footrests. She inhaled the slight aroma of sandalwood, mixed with piñon. Outside the window a few snowflakes were beginning to fall. She was suddenly worried about getting her car back down that rutted hill. The silence lingered. The green-eyed woman seemed to be studying her.

"You've been on a long search," Luna said at last. "Long—and so far, disappointing." It wasn't a question. Lucie nodded. Luna's voice dropped. "You bear a terrible wound. You know what it is, don't you?"

Lucie shook her head. If she'd known what it was, why would she be here?

"It's called the mother wound. You had no mother. Ever. Of course you were of woman born, but she was no mother to you."

The mother wound. Lucie pressed herself against the back of her armchair, willing herself not to hear this, not to understand. Yet the phrase persisted.

"Someone else came later, but she was no mother either." Luna closed her eyes, and Lucie stared at the pale green eye shadow smoothed over the eyelids, wondered how you could apply it so well with your eyes closed. The psychic lifted a hand, and the ringed fingers flared. "The father—the father was better. That may be all that kept you whole. You know that. But the mother wound is... dreadful. I am so sorry." She opened her eyes, which were full of tears. "So very sorry."

Lucie could hardly breathe. "How do you know this?"

Luna dismissed the question with her silver-ringed fingers. Her nails too were silver. "I think others have told you this. I happen to be the one you're ready to hear." She closed her eyes. "Many women with such a wound find solace in other women, but you never have. No, it's all right—I feel your apprehension—you're safe here. You've tried to stop the pain of this wound with men. They're men—you ask more of them than they can give. So they're bound to let you down. Recently..." The psychic hesitated, then went on: "You've recently been with a man—maybe you still are; this is a very strong presence—who nurses a wound himself. Perhaps...yes, his own mother wound. He loves you deeply, but these wounds call out to each other, cause you both great pain. So he distrusts it, this love. He's never loved like this before; its power frightens him. You distrust it too. You keep each other at a distance. For now, that's a good thing. In the future, it might be different, but for now, a good thing. Neither of you will find each other, be complete for each other, until each of you heals. Instead, you—you really could do more damage to each other. More than you already have. I wish I could tell you that you might heal each other, but...no, I don't see that. You must heal yourself."

"How?"

Luna's eyes grew wide. "That is so difficult. So very difficult. I must tell you, you will suffer in healing." From a pocket somewhere in the long green gown, she drew out a string of amber beads and began to slip them through her fingers. They clicked softly against the silver rings. "In the beginning..." She trailed off and did not finish aloud, though she seemed to be murmuring something under her breath to herself as the beads clicked against her rings, through her fingers.

"What are you saying?" Lucie cried impatiently. "I can't hear you!"

Luna seemed unwillingly pulled back from somewhere else. She shook her head as if to clear it, whispered, "Please, Lucie. I grasp your pain. But please do not raise your voice in this room. This is a space for quiet and, if possible, healing. Quiet. So if the messengers bring word, they can be heard."

Lucie covered her face with both her hands. "This is ridiculous. This is the twenty-first century. I don't believe in messengers from afar. I don't believe your real name is Luna. I don't believe—but yes, the rest of it, the mother wound. That part is true. I had no real mother." The meaning of the two journeys suddenly became manifest. She'd been sent away from Borneo, was turned away in London, because she wasn't wanted. She'd never been wanted. Aunt Evelyn had been Grace's mother, not hers, which put her in opposition to Lucie. She'd had no mother. How had she failed to know this, accept its deep truth until now? The knowledge was knife-like in its pain, its unsparing clarity.

Luna spoke slowly, as if she were instructing a child. "The messengers aren't from afar, Lucie. They're within. They long to emerge and say what must be said. Take your hands from your eyes, your ears, and listen to them, my dear. And yes, Luna is my real name. It wasn't the name I was given at birth, but it's my real name. Life is a journey toward the deepest parts of reality. You came here because you finally want to begin that journey."

"I cannot," Lucie said, though she was beginning to cry.

"You can," Luna said kindly. "Be patient with yourself."

Lucie felt as if she were somewhere else, not up a rutted road, sitting in a small, tumbledown adobe, a fire in the corner, snow accumulating outside on the windowsill. Her voice seemed very distant from her, not her own at all. Memories were pushing in on her, the heat and hot life of the Borneo forests, the sterility of her time in Connecticut, the visit to London, which she hardly dared recollect. "I don't even know where to begin."

"A wound must be cleansed before it can begin to heal. But the cleansing can be painful in itself. I hope you won't lose heart."

7

As the first real winter clouds bore down on Santa Fe, Judith called her old friend Ron, who invited her over for a glass of wine that very afternoon. She climbed the steps wearily to what they'd jokingly used to call Casa Rongabe, the House of Ron and Gabe, a house on the shoulder of the hill that looked over the neighbors' little private adobe chapel with the mural of the *Virgen de Guadalupe*, and north, all the way to Colorado. She'd once bounced up these steps in a happier time, a younger time. How long since she'd been here? Since she'd just sat down and had a conversation with this dear man who'd known her most of her life?

He opened the door before she had a chance to knock, hugged her warmly. "Hello, darlin'. Been a while. Come sit by the fire." She was touched by the familiarity of his slightly stooped shoulders, his smile as he turned to her. Inside that pale, lined face she still saw the boy, not yet man, he'd been when they were in the American high school together in Munich, but an older, more knowing man had emerged too, the two faces melding back and forth in her mind like some Victorian optical illusion.

"Gabe's not here?"

"With his infinite tact, Gabes decided these two old friends needed some time alone together. He's—well, I don't know where he is. The shop, probably." Ron and Gabe ran a small bookshop that was doing well despite the big box stores and the Internet.

They sat, staring at the fire, such a pleasant luxury in the afternoon. She didn't want wine, gladly took a cup of tea instead. He spoke quietly, with great kindness. "I said so at the time, and I'll say it again. I'm so very sorry Nikki has died. It must be very hard on you both."

His kind words were an invitation to cry, but she'd exhausted tears. Still, Ron handed her a box of tissues. "Oh, dearest Queen Judith. We so wanted you to be happy. I didn't think it would be like this."

"Who did?"

"I haven't seen him for months. How's he doing?"

"It'll be a year in November, Ron. It's terrible. He's not doing well at all."

"How so?"

"He's just collapsed in on himself. Totally closed off. I can hardly get him to talk. I never thought I'd say this, but for the first time I can see why his first wife went the drug route."

Ron clucked sympathetically. "He getting some exercise? Endorphins are a natural upper, help a lot."

Judith shook her head. "He still walks to work, but he used to run every morning before work, too. He's sleeping so badly now he can't get up early enough to run. Then he crashes weekends and sleeps the entire weekend away. Anyway, he seems to have lost interest in running. In that, and everything else. Except the foundation." She looked across the couch at her old friend. "Don't think I say that out of jealousy. I'm grateful he's got something to keep him going."

"Yeah, I saw that interview in the *New Mexican*. They said ascetic-looking, but what does the *New Mexican* know? Is he gaining weight, then? That would sure add to the depression." Ron, always in this world, here and now.

"No, he's hardly eating. I think that's worse. He looks like a scarecrow. Ascetic was a polite word for gaunt. Even the goddam dog is losing its hair in patches. Jack, on the other hand, who used to shave twice a day, three times if something was happening at night, these days he hardly manages it once a day. At least he's still taking showers."

"Drinking?"

She made a face. "Jack's never been a big drinker, Ron. You know that. He's got strong ideas, puritanical, about mind-altering substances of any kind."

Ron kept silent for a while. "And your—well, what the shrinks would call your intimate life?"

"On hold. To tell the truth, gone."

He reached for her hand, spared her the embarrassment of looking at her. "How are you handling that, you horny babe?"

At least she could smile. "Only a very old, very dear friend would have the chutzpah to ask that." Her late friend Sophie would have asked impertinently and at once. She felt the pain of that loss all over again. "How well you know me. Not handling it very well. Not very well at all. I miss it. Not the sex so much as what it stands for. Stood for. The intimacy. I miss being close to him. Well, okay, the sex. It was a tremendous part of our marriage. When I stop missing it—and I'm so afraid that will happen, Ronnie—I'll know I've crossed over, closed down something vital." She stopped. "I couldn't tell anyone else this, but you've known us both. Loved us both. You wanted this marriage to happen, I know that."

"We were thrilled, Gabe and I. I mean it. Match made in heaven and all that. Well, so we thought." His voice was so soft, so familiar, after all these years. Had delivered endless praise, a few admonishments, always great love. She savored the sound in her ears, without really hearing what he said. "We also thought—Gabe saw it first, I came around to seeing it—that for all that he butted his way through the world, and very successfully, of course, he was the fragile one. You were going to be called on to—protect that fragility."

She took a deep breath, sat up erectly. "Your old friend Judith is a damn fool. I fell in love like a teenager. I am not a teenager and haven't been one for years. Nobody to blame for that one but me." She stopped, reconsidered. "For a while, it really was paradise. Oh, the libidinous rush! The sheer breathtaking joy of it all! He'd phone me from the airport, and I'd just have time to get home and—oh, the hormone cascades! Awash in testosterone, the two of us. Drowning in dopamine! High on—oh, God, I don't know."

Ron's long pale hand squeezed hers gently. "Don't do that, sweetheart. In all that self-mockery, I hear a lot of pain."

She nodded. She'd come here to offer this pain to him, somehow hoping he'd take it away. Now she had to laugh because she felt called upon to defend herself. "It wasn't just sex. Talking, talking, talking, day and night. The past, the present, the future. Such exquisite joy in each other. Congratulating ourselves for finding each other. Did I think it would go on forever? No. Someday the four-alarm fire had to drop to three, to two. But I thought by that time we'd have something as mellow as old music." She was close to tears after all, and pulled herself back. "So inappropriate. Unseemly. Unbecoming. We're grownups, with grownup concerns. Not teenagers. Not Romeo and Juliet. As this catastrophe arrived in such a timely way to remind us."

"Oh—" Ron began, and was interrupted.

"Did I not know him, Ron? Of course I learned things about him the last few years. How fundamentally serious he is—but that's fine, I love that. I'm not exactly the class clown myself. How—" and here she smiled "—there's a deep insecurity hidden from most people, only shows to someone who loves him. It's all right. It's all right. He'd hidden behind such a rigid mask the first year he was here, self-protective, so unreadable. Us together, the mask fell away. He lightened up so beautifully, full of fun—does that contradict what I just said? No, day-to-day, full of fun; singing silly songs in the shower, nonsense nicknames for everyone. Yet fundamentally so serious. Discoveries I was happy to make. All of them. But with Nikki's death, he's a different man. The mask, the helmet, is back. Unreadable. Untouchable. He had a close friendship with Leandro Torres that he suddenly dropped. Sorry, Lee, you're just not there anymore. Brutal for Lee. Who was having his own problems then." She was silent for a moment. "It would sadden me immensely to think he's one of these guys who has enthusiasms and then abruptly loses interest, drops them. It would sadden me deeply."

She stopped, collected herself. "He's suddenly—an old man. Sometimes he walks with great effort, like someone beat him with a stick. He'll stop, look around at the world, almost baffled. I don't even recognize that old guy. I know what you're thinking, Ronnie. What is it with me and old guys?" Her elderly first husband, a prominent mathematician. "I thought this one would be there to bury me."

Ron smiled, shook his head gently. "And you?"

"I—I miss paradise more than I can say. Things are going on with me that I don't understand. Well, as Herr Wittgenstein once said, what can be said at all can be said clearly, but what we cannot talk about we must pass over in silence. I'm washed out, a hangover state. Burned out, frankly."

Ron sighed. "I gotta ask you something hard. Does he seem self-destructive? Do you think he'd do anything to harm himself, or even you?"

Judith felt the tears begin to push behind her eyes yet again. Would she ever stop wanting to cry? "Ron. Of course not." An automatic response. She thought suddenly of an admission once made in a beautiful hotel room in the ancient city of Siracusa, where he'd brought tears to her eyes, that he could ever have been that unhappy. "How do I know? I've never seen him like this. I'm not afraid for myself; I think he loves me deeply. Or did. But to himself? I don't know. I honestly don't know. His first wife was probably a suicide. Now his daughter. Char says his own mother was none too stable. He was brought up by his aunt, a salt-of-the-earth woman. You've met Char, right? Even so, before all this I'd have said no, not self-destructive at all. Finding himself for the first time these last few years. Genuinely content for the first time. But now—I just don't know."

"Oh, sweet *Königin*." The old nickname, sweet queen. "I don't remember, does he still have guns around the house?"

Judith gasped. "My God. Well, yes. Remember, he was a hunter in Germany. We have some rifles in a gun safe. Fine pieces; he's talked about selling them in Europe because he doesn't hunt anymore. He has a permit to carry a concealed weapon. Some kind of Glock, I think it is. He never carries it; just down to the shooting range for practice every once in a while." She stared at her old friend, letting the implications of these questions sink in. She was unmoored, lightheaded.

"Is he getting help?"

"Jack? No way. He thinks any therapist is only going to give him pills, which he has—a great resistance to. To be blunt, the devil's spawn, he thinks. His first wife went under with drugs. Nikki was on medications when she died. So papa's little endocrine imbalance is just going to have to fix itself."

Ron was silent for a while, still holding her hand. "It's not gonna fix itself. You need to push on him, get him to a doc."

"You really don't know him if you think I can do that."

"Know him? Or you?" He left her with that for a moment. "I don't know him well enough, so I have to ask. Does he have any kind of spiritual beliefs to—well, to turn to?"

"Not really. He's always cherished the Stoics, Epictetus, Marcus Aurelius. I think they counsel detachment. God knows he's become detached."

"Oh, darling Judith. What a fucking turn of events. I'm no shrink, but I'm sure one would tell you there's so much anger and guilt to deal with for a parent whose child has committed suicide. It's profound. For him, lifelong. But probably not always so painful for you both as it is now."

"Then I suppose I'd better start reading the Stoics," Judith said sadly. "Learn to detach."

He kissed her hand in his. "Honey, I've been evading asking you what you're doing yourself to cope."

"Me? At first I just tiptoed around, afraid to say boo. The whole thing seemed so completely—overwhelming. There wasn't any right thing to say. I was just getting to know Nikki. Oddly, strangely, I was the one she seemed most comfortable with. She phoned me from New York so often that, frankly Ronnie, I began to dodge her calls—she seemed to have no idea I was at work, that I couldn't have an hour-long conversation any time she felt like hanging out on the phone. I'd return those calls, but I couldn't be there like she wanted me to be there. Maybe if I'd understood her needs better."

"Her mother died. When?" Despite her raised hand, he refilled her tea cup.

"Nikki was still in high school—a boarding school in Germany. Jack had put her and her brother there when their mother got too sick—that's a euphemism:

was too strung out—to look after them. I think that went on for five years, maybe more for Nikki. Losing your mother at that age, even one who never actually mothered you in any real sense, has to be tough. No one would ever say my name and maternal in the same breath, but my heart went out to her as another human being in sad straits. I tried to be some help, some company. A female adult she could look to."

She thought. "Actually, I learned something in those talks, Ronnie. She'd had to be the adult supervision for her own mother all her young life. So she automatically sponged up all her mother's complaints against Jack. When she actually dealt with her father, the reality seemed weird—at odds—with the image. That mismatch never went away. Sometimes she'd say something quite nasty about him, and I'd say, Nikki, give me an example, and—nothing. It was just a 'feeling' she had. She imputed all kinds of ludicrous opinions to him about everything. I'd be saying, no, Nikki, that's not what your papa thinks at all. Ask him yourself if you don't believe me. Well, maybe he's changed, she'd say grudgingly. It was all this vestigial crap from her mother. I finally told her to discover him for herself, that in my view he was an extraordinary human being who'd been formed under extraordinary circumstances. She'd go: You're his wife; you're going to say that. But actually, she wanted to know him, wanted me to tell her about him, the real Jackster, as she called him behind his back. Her father is an agent, acts upon the world: Nikki and, for that matter, her mother, were always subject to the world. Its events. Its ebbs and flows."

Judith got up, walked to a bookcase, stared unseeingly at the books, moved her hand absently over their spines. "Jack had some issues with her, no question. He has ridiculously high standards, starting with himself. He sometimes said to me that while he loved her—in a dutiful-father kind of way—he didn't always like her. Well, hell, she wasn't always likable—very volatile, more than a bit whiny. Always so very needy. Nothing that drove her, like me, like her father, at that age—and sure, ever since—to excel at something unique. She had some artsy-fartsy ideas about herself as a painter, but they were dreams, never happened, and Jack was really troubled by that. At the same time, he saw in her his crazy younger self, the self he never was allowed to be. So I don't know. Maybe there was a little jealousy about that on his part?" Judith turned to look back at Ron on the couch. "She looked very much like him. That complicated things too. Now it's never going to get resolved. She made sure of that."

8

The sky was threatening—maybe rain, probably snow. Through the windows, they could see an enormous cloudbank obscuring the mountaintops. Snowing at the higher elevations. Ron Gresham cocked his head as if he were trying to get a better angle to view her. Frowned. "Have you salvaged anything from all this, Jay?"

She came back to the couch, sat down heavily, turned her face away. In shame? he wondered. Turned back to him. "Learned a few things about myself, I guess. First, that I'm not a particularly patient or generous-hearted woman. I run out of sympathy real quick. I want to say: pull up your socks, stop whining, what's done is done. He doesn't whine, of course. He goes silent. Deathly silent. But I'm not all warm and fuzzy either. It's not my nature. This worries me."

"How so?"

"Let me tell you a story." She stopped. "When I was newly married to Jonathan, when I was a very young mathematician, he invited a couple to dinner that I was very eager to meet. Forty years before, they'd had a shocking affair—everyone knew about it, even after all that time. The guy was her husband's student then. Not only did he crack a great problem, one that his professor had been working on without luck for years, but he ran off with the professor's wife in the bargain. She left her husband, and her infants—a legendary grand passion. Maybe I expected her to arrive with a rose in her teeth, or décolletage down to here. What I saw, what I learned, was a little subtler than that. Women who've been part of a grand passion carry themselves differently from other women. Reckless desire, that wild yearning; above all, giving in to it, surrendering to it totally...all that injects something into the bloodstream that never goes away. A kind of pride. Self-satisfaction. A special confidence maybe, so that whatever happens to her from then on, she's—well, different from the rest, okay? So, young as I was, I could see this, detect it in her at some level. But him. He was old by then. Irksome. Repeating himself. Whimpering, picking his nose, scratching his crotch, randomly absent from the conversation. No. She was the one I watched. She was snappish, impatient, scolding him for infractions I didn't even see, never mind the ones I did. And I thought, is this what it comes to? Is this what happens to a grand passion? I didn't wait around for it to happen with Jonathan, which wasn't a grand passion in the first place. But with Jack. I hoped to feast on that grand passion for many years to come. I don't want to be that bitch. Ever."

Judith sat back, her arms folded across her chest, looking into some middle distance. "Then I also learned that some things aren't quite amenable to the way I usually think."

"How do you mean?"

She smiled apologetically. "I'm what's called a computational thinker. I always was. My professional training just gave me a vocabulary for it, and a whole hell of a lot more practice at it. First thing with a problem, you ask, how big is this? How can I make it tractable? Can I decompose it, solve little bits of it at least? Can I reduce it to a problem I've already solved? You know, transform it somehow, reformulate it? Is there some way of abstracting this to a simpler problem, so I can operate on multiple levels simultaneously?" She sighed "In this case . . . the answer to all those is no. Hell no. Okay, okay; can I settle for an approximate solution? The answer to that is yes. Maybe. Depends how approximate. But I couldn't even get to that. Okay. Is there some way to recover from a worst-case crash? Contain the damage, correct the errors? The girl is fucking dead. No way to correct that. If there's a way to contain the damage, I haven't been able to think of it. He's not the kind of guy you can say, no problem, honey, it's just brain area 25 out of whack, making mischief with the serotonin transporters; a little circuit disorder. Take two Zoloft and call me in the morning."

Ron's eyebrows flew up. "Praise God from whom all blessings flow." He was trying to conceal a smile, and she waved her hand: feel free. He gave in with a big grin. "Queen Judith, you're brainy, you're beautiful, and no doubt you're sexy, but when it comes to interpersonal relations, you could use a tutorial. Maybe even a makeover."

She wasn't listening. "I really tried to re-conceptualize this. Tried to draw on what it felt like when my father died. When Sophie died. The analogies are bad, totally inappropriate. My father was old, and his death a blessed release from dementia. Sophie died too young, but it was a natural death. Neither of them was my own kid. This is all about his own kid. He'd had a rocky relationship with her, which was already generating guilt even before she killed herself. My grief for my father, my grief for Sophie—it just didn't commute. Very different. So I couldn't really get into Jack's head that way."

She thought for a while, and Ron kept silent, sensing there was more, maybe something even more difficult. She evaded looking at him. "I hardly know how to say this. You know I resisted Jack, resisted him for so long. When I finally stopped resisting, I thought—that was stupid. He's wonderful. This is the life I was meant for. But maybe…maybe those original instincts, inchoate as they were, were right on target."

She was remembering, trying to figure things out as she went along. "In the beginning, I thought of him as a thug. That softened to maybe only desperado—and yeah, I got that right. But he—he had me right away with a question he raised the first time I ever saw him. A dinner party at ghastly Maya's, and he stopped everyone with a simple question. *Why are you here?* You could take it as, how come you're in Santa Fe? Some people did. But I knew he was asking—sounds pompous, but a metaphysical question, waiting to see who'd rise to that level. I wanted to. I wanted a man who'd ask such a question. But I was deeply, deeply afraid. About him was also—an air of menace. Yet little by little, he got me. He said he wasn't interested in the past, only in the future. He pulled out of me things I'd never told anyone, not even you. What my work has been to me. That sometimes it seems—it used to seem—sacred. How that humbled me. He dug that out. Made me put it into words. He laid claim to so much of me, and I—I said yes. Yours, Jack Molloy. All yours."

Ron kept silent, but his expectant look pushed her on. "So I've—well, I've withdrawn. Gone to work on something else in the hopes that he'll heal himself, solve the problem himself. Neither courageous nor glorious. In no way edifying. But goddam, Ronnie, what should I do?"

He didn't think she was asking for advice.

"Jack has one of the great contemporary art collections."

"Well, yeah?" he said, not following. "Everyone knows."

"He's always bought emerging artists, wanted to be there first. For him, the fun was in the finding, the getting. Maybe not so much the keeping. I sometimes wonder if, by capitulating the way I did, by saying yes, I doomed myself. That's such a crap thing to say about him. He's not that way, not about human beings."

Ron shook his head sadly. "You gotta get some help yourself, dear one. You gotta. There's a Dr. Feldman who's getting ready to retire, but you'd respect her mind, which I know is important to you if you're going to get anything out of it. And Jay? There's something else. Last time I saw Molloy one-on-one, we did a hike at Tent Rocks. Jesus, that's more than a year ago, before Nikki died. Maybe early last fall already? I told him then that I'd noticed something was bothering you, and he better pay attention. Tell me what I was picking up from you then."

She hissed. "Judith's little problems got swamped in the tsunami."

Again, he kissed her hand affectionately. "Judith's little problems? They're more important to me than anything else."

She turned to him, studied him. His pallor had never changed, from the time he'd been a teenager and they'd cruelly nicknamed him *der Spargel*, the white asparagus. Age and some physical activity had put beef on him, and the face was finally creasing, though she had to make an effort to see that, to stop seeing him as he'd been all those decades ago in their adolescence. Thought of how they'd met, their enduring friendship built on a kind of secret, implicit understanding that they were each one thing to the world, but another, hidden thing in their hearts. Not hidden to each other. "You're such a good and loyal friend, Ronnie. You make me understand why friendship is so dear, so precious. Thank you."

He smiled and didn't have to say she'd once saved his life. "So tell me Judith's little problems. At least we can laugh."

"Nothing but old age. I'm losing it. My mathematical gift. Losing the power. For a few more years I can fake it ten different ways—committees, consulting, all that. But that great surge of mathematical power has gone, baby, gone. Dried up. Disappeared. That's bad. I know I'm grieving for it. But the worst thing is, I don't really know who I am without it. My identity." She said the word half sarcastically. "Then on top of that...all this. Sometimes I wonder, Ronnie. When I was in graduate school, I watched my female colleagues dropping out in droves—they'd drop out because they just must marry some guy; they had to have a baby; they had to—well, anything to get out from under the pressure. I wasn't—generous to them about that. But now it occurs to me that I might have married Jack for something similar. Did I sense I might not be able to cut it in mathematics anymore? Then along comes an easy alternative, so I take that way out?"

"You're asking me?" He looked at her with genuine curiosity, and when she nodded, he took a deep breath. "Okay. I think by saying that, you dishonor the noble occasion your career has been. And you dishonor the grand experiment of your marriage. I also think you're being as unjustly hard on yourself, as you once were on those young women colleagues of yours. That's what I think." They kept silent, listening to the piñon crackling in the fireplace, the wind picking up.

Finally he spoke again. "You never asked me why I quit making movies." She looked at him sharply. "Yeah, of course. I could see the end coming. I didn't want to repeat myself—well, anymore than I already had. So Gabe conveniently had a wipeout on his surfboard, and Gabe and Ron conveniently picked up and went to Morocco for a few years. He still thinks I threw over everything for him, and while I've told him no, it was for me, in a very touching way he doesn't believe that. Don't want to say more about it, except I understand where you're coming from. That's our next job, Jay. To be the next thing we have to be, whatever it is. We don't know. We can't reason our way forward. To quote my favorite scientist, change is inevitable; the nature of that change is not." He squeezed the hand he had not let go of. "Say that for Molloy, he moved elegantly into the next thing he had to be—until this came along. Now he'll have to move into a different thing. Adaptation. Adaptation matters. Do you want me to say something to him?"

She looked fearful. "Oh, God. No. Please don't. He'd hate it that I've even confided this much in you. He's such a private person."

"I know." He smiled in affectionate recollection. "Before you guys were an item, I once had a funny conversation with him. He actually invited me over, we had a scotch. He was trying so hard to find out from me if he had a chance with you, and he just couldn't bring himself to ask it outright. The feints and maneuvers were a stitch. But I also kind of liked him for it. When you're a grownup, life shouldn't be an Oprah episode. In that, Jack Molloy and I are alike—at least we honor the Stoics, even if we can't always live up to the precepts. He'd been *l'Homme au Masque de Fer* to all of us until then, and that's the first time I saw that iron mask melt a little. First time I saw this could be something more than one of his notorious one-night stands. Or one of yours, for that matter. The funny thing is, I remember thinking back then, as he was struggling to ask about you, I remember thinking, if you hurt my Judith in any way, man, I'm quite capable of killing you. Oh, yes. And here we are. I see you hurting more than I've ever seen, even more than when Sophie threw you out before she died. He's caused the pain. And I don't hold it against him at all, Judith. Life—and death—it just turned out that way. I worry about him instead. I want an end to this for you both. A happy ending. We never let go of being children in that sense, do we?"

She closed her eyes, her head back on the couch. "It helps to have someone to tell. Doesn't change things, but it helps."

"We take strength from each other's strengths, dear one. You, happily married. It was a source of joy and strength for all of us. Everybody loved to come over on a Sunday night, such great talk at your table. I loved the way he always looked at you, downright worshipfully. How proud he was of you. Part of the network goes down, we can't just re-route. We need to fix it."

When she got up to go, he held on to both her hands, scrutinized her. "We've known each other so very long, Jay. I love you; it kills me to see you hurting like this. But I also think you're probably the only one who can pull him out of all this. You two do belong together. Gabe and I were right about that. Maybe that's your next thing to be."

"Jack Molloy's caseworker? Oh, I don't think so. God help us, no. But Ron, there's one more thing. I'm so afraid—afraid that this is the end for Jack and me. That maybe he thinks if he just changes the old wife, everything else will change magically too. He wouldn't be the first."

Her old friend stared at her for a long time. "Nothing's impossible," he finally said, "Nothing's impossible. But somehow I doubt it. I think he's hurting beyond hurt, and your job is to find a way to reach through all that and pull him back to us." In the tone of voice they used to use when they were playing their old etymology game, he added, "Uxurious?"

She shook her head. Not willing to play. Not knowing the answer. Maybe not even knowing the word.

"It means loving your wife excessively. Odd word. Etymology from the Latin, *uxor*, wife, then Middle English. I don't think there's a female equivalent, loving your husband excessively. Anyway, your husband is uxurious. For what it's worth."

9

"I read *The Birth of Tragedy* since we saw each other last."

And of course you can read it in the original. I envy that.

"In the original. Not that it helped. All that stuff about purifying the German spirit. Embarrassing. Even worse in German. The author said so himself later. About the role of music in our brains I'll leave to the neuroscientists, thanks. Well, he was my age when he wrote it. Maybe you get a pass for youthful nonsense. But the central nugget fascinated me. I suppose that's why people still read it and argue with it to this day."

The central nugget?

"The major idea—that tragedy is born out of the complementary aspects of the Dionysian and the Apollonian. Passion and order. Tragedy doesn't, can't exist without both. Tragedy synthesizes both. Horrible things happen in tragedy; you can't escape them. Horrible things happen in life. Yet paradoxically, tragedy is life-affirming. Tragedy compels you to stare into the abyss. Then shows you how you can step back from it. It takes you beneath the ever-changing surface to what's eternal, what old Fritz calls the creative primordial mother. Whew. But I sort of get what he means."

A lot to talk about here. Do you remember telling me about your daydream, wanting to be Hans Castorp, who saw himself as a little goat-man, a faun, lying in the meadow, making beautiful music?

"Did I mention that to you? I didn't remember I had."

Yes. What's Nietzsche's take on the goat-man, the faun? The satyr? Faun is what the Romans called these woodland creatures, these satyrs.

"Oh, my God. Yes. I didn't make that connection at all."

Tell me what you're thinking as it occurs to you.

"Nietzsche calls the satyr a—well, it's very complicated. An emblem, I guess, of primitive nature. A human archetype, the symbol, the embodiment, of our highest, most intense emotions. There's a unique intimacy between the satyr and his god, Dionysius. The god leads, and the satyr flings himself into the bacchanalia of those extreme emotions, is carried away to the point where he actually destroys his god, dismembers him. The passions are violent and sexual.

Very, very sexual. Murderous. Extreme. Along with all of nature. And the ancient Greeks regarded that as sacred."

That?

"The sexual powers of nature. Including humans. Even though it inevitably leads to destruction."

Go on.

"The satyr was both sublime and divine. Nietzsche says that when the ancient Greeks participated in the theater, they transformed themselves, changed from ordinary life to the heightened life of the satyr—maybe we'd say identified themselves with satyrs... Anyway, to become a satyr was to change to a truer, heightened life. It was a way to encounter truth and nature in its most forceful form. Is that what you're getting at?"

It's a beginning.

"Okay. The satyr seems extreme in his passions, maybe excessively so. He's not a god himself, but he's so near to his god that it opens him to the deep wisdom of nature."

What is that wisdom?

"That however noble our intentions are, we'll commit terrible acts, suffer enormously... We'll come to believe that life is meaningless, unendurable; we'll long to end it. Yet all that suffering will bring about a greater good. Somehow it will bring to life a new world. Somehow. We look into the abyss, which is real, and awful, but nature—and art—heal us. Well, console us."

And isn't it the case, doesn't Nietzsche make the point, that natural laws must be broken to achieve this wisdom? That we can't learn nature's wisdom without breaking its rules? That to achieve wisdom we must commit a crime against nature? Please, I think we're on to something important here. I know there are acts, even thoughts, of yours that you're deeply ashamed of. That you consider unnatural.

"Well, yes. Yes. No need to name them all. You've heard them."

It was an ancient belief—again, according to Nietzsche—that the magus, the wise man, must be born of an incestuous union. Who do you think has been symbolically born from these incestuous unions, these acts against nature?

"I don't know."

I think you do, Stephen. But the knowledge is very hard for you to accept. You came to me because you wanted help with some vivid dreams. What does the philosopher say about dreams?

"He calls dreams the Apollonian world. Clearer, more intense, than the everyday world."

He says more.

"Much more. I'm trying to remember. Apollo is the god of individuation, but in pulling us apart, one from another, he violates the fundamental oneness of the world. He's both right and wrong about this. That's the essence of tragedy. Yet tragedy is a place of continuous rebirth for us. Rebirth. I like that."

Can you connect that notion to the dreams you first brought to me?

"Well, that's what I've been trying to do all along, isn't it?"

Nietzsche isn't the last word, Stephen, but the framework he offers in *The Birth of Tragedy* might be helpful for you as you try to decrypt the messages of these dreams. Try this framework when you think about the lives of the people you love—your father. Your sister. Your stepmother, Judith. Daniella, of course. The architect, Leandro Torres. Finally, you yourself. Hasn't each of you been led to the edge of the abyss? Who's looked in and yet redeemed themselves? Who's failed, or refused, to look in? Where are the connections among you? What will rebirth look like?

"I'll think about it...some more."

And especially think along the lines you were talking about at our last meeting—that creativity is sacred. The creators are holy ones. Touched by divinity. Ask yourself how those creators nurture the flame, connect with the creative primordial mother, as Nietzsche calls that fundamental will to exist. To create. To be reborn. How did they dare to look into the abyss? What have they seen when they looked there? What price do they pay for reaching for the divine? How will they keep the flame from consuming them?

"Maybe they can't."

Maybe not, Stephen. Maybe not.

"But Nietzsche would claim that to know that raging desire to exist, to be, directly, immediately, without intervention, is to be at one with the fundamental nature of life. United with its creative joy. If the time ever comes I feel that, I'll let you know."

10

One afternoon later that winter, Molloy realizes he cannot remember a word of whatever's in front of him, though five densely printed pages have apparently turned under his hand, his eyes. What he does understand is that he's on the verge of losing everything. The hands holding everything together for so long, no matter what the sacrifice, cannot hold much longer, are beginning to let slip. He examines his desperation with an almost clinical detachment. For all the crises he's faced in his life, a narcotics-addled wife who couldn't care for their children; a hundred and one maulings from one market or another that threatened his very livelihood; the sudden murder of his closest friend; periods then of loneliness so extreme they almost paralyzed him; for all those, which, one by one he had overcome, he doesn't know how to prevent this coming catastrophe.

For he can see it coming. He can see the woman he loves—and oh how he loves her, as mute as he's been; how he fears her absence more than anything—withdrawing from his life, first gradually, and then forever. The earworm that grabs hold of him most often is Jacques Brel, usually in English, If you go away. Sometimes in French, *Ne me quitte pas*. Life reduced to sentimental pop songs. His son too will be lost to him. He'll have nothing, nobody. At least he talks less to Nikki in his head; the arguments haven't changed, but repeating them no longer gives him comfort.

Outside his office window, the winter sky is darkening. The sunset will be what, in happier times, he and Judith used to call the work of the *Kitschmeister*, so florid in its purples, golds, reds and oranges, so much wretched excess, that it mocks good taste.

Impulsively, he calls Nola, asks to see her. He'll come over, he says. Her silence humiliates, discourages him. He goes on: it's nothing to discuss in public, like in a restaurant or something.

"All right," she says at last.

He cancels his late afternoon appointments, tells Wally he'll be unreachable, and whistles to Wotan to follow him. At the foundation's front door he stops, comes back to Wally. "If Judith calls, she can reach me on my mobile." But he knows sadly that Judith will not call. She's leaving him alone. For his sake. For her own sake too, he assumes. He knows he's, if not infectious, certainly repellent.

On the walk to Nola's, he thinks about Brand X being back in town. That's how he thinks of Benito: Brand X, the unnamable, the lesser alternative. Brand X would do the reptile thing if Judith gives him even the slightest opening. But why blame Brand X? Queen Judith has always called the shots in her life. Poor old Brand X is as helpless before Judith as Molloy himself is. If Queen Judith wants Brand X, then she'll have him, and neither he nor Brand X can do a fucking thing about it. That idea makes him even more wretched. He wills himself not to think about it.

Nola lives just off Acequia Madre, the road that has run for four hundred years or more past the mother ditch. It's not far from his office. He and Wotan walk the distance in less than ten minutes. Even in his misery, he can be grateful for the beauty of the bare cottonwoods above his head, the solid tranquility of the high, earth-colored walls that shelter and protect so much. He walks alongside the *acequia*, frozen now, but he knows the sound it makes in the summer, feels momentarily comforted by history, at least. Maybe he isn't in such bad shape after all. Maybe he doesn't need to make this visit. When Wotan tries to scramble down the steep banks of the *acequia*, the dog gets a sharp *"Nein!"* from his master, who doesn't relish scrambling down after him if Wotan can't get himself out. Which is silly. Of course he can. What Molloy wants is concentration of purpose, and poor Wotan will just have to go along with it.

He pushes open Nola's front gate, and suddenly remembers one of the first things he ever heard Judith say, that gates were provisional, allowed you to back out. He thinks he could still back out from this, pretend it was just a social visit, a chance to drink tea. Knows he can't. He stops on the pathway. In the summer, in the autumn, Nola's garden is particularly beautiful: restful, well-tended, rich in blossoms, texture, color. Now he sees that in the bleak winter, its dormant branches are an intricate gray sculpture. Dead.

What is it about the desert winter that seems so much more final than the northern gardens, the hardwood forests he's known all his life? In the Pennsylvania woods with his uncle, carrying his deer rifle, he learned the trees by the bark alone, since the leaves had long gone: black oak, elm, sycamore, the ash trees, black and white, the different maples. Their barks are as distinct as their names, for in the east, tree bark has color, texture, signs of life, even in the dead of winter. In the high desert winter, all is bleached out, monochrome gray. Driftwood of the unforgiving sun. A vague promise for the spring is intellectual, not something he really feels.

Nola opens the stout turquoise blue front door, a welcoming smile; holds out a hand.

Why am I here? he asks himself in despair, cannot answer. Pulls himself together. "Thanks for seeing me on the spur of the moment. Jesus. It feels like it's been winter for a year." He looks over his shoulder. "Your garden. Hard to remember how it flowers."

"It's just asleep now. Resting. Let me take your coat."

He sits across from Nola on her couch, thinks that Lee Torres had sat here a long time ago, wounded in body. He feels a sudden sadness that he's been such a poor friend to Leandro Torres. Whose body must be mended by now, while he himself has brought to Nola a mortally wounded soul. To Nola, he has always been able to talk.

He inhales the cedary smell of the interior, drifting down from the latillas overhead, the scent of the small piñon fire in the corner fireplace. How dark, how restful the house is, compared to the bright light of his own house. Though once, when everything in life was bright, he loved his own luminous rooms, the rooms he shares with his wife. Nola's house is old, and she's done little to change the small windows, the thick walls. It had been a farmhouse. Fields irrigated by the *acequia madre*, the mother ditch, had once surrounded it in all directions. No agriculture here anymore, but Nola still has water rights, irrigates her summer garden from the mother ditch.

He hasn't been here since the day her son died. A year and a half ago, or more. The dreadful phrenology heads, the work of her former husband, have disappeared from the shelves, replaced by exquisite things she owns herself, or the work of artists she'd represented when her gallery was open. Or maybe she's reopened it. Did he and Judith go to a reopening this summer? He can't remember, is embarrassed to ask.

She serves hot tea, a bowl of water for the panting Wotan. Even in winter, the desert dehydrates living creatures. He thanks her silently for her own silence. Sipping his tea, he procrastinates some more, sighs, looks at her bleakly. "Tell me it will get better."

Nola studies him. He cringes a little under that scrutiny, knows exactly what she sees, for he looks at himself daily with disbelief: his skin slack and pale, the enormous crescent moons of darkness under his red-rimmed eyes; the creases from nose to mouth like arroyos, eroded by tears that remain unshed. He's graying rapidly. She hasn't seen him for a while; the decline must be a grim surprise. He can imagine her thinking, once such a handsome man. Well, she'd thought so once, hadn't she? She nods slowly, as if saying yes, she'd thought so once. "I suppose it will, eventually."

"Eventually." He says it like a curse. "One of the last times I dropped her off at the airport... She was carrying on about something, and I thought, maybe it isn't so bad to have all that hysteria on the other side of the country. Her father. That's what I actually thought."

"Don't beat yourself up about it."

"Don't beat myself up about it? Your son died despite everything you and a team of doctors could do. I watched you then, at the edge, month after month after month. Whereas my daughter died because I turned my back, pushed her away."

"I don't think so, no. Did she leave a note?"

He doesn't answer. Nikki did not leave a note. Not in so many words.

"She was in New York. You couldn't have done anything from here."

"We didn't take phone calls for three or four days after she left us in Colorado. It was our way of keeping the world at bay for a while. We thought we were entitled to a little down time. Even when we got home to Santa Fe, we didn't turn on the phones until the next day. So it was several days before—before I knew." He looks at her hopelessly, says nothing. Please, Nola. Help.

"Did you have any inkling this might be coming?

He shakes his head. "Not at all. We'd all been skiing up in Colorado over that Thanksgiving. She seemed pretty happy. In fact, it was the happiest family time we'd spent in years. Maybe ever." He looks at the wall above her head. "Well, sure. Always signs in retrospect. Her mother probably committed suicide, did you know that?" Nola nods. He'd spoken of this once before, in an eerie rose-colored cave in far northern New Mexico. He's forgotten, but Nola hasn't. "It isn't for sure," he goes on. "Lindy was addicted to every upper and downer under the sun, legal and illegal, and she finally overdosed. I was abroad, in Turkey on business. Nikki never forgave me for not being there for her mother. Wherever my Nikki is now, she won't ever forgive me for not being there for her, either." He covers his eyes with a hand, thinks this dull pressure behind his eyes means he wants to weep. But he cannot. Nola is still, waiting to hear more. Surely there's more, but where will it come from? He's empty.

After a while he lifts his head. "I always blamed Lindy for Nikki's problems. Instabilities. I never said it out loud, but it's true, I always did. That was so wrong. Maybe not wrong. Not completely right." He turns toward her, but looks past her, not seeing her in any way. "My own mother was a kind of small-town tragedy. After I was born, she nearly never came out of her bedroom. We weren't sophisticated people. Nobody thought she should see a doctor, or if she should, what kind of doctor. My aunt and uncle raised me. So whatever's genetic—my poor darling Nikki was cursed on both sides. Don't ask me how I escaped it. How my son has escaped it. At least so far. Though Jesus, the big sleep looks very, very attractive just now."

"Molloy—"

"I was older than Nikki when I wanted to—put an end to it. Nothing had any meaning. I was trapped in a horror of a marriage. I hated my work. I could feel myself closing down, month after month. Year after year. I thought, why not just finish the job? What could the future hold, if the present was intolerable, getting worse all the time?"

"I had no idea."

"Are you shocked?" he asks without interest. "Nobody knows this except a doc I used to see. Well, Judith kind of guessed once. It was long after the fact when—when I finally saw that doc. To this day, I don't know what stopped me. The kids, I guess. I had two little kids, two little hostages to fortune. Who was going to look after them if I was gone? I sure as hell wasn't going to be my father, so long, it's been good to know you." He shifts uneasily on the couch, rubs his fingertips on a Two Gray Hills rug that's thrown over the couch back.

"Then sometimes I think the papa's just a spear-carrier in this production. Nikki didn't know how much I loved her, and if she had, she wouldn't have cared. Lindy? My mother? It's like they never saw me. I'm a bit player in this whole drama—except what they all have in common is Jack Molloy. What's the matter with me, Nola, that I carry death with me like this?"

Nola shakes her head. "It's not you. You have a big heart, dear friend. You've suffered unusual—misfortunes."

"Misfortunes? Every one of these women has said, in no uncertain terms, fuck you, Jack Molloy. My mother. My first wife. My daughter. Am I so evil? Nola?"

She remains silent. Maybe she thinks it's only a rhetorical question. Maybe she agrees. He shifts his gaze so he can actually see her. The oversize glasses have been replaced with something more chic. She's put on a little weight, which suits her. "You look well, Nola. You look…"

She crosses her legs, smooths her skirt self-consciously. "I have someone now."

"Good. I'm very glad to hear it. A lover."

"Lover? Well, in some limited way." She smiles almost coyly, winks for emphasis. "At a certain age we finally get it, that Mr. Right is—whaddya know?—Mr. Impossible. So we settle instead for Mr. Possible. My friend is my Mr. Possible. Since he also yearns for someone he can't have, I'm his Miss Possible. It's an accommodation, Molloy, a mutual convenience. Life's like that." She pauses. "It's your friend Torres. If I'm not his first choice, at least he finds me desirable. To be thought desirable after all these years—well, it's good for your complexion, as they say."

"I wish you both joy," he says flatly. His mind wanders. Torres had moved out of the compound right after Nikki's death, saying he was sure they wanted to be alone in their grief. He'd hardly noticed. He doesn't even know where Torres has gone, though someone must have told him. He can't think about that; his mind flashes compulsively back to the three dead women. "I'd give the world to be able to hear it from each of these women—what did I do to you to deserve this? Just tell me. Just tell me. Maybe I can't fix it. Maybe I'm such a grim companion that three women have—"

"It's not about you. You didn't choose your mother and you didn't choose your daughter. Your first wife? Well, that I can't help you with. Maybe that's how you thought women were supposed to be."

He listens, knows he's not hearing. "The last time we were together, Nikki accused me of being brutal about her art. Yeah, I probably was. You yourself said that I'd better not do that. Remember?"

She shakes her head.

"You don't remember? In the pink cave? You said 'One day this daughter will come to you with the knowledge that the collector's eye and the artist's eye are entirely different things. If you've been wise and kind, she'll tell you this wisely and kindly. If you haven't, she'll tell you this as she slices out your heart.' I guess I wasn't wise and kind. I couldn't seem to help it then. I didn't think it would—and then she stopped painting. But at Thanksgiving she told us she'd started up again; that this was good new stuff. Even I might like it. Even I, the great almighty and final judge of all art under the sun. She said she'd set up a studio in her brother's room at our New York place; she hadn't been able to get to her loft in Tribeca since 9/11. But when Judith and I got to the apartment afterwards, there was no art. No studio. No nothing. She couldn't after all—oh fuck it, nobody kills themselves over their art. You hit a rough patch, slice your ear off, and go on. It's only a painting. But she sure as hell sliced out my heart, didn't she?"

He's silent for a while, his eyes moving from place to place around the room. He can see the paintings, the refined ceramics, but hardly registers them. He knows he's almost twitching in his misery. When he resumes, the voice is not his own, a whisper, the sins of his life in a rushed confession. "Nola, I didn't want Nikki to be born. I begged her mother to abort. Lindy had been so sick, so goddamned deranged after Stevie was born that I just couldn't face another. I didn't think she could face another. I begged her to abort. Me, raised a good Catholic boy. It's stupid, I know, but I sometimes wondered if Nikki heard this, felt it somehow, while she was lying there in her mother's womb. Knew that her papa didn't want her, refused to accept her on any terms. But once she was born, everything changed. I loved her ridiculously. Wouldn't that cancel out... No, I'm not saying that right. I loved her ridiculously. I often—didn't particularly like her.

"You saw her, right? At your boy's funeral? Maybe you didn't notice; you had enough on your mind that day. She was the image of me, her papa. Everyone always said so. When she was driving me crazy with her hysterics, I still loved her because—because she was my kid, and because it was like loving yourself, your younger crazy self. The younger crazy self you could never be. You couldn't let yourself be. Life hadn't let you be. Did she know her father hadn't wanted her? Did she never forgive me for that? Nothing was going to alter that first principle? Well, she had her revenge, didn't she? She turned around and rejected me in the most unequivocal, ultimate way she could've. Oh, sweet Jesus, did she reject me." The whisper was gone with a shout: "I am so fucking angry at her for that!"

"My friend..."

"Your boy dies, you grieve. It's all so straightforward. My girl dies, and now we only begin with settling the shit. She thinks she's settled mine. Well, yeah. I thought when my father showed up last fall, no, a year ago last fall, whenever it was—that I'd never felt such rage. Mother of God, I didn't know what rage was! I could kill that kid." He sees Nola is stifling a smile. No wonder. Even he'd laugh.

"And Judith?" she eventually asks.

The groan is forced out of him. "She's been—she's trying her best. But she's not a mother, a parent. She can't know what it's like to lose a child."

"How much of this have you told her?"

"Nothing. Can you picture me telling the imperial Judith any of this?"

"You're quite in awe of your wife, aren't you?"

He ignores the asperity in that question. "Yes. In awe. More than ever. It was a kind of schoolboy crush at first. Now it's the real deal." He shakes his head sorrowfully. "I'm not really doing her justice. She'd listen. I think she would. I just—don't want her to know this. Oh shit, I know it's a nightmare for her too; really I do. What a life I'm giving her. But I can't help it. When she comes to me with some idea to make things better, let's go to Europe, let's try a long stay in Manhattan—to me she's just being a pest. I wish she'd go away and leave me alone already. No, I don't really want that. I want... This woman is the love of my life, and I can't even—" He doesn't want to say more, and changes the subject. "Thanks for listening. You, at least..." he trails off.

"Yes. I, at least, understand." She says it slowly, regretfully.

"She'd listen; she might even understand. I don't know. But she's leaving me, Nola. Not a packed suitcase and slamming the door, but the distance between us just grows and grows. She takes on more outside stuff—consulting, committees. She travels more. I see less and less of her. Jesus, can I blame her? It's a survival mechanism. Judith comes home every night to the house of the dead. The most exciting thing I've got the energy to do is maybe listen to some Bach. Mahler if it's been a good day. For the first few months, she was just so quiet and understanding. Never asked—now she's—I know she's spending more time at her own little place. She's writing a book, she says. Needs her library. I guess it's true. I don't let myself think otherwise."

"Isn't that stuff all on the Internet now? You have high-speed connections at your house, don't you?"

He takes a painful breath. Is Nola trying to tell him something? He flashes on Benito's small house on Canyon Road, and pushes the image out of his mind. Won't pursue that. Just won't. "God knows I'm no husband to her, Nola. We had—we had a very satisfying married life before all this happened. Deeply passionate. Splendid, to tell the truth. Now I can't even—"

Nola turns her face away, saying silently that this is a part she doesn't want to hear.

11

Having silenced Molloy by turning her face away, Nola changes the subject. "And the foundation?"

What's he doing here, anyway? She can hardly bear to look at his ravaged face, the thinness that looks like a wasting disease. Her feelings are so mixed she can't begin to sort them out. Love. Frustration. Longing. Irritation. Disappointment. The tangle is ridiculous, full of conflicts, impenetrable.

He's calmed himself. "The foundation? Running on its own momentum for now. That won't last. Well, no. I'm there for that. It's about the only place I feel alive, can actually function. My strategy's been to look deep; focus on stuff that moves and changes. Never ask the usual questions. Kind of the way I look at a painting."

He falls into thought for a moment. "Since I started the foundation, I've come to see something. All the paintings I own, I love, have this in common: the background is as important as the foreground, the figure as important as the ground. If the two shift places while I'm looking, it's an even more significant piece. In a way it's like how I saw the world as a trader. What was happening I discounted. I was looking for what *would* happen. Well, same in philanthropy."

Now she can look at him, push down all that rioting tumult inside her. He's beginning to sound almost like his old self. She smiles. "What, in Chinese painting, they call the moment of incipience."

"Is that what it's called? The advantages of a first-rate education."

Molloy and his touching lapses of self-confidence. It makes him sound shallow and envious, when in fact he's neither, she thinks. Does he let Judith see those moments? The imperial Judith. The goddamned imperial Judith. A flash of anger, jealousy, yet a little triumph too, because this is when she and this man are at their most intimate. When she sees a part of him no one else, including the imperial Judith, may see.

He's gone back to what he feels confident about, seems to draw some strength from it, his voice more natural. "You have to see the world as always moving, about to change. Its parts affect each other in ways you might not even guess. You experiment. Put things in a bigger context. You blend deduction, insight, inference. The interactions are deeply challenging. You get hierarchies with different causes at different levels. You've got to be on the lookout at the micro-level for enormous changes at the macro-level. Thus saith the syllabus of the Center for Innovative Philanthropy."

He shrugs, collapses into himself. "I can do this in the world—buy a painting, do a deal, decide which head of which foundation should be invited to spend a little time in Santa Fe, so he can go to complexity boot camp, learn how to approach his mission differently. Feed the results back to us. *His* mission, no. No, they're mostly all women, the foundation heads who come to us, because women are the most open-minded about these things. These days."

"Is that what you're doing at the Center?"

He looks up. "Yeah, that's what we're doing now. We're all learning. In five years we'll be doing something different. I'm sure we will. Right now we've taken to calling ourselves a meta-foundation, a foundation about foundations." He shakes his head. "But for me personally...for me personally, this is not working. Simply not working."

His head drops against the back of the couch, against the Two Gray Hills rug, its geometric patterns of gray, beige and black providing a picturesque setting for him, she thinks—does not want to think, no, not really. She must lean forward to hear him. "I am such a complete and utter failure, Nola. Every way I turn. I can't even face myself in the mirror." He's quiet for a while, and Nola keeps silence too, waiting. "I always loved the Stoics," he goes on almost tangentially. "I have Epictetus in the bathroom so I can read him every day. I thought they had all the wisdom, and stupidly, I somehow believed—I believed I'd made it my own. No. I haven't. I cannot practice detachment. I cannot. This has wrecked me. Not just the grief. Not just the grief, but what she was saying about me, about all of us. The Stoics say happiness only comes from within."

He stops, recollects. "One night, when Nikki and I were cooped up together in the New York place on account of 9/11, she was asking me about happiness. She said—she too said she knew it was supposed to come from within, but she couldn't find it there. Ever. I was so happy myself. My life with Judith here in Santa Fe. The foundation taking off. Everything...everything coming up roses. I'd forgotten how sad I'd been for so much of my life. Amnesia, brought on by total bliss. I couldn't see why she couldn't find it, but I was deeply sorry. It had come so abundantly for me after so long that I was stupid enough to think, it will come for you, honey, just wait."

Nola wants to soothe this raw misery, lessen it somehow, comfort it away, like she once did for her dead son's pain. She reaches for his hand, hirsute down to its knuckles, and its warmth gives her a sharp pleasure that, at this moment, seems illicit.

He's pulled his head from the back of the couch and dropped it down toward his chest, making it even harder to hear him. "Epictetus says we should learn the will of nature, and make it our own. Learn to accept events with intelligence, even the death of those we love. Master ourselves." At last he lifts his head level, faces her, puts another hand over hers already on his. For a moment they are deeply joined. His onyx eyes, gone far too large in his thinning face, are supplicating.

Then he wrenches away from her, jumps up to pace. His voice rises. "Nola, I thought I had. I'd been through avalanches of shit and got out the other side. Not just that. By most people's lights, I was very successful. A hero. I didn't love what I did, but I did it well, and now I could—I'd earned the right to do something different. I found a woman I adored, and she seemed to adore me back. A master of myself, and for that matter, of the universe, in a way those guys I left on Wall Street hadn't a fucking clue about. But...Nikki's death...Nikki's death ended everything. It's all illusion, self-deception, this being master of myself, my life. I'm a failure. A failure as father. As a husband. As master of myself. The first time I'm really tested, everything falls apart. How can I be so angry with that poor little child who could find no way to end her pain except to end her life? How can I? Because she exposed me as nothing but a fucking fraud?" He stops pacing, eyes closed, face crumpled in agony. "Can you imagine me saying this to Judith?"

He resumes pacing, voicing aloud what she suspects are some of the monologues he's had in his head with his daughter. "Why did she do it? Why, Nola? Why? I'd have helped her. We'd all have helped her. I gave her the name of a shrink I'd seen, and Stevie told me she'd gone to him. Everyone was trying." Suddenly she hears rage. "Back to the factory floor? Sold insurance in Mount Lebanon? Is that what I should have done? Is it?"

He's grabbed a nearby sofa pillow, pounds it rhythmically. "No!...No!... No!..." The volume rises with each syllable. With a mighty strength, he hurls the pillow against the wall. A nearby lamp falls over. "No!" He moves as if to pick up the pillow, but instead pounds his fist against the wall, over and over. "No!...No!... No!...No!...No!...No!"

His dog has jumped up in alarm, whimpers.

Nola is terrified by this eruption. Fascinated by it. Thrilled by it. A warrior, hand-to-hand, an animal, tooth and claw, up against a foe that will kill—or be killed. She watches with fear, but also knows she's aroused, provoked, beginning to be seduced by a force in this room so primitive, so wild, it's been buried under civilization for millennia. Molloy is its conduit. Its keeper. A Molloy no one has ever seen is releasing it, loosing its power into the world. She stops breathing. He thrashes, grappling with invisible enemies that will give him no quarter. He will win. He will win. There's a madness about him now, a black energy that sends the teacups flying, a painting awry.

An elegant Rick Dillingham ceramic hits against a Nampeyo pot, and both of them shatter on the tile floor.

The sound of this stops him abruptly. He stares at the earth-toned shards at his feet, two priceless pots by dead masters, the pieces quivering as they come to rest in destruction. He's drenched, still sweating, his chest heaving, gasping for breath. His eyes shift from the shards to the rest of the room, as if he doesn't quite know where he is. Certainly not where he's just been. He looks back at the shards, glorious gold from the Dillingham piece glowing among the earth tones from the Hopi Nampeyo pot, earth tones that seem to soothe him, maybe, at last, even ground him.

Into those shards he drops to his knees, his hands clasped between his legs. He howls like an animal, a howl that echoes around the room in desolation. Its name is loss.

Nola rises to comfort him, kneels beside him, her arms around his shoulders. She can feel the power of what he's trying to stifle. "Let it go," she murmurs. "Just let it go." He sobs then without restraint, great wracking gasps that fill the room, empty him out. She's never seen a man cry before. Ernie was dry-eyed at Pete's death, whatever he was feeling. How much more profound, tragic, to hear these cries bursting out of a male chest. She holds him to her, stroking him, whispering to him, words of comfort, words of endearment. Thanks to Torres, holding a man close has become easy again, not strange.

At long last he calms. She helps him back to the couch, sits him down like a child. He still seems confused by what's possessed him. She kisses him affectionately on his forehead, his moist eyes, finally finds his mouth and kisses him long and lovingly, then cradles his head on her chest, rocks him gently. He's like a child at that moment, his arms around her, seeking comfort. Yet not a child. No, a man who's suffered greatly, from circumstances, from ego, from— well, God knows what. From life itself.

Softly, as if she were speaking to herself alone, almost crooning, she says: "Did you know I loved you from the moment I first saw you, Jack Molloy? Years ago at that Christmas holiday dinner at Maya's? That I've loved you ever since? Did you know that making love with you inside the pink cave was one of the sweetest experiences of my life? Did you know that?" She stops, sighs, strokes his head. "You talked that day about being a kind of Theseus—you love that mythical character, don't you? But I thought, no, it's further back than that. He's Osiris, come to be revived in the desert by his sister, his lover, his mate, Isis. I thought I could be—" she takes a deep breath and continues quickly. "I imagined myself as your Isis. That's because you're my impossible Mr. Right."

He tries to evade this, pull away, but not very forcefully. She senses the change. The terrible emptiness might be starting to fill. As his face relaxes, she knows it's something more than comfort he feels. A lightening. Perhaps relief.

"And now we've suffered the same way," she murmurs to him. "A way that no one else can understand. A bad marriage for each of us, yes. A dead child, yes. Don't we belong together, dear one? Ah, my poor Jack. Let me heal you." She pulls his head gently upward to her again, strokes it, kisses his earlobe, the side of his neck, reaches down to kiss his slack mouth. He doesn't resist. She can feel his warmth, takes in the sulfurous tang of his skin, senses that he's almost happy, yes, responding to her kiss. "Dear Jack. Dear Jack. Dear Jack." He groans softly. "Dear Jack, are you feeling desire for me now, even a little?" His eyes are closed. He's breathing heavily, winded from those cathartic sobs. She begins to feel sweet arousal, knows it can't just be hers alone. She's back in practice now; knows how to release herself, yield to desire and its demands. Desire? No. This is a ferocious greed; her core is raging for him. She might die if she doesn't have this man right now. She slips her hand into his groin. He yelps and jumps at the intrusion.

"Oh, yes. Oh, yes!" She pulls herself violently away from him, looks at her bare open hand. "You take that home and fuck your wife. She probably needs it even more than I do."

She doesn't allow herself to cry when he gets up, almost staggering, his dog herding him with tender worry. Silently, she helps him into his coat, wonders if, with that soaking shirt, he'll catch a chill if she doesn't drive him home. But she doesn't offer. He's still on the portal when she hears he's got his phone out, making a husky plea: "My love. My love. I'm on my way home. Please come home and—just be with me."

12

"Where's papa?" Judith asks Wotan as he bounds to the front door to meet her. On the sound system she can hear the waltzes from *Rosenkavalier*.

"Here. In here." Molloy is in the living room. He's got a fire going, fixed cinnamon tea, even found in the freezer some *biscochitos*, the local anise cookies, left over from what he seems to recall was the second of two very gloomy Christmases. He gazes up at her. "Thanks. Thanks for coming home. Hope I didn't interrupt anything crucial."

"This is crucial." She drops to the couch beside him.

"I need to tell you some things." But he looks away, his hands clasped between his knees, wondering where the words will come from. When he turns back to her, he can see she's retreated far away from him, far behind her eyes, is expecting what for him would be the worst. A final rupture.

He addresses that head on. "If you were to end this all..."

No reaction from her.

"Nobody would blame you."

She's impassive. "Is that what you want?"

"Me? Is that what I want? Oh, no." He takes both her hands, folds his own around them, a kind of prayer. Her distance is palpable and chills him. "Judith, my love. *Geliebte Göttin*."

She closes her eyes and her pain assaults him, a pain he's been largely unaware of. No. A pain he's ignored, discounted, convinced his own was so much greater.

"Let me try again. Judith, my love. *Meine Göttin*. I am so very sorry."

She watches him warily. He knows how wrong this sounds. How, if she's expecting a rupture, she could see this as prelude. He shakes his head. "Jesus, Jacko. You're saying this all wrong. Judith, I love you. I hate that I've caused you so much grief. I want to make it right again."

She exhales mightily but says nothing.

The clouds have delivered no storm and are drifting away. The last sun of the afternoon comes through the French doors, a cruel light. Something is coming over him, nagging to be acknowledged, that if something terrible has been weighting him, pulling him down, suffocating him, it isn't entirely what he thought. It's his daughter's death, yes. But it's also his own ego, which has belittled, diminished, mocked everything he's tried to do until now. He feels a sudden and deep shame. But realization, shame, isn't sufficient. How to find the way beyond the petty subversive self? The lightness he felt when he left Nola is dissolving, despair settling in again.

Judith has pulled her hands from his. She keeps her silence, sipping the tea, looking out through the French doors to the bare cottonwoods that line the Santa Fe River, to the city beyond it. "This is good," she says at last, and lets him decide whether she means the tea; his clumsy attempts at apology; the pleasure of sitting beside him late in the afternoon on a cold winter's day; or that, for the first time in so long, he's asked her to be with him. She's certainly understood that this isn't one of the old-time erotic summonses. This is exactly and only what it is: be with me.

"I just came from Nola's," he says. He feels the flash of anger from her, and she will not let him take her hands again. He accepts this sadly. Slowly, more coherently, he repeats to her what he'd said to Nola. She listens, sighing in sympathy at some things, shakes her head at others. He tells her he's called the man who got him out of his last great depression, hoping the guy can work his magic again. "Although," he says sorrowfully, "it'll take some face time. He's in New York. I'm sure it can't all be done by phone. I don't know if I can stay in the place where Nikki—"

Judith speaks at last, her voice pulled up from some distant place. "Let's wait and see."

Rosenkavalier's waltzes have finished. They sit together in a long silence until he says what she must be wondering.

"Why could I tell all this to Nola, and not to you?" She assesses him, waiting for an answer. He can see the soreness in her eyes. Why indeed? She hasn't reproached him for it, though she'd have the right. "Because you—because for you—I never wanted to be less than—because your good opinion means everything to me."

She continues to stare at him. "Do I seem so judgmental to you?"

"No, not at all. The—the judgments are mine. Mine. It's very hard to be around someone so altogether poised—"

She turns away, her arm across the back of the couch. He doesn't know what she's thinking. He'd like to touch her shoulder, but is afraid. At last she reveals her weary face, this time reaches for his hand, presses it lightly, lets it go.

So they sit in further silence as the afternoon dwindles, exhaustion in this silence, maybe some relief. Not the terrible tense silences of the last year and more. "I'm glad you've told me all this," she says at last. "Good for you. Good for me to know where you're at."

Now he has the courage to look at her. "Did anything really surprise you?"

She shakes her head. "I could certainly argue about some things. Utter failure as a human being?" She moans softly, composes herself. "For now, I'll just register my objection, let it go at that. One of these days, tell you about my own failures."

"No," he says uneasily. "You're strong and can listen to mine. I'm—not so strong." He's thinking of that cozy house on Canyon Road, that so fucking hot guy in the cowboy boots. If she's sought comfort there, he doesn't want to know.

The silence continues, but its nature has changed. At last it comforts. In a gesture that seems to him momentous, she takes his hand to keep. Forgiving. Loving. She strokes the hair on it down to the first knuckle, looks at it, murmurs. "More than once the past few months, I've asked myself the central Molloy question: why am I here?"

"The central—and do you know?"

She nods her head. "I know. Oh yes, I know." A weary answer, but he lets himself feel hope. "I'd like to say everything will be all right. That's only a wish. No guarantees. Maybe everything will be all right. Eventually." But how, her face says, how, after all this pain? After all the speeches to him she's made in her head, how she's prepared to end this civilly, no fuss; all to be reset to what it was before they met and married. A speech still in reserve. Instead she says: "We've been—concerned about you."

"I don't even want to parse that sentence. We? Concerned?"

"Jack, this is a drag. Can I use plain English? You haven't always seemed completely stable."

"Yeah. I haven't been. Always."

She nods wearily. "I've traveled quite a distance from you these past few months. I was ready to end this marriage if that's what you want. No muss, no fuss. Perfectly civilized. I'd go back to my *casita*, continue my life as if I'd never known you." Her voice, quiet up to now, suddenly cries out: "As if!"

He grabs her shoulders, makes her look at him, his sunken eyes, his emaciation. "Let me say this in English, because I want to say it exactly right.

I appreciate more than I can say how you've stood by me through all this. My greatest fear, always, was that you'd leave me. I couldn't think of any reason why you'd bother to stay. But life without you—that really would've put me over the edge. Thanks. Thanks for hanging in...my love."

She nods. He knows this is not enough to bridge the distance, but it's a beginning. Behind the bare trees, the sun is dropping. He looks up. "A New Mexico sunset tonight. The *Kitschmeister* at work."

More time passes. Finally she asks, "Are you hungry? Could you eat some dinner? I think there's some cheese and stuff in the fridge."

They sit together in the kitchen at a small bar, dividing cheese, leftover cold chicken, bread, wine. Her head is turned away from him again, and he can't tell where this will go next. She says: "Do you remember the first time we sat here?"

He smiles at last, the helmet of his face softening. "Like it was yesterday." The first time they'd ever made love was in a beautiful desert garden where they'd attended a reception, meant to launch Molloy's foundation. "It was all so fast, so ecstatic. I thought, this woman's gonna believe I don't know shit about love-making. November! What were we thinking, fucking outside at night in November?"

For the first time since she's come home, she smiles too. "We weren't thinking; we were swept away."

"Then when you said you needed to go home to change your clothes, and you'd come over after that, first, I had to tell a lot of people I was supposed to have dinner with that I couldn't; and then I spent thirty horrible minutes, like a century, wondering if you'd even show up. I kept obsessing, why didn't I follow her home? Why take a chance that she'll change her mind after all this time?"

Judith allows herself to smile again. "Did you?"

"When I heard your car in the driveway, I was even more nervous that it all might actually happen."

"We were both so totally uncool, right? I think we could barely look at each other. All those months of being so hungry for—for each other. So scared of it." She's still smiling.

"You were scared. Okay, me too, but in a different way."

She looks at him, and he thinks he might see love in her eyes. At least her voice is tender. "You said, are you hungry? Because neither of us had eaten at the reception. You brought me in here, to this very spot, laid out a meal like this—bread, cheese, the fruit, and a bottle of wine that was already open." She leans across the bar toward him. "I loved it that you were so provident—if you'd followed me home, we'd have been sharing a yogurt cup that was already half gone; that's exactly the total of what was in my fridge—but here was a sweet little feast, all laid out just for me. I loved it that I wasn't someone to open a new bottle of wine for, or cut into a fresh loaf of bread. Just family. It was so deliciously intimate. I'd never seen you in jeans before. Always so starchy-proper Molloy in his bespoke suits, bespoke slacks and jackets. Levis! Not designer jeans. I loved that."

He concedes it. "Still just a poor boy from the Mon Valley who's appalled by conspicuous consumption."

"Is that why I sometimes come home to find the rich guy on his back under the sink, muttering about crescent wrenches?"

"Not gonna call some guy for ninety bucks an hour when—"

"Yeah, yeah. Right." She laughs merrily, perhaps a kaleidoscope of memory before her eyes. "That night. That night, you were wearing moccasins, boat shoes, whatever they're called, no socks—very preppy, Molloy—and I thought I'd never seen such delicate, beautifully sculpted ankles in my life. I'd have killed for them for myself. And I also thought, those will be so delicious to nibble."

"Really?" He's sitting on a kitchen stool and rubs his ankle unconsciously, grins, recollects. "You took off your sweater after a while, and the front of your tee shirt said Black Death, the European Tour, and I'm thinking Black who? Maybe Black Sabbath? Don't know this group, but what the hell, this lady and I share some more music. It isn't gonna be all opera and chamber music. Then when you turned around to put the sweater down, I saw the back of it: Crimea, Rhine Valley, Calais, Dorset, and so on, and the dates, 1347 to whatever it was. Inside I was laughing, and loving you for yet one more thing. And being a guy, I also noticed you weren't wearing a bra under that tee shirt, so I knew it was when, not if."

"It was one of my workout tees, the only thing that was clean. Whoa, I had no idea you were so observant, Jack. Let alone so calculating."

"And you weren't?"

"Would you call unbridled lust calculating? Oh babe, was I hot for you that night!" Her knuckles go up to her mouth.

Some of these stories are old and familiar encantations. But not all of them.

He's grinning in delighted recollection. "Here's something else I loved.

We're finally down on the floor getting to it, and you say, 'um, Molloy—you still called me that then—do you, like, have a bed? I'm long past the stage of fooling around on the floor.' I did love that. Frankly, me too. One fuck out in nature's wonderland was plenty for one night. I didn't want to risk putting my back out. I was glad to get you up the stairs."

"Yes? Because I'm thinking, I bet that bitch Inéz would fuck him anywhere he wanted, up the chimney if asked, a walking *Kama Sutra*; so let's set a few ground rules here. Upstairs when we finally do get to a bed, I'm expecting the usual disgusting man-cave, sheets unchanged since the Paleozoic, but no, holy shit, fresh sheets and they're linen. What a guy! I didn't know then that you made your housekeeper change the sheets every day whether you were expecting company or not."

"My love. You weren't jealous of Inéz, surely?"

"That ever so young, ever so gorgeous, ever so dumb bitch? Of course I was. I felt like Methusaleh's mother every time I saw her."

"Oh, sweetheart." He shakes his head slowly. They're almost giggling together, demolishing the cheese, the chicken, the wine. "That turned out to be quite a night. Beyond all expectations. And my love, let me tell you, I'd fantasized some high expectations." He strokes her cheek.

"You're embarrassing me, Jack, and I'm your legally wedded wife."

"Another great moment in our erotic life. We're in Europe the first time; it's early on; you're still more rag doll than human being. We're just getting ready to make love, and I say, hey, I've brought you here to make you well, not molest you, and if ever—and Jesus, I feel you tonguing your way down my torso, and next thing I know you're delivering the greatest blowjob I've ever had, maybe the greatest blowjob of all time. *Guinness Book of Records*; shatters all previous. So I fall in love all over again. Without letting myself wonder where you ever learned some of those tricks."

"Tricks? I was just doing what made you happy. It meant a lot to me to make you happy, love." She pauses. "It still does."

This hits him with the force of an epiphany. So many women in his life have been eager to say how he failed them. His first wife. His former mother-in-law. His daughter. Even, somehow, his own mother, immured in her bedroom all her life after she gave birth to him. Not one of them had ever said they didn't want to fail him. That they wanted to make him happy. Whereas Judith says it, has done it as long as they've been together. He could cry again. He stands up, begins putting dishes in the dishwasher, his back to her. "I haven't been much of a husband to you the past months. First Jerry McCarthy."

"Your father."

He's reluctant to use the words. "My father. Yes... Then Nikki."

"Then Nikki."

"My entire life—got turned inside out. I tried to reason my way out of it. Don't seem to have the resilience I once had." Long silence. "My desire—it's mostly been missing in action. Nothing to do with you."

"I know. At least I think I know."

He turns to face her. "This conversation—I hope we can someday—"

"Yes."

He shakes his head sadly. "No matter what I do to spring myself out of this, I've got this new pain that's never going away. Acid rain. Eating away. Don't think I'm saying that to feel sorry for myself. Though I do. Truth is, I do."

She nods, sees, as if for the first time, how the last year and more has ravaged him. *Defaced* him. "You're entitled. This is about the worst thing that can happen to a parent. I hear."

"You hear?"

"Jack, things have been difficult. I've needed a little help myself."

He swears softly, bitterly. She slides off her stool. "Looks like you've got everything under control here. I'm wiped out; totally blitzed. I'm going up to read before I go to sleep. I hope you'll come up and—just be with me." It's her way of telling him that all she wants is his company. She reaches over to kiss him, a chaste but loving kiss, the way you might kiss a child, stares at him thoughtfully, goes up the stairs.

Somehow he remembers that it's the night to roll out the green garbage bin, put out the recyclables. He asks himself why the cook doesn't do this, like Annamarie always did. This one just leaves food in the freezer. Doing as he was told, not lingering in the house a moment more than he needs to, because Molloy has found his presence irritating. Would Annamarie consider coming back? Why in the hell is he rolling out his own garbage bin anyway? The enormous wealth is public now; no secret; he could call a plumber, increase the household staff. What part of general mastery is he trying to prove? But he's revolted at the thought of more people, strangers, breathing the same air as him in his refuge, his home. The very idea repels him.

He stops to add up the other damage. His son, distant. No blame there; it's self-protective. But he's distant. His friendship with Torres all but destroyed from neglect. Where to begin with each of those? But by God, begin he will.

As he's putting the dog in its kennel, he murmurs to it in German. "I know she lets you sleep on the bed when I'm away, but not tonight, Wotanle." By the time he's got back inside, set the alarm, cleaned himself up and got upstairs to her, she's fallen asleep over her book.

He takes her book gently from her hands, turns off the lights, stands beside her until his eyes adjust. He can see that Gainsborough nose, beneath it, her knuckles at her mouth, as she often sleeps. In someone else, a cosmic fear; in his Judith, an enduring cosmic awe. At last he strips, and crawls in beside her, fits himself around her back. Her body is deliciously familiar, her scent sweet in his nose. It evokes a few precious years of joy, tenderness and passion. Far too few. It evokes the beginning, when they'd evaded each other fearfully. *Did you think we might explode?* For months he's barely been able to tolerate her next to him, and yet couldn't bear not having her, either.

Now he wants very much to make love to her. Very much. He slips a hand under her arm, on to her breast, nuzzles her neck. She moves away, a little grumble of complaint. He persists. She murmurs, "*Arschloch. Schlaf schon.*" You asshole. I'm already asleep."

"You don't have to wake up," he whispers. "I'll take care of everything." He moves closer. "No one but you. Ever. This life. Former lives. Future lives."

He can sense her smiling even in the dark. But he knows that behind that smile lies deep skepticism. Disillusionment. They will have to remake it all.

ACKNOWLEDGMENTS

The title of this book, *Bounded Rationality*, is a phrase coined by the Nobel laureate, Herbert A. Simon, when he observed that humans generally aim to behave rationally, but such rationality is bounded—limited—by the place where they find themselves in, say, an organization (the head of production does not see things exactly as the head of sales does); limited by their own predispositions, psychological and social; or by any number of other idiosyncrasies. Though it began as a concept in economics and organizational theory, it has since found a place everywhere in the study of social behavior. I'm proud to have called Herb Simon a friend, and think he wouldn't mind having his famous phrase attached to a novel. It's a modest tribute to a one of the grandest thinkers I was ever privileged to know.

Stewart Brand first suggested that I write this book by saying: "Okay. Now that guy has to learn that spending money wisely is much harder than making it." He meant the character called Molloy, who first appeared in my novel, *The Edge of Chaos*, and Stewart Brand was right. For insight into current trends in philanthropy, I am grateful for conversations with Gara LaMarche, Morton Meyerson, and James Allen Smith; and also for the work of Kathryn Fulton at the Global Business Network/Monitor Group.

Though Leandro Torres and his story are entirely invented, Roberto Batista helped me enormously by opening his past and his heart to me. *Muchas gracias, amigo. Muchas gracias también* to my Spanish tutor, Adam Winkel, who kept his sense of humor even with such a recalcitrant student as I am. Adam also read parts of this work and made useful suggestions. *Vielen danke auch* to Dieter Baumeister for correcting and refining my German—and for a long and affectionate friendship.

Stuart Kauffman and I enjoyed many stimulating conversations about reinventing the sacred, and Jill Fineberg, who embodies that reinvention, guided me in other important ways. Hillel Swiller, M.D., a psychiatrist whose specialty is clinical depression, read parts of the manuscript and offered illuminating and witty commentary.

Margot Wellington tutored me, and guided my reading in current architecture and city planning. She was even generous enough to spend time walking me around New York City architecture. She resumed an education in that field that began for me with Tom Tellefsen, and with her late uncle, Winfield Scott Wellington. The work of Mikey Torres in this book, an attempt to understand in some scientific way the dynamics of cities, is actually the work of Luís M. A. Bettencourt, Los Alamos National Laboratory; José Lobo, Arizona State University; Dirk Helbing and Christian Kühnert, Dresden University of Technology; and Geoffrey West, the Santa Fe Institute. I hope I have not misrepresented it in any serious way.

The passages where Leandro Torres describes his creative methods are inspired by the very fine *Dialogues with Boulez*, between Pierre Boulez and Rocco diPietro, brought to my attention by Polly Valenzuela. The poem by Ausonius that Molloy recites to Judith at their wedding was in fact translated and recited by Andrew Stewart to his wife, Darlis Wood, at their wedding, and is used with permission. I am also grateful for Stewart's *Classical Greece and the Birth of Western Art*, which I joyfully plundered for background.

Two of the images in Stephen's dreams, the figures at the White Place that move toward him, draped in long robes, and the nude figure ascending from White Sands, are images that hang on my walls, Iris prints created by Eddie Dayan. But I acquired those prints because I'd dreamed those images myself, and was shocked to find them later in Eddie's studio.

I owe thanks to Claudette Mayer, whom I met after publishing *The Edge of Chaos*. Some parts of the life of my character Judith so parallel Claudette's life that she might plausibly have sued me for invasion of privacy. Fortunately, she didn't, and instead has enriched my understanding of what life was like for a young American girl in mid-20th-century Munich. Claudette also pointed me to the unusual life her father had led, as one of a group of immigrant American Jews who went back behind Nazi war lines, and, at enormous risk to themselves, transmitted important intelligence to the Allies. Henry Greenwood, Judith Greenwood's father in this book, is a fictional addition to that real-life brave band, though Henry's story isn't so heroic.

My husband Joseph Traub read two different drafts, and helped in countless ways, as he always does. Genevieve Young read the entire manuscript and made penetrating comments and suggestions, most of which I have taken to heart.

Others whose help has been important in so many other ways are Michael Collins, Judith Gorog, Richard Hertz, David Krakauer, Jim Rutt, Anne Werner, and William Zinsser. It truly is a small world network.

READERS GUIDE TO
BOUNDED RATIONALITY

1. Bounded rationality is a concept that originated in economics, but has been adapted by many other fields, including the sciences of complexity. It means that though an agent (human or otherwise) may *intend* to behave rationally, such intentions are bounded by limited information, or limited time to explore possibilities before a decision must be made, or various psychological and personal predispositions. For example, Judith, a mathematician, usually behaves rationally. But where does rationality fail her? Is this a good or a bad thing? Each of the other principal characters also behaves rationally until he or she runs up against certain limits. What are some examples of these?

2. The opening passage of *Bounded Rationality* describes geologic features of Santa Fe—the mountains, the desert, and a deep fault in the North American tectonic plate that is gradually but invisibly pushing mountains apart from each other. Do these geologic features prefigure parts of the story to come?

3. During the long European trip he takes with Judith to bring her back to health, Molloy is haunted by two phrases: *Et in Arcadia ego*, and *Verweile doch! Du bist so Schön!* The first phrase can be translated as "I once lived in Arcadia," or "I, death, am here in Arcadia (paradise) too." The second phrase is "Stay, moment! You are so beautiful!" This last is key to Goethe's poem *Faust*. If Faust utters these words, he loses everything. Does Molloy have presentiments about the future, or does he simply understand the human condition?

4. All the main characters in *Bounded Rationality* feel compelled to conceal important personal information. Sometimes that information emerges anyway, with varied consequences. What is concealed, what revealed, and what are the consequences?

5. A major theme of this book is the complicated, often vexed, relationship between fathers and sons. Consider each of the fathers and sons in this book and compare their relationships.

6. Molloy is nearly undone by the appearance of his father for the first time in his life. He cannot forgive Jerry McCarthy for abandoning all responsibility, or duty, as a father. Is Molloy justified to be so unforgiving? Duty plays a role in the lives of other characters too. What conflicting ideas of duty estrange Torres from his son, Mikey? Do Stephen's views of his father's duties to him change over time? Stephen's view of his own responsibilities? As Molloy's wife, does Judith meet her responsibilities during her husband's great crisis? Does Molloy himself?

7. Mothers and children also figure in this book. Are their relationships different from those between fathers and sons? Partly from exasperation with her stepson, partly out of genuine puzzlement, Judith speculates that the common wisdom has, in her lifetime, changed from the dictum that women must invariably sacrifice themselves for men, to the dictum that parents must invariably sacrifice themselves for their children. In your experience, is this an accurate description of a late twentieth-century cultural change? Is either dictum reasonable?

8. Leandro Torres seems single-mindedly devoted to his profession, but something has caused him to change his life and settle in Santa Fe. He admits he's lonely and needs his son and family. Is that all there is to it?

9. The visual arts are central to the lives of several characters. Molloy, for example, has a celebrated art collection, and is quietly pursuing why humans make art in the first place. Torres, who makes art on both an architectural and a personal scale, is especially eloquent about his art to anyone within earshot. Nola Holliman, a friend to them both, runs a major gallery in Santa Fe, a city which is, depending on how it's calculated, said to be the third or fifth largest art market in the United States. Besides offering aesthetic satisfaction, what larger role do the arts play in the lives of these and other characters? Might Judith say some of the same things about doing science as Torres says about doing architecture?

10. Another theme in this book is the yearning for home—sometimes as an actual geographical location, sometimes as a psychological place where people will always receive, love and comfort you. Describe the sense of home each of the principal characters yearns for.

11. When Nola's young son dies, a star-crossed love affair is revealed. This is not the only one among these characters. What do you think the future holds for Torres and Lucie? For Torres and Nola? For Benito Jiménez and Judith? For that matter, for Molloy and Judith?

12. Molloy's motives in setting up his foundation are somewhat mixed. Though he wants to spend his great fortune in a beneficial way, he confesses that a certain amount of ego is also involved. What does this say about Molloy's character? Does it surprise or offend you? Do you see parallels between the reasons why Molloy pursues philanthropy, and why Torres designs monumental architecture? Why Judith works so hard at her mathematical research?

13. Lucie Marchmont considers her work as a legal translator a retreat from her own best and earliest ambitions—even the words she translates aren't her own. As she and Torres gradually reveal their pasts, they recognize similarities. Each has been driven from home by political events beyond their control, and as a consequence, each suffers a troubled and rootless childhood. This has inflicted upon each of them a great wound. How do these histories and wounds shape their subsequent love affair? How does Torres deal with his past? When Lucie finally seeks help from healers for the spiritual paralysis that has overtaken her, what makes her receptive at last to confronting her own past?

14. The shock of the September 11, 2001 attacks on the World Trade Center, and the Pentagon, affects each of the characters differently, and is a turning point in the book. Describe those effects, and how each character's life changes.

15. After an idyllic family Thanksgiving, Molloy and Judith drive back to Santa Fe listening to a dramatization of Milton's *Paradise Lost*. Since they agree that the fundamental question in the poem is free will, can we ask whether their own paradise—soon to be lost—is something that they might have had a choice about losing? Does Nikki Molloy actually choose her destiny?

16. What Molloy suffers from after his daughter's death is classic clinical depression. He concedes to himself that his daughter's disorder is a sickness, but in its own terms, it still evokes from him and others an emotional, not necessarily rational, or even compassionate, response. Does he recognize this with his own illness? Why do you

think he refuses to get medical help for so long? Why does he find it impossible to tell Judith what he's suffering? Stephen's girlfriend, Daniella, gives him an ultimatum, and Stephen backs off from his father at this time. If even the cook quits, why doesn't Judith?

17. Both Lucie Marchmont and Judith Greenwood are haunted by the fear of professional failure. How does such fear of failure manifest itself in them? The fear of failure haunts others in this book too. Who are they, and what failures do they fear?

18. Stephen Molloy embarks on a quest that begins with a dream both violent and erotic. He pursues the meaning of his dreams with a tutor, who guides him without making definitive interpretations. Make some guesses about what this dream might mean to Stephen, and what he ultimately seeks.

19. As each person in the Molloy family reacted differently to 9/11, each person reacts differently to Nikki's death. Are these reactions consistent with who they are? Does Nikki's death change the fundamentals of her family? If Judith's eulogy for Nikki Molloy makes scientific sense to a researcher involved with the sciences of complexity, does it make sense to you in a spiritual way?

20. Toward the end of his studies, Stephen's tutor asks profound questions about Stephen's family and friends. *Hasn't each of you been led to the edge of the abyss? Who's looked in, and yet redeemed themselves? How did they dare to look into it? What have they seen when they looked there? What price do they pay for reaching for the divine? How will they keep the flame from consuming them? Who's failed, or refused, to look in? Where are the connections among you? What will rebirth look like?* Then Stephen's tutor continues: *Creativity is sacred. The creators are holy ones. Touched by divinity. How do those creators nurture the flame, connect with that fundamental will to exist, to create, to be reborn?* Perhaps these are fair questions to ask about the principal characters in this book.

www.ingramcontent.com/pod-product-compliance
Lightning Source LLC
Chambersburg PA
CBHW020416030726
47495CB00006B/1523